Julian Hawthorne

American Riddle Stories

Julian Hawthorne

American Riddle Stories

ISBN/EAN: 9783955630485

Auflage: 1

Erscheinungsjahr: 2013

Erscheinungsort: Bremen, Deutschland

@ Leseklassiker in Access Verlag GmbH, Fahrenheitstr. 1, 28359 Bremen. Alle Rechte beim Verlag und bei den jeweiligen Lizenzgebern.

Leseklassiker

Table of Contents

"Riddle Stories" *Introduction by Julian Hawthorne*	1
F. Marion Crawford By the Waters of Paradise	11
Mary E. Wilkins Freeman The Shadows on the Wall	36
Melville Davisson Post The Corpus Delicti	57
Ambrose Bierce An Heiress from Redhorse The Man and the Snake	86 93
Edgar Allan Poe The Oblong Box The Gold-Bug	100 112
Washington Irving Wolfert Webber, or Golden Dreams	150
Charles Brockden Brown Wieland's Madness	205
Fitzjames O'Brien The Golden Ingot My Wife's Tempter	284 300
Nathaniel Hawthorne The Minister's Black Veil	312
Anonymous Horror: A True Tale	326

"Riddle Stories"

Introduction by Julian Hawthorne

When Poe wrote his immortal Dupin tales, the name "Detective" stories had not been invented; the detective of fiction not having been as yet discovered. And the title is still something of a misnomer, for many narratives involving a puzzle of some sort, though belonging to the category which I wish to discuss, are handled by the writer without expert detective aid. Sometimes the puzzle solves itself through operation of circumstance; sometimes somebody who professes no special detective skill happens upon the secret of its mystery; once in a while some venturesome genius has the courage to leave his enigma unexplained. But ever since Gaboriau created his Lecoq, the transcendent detective has been in favor; and Conan Doyle's famous gentleman analyst has given him a fresh lease of life, and reanimated the stage by reverting to the method of Poe. Sherlock Holmes is Dupin redivivus, and mutatus mutandis; personally he is a more stirring and engaging companion, but so far as kinship to probabilities or even possibilities is concerned, perhaps the older version of him is the more presentable. But in this age of marvels we seem less difficult to suit in this respect than our forefathers were.

The fact is, meanwhile, that, in the riddle story, the detective was an afterthought, or, more accurately, a deus ex machina to make the story go. The riddle had to be unriddled; and who could do it so naturally and readily as a detective? The detective, as Poe saw him, was a means to this end; and it was only afterwards that writers perceived his availability as a character. Lecoq accordingly becomes a figure in fiction, and Sherlock, while he was as yet a novelty, was nearly as attractive as the complications in which he involved himself. Riddle-story writers in general, however, encounter the obvious embarrassment that their detective is obliged to lavish so much attention on the professional services which the exigencies of the tale demand of him, that he has very little leisure to expound his own personal equation – the rather since the attitude of peering into a millstone is not, of itself, conducive to elucidations of oneself; the professional endowment obscures all the others. We ordinarily find, therefore, our author dismissing the individuality of his detective with a few strong black-chalk outlines, and devoting his main labor upon what he feels the reader will chiefly occupy his own ingenuity with, – namely, the elaboration of the riddle itself. Reader and writer sit down to a game, as it were, with the odds, of course, altogether on the latter's side, – apart from the fact that a writer sometimes permits himself a little cheating. It more often happens that the detective appears to be in the writer's pay, and aids the deception by leading the reader off on false scents. Be that as it may, the professional sleuth is in nine cases out of ten a dummy by malice prepense; and it might be plausibly argued that, in the interests of pure art, that is what he ought to be. But genius always finds a way that is better than the rules, and I think it will be found that the very best riddle stories contrive to drive character and riddle side by side, and to make each somehow enhance the effect of the other. – The intention of the above paragraph will be more precisely conveyed if I include under the name of detective not only the man from the central office, but also anybody whom the writer may, for ends of his own, consider better qualified for that function. The latter is a professional detective so far as the exigencies of the tale are concerned, and what becomes of him after that nobody need care, – there is no longer anything to prevent his becoming, in his own right, the most fascinating of mankind.

But in addition to the dummyship of the detective, or to the cases in which the mere slip of circumstance takes his place, there is another reason against narrowing our conception of the riddle story to the degree which the alternative appellation would imply. And that is, that it would exclude not a few of the most captivating riddle stories in existence; for in De Quincey's "Avenger," for example, the interest is not in the unraveling of the web, but in the weaving of it. The same remark applies to Bulwer's "Strange Story"; it is the strangeness that is the thing. There is, in short, an inalienable charm in the mere contemplation of mystery and the hazard of fortunes; and it would be a pity to shut them out from our consideration only because there is no second-sighted conjurer on hand to turn them into plain matter of fact.

Yet we must not be too liberal; and a ghost story can be brought into our charmed and charming circle only if we have made up our minds to believe in the ghosts; otherwise their introduction would not be a square deal. It would not be fair, in other words, to propose a conundrum on a basis of ostensible materialism, and then, when no other key would fit, to palm off a disembodied spirit on us. Tell me beforehand that your scenario is to include both worlds, and I have no objection to make; I simply attune my mind to the more extensive scope. But I rebel at an unheralded ghostland, and declare frankly that your tale is incredible. And I must confess that I would as lief have ghosts kept out altogether; their stories make a very good library in themselves, and have no need to tag themselves on to what is really another department of fiction. Nevertheless, when a ghost story is told with the consummate art of a Miss Wilkins, and of one or two others on our list, consistency in this regard ceases to be a jewel; art proves irresistible. As for adventure stories, there is a fringe of them that comes under the riddle-story head; but for the most part the riddle story begins after the adventures have finished. We are to contemplate a condition, not to watch the events that ultimate in it. Our detective, or anyone else, may of course meet with haps and mishaps on his way to the solution of his puzzle; but an astute writer will not color such incidents too vividly, lest he risk forfeiting our preoccupation with the problem that we came forth for to study. In a word, One thing at a time!

The foregoing disquisition may seem uncalled for by such rigid moralists as have made up their minds not to regard detective, or riddle stories, as any part of respectable literature at all. With that sect, I announce at the outset that I am entirely out of sympathy. It is not needed to compare "The Gold Bug" with "Paradise Lost"; nobody denies the superior literary stature of the latter, although, as the Oxford Senior Wrangler objected, "What does it prove?" But I appeal to Emerson, who, in his poem of "The Mountain and the Squirrel," states the nub of the argument, with incomparable felicity, as follows: – you will recall that the two protagonists had a difference, originating in the fact that the former called the latter "Little Prig." Bun made a very sprightly retort, summing up to this effect: –

> "Talents differ; all is well and wisely put;
> If I cannot carry forests on my back,
> Neither can you crack a nut."

Andes and Paradises Lost are expedient and perhaps necessary in their proper atmosphere and function; but Squirrels and Gold Bugs are indispensable in our daily walk. There is as fine and as true literature in Poe's Tales as in Milton's epics; only the elevation and dimensions differ. But I would rather live in a world that possessed only literature of the Poe caliber, than shiver in one echoing solely the strains of the Miltonian muse. Mere human beings are not constructed to stand all day a-tiptoe on the misty mountain tops; they like to walk the streets most of the time and sit in easy chairs. And writings that picture the human mind and nature, in true colors and in artistic proportions, are literature, and nobody has any business to pooh-pooh them. In fact, I feel as if I were knocking down a man of straw. I look in vain for any genuine resistance. Of course "The Gold Bug" is literature; of course any other story of mystery and puzzle is also literature, provided it is as good as "The Gold Bug," – or I will say, since that standard has never since been quite attained, provided it is a half or a tenth as good. It is goldsmith's work; it is Chinese carving; it is Daedalian; it is fine. It is the product of the ingenuity lobe of the human brain working and expatiating in freedom. It is art; not spiritual or transcendental art, but solid art, to be felt and experienced. You may examine it at your leisure, it will be always ready for you; you need not fast or watch your arms overnight in order to understand it. Look at the nice setting of the mortises; mark how the cover fits; how smooth is the working of that spring drawer. Observe that this bit of carving, which seemed mere ornament, is really a vital part of the mechanism. Note, moreover, how balanced and symmetrical the whole design is, with what economy and foresight every part is fashioned. It is not only an ingenious structure, it is a handsome bit of furniture, and will materially improve the looks of the empty chambers, or disorderly or ungainly chambers that you carry under your crown. Or if it happen that these apartments are noble in decoration and proportions, then this captivating little object will find a suitable place in some spare nook or other, and will rest or entertain eyes too long focused on the severely sublime and beautiful. I need not, however, rely upon abstract argument to support my contention. Many of the best writers of all time have used their skill in the inverted form of story telling, as a glance at our table of contents will show; and many of their tales depend for their effect as much on character and atmosphere as on the play and complication of events.

The statement that a good detective or riddle story is good in art is supported by the fact that the supply of really good ones is relatively small, while the number of writers who would write good ones if they could, and who have tried and failed to write them, is past computation. And one reason probably is that such stories, for their success, must depend primarily upon structure – a sound and perfect plot – which is one of the rare things in our contemporary fiction. Our writers get hold of an incident, or a sentiment, or a character, or a moral principle, or a hit of technical knowledge, or a splotch of local color, or even of a new version of dialect, and they will do something in two to ten thousand words out of that and call it a short story. Magazines may be found to print it – for there are all manner of magazines; but nothing of that sort will serve for a riddle story. You cannot make a riddle story by beginning it and then trusting to luck to bring it to an end. You must know all about the end and the middle before thinking, even, of the beginning; the beginning of a riddle story, unlike those of other stories and of other enterprises, is not half the battle; it is next to being quite unimportant, and, moreover, it is always easy. The unexplained corpse lies weltering in its gore in the first paragraph; the inexplicable cipher presents its enigma at the turning of the opening page. The writer who is secure in the knowledge that he has got a good thing coming, and has arranged the manner and details of its coming, cannot go far wrong with his exordium; he wants to get into action at once, and that is his best assurance that he will do it in the right way. But O! what a labor and sweat it is; what a planning and trimming; what a remodeling, curtailing, interlining; what despairs succeeded by new lights, what heroic expedients tried at the last moment, and dismissed the moment after; what wastepaper baskets full of futilities, and what gallant commencements all over again! Did the reader know, or remotely suspect, what terrific struggles the writer of a really good detective story had sustained, he would regard the final product with a new wonder and respect, and read it all over once more to find out how the troubles occurred. But he will search in vain; there are no signs of them left; no, not so much as a scar. The tale moves along as smoothly and inevitably as oiled machinery; obviously, it could not have been arranged otherwise than it is; and the wise reader is convinced that he could have done the thing himself without half trying. At that, the weary writer smiles a bitter smile; but it is one of the spurns that patient merit of the unworthy takes. Nobody, except him who has tried it, will ever know how hard it is to write a really good detective story. The man or woman who can do it can also write a good play (according to modern ideas of plays), and possesses force of character, individuality, and mental ability. He or she must combine the intuition of the artist with the talent of the master mechanic, but will seldom be a poet, and will generally care more for things and events than for fellow creatures. For, although the story is often concerned with righting some wrong, or avenging some murder, yet it must be confessed that the author commonly succeeds better in the measure of his ruthlessness in devising crimes and giving his portraits of devils an extra touch of black. Mercy is not his strong point, however he may abound in justice; and he will not stickle at piling up the agony, if thereby he provides opportunity for enhancing the picturesqueness and completeness of the evil doer's due.

But this leads me to the admission that one charge, at least, does lie against the door of the riddle-story writer; and that is, that he is not sincere; he makes his mysteries backward, and knows the answer to his riddle before he states its terms. He deliberately supplies his reader, also, with all manner of false scents, well knowing them to be such; and concocts various seeming artless and innocent remarks and allusions, which in reality are diabolically artful, and would deceive the very elect. All this, I say, must be conceded; but it is not unfair; the very object, ostensibly, of the riddle story is to prompt you to sharpen your wits; and as you are yourself the real detective in the case, so you must regard your author as the real criminal whom you are to detect.

Credit no statement of his save as supported by the clearest evidence; be continually repeating to yourself, "Timeo Danaos et dona ferentes," – nay, never so much as then. But, as I said before, when the game is well set, you have no chance whatever against the dealer; and for my own part, I never try to be clever when I go up against these thimble-riggers; I believe all they tell me, and accept the most insolent gold bricks; and in that way I occasionally catch some of the very ablest of them napping; for they are so subtle that they will sometimes tell you the truth because they think you will suppose it to be a lie. I do not wish to catch them napping, however; I cling to the wisdom of ignorance, and childishly enjoy the way in which things work themselves out – the cul-de-sac resolving itself at the very last moment into a promising corridor toward the outer air. At every rebuff it is my happiness to be hopelessly bewildered; and I gape with admiration when the Gordian knot is untied. If the author be old-fashioned enough to apostrophize the Gentle Reader, I know he must mean me, and docilely give ear, and presently tumble head-foremost into the treacherous pit he has digged for me. In brief, I am there to be sold, and I get my money's worth. No one can thoroughly enjoy riddle stories unless he is old enough, or young enough, or, at any rate, wise enough to appreciate the value of the faculty of being surprised. Those sardonic and omniscient persons who know everything beforehand, and smile compassionately or scornfully at the artless outcries of astonishment of those who are uninformed, may get an ill-natured satisfaction out of the persuasion that they are superior beings; but there is very little meat in that sort of happiness, and the uninformed have the better lot after all.

    I need hardly point out that there is a distinction and a difference between short riddle stories and long ones – novels. The former require far more technical art for their proper development; the enigma cannot be posed in so many ways, but must be stated once for all; there cannot be false scents, or but a few of them; there can be small opportunity for character drawing, and all kinds of ornament and comment must be reduced to their very lowest terms. Here, indeed, as everywhere, genius will have its way; and while a merely talented writer would deem it impossible to tell the story of "The Gold Bug" in less than a volume, Poe could do it in a few thousand words, and yet appear to have said everything worth saying. In the case of the Sherlock Holmes tales, they form a series, and our previous knowledge of the hero enables the writer to dispense with much description and accompaniment that would be necessary had that eminent personage been presented in only a single complication of events. Each special episode of the great analyst's career can therefore be handled with the utmost economy, and yet fill all the requirements of intelligent interest and comprehension. But, as a rule, the riddle novel approaches its theme in a spirit essentially other than that which inspires the short tale. We are given, as it were, a wide landscape instead of a detailed genre picture. The number of the dramatis personae is much larger, and the parts given to many of them may be very small, though each should have his or her necessary function in the general plan. It is much easier to create perplexity on these terms; but on the other hand, the riddle novel demands a power of vivid character portrayal and of telling description which are not indispensable in the briefer narrative. A famous tale, published perhaps forty years ago, but which cannot be included in our series, tells the story of a murder the secret of which is admirably concealed till the last; and much of the fascination of the book is due to the ability with which the leading character, and some of the subordinate ones, are drawn. The author was a woman, and I have often marveled that women so seldom attempt this form of literature; many of them possess a good constructive faculty, and their love of detail and of mystery is notorious. Perhaps they are too fond of sentiment; and sentiment must be handled with caution in riddle stories. The fault of all riddle novels is that they inevitably involve two kinds of interest, and can seldom balance these so perfectly that one or the other of them shall not suffer. The mind of the reader becomes weary in its frequent journeys between human characters on one side the mysterious events on the other, and would prefer the more single- eyed treatment of the short tale. Wonder, too, is a very tender and short-lived emotion, and sometimes perishes after a few pages. Curiosity is tougher; but that too may be baffled too long, and end by tiring of the pursuit while it is yet in its early stages. Many excellent plots, admirable from the constructive point of view, have been wasted by stringing them out too far; the reader recognizes their merit, but loses his enthusiasm on account of a sort of monotony of strain; he wickedly turns to the concluding chapter, and the game is up. "The Woman in White," by Wilkie Collins, was published about 1860, I think, in weekly installments, and certainly they were devoured with insatiable appetite by many thousands of readers. But I doubt whether a book of similar merit could command such a following to-day; and I will even confess that I have myself never read the concluding parts, and do not know to this day who the woman was or what were the wrongs from which she so poignantly suffered.

The tales contained in the volumes herewith offered are the best riddle or detective stories in the world, according to the best judgment of the editors. They are the product of writers of all nations; and translation, in this case, is less apt to be misleading than with most other forms of literature, for a mystery or a riddle is equally captivating in all languages. Many of the good ones – perhaps some of the best ones – have been left out, either because we missed them in our search, or because we had to choose between them and others seemingly of equal excellence, and were obliged to consider space limitations which, however generously laid out, must have some end at last. Be that as it may, we believe that there are enough good stories here to satisfy the most Gargantuan hunger, and we feel sure that our volumes will never be crowded off the shelf which has once made room for them. If we have, now and then, a little transcended the strict definition of the class of fiction which our title would promise, we shall nevertheless not anticipate any serious quarrel with our readers; if there be room to question the right of any given story to appear in this company, there will be all the more reason for accepting it on its own merits; for it had to be very good indeed in order to overcome its technical disqualification. And if it did not rightfully belong here, there would probably be objections as strong to admitting it in any other collection. Between two or more stools, it would be a pity to let it fall to the ground; so let it be forgiven, and please us with whatever gift it has.

In many cases where copyrights were still unexpired, we have to express our acknowledgments to writers and publishers who have accorded us the courtesy of their leave to reproduce what their genius or enterprise has created and put forth. To our readers we take pleasure in presenting what we know cannot fail to give them pleasure – a collection of the fruits of the finest literary ingenuity and nicest art accessible to the human mind. Gaudeat, non caveat emptor!

JULIAN HAWTHORNE.

American Mystery Stories

F. Marion Crawford

By the Waters of Paradise

I

I remember my childhood very distinctly. I do not think that the fact argues a good memory, for I have never been clever at learning words by heart, in prose or rhyme; so that I believe my remembrance of events depends much more upon the events themselves than upon my possessing any special facility for recalling them. Perhaps I am too imaginative, and the earliest impressions I received were of a kind to stimulate the imagination abnormally. A long series of little misfortunes, so connected with each other as to suggest a sort of weird fatality, so worked upon my melancholy temperament when I was a boy that, before I was of age, I sincerely believed myself to be under a curse, and not only myself, but my whole family and every individual who bore my name.

I was born in the old place where my father, and his father, and all his predecessors had been born, beyond the memory of man. It is a very old house, and the greater part of it was originally a castle, strongly fortified, and surrounded by a deep moat supplied with abundant water from the hills by a hidden aqueduct. Many of the fortifications have been destroyed, and the moat has been filled up. The water from the aqueduct supplies great fountains, and runs down into huge oblong basins in the terraced gardens, one below the other, each surrounded by a broad pavement of marble between the water and the flower-beds. The waste surplus finally escapes through an artificial grotto, some thirty yards long, into a stream, flowing down through the park to the meadows beyond, and thence to the distant river. The buildings were extended a little and greatly altered more than two hundred years ago, in the time of Charles II., but since then little has been done to improve them, though they have been kept in fairly good repair, according to our fortunes.

In the gardens there are terraces and huge hedges of box and evergreen, some of which used to be clipped into shapes of animals, in the Italian style. I can remember when I was a lad how I used to try to make out what the trees were cut to represent, and how I used to appeal for explanations to Judith, my Welsh nurse. She dealt in a strange mythology of her own, and peopled the gardens with griffins, dragons, good genii and bad, and filled my mind with them at the same time. My nursery window afforded a view of the great fountains at the head of the upper basin, and on moonlight nights the Welshwoman would hold me up to the glass and bid me look at the mist and spray rising into mysterious shapes, moving mystically in the white light like living things.

"It's the Woman of the Water," she used to say; and sometimes she would threaten that if I did not go to sleep the Woman of the Water would steal up to the high window and carry me away in her wet arms.

The place was gloomy. The broad basins of water and the tall evergreen hedges gave it a funereal look, and the damp-stained marble causeways by the pools might have been made of tombstones. The gray and weather-beaten walls and towers without, the dark and massively furnished rooms within, the deep, mysterious recesses and the heavy curtains, all affected my spirits. I was silent and sad from my childhood. There was a great clock tower above, from which the hours rang dismally during the day, and tolled like a knell in the dead of night. There was no light nor life in the house, for my mother was a helpless invalid, and my father had grown melancholy in his long task of caring for her. He was a thin, dark man, with sad eyes; kind, I think, but silent and unhappy. Next to my mother, I believe he loved me better than anything on earth, for he took immense pains and trouble in teaching me, and what he taught me I have never forgotten. Perhaps it was his only amusement, and that may be the reason why I had no nursery governess or teacher of any kind while he lived.

I used to be taken to see my mother every day, and sometimes twice a day, for an hour at a time. Then I sat upon a little stool near her feet, and she would ask me what I had been doing, and what I wanted to do. I dare say she saw already the seeds of a profound melancholy in my nature, for she looked at me always with a sad smile, and kissed me with a sigh when I was taken away.

One night, when I was just six years old, I lay awake in the nursery. The door was not quite shut, and the Welsh nurse was sitting sewing in the next room. Suddenly I heard her groan, and say in a strange voice, "One – two – one – two!" I was frightened, and I jumped up and ran to the door, barefooted as I was.

"What is it, Judith?" I cried, clinging to her skirts. I can remember the look in her strange dark eyes as she answered:

"One – two leaden coffins, fallen from the ceiling!" she crooned, working herself in her chair. "One – two – a light coffin and a heavy coffin, falling to the floor!"

Then she seemed to notice me, and she took me back to bed and sang me to sleep with a queer old Welsh song.

I do not know how it was, but the impression got hold of me that she had meant that my father and mother were going to die very soon. They died in the very room where she had been sitting that night. It was a great room, my day nursery, full of sun when there was any; and when the days were dark it was the most cheerful place in the house. My mother grew rapidly worse, and I was transferred to another part of the building to make place for her. They thought my nursery was gayer for her, I suppose; but she could not live. She was beautiful when she was dead, and I cried bitterly.

The light one, the light one – the heavy one to come," crooned the Welshwoman. And she was right. My father took the room after my mother was gone, and day by day he grew thinner and paler and sadder.

"The heavy one, the heavy one – all of lead," moaned my nurse, one night in December, standing still, just as she was going to take away the light after putting me to bed. Then she took me up again and wrapped me in a little gown, and led me away to my father's room. She knocked, but no one answered. She opened the door, and we found him in his easy chair before the fire, very white, quite dead.

So I was alone with the Welshwoman till strange people came, and relations whom I had never seen; and then I heard them saying that I must be taken away to some more cheerful place. They were kind people, and I will not believe that they were kind only because I was to be very rich when I grew to be a man. The world never seemed to be a very bad place to me, nor all the people to be miserable sinners, even when I was most melancholy. I do not remember that anyone ever did me any great injustice, nor that I was ever oppressed or ill treated in any way, even by the boys at school. I was sad, I suppose, because my childhood was so gloomy, and, later, because I was unlucky in everything I undertook, till I finally believed I was pursued by fate, and I used to dream that the old Welsh nurse and the Woman of the Water between them had vowed to pursue me to my end. But my natural disposition should have been cheerful, as I have often thought.

Among the lads of my age I was never last, or even among the last, in anything; but I was never first. If I trained for a race, I was sure to sprain my ankle on the day when I was to run. If I pulled an oar with others, my oar was sure to break. If I competed for a prize, some unforeseen accident prevented my winning it at the last moment. Nothing to which I put my hand succeeded, and I got the reputation of being unlucky, until my companions felt it was always safe to bet against me, no matter what the appearances might be. I became discouraged and listless in everything. I gave up the idea of competing for any distinction at the University, comforting myself with the thought that I could not fail in the examination for the ordinary degree. The day before the examination began I fell ill; and when at last I recovered, after a narrow escape from death, I turned my back upon Oxford, and went down alone to visit the old place where I had been born, feeble in health and profoundly disgusted and discouraged. I was twenty-one years of age, master of myself and of my fortune; but so deeply had the long chain of small unlucky circumstances affected me that I thought seriously of shutting myself up from the world to live the life of a hermit and to die as soon as possible. Death seemed the only cheerful possibility in my existence, and my thoughts soon dwelt upon it altogether.

I had never shown any wish to return to my own home since I had been taken away as a little boy, and no one had ever pressed me to do so. The place had been kept in order after a fashion, and did not seem to have suffered during the fifteen years or more of my absence. Nothing earthly could affect those old gray walls that had fought the elements for so many centuries. The garden was more wild than I remembered it; the marble causeways about the pools looked more yellow and damp than of old, and the whole place at first looked smaller. It was not until I had wandered about the house and grounds for many hours that I realized the huge size of the home where I was to live in solitude. Then I began to delight in it, and my resolution to live alone grew stronger.

The people had turned out to welcome me, of course, and I tried to recognize the changed faces of the old gardener and the old housekeeper, and to call them by name. My old nurse I knew at once. She had grown very gray since she heard the coffins fall in the nursery fifteen years before, but her strange eyes were the same, and the look in them woke all my old memories. She went over the house with me.

"And how is the Woman of the Water?" I asked, trying to laugh a little. "Does she still play in the moonlight?"

"She is hungry," answered the Welshwoman, in a low voice.

"Hungry? Then we will feed her." I laughed. But old Judith turned very pale, and looked at me strangely.

"Feed her? Aye – you will feed her well," she muttered, glancing behind her at the ancient housekeeper, who tottered after us with feeble steps through the halls and passages.

I did not think much of her words. She had always talked oddly, as Welshwomen will, and though I was very melancholy I am sure I was not superstitious, and I was certainly not timid. Only, as in a far-off dream, I seemed to see her standing with the light in her hand and muttering, "The heavy one – all of lead," and then leading a little boy through the long corridors to see his father lying dead in a great easy chair before a smoldering fire. So we went over the house, and I chose the rooms where I would live; and the servants I had brought with me ordered and arranged everything, and I had no more trouble. I did not care what they did provided I was left in peace and was not expected to give directions; for I was more listless than ever, owing to the effects of my illness at college.

I dined in solitary state, and the melancholy grandeur of the vast old dining-room pleased me. Then I went to the room I had selected for my study, and sat down in a deep chair, under a bright light, to think, or to let my thoughts meander through labyrinths of their own choosing, utterly indifferent to the course they might take.

The tall windows of the room opened to the level of the ground upon the terrace at the head of the garden. It was in the end of July, and everything was open, for the weather was warm. As I sat alone I heard the unceasing splash of the great fountains, and I fell to thinking of the Woman of the Water. I rose and went out into the still night, and sat down upon a seat on the terrace, between two gigantic Italian flower pots. The air was deliciously soft and sweet with the smell of the flowers, and the garden was more congenial to me than the house. Sad people always like running water and the sound of it at night, though I cannot tell why. I sat and listened in the gloom, for it was dark below, and the pale moon had not yet climbed over the hills in front of me, though all the air above was light with her rising beams. Slowly the white halo in the eastern sky ascended in an arch above the wooded crests, making the outlines of the mountains more intensely black by contrast, as though the head of some great white saint were rising from behind a screen in a vast cathedral, throwing misty glories from below. I longed to see the moon herself, and I tried to reckon the seconds before she must appear. Then she sprang up quickly, and in a moment more hung round and perfect in the sky. I gazed at her, and then at the floating spray of the tall fountains, and down at the pools, where the water lilies were rocking softly in their sleep on the velvet surface of the moonlit water. Just then a great swan floated out silently into the midst of the basin, and wreathed his long neck, catching the water in his broad bill, and scattering showers of diamonds around him.

Suddenly, as I gazed, something came between me and the light. I looked up instantly. Between me and the round disk of the moon rose a luminous face of a woman, with great strange eyes, and a woman's mouth, full and soft, but not smiling, hooded in black, staring at me as I sat still upon my bench. She was close to me – so close that I could have touched her with my hand. But I was transfixed and helpless. She stood still for a moment, but her expression did not change. Then she passed swiftly away, and my hair stood up on my head, while the cold breeze from her white dress was wafted to my temples as she moved. The moonlight, shining through the tossing spray of the fountain, made traceries of shadow on the gleaming folds of her garments. In an instant she was gone and I was alone.

I was strangely shaken by the vision, and some time passed before I could rise to my feet, for I was still weak from my illness, and the sight I had seen would have startled anyone. I did not reason with myself, for I was certain that I had looked on the unearthly, and no argument could have destroyed that belief. At last I got up and stood unsteadily, gazing in the direction in which I thought the face had gone; but there was nothing to be seen – nothing but the broad paths, the tall, dark evergreen hedges, the tossing water of the fountains and the smooth pool below. I fell back upon the seat and recalled the face I had seen. Strange to say, now that the first impression had passed, there was nothing startling in the recollection; on the contrary, I felt that I was fascinated by the face, and would give anything to see it again. I could retrace the beautiful straight features, the long dark eyes, and the wonderful mouth most exactly in my mind, and when I had reconstructed every detail from memory I knew that the whole was beautiful, and that I should love a woman with such a face.

"I wonder whether she is the Woman of the Water!" I said to myself. Then rising once more, I wandered down the garden, descending one short flight of steps after another from terrace to terrace by the edge of the marble basins, through the shadow and through the moonlight; and I crossed the water by the rustic bridge above the artificial grotto, and climbed slowly up again to the highest terrace by the other side. The air seemed sweeter, and I was very calm, so that I think I smiled to myself as I walked, as though a new happiness had come to me. The woman's face seemed always before me, and the thought of it gave me an unwonted thrill of pleasure, unlike anything I had ever felt before.

I turned as I reached the house, and looked back upon the scene. It had certainly changed in the short hour since I had come out, and my mood had changed with it. Just like my luck, I thought, to fall in love with a ghost! But in old times I would have sighed, and gone to bed more sad than ever, at such a melancholy conclusion. To-night I felt happy, almost for the first time in my life. The gloomy old study seemed cheerful when I went in. The old pictures on the walls smiled at me, and I sat down in my deep chair with a new and delightful sensation that I was not alone. The idea of having seen a ghost, and of feeling much the better for it, was so absurd that I laughed softly, as I took up one of the books I had brought with me and began to read.

That impression did not wear off. I slept peacefully, and in the morning I threw open my windows to the summer air and looked down at the garden, at the stretches of green and at the colored flower- beds, at the circling swallows and at the bright water.

"A man might make a paradise of this place," I exclaimed. "A man and a woman together!"

From that day the old Castle no longer seemed gloomy, and I think I ceased to be sad; for some time, too, I began to take an interest in the place, and to try and make it more alive. I avoided my old Welsh nurse, lest she should damp my humor with some dismal prophecy, and recall my old self by bringing back memories of my dismal childhood. But what I thought of most was the ghostly figure I had seen in the garden that first night after my arrival. I went out every evening and wandered through the walks and paths; but, try as I might, I did not see my vision again. At last, after many days, the memory grew more faint, and my old moody nature gradually overcame the temporary sense of lightness I had experienced. The summer turned to autumn, and I grew restless. It began to rain. The dampness pervaded the gardens, and the outer halls smelled musty, like tombs; the gray sky oppressed me intolerably. I left the place as it was and went abroad, determined to try anything which might possibly make a second break in the monotonous melancholy from which I suffered.

II

Most people would be struck by the utter insignificance of the small events which, after the death of my parents, influenced my life and made me unhappy. The grewsome forebodings of a Welsh nurse, which chanced to be realized by an odd coincidence of events, should not seem enough to change the nature of a child and to direct the bent of his character in after years. The little disappointments of schoolboy life, and the somewhat less childish ones of an uneventful and undistinguished academic career, should not have sufficed to turn me out at one-and-twenty years of age a melancholic, listless idler. Some weakness of my own character may have contributed to the result, but in a greater degree it was due to my having a reputation for bad luck. However, I will not try to analyze the causes of my state, for I should satisfy nobody, least of all myself. Still less will I attempt to explain why I felt a temporary revival of my spirits after my adventure in the garden. It is certain that I was in love with the face I had seen, and that I longed to see it again; that I gave up all hope of a second visitation, grew more sad than ever, packed up my traps, and finally went abroad. But in my dreams I went back to my home, and it always appeared to me sunny and bright, as it had looked on that summer's morning after I had seen the woman by the fountain.

I went to Paris. I went farther, and wandered about Germany. I tried to amuse myself, and I failed miserably. With the aimless whims of an idle and useless man come all sorts of suggestions for good resolutions. One day I made up my mind that I would go and bury myself in a German university for a time, and live simply like a poor student. I started with the intention of going to Leipzig, determined to stay there until some event should direct my life or change my humor, or make an end of me altogether. The express train stopped at some station of which I did not know the name. It was dusk on a winter's afternoon, and I peered through the thick glass from my seat. Suddenly another train came gliding in from the opposite direction, and stopped alongside of ours. I looked at the carriage which chanced to be abreast of mine, and idly read the black letters painted on a white board swinging from the brass handrail: BERLIN – COLOGNE – PARIS. Then I looked up at the window above. I started violently, and the cold perspiration broke out upon my forehead. In the dim light, not six feet from where I sat, I saw the face of a woman, the face I loved, the straight, fine features, the strange eyes, the wonderful mouth, the pale skin. Her head-dress was a dark veil which seemed to be tied about her head and passed over the shoulders under her chin. As I threw down the window and knelt on the cushioned seat, leaning far out to get a better view, a long whistle screamed through the station, followed by a quick series of dull, clanking sounds; then there was a slight jerk, and my train moved on. Luckily the window was narrow, being the one over the seat, beside the door, or I believe I would have jumped out of it then and there. In an instant the speed increased, and I was being carried swiftly away in the opposite direction from the thing I loved.

For a quarter of an hour I lay back in my place, stunned by the suddenness of the apparition. At last one of the two other passengers, a large and gorgeous captain of the White Konigsberg Cuirassiers, civilly but firmly suggested that I might shut my window, as the evening was cold. I did so, with an apology, and relapsed into silence. The train ran swiftly on for a long time, and it was already beginning to slacken speed before entering another station, when I roused myself and made a sudden resolution. As the carriage stopped before the brilliantly lighted platform, I seized my belongings, saluted my fellow-passengers, and got out, determined to take the first express back to Paris.

This time the circumstances of the vision had been so natural that it did not strike me that there was anything unreal about the face, or about the woman to whom it belonged. I did not try to explain to myself how the face, and the woman, could be traveling by a fast train from Berlin to Paris on a winter's afternoon, when both were in my mind indelibly associated with the moonlight and the fountains in my own English home. I certainly would not have admitted that I had been mistaken in the dusk, attributing to what I had seen a resemblance to my former vision which did not really exist. There was not the slightest doubt in my mind, and I was positively sure that I had again seen the face I loved. I did not hesitate, and in a few hours I was on my way back to Paris. I could not help reflecting on my ill luck. Wandering as I had been for many months, it might as easily have chanced that I should be traveling in the same train with that woman, instead of going the other way. But my luck was destined to turn for a time.

I searched Paris for several days. I dined at the principal hotels; I went to the theaters; I rode in the Bois de Boulogne in the morning, and picked up an acquaintance, whom I forced to drive with me in the afternoon. I went to mass at the Madeleine, and I attended the services at the English Church. I hung about the Louvre and Notre Dame. I went to Versailles. I spent hours in parading the Rue de Rivoli, in the neighborhood of Meurice's corner, where foreigners pass and repass from morning till night. At last I received an invitation to a reception at the English Embassy. I went, and I found what I had sought so long.

There she was, sitting by an old lady in gray satin and diamonds, who had a wrinkled but kindly face and keen gray eyes that seemed to take in everything they saw, with very little inclination to give much in return. But I did not notice the chaperon. I saw only the face that had haunted me for months, and in the excitement of the moment I walked quickly toward the pair, forgetting such a trifle as the necessity for an introduction.

She was far more beautiful than I had thought, but I never doubted that it was she herself and no other. Vision or no vision before, this was the reality, and I knew it. Twice her hair had been covered, now at last I saw it, and the added beauty of its magnificence glorified the whole woman. It was rich hair, fine and abundant, golden, with deep ruddy tints in it like red bronze spun fine. There was no ornament in it, not a rose, not a thread of gold, and I felt that it needed nothing to enhance its splendor; nothing but her pale face, her dark strange eyes, and her heavy eyebrows. I could see that she was slender too, but strong withal, as she sat there quietly gazing at the moving scene in the midst of the brilliant lights and the hum of perpetual conversation.

I recollected the detail of introduction in time, and turned aside to look for my host. I found him at last. I begged him to present me to the two ladies, pointing them out to him at the same time.

"Yes – uh – by all means – uh," replied his Excellency with a pleasant smile. He evidently had no idea of my name, which was not to be wondered at.

"I am Lord Cairngorm," I observed.

"Oh – by all means," answered the Ambassador with the same hospitable smile. "Yes – uh – the fact is, I must try and find out who they are; such lots of people, you know."

"Oh, if you will present me, I will try and find out for you," said I, laughing.

"Ah, yes – so kind of you – come along," said my host. We threaded the crowd, and in a few minutes we stood before the two ladies.

"'Lowmintrduce L'd Cairngorm," he said; then, adding quickly to me, "Come and dine to-morrow, won't you?" he glided away with his pleasant smile and disappeared in the crowd.

I sat down beside the beautiful girl, conscious that the eyes of the duenna were upon me.

"I think we have been very near meeting before," I remarked, by way of opening the conversation.

My companion turned her eyes full upon me with an air of inquiry. She evidently did not recall my face, if she had ever seen me.

"Really – I cannot remember," she observed, in a low and musical voice. "When?"

"In the first place, you came down from Berlin by the express ten days ago. I was going the other way, and our carriages stopped opposite each other. I saw you at the window."

"Yes – we came that way, but I do not remember – " She hesitated.

"Secondly," I continued, "I was sitting alone in my garden last summer – near the end of July – do you remember? You must have wandered in there through the park; you came up to the house and looked at me – "

"Was that you?" she asked, in evident surprise. Then she broke into a laugh. "I told everybody I had seen a ghost; there had never been any Cairngorms in the place since the memory of man. We left the next day, and never heard that you had come there; indeed, I did not know the castle belonged to you."

"Where were you staying?" I asked.

"Where? Why, with my aunt, where I always stay. She is your neighbor, since it IS you."

"I – beg your pardon – but then – is your aunt Lady Bluebell? I did not quite catch – "

"Don't be afraid. She is amazingly deaf. Yes. She is the relict of my beloved uncle, the sixteenth or seventeenth Baron Bluebell – I forget exactly how many of them there have been. And I – do you know who I am?" She laughed, well knowing that I did not.

"No," I answered frankly. "I have not the least idea. I asked to be introduced because I recognized you. Perhaps – perhaps you are a Miss Bluebell?"

"Considering that you are a neighbor, I will tell you who I am," she answered. "No; I am of the tribe of Bluebells, but my name is Lammas, and I have been given to understand that I was christened Margaret. Being a floral family, they call me Daisy. A dreadful American man once told me that my aunt was a Bluebell and that I was a Harebell – with two l's and an e – because my hair is so thick. I warn you, so that you may avoid making such a bad pun."

"Do I look like a man who makes puns?" I asked, being very conscious of my melancholy face and sad looks.

Miss Lammas eyed me critically.

"No; you have a mournful temperament. I think I can trust you," she answered. "Do you think you could communicate to my aunt the fact that you are a Cairngorm and a neighbor? I am sure she would like to know."

I leaned toward the old lady, inflating my lungs for a yell. But Miss Lammas stopped me.

"That is not of the slightest use," she remarked. "You can write it on a bit of paper. She is utterly deaf."

"I have a pencil," I answered; "but I have no paper. Would my cuff do, do you think?"

"Oh, yes!" replied Miss Lammas, with alacrity; "men often do that."

I wrote on my cuff: "Miss Lammas wishes me to explain that I am your neighbor, Cairngorm." Then I held out my arm before the old lady's nose. She seemed perfectly accustomed to the proceeding, put up her glasses, read the words, smiled, nodded, and addressed me in the unearthly voice peculiar to people who hear nothing.

"I knew your grandfather very well," she said. Then she smiled and nodded to me again, and to her niece, and relapsed into silence.

"It is all right," remarked Miss Lammas. "Aunt Bluebell knows she is deaf, and does not say much, like the parrot. You see, she knew your grandfather. How odd that we should be neighbors! Why have we never met before?"

"If you had told me you knew my grandfather when you appeared in the garden, I should not have been in the least surprised," I answered rather irrelevantly. "I really thought you were the ghost of the old fountain. How in the world did you come there at that hour?"

"We were a large party and we went out for a walk. Then we thought we should like to see what your park was like in the moonlight, and so we trespassed. I got separated from the rest, and came upon you by accident, just as I was admiring the extremely ghostly look of your house, and wondering whether anybody would ever come and live there again. It looks like the castle of Macbeth, or a scene from the opera. Do you know anybody here?"

"Hardly a soul! Do you?"

"No. Aunt Bluebell said it was our duty to come. It is easy for her to go out; she does not bear the burden of the conversation."

"I am sorry you find it a burden," said I. "Shall I go away?"

Miss Lammas looked at me with a sudden gravity in her beautiful eyes, and there was a sort of hesitation about the lines of her full, soft mouth.

"No," she said at last, quite simply, "don't go away. We may like each other, if you stay a little longer – and we ought to, because we are neighbors in the country."

I suppose I ought to have thought Miss Lammas a very odd girl. There is, indeed, a sort of freemasonry between people who discover that they live near each other and that they ought to have known each other before. But there was a sort of unexpected frankness and simplicity in the girl's amusing manner which would have struck anyone else as being singular, to say the least of it. To me, however, it all seemed natural enough. I had dreamed of her face too long not to be utterly happy when I met her at last and could talk to her as much as I pleased. To me, the man of ill luck in everything, the whole meeting seemed too good to be true. I felt again that strange sensation of lightness which I had experienced after I had seen her face in the garden. The great rooms seemed brighter, life seemed worth living; my sluggish, melancholy blood ran faster, and filled me with a new sense of strength. I said to myself that without this woman I was but an imperfect being, but that with her I could accomplish everything to which I should set my hand. Like the great Doctor, when he thought he had cheated Mephistopheles at last, I could have cried aloud to the fleeting moment, Verweile doch, du bist so schön!

"Are you always gay?" I asked, suddenly. "How happy you must be!"

"The days would sometimes seem very long if I were gloomy," she answered, thoughtfully. "Yes, I think I find life very pleasant, and I tell it so."

"How can you 'tell life' anything?" I inquired. "If I could catch my life and talk to it, I would abuse it prodigiously, I assure you."

"I dare say. You have a melancholy temper. You ought to live out-of-doors, dig potatoes, make hay, shoot, hunt, tumble into ditches, and come home muddy and hungry for dinner. It would be much better for you than moping in your rook tower and hating everything."

"It is rather lonely down there," I murmured, apologetically, feeling that Miss Lammas was quite right.

"Then marry, and quarrel with your wife," she laughed. "Anything is better than being alone."

"I am a very peaceable person. I never quarrel with anybody. You can try it. You will find it quite impossible."

"Will you let me try?" she asked, still smiling.

"By all means – especially if it is to be only a preliminary canter," I answered, rashly.

"What do you mean?" she inquired, turning quickly upon me.

"Oh – nothing. You might try my paces with a view to quarreling in the future. I cannot imagine how you are going to do it. You will have to resort to immediate and direct abuse."

"No. I will only say that if you do not like your life, it is your own fault. How can a man of your age talk of being melancholy, or of the hollowness of existence? Are you consumptive? Are you subject to hereditary insanity? Are you deaf, like Aunt Bluebell? Are you poor, like – lots of people? Have you been crossed in love? Have you lost the world for a woman, or any particular woman for the sake of the world? Are you feeble-minded, a cripple, an outcast? Are you – repulsively ugly?" She laughed again. "Is there any reason in the world why you should not enjoy all you have got in life?"

"No. There is no reason whatever, except that I am dreadfully unlucky, especially in small things."

"Then try big things, just for a change," suggested Miss Lammas. "Try and get married, for instance, and see how it turns out."

"If it turned out badly it would be rather serious."

"Not half so serious as it is to abuse everything unreasonably. If abuse is your particular talent, abuse something that ought to be abused. Abuse the Conservatives – or the Liberals – it does not matter which, since they are always abusing each other. Make yourself felt by other people. You will like it, if they don't. It will make a man of you. Fill your mouth with pebbles, and howl at the sea, if you cannot do anything else. It did Demosthenes no end of good, you know. You will have the satisfaction of imitating a great man."

"Really, Miss Lammas, I think the list of innocent exercises you propose – "

"Very well – if you don't care for that sort of thing, care for some other sort of thing. Care for something, or hate something. Don't be idle. Life is short, and though art may be long, plenty of noise answers nearly as well."

"I do care for something – I mean, somebody," I said.

"A woman? Then marry her. Don't hesitate."

"I do not know whether she would marry me," I replied. "I

have never asked her."

"Then ask her at once," answered Miss Lammas. "I shall die happy if I feel I have persuaded a melancholy fellow creature to rouse himself to action. Ask her, by all means, and see what she says. If she does not accept you at once, she may take you the next time. Meanwhile, you will have entered for the race. If you lose, there are the 'All-aged Trial Stakes,' and the 'Consolation Race.'"

"And plenty of selling races into the bargain. Shall I take you at your word, Miss Lammas?"

"I hope you will," she answered.

"Since you yourself advise me, I will. Miss Lammas, will you do me the honor to marry me?"

For the first time in my life the blood rushed to my head and my sight swam. I cannot tell why I said it. It would be useless to try to explain the extraordinary fascination the girl exercised over me, or the still more extraordinary feeling of intimacy with her which had grown in me during that half hour. Lonely, sad, unlucky as I had been all my life, I was certainly not timid, nor even shy. But to propose to marry a woman after half an hour's acquaintance was a piece of madness of which I never believed myself capable, and of which I should never be capable again, could I be placed in the same situation. It was as though my whole being had been changed in a moment by magic – by the white magic of her nature brought into contact with mine. The blood sank back to my heart, and a moment later I found myself staring at her with anxious eyes. To my amazement she was as calm as ever, but her beautiful mouth smiled, and there was a mischievous light in her dark-brown eyes.

"Fairly caught," she answered. "For an individual who pretends to be listless and sad you are not lacking in humor. I had really not the least idea what you were going to say. Wouldn't it be singularly awkward for you if I had said 'Yes'? I never saw anybody begin to practice so sharply what was preached to him – with so very little loss of time!"

"You probably never met a man who had dreamed of you for seven months before being introduced."

"No, I never did," she answered gayly. "It smacks of the romantic. Perhaps you are a romantic character, after all. I should think you were if I believed you. Very well; you have taken my advice, entered for a Stranger's Race and lost it. Try the All-aged Trial Stakes. You have another cuff, and a pencil. Propose to Aunt Bluebell; she would dance with astonishment, and she might recover her hearing."

III

That was how I first asked Margaret Lammas to be my wife, and I will agree with anyone who says I behaved very foolishly. But I have not repented of it, and I never shall. I have long ago understood that I was out of my mind that evening, but I think my temporary insanity on that occasion has had the effect of making me a saner man ever since. Her manner turned my head, for it was so different from what I had expected. To hear this lovely creature, who, in my imagination, was a heroine of romance, if not of tragedy, talking familiarly and laughing readily was more than my equanimity could bear, and I lost my head as well as my heart. But when I went back to England in the spring, I went to make certain arrangements at the Castle – certain changes and improvements which would be absolutely necessary. I had won the race for which I had entered myself so rashly, and we were to be married in June.

Whether the change was due to the orders I had left with the gardener and the rest of the servants, or to my own state of mind, I cannot tell. At all events, the old place did not look the same to me when I opened my window on the morning after my arrival. There were the gray walls below me and the gray turrets flanking the huge building; there were the fountains, the marble causeways, the smooth basins, the tall box hedges, the water lilies and the swans, just as of old. But there was something else there, too – something in the air, in the water, and in the greenness that I did not recognize – a light over everything by which everything was transfigured. The clock in the tower struck seven, and the strokes of the ancient bell sounded like a wedding chime. The air sang with the thrilling treble of the song-birds, with the silvery music of the plashing water and the softer harmony of the leaves stirred by the fresh morning wind. There was a smell of new-mown hay from the distant meadows, and of blooming roses from the beds below, wafted up together to my window. I stood in the pure sunshine and drank the air and all the sounds and the odors that were in it; and I looked down at my garden and said: "It is Paradise, after all." I think the men of old were right when they called heaven a garden, and Eden a garden inhabited by one man and one woman, the Earthly Paradise.

I turned away, wondering what had become of the gloomy memories I had always associated with my home. I tried to recall the impression of my nurse's horrible prophecy before the death of my parents – an impression which hitherto had been vivid enough. I tried to remember my old self, my dejection, my listlessness, my bad luck, my petty disappointments. I endeavored to force myself to think as I used to think, if only to satisfy myself that I had not lost my individuality. But I succeeded in none of these efforts. I was a different man, a changed being, incapable of sorrow, of ill luck, or of sadness. My life had been a dream, not evil, but infinitely gloomy and hopeless. It was now a reality, full of hope, gladness, and all manner of good. My home had been like a tomb; to-day it was Paradise. My heart had been as though it had not existed; to-day it beat with strength and youth and the certainty of realized happiness. I reveled in the beauty of the world, and called loveliness out of the future to enjoy it before time should bring it to me, as a traveler in the plains looks up to the mountains, and already tastes the cool air through the dust of the road.

Here, I thought, we will live and live for years. There we will sit by the fountain toward evening and in the deep moonlight. Down those paths we will wander together. On those benches we will rest and talk. Among those eastern hills we will ride through the soft twilight, and in the old house we will tell tales on winter nights, when the logs burn high, and the holly berries are red, and the old clock tolls out the dying year. On these old steps, in these dark passages and stately rooms, there will one day be the sound of little pattering feet, and laughing child voices will ring up to the vaults of the ancient hall. Those tiny footsteps shall not be slow and sad as mine were, nor shall the childish words be spoken in an awed whisper. No gloomy Welshwoman shall people the dusky corners with weird horrors, nor utter horrid prophecies of death and ghastly things. All shall be young, and fresh, and joyful, and happy, and we will turn the old luck again, and forget that there was ever any sadness.

So I thought, as I looked out of my window that morning and for many mornings after that, and every day it all seemed more real than ever before, and much nearer. But the old nurse looked at me askance, and muttered odd sayings about the Woman of the Water. I cared little what she said, for I was far too happy.

At last the time came near for the wedding. Lady Bluebell and all the tribe of Bluebells, as Margaret called them, were at Bluebell Grange, for we had determined to be married in the country, and to come straight to the Castle afterwards. We cared little for traveling, and not at all for a crowded ceremony at St. George's in Hanover Square, with all the tiresome formalities afterwards. I used to ride over to the Grange every day, and very often Margaret would come with her aunt and some of her cousins to the Castle. I was suspicious of my own taste, and was only too glad to let her have her way about the alterations and improvements in our home.

We were to be married on the thirtieth of July, and on the evening of the twenty-eighth Margaret drove over with some of the Bluebell party. In the long summer twilight we all went out into the garden. Naturally enough, Margaret and I were left to ourselves, and we wandered down by the marble basins.

"It is an odd coincidence," I said; "it was on this very night last year that I first saw you."

"Considering that it is the month of July," answered Margaret with a laugh, "and that we have been here almost every day, I don't think the coincidence is so extraordinary, after all."

"No, dear," said I, "I suppose not. I don't know why it struck me. We shall very likely be here a year from today, and a year from that. The odd thing, when I think of it, is that you should be here at all. But my luck has turned. I ought not to think anything odd that happens now that I have you. It is all sure to be good."

"A slight change in your ideas since that remarkable performance of yours in Paris," said Margaret. "Do you know, I thought you were the most extraordinary man I had ever met."

"I thought you were the most charming woman I had ever seen. I naturally did not want to lose any time in frivolities. I took you at your word, I followed your advice, I asked you to marry me, and this is the delightful result – what's the matter?"

Margaret had started suddenly, and her hand tightened on my arm. An old woman was coming up the path, and was close to us before we saw her, for the moon had risen, and was shining full in our faces. The woman turned out to be my old nurse.

"It's only Judith, dear – don't be frightened," I said. Then I spoke to the Welshwoman: "What are you about, Judith? Have you been feeding the Woman of the Water?"

"Aye – when the clock strikes, Willie – my Lord, I mean," muttered the old creature, drawing aside to let us pass, and fixing her strange eyes on Margaret's face.

"What does she mean?" asked Margaret, when we had gone by.

"Nothing, darling. The old thing is mildly crazy, but she is a good soul."

We went on in silence for a few moments, and came to the rustic bridge just above the artificial grotto through which the water ran out into the park, dark and swift in its narrow channel. We stopped, and leaned on the wooden rail. The moon was now behind us, and shone full upon the long vista of basins and on the huge walls and towers of the Castle above.

"How proud you ought to be of such a grand old place!" said Margaret, softly.

"It is yours now, darling," I answered. "You have as good a right to love it as I – but I only love it because you are to live in it, dear."

Her hand stole out and lay on mine, and we were both silent. Just then the clock began to strike far off in the tower. I counted – eight – nine – ten – eleven – I looked at my watch – twelve – thirteen – I laughed. The bell went on striking.

"The old clock has gone crazy, like Judith," I exclaimed. Still it went on, note after note ringing out monotonously through the still air. We leaned over the rail, instinctively looking in the direction whence the sound came. On and on it went. I counted nearly a hundred, out of sheer curiosity, for I understood that something had broken and that the thing was running itself down.

Suddenly there was a crack as of breaking wood, a cry and a heavy splash, and I was alone, clinging to the broken end of the rail of the rustic bridge.

I do not think I hesitated while my pulse beat twice. I sprang clear of the bridge into the black rushing water, dived to the bottom, came up again with empty hands, turned and swam downward through the grotto in the thick darkness, plunging and diving at every stroke, striking my head and hands against jagged stones and sharp corners, clutching at last something in my fingers and dragging it up with all my might. I spoke, I cried aloud, but there was no answer. I was alone in the pitchy darkness with my burden, and the house was five hundred yards away. Struggling still, I felt the ground beneath my feet, I saw a ray of moonlight- -the grotto widened, and the deep water became a broad and shallow brook as I stumbled over the stones and at last laid Margaret's body on the bank in the park beyond.

"Aye, Willie, as the clock struck!" said the voice of Judith, the Welsh nurse, as she bent down and looked at the white face. The old woman must have turned back and followed us, seen the accident, and slipped out by the lower gate of the garden. "Aye," she groaned, "you have fed the Woman of the Water this night, Willie, while the clock was striking."

I scarcely heard her as I knelt beside the lifeless body of the woman I loved, chafing the wet white temples and gazing wildly into the wide-staring eyes. I remember only the first returning look of consciousness, the first heaving breath, the first movement of those dear hands stretching out toward me.

That is not much of a story, you say. It is the story of my life. That is all. It does not pretend to be anything else. Old Judith says my luck turned on that summer's night when I was struggling in the water to save all that was worth living for. A month later there was a stone bridge above the grotto, and Margaret and I stood on it and looked up at the moonlit Castle, as we had done once before, and as we have done many times since. For all those things happened ten years ago last summer, and this is the tenth Christmas Eve we have spent together by the roaring logs in the old hall, talking of old times; and every year there are more old times to talk of. There are curly-headed boys, too, with red-gold hair and dark-brown eyes like their mother's, and a little Margaret, with solemn black eyes like mine. Why could not she look like her mother, too, as well as the rest of them?

The world is very bright at this glorious Christmas time, and perhaps there is little use in calling up the sadness of long ago, unless it be to make the jolly firelight seem more cheerful, the good wife's face look gladder, and to give the children's laughter a merrier ring, by contrast with all that is gone. Perhaps, too, some sad-faced, listless, melancholy youth, who feels that the world is very hollow, and that life is like a perpetual funeral service, just as I used to feel myself, may take courage from my example, and having found the woman of his heart, ask her to marry him after half an hour's acquaintance. But, on the whole, I would not advise any man to marry, for the simple reason that no man will ever find a wife like mine, and being obliged to go farther, he will necessarily fare worse. My wife has done miracles, but I will not assert that any other woman is able to follow her example.

Margaret always said that the old place was beautiful, and that I ought to be proud of it. I dare say she is right. She has even more imagination than I. But I have a good answer and a plain one, which is this, – that all the beauty of the Castle comes from her. She has breathed upon it all, as the children blow upon the cold glass window panes in winter; and as their warm breath crystallizes into landscapes from fairyland, full of exquisite shapes and traceries upon the blank surface, so her spirit has transformed every gray stone of the old towers, every ancient tree and hedge in the gardens, every thought in my once melancholy self. All that was old is young, and all that was sad is glad, and I am the gladdest of all. Whatever heaven may be, there is no earthly paradise without woman, nor is there anywhere a place so desolate, so dreary, so unutterably miserable that a woman cannot make it seem heaven to the man she loves and who loves her.

I hear certain cynics laugh, and cry that all that has been said before. Do not laugh, my good cynic. You are too small a man to laugh at such a great thing as love. Prayers have been said before now by many, and perhaps you say yours, too. I do not think they lose anything by being repeated, nor you by repeating them. You say that the world is bitter, and full of the Waters of Bitterness. Love, and so live that you may be loved – the world will turn sweet for you, and you shall rest like me by the Waters of Paradise.

From "The Play-Actress and the Upper Berth," by F. Marion Crawford.

Mary E. Wilkins Freeman

The Shadows on the Wall

"Henry had words with Edward in the study the night before Edward died," said Caroline Glynn.

She was elderly, tall, and harshly thin, with a hard colourlessness of face. She spoke not with acrimony, but with grave severity. Rebecca Ann Glynn, younger, stouter and rosy of face between her crinkling puffs of gray hair, gasped, by way of assent. She sat in a wide flounce of black silk in the corner of the sofa, and rolled terrified eyes from her sister Caroline to her sister Mrs. Stephen Brigham, who had been Emma Glynn, the one beauty of the family. She was beautiful still, with a large, splendid, full-blown beauty; she filled a great rocking-chair with her superb bulk of femininity, and swayed gently back and forth, her black silks whispering and her black frills fluttering. Even the shock of death (for her brother Edward lay dead in the house,) could not disturb her outward serenity of demeanor. She was grieved over the loss of her brother: he had been the youngest, and she had been fond of him, but never had Emma Brigham lost sight of her own importance amidst the waters of tribulation. She was always awake to the consciousness of her own stability in the midst of vicissitudes and the splendor of her permanent bearing.

But even her expression of masterly placidity changed before her sister Caroline's announcement and her sister Rebecca Ann's gasp of terror and distress in response.

"I think Henry might have controlled his temper, when poor Edward was so near his end," said she with an asperity which disturbed slightly the roseate curves of her beautiful mouth.

"Of course he did not KNOW," murmured Rebecca Ann in a faint tone strangely out of keeping with her appearance.

One involuntarily looked again to be sure that such a feeble pipe came from that full-swelling chest.

"Of course he did not know it," said Caroline quickly. She turned on her sister with a strange sharp look of suspicion. "How could he have known it?" said she. Then she shrank as if from the other's possible answer. "Of course you and I both know he could not," said she conclusively, but her pale face was paler than it had been before.

Rebecca gasped again. The married sister, Mrs. Emma Brigham, was now sitting up straight in her chair; she had ceased rocking, and was eyeing them both intently with a sudden accentuation of family likeness in her face. Given one common intensity of emotion and similar lines showed forth, and the three sisters of one race were evident.

"What do you mean?" said she impartially to them both. Then she, too, seemed to shrink before a possible answer. She even laughed an evasive sort of laugh. "I guess you don't mean anything," said she, but her face wore still the expression of shrinking horror.

"Nobody means anything," said Caroline firmly. She rose and crossed the room toward the door with grim decisiveness.

"Where are you going?" asked Mrs. Brigham.

"I have something to see to," replied Caroline, and the others at once knew by her tone that she had some solemn and sad duty to perform in the chamber of death.

"Oh," said Mrs. Brigham.

After the door had closed behind Caroline, she turned to Rebecca.

"Did Henry have many words with him?" she asked.

"They were talking very loud," replied Rebecca evasively, yet with an answering gleam of ready response to the other's curiosity in the quick lift of her soft blue eyes.

Mrs. Brigham looked at her. She had not resumed rocking. She still sat up straight with a slight knitting of intensity on her fair forehead, between the pretty rippling curves of her auburn hair.

"Did you – hear anything?" she asked in a low voice with a

glance toward the door.

"I was just across the hall in the south parlor, and that door was open and this door ajar," replied Rebecca with a slight flush.

"Then you must have – "

"I couldn't help it."

"Everything?"

"Most of it."

"What was it?"

"The old story."

"I suppose Henry was mad, as he always was, because Edward was living on here for nothing, when he had wasted all the money father left him."

Rebecca nodded with a fearful glance at the door.

When Emma spoke again her voice was still more hushed. "I know how he felt," said she. "He had always been so prudent himself, and worked hard at his profession, and there Edward had never done anything but spend, and it must have looked to him as if Edward was living at his expense, but he wasn't."

"No, he wasn't."

"It was the way father left the property – that all the children should have a home here – and he left money enough to buy the food and all if we had all come home."

"Yes."

"And Edward had a right here according to the terms of father's will, and Henry ought to have remembered it."

"Yes, he ought."

"Did he say hard things?"

"Pretty hard from what I heard."

"What?"

"I heard him tell Edward that he had no business here at all, and he thought he had better go away."

"What did Edward say?"

"That he would stay here as long as he lived and afterward, too, if he was a mind to, and he would like to see Henry get him out; and then – "

"What?"

"Then he laughed."

"What did Henry say."

"I didn't hear him say anything, but – "

"But what?"

"I saw him when he came out of this room."

"He looked mad?"

"You've seen him when he looked so."

Emma nodded; the expression of horror on her face had deepened.

"Do you remember that time he killed the cat because she had scratched him?"

"Yes. Don't!"

Then Caroline reentered the room. She went up to the stove in which a wood fire was burning – it was a cold, gloomy day of fall – and she warmed her hands, which were reddened from recent washing in cold water.

Mrs. Brigham looked at her and hesitated. She glanced at the door, which was still ajar, as it did not easily shut, being still swollen with the damp weather of the summer. She rose and pushed it together with a sharp thud which jarred the house. Rebecca started painfully with a half exclamation. Caroline looked at her disapprovingly.

"It is time you controlled your nerves, Rebecca," said she.

"I can't help it," replied Rebecca with almost a wail. "I am nervous. There's enough to make me so, the Lord knows."

"What do you mean by that?" asked Caroline with her old air of sharp suspicion, and something between challenge and dread of its being met.

Rebecca shrank.

"Nothing," said she.

"Then I wouldn't keep speaking in such a fashion."

Emma, returning from the closed door, said imperiously that it ought to be fixed, it shut so hard.

"It will shrink enough after we have had the fire a few days," replied Caroline. "If anything is done to it it will be too small; there will be a crack at the sill."

"I think Henry ought to be ashamed of himself for talking as he did to Edward," said Mrs. Brigham abruptly, but in an almost inaudible voice.

"Hush!" said Caroline, with a glance of actual fear at the closed door.

"Nobody can hear with the door shut."

"He must have heard it shut, and – "

"Well, I can say what I want to before he comes down, and I am not afraid of him."

"I don't know who is afraid of him! What reason is there for anybody to be afraid of Henry?" demanded Caroline.

Mrs. Brigham trembled before her sister's look. Rebecca gasped again. "There isn't any reason, of course. Why should there be?"

"I wouldn't speak so, then. Somebody might overhear you and think it was queer. Miranda Joy is in the south parlor sewing, you know."

"I thought she went upstairs to stitch on the machine."

"She did, but she has come down again."

"Well, she can't hear."

"I say again I think Henry ought to be ashamed of himself. I shouldn't think he'd ever get over it, having words with poor Edward the very night before he died. Edward was enough sight better disposition than Henry, with all his faults. I always thought a great deal of poor Edward, myself."

Mrs. Brigham passed a large fluff of handkerchief across her eyes; Rebecca sobbed outright.

"Rebecca," said Caroline admonishingly, keeping her mouth stiff and swallowing determinately.

"I never heard him speak a cross word, unless he spoke cross to Henry that last night. I don't know, but he did from what Rebecca overheard," said Emma.

"Not so much cross as sort of soft, and sweet, and aggravating," sniffled Rebecca.

"He never raised his voice," said Caroline; "but he had his way."

"He had a right to in this case."

"Yes, he did."

"He had as much of a right here as Henry," sobbed Rebecca, "and now he's gone, and he will never be in this home that poor father left him and the rest of us again."

"What do you really think ailed Edward?" asked Emma in hardly more than a whisper. She did not look at her sister.

Caroline sat down in a nearby armchair, and clutched the arms convulsively until her thin knuckles whitened.

"I told you," said she.

Rebecca held her handkerchief over her mouth, and looked at them above it with terrified, streaming eyes.

"I know you said that he had terrible pains in his stomach,

and had spasms, but what do you think made him have them?"

"Henry called it gastric trouble. You know Edward has always had dyspepsia."

Mrs. Brigham hesitated a moment. "Was there any talk of an – examination?" said she.

Then Caroline turned on her fiercely.

"No," said she in a terrible voice. "No."

The three sisters' souls seemed to meet on one common ground of terrified understanding through their eyes. The old-fashioned latch of the door was heard to rattle, and a push from without made the door shake ineffectually. "It's Henry," Rebecca sighed rather than whispered. Mrs. Brigham settled herself after a noiseless rush across the floor into her rocking-chair again, and was swaying back and forth with her head comfortably leaning back, when the door at last yielded and Henry Glynn entered. He cast a covertly sharp, comprehensive glance at Mrs. Brigham with her elaborate calm; at Rebecca quietly huddled in the corner of the sofa with her handkerchief to her face and only one small reddened ear as attentive as a dog's uncovered and revealing her alertness for his presence; at Caroline sitting with a strained composure in her armchair by the stove. She met his eyes quite firmly with a look of inscrutable fear, and defiance of the fear and of him.

Henry Glynn looked more like this sister than the others. Both had the same hard delicacy of form and feature, both were tall and almost emaciated, both had a sparse growth of gray blond hair far back from high intellectual foreheads, both had an almost noble aquilinity of feature. They confronted each other with the pitiless immovability of two statues in whose marble lineaments emotions were fixed for all eternity.

Then Henry Glynn smiled and the smile transformed his face. He looked suddenly years younger, and an almost boyish recklessness and irresolution appeared in his face. He flung himself into a chair with a gesture which was bewildering from its incongruity with his general appearance. He leaned his head back, flung one leg over the other, and looked laughingly at Mrs. Brigham.

"I declare, Emma, you grow younger every year," he said.

She flushed a little, and her placid mouth widened at the corners. She was susceptible to praise.

"Our thoughts to-day ought to belong to the one of us who will NEVER grow older," said Caroline in a hard voice.

Henry looked at her, still smiling. "Of course, we none of us forget that," said he, in a deep, gentle voice, "but we have to speak to the living, Caroline, and I have not seen Emma for a long time, and the living are as dear as the dead."

"Not to me," said Caroline.

She rose, and went abruptly out of the room again. Rebecca also rose and hurried after her, sobbing loudly.

Henry looked slowly after them.

"Caroline is completely unstrung," said he. Mrs. Brigham rocked. A confidence in him inspired by his manner was stealing over her. Out of that confidence she spoke quite easily and naturally.

"His death was very sudden," said she.

Henry's eyelids quivered slightly but his gaze was unswerving.

"Yes," said he; "it was very sudden. He was sick only a few hours."

"What did you call it?"

"Gastric."

"You did not think of an examination?"

"There was no need. I am perfectly certain as to the cause of his death."

Suddenly Mrs. Brigham felt a creep as of some live horror over her very soul. Her flesh prickled with cold, before an inflection of his voice. She rose, tottering on weak knees.

"Where are you going?" asked Henry in a strange, breathless voice.

Mrs. Brigham said something incoherent about some sewing which she had to do, some black for the funeral, and was out of the room. She went up to the front chamber which she occupied. Caroline was there. She went close to her and took her hands, and the two sisters looked at each other.

"Don't speak, don't, I won't have it!" said Caroline finally in an awful whisper.

"I won't," replied Emma.

That afternoon the three sisters were in the study, the large front room on the ground floor across the hall from the south parlor, when the dusk deepened.

Mrs. Brigham was hemming some black material. She sat close to the west window for the waning light. At last she laid her work on her lap.

"It's no use, I cannot see to sew another stitch until we have a light," said she.

Caroline, who was writing some letters at the table, turned to Rebecca, in her usual place on the sofa.

"Rebecca, you had better get a lamp," she said.

Rebecca started up; even in the dusk her face showed her agitation.

"It doesn't seem to me that we need a lamp quite yet," she said in a piteous, pleading voice like a child's.

"Yes, we do," returned Mrs. Brigham peremptorily. "We must have a light. I must finish this to-night or I can't go to the funeral, and I can't see to sew another stitch."

"Caroline can see to write letters, and she is farther from the window than you are," said Rebecca.

"Are you trying to save kerosene or are you lazy, Rebecca

Glynn?" cried Mrs. Brigham. "I can go and get the light myself, but I have this work all in my lap."

Caroline's pen stopped scratching.

"Rebecca, we must have the light," said she.

"Had we better have it in here?" asked Rebecca weakly.

"Of course! Why not?" cried Caroline sternly.

"I am sure I don't want to take my sewing into the other room, when it is all cleaned up for to-morrow," said Mrs. Brigham.

"Why, I never heard such a to-do about lighting a lamp."

Rebecca rose and left the room. Presently she entered with a lamp – a large one with a white porcelain shade. She set it on a table, an old-fashioned card-table which was placed against the opposite wall from the window. That wall was clear of bookcases and books, which were only on three sides of the room. That opposite wall was taken up with three doors, the one small space being occupied by the table. Above the table on the old-fashioned paper, of a white satin gloss, traversed by an indeterminate green scroll, hung quite high a small gilt and black-framed ivory miniature taken in her girlhood of the mother of the family. When the lamp was set on the table beneath it, the tiny pretty face painted on the ivory seemed to gleam out with a look of intelligence.

"What have you put that lamp over there for?" asked Mrs. Brigham, with more of impatience than her voice usually revealed. "Why didn't you set it in the hall and have done with it. Neither Caroline nor I can see if it is on that table."

"I thought perhaps you would move," replied Rebecca hoarsely.

"If I do move, we can't both sit at that table. Caroline has her paper all spread around. Why don't you set the lamp on the study table in the middle of the room, then we can both see?"

Rebecca hesitated. Her face was very pale. She looked with an appeal that was fairly agonizing at her sister Caroline.

"Why don't you put the lamp on this table, as she says?" asked Caroline, almost fiercely. "Why do you act so, Rebecca?"

"I should think you WOULD ask her that," said Mrs. Brigham. "She doesn't act like herself at all."

Rebecca took the lamp and set it on the table in the middle of the room without another word. Then she turned her back upon it quickly and seated herself on the sofa, and placed a hand over her eyes as if to shade them, and remained so.

"Does the light hurt your eyes, and is that the reason why you didn't want the lamp?" asked Mrs. Brigham kindly.

"I always like to sit in the dark," replied Rebecca chokingly. Then she snatched her handkerchief hastily from her pocket and began to weep. Caroline continued to write, Mrs. Brigham to sew.

Suddenly Mrs. Brigham as she sewed glanced at the opposite wall. The glance became a steady stare. She looked intently, her work suspended in her hands. Then she looked away again and took a few more stitches, then she looked again, and again turned to her task. At last she laid her work in her lap and stared concentratedly. She looked from the wall around the room, taking note of the various objects; she looked at the wall long and intently. Then she turned to her sisters.

"What IS that?" said she.

"What?" asked Caroline harshly; her pen scratched loudly across the paper.

Rebecca gave one of her convulsive gasps.

"That strange shadow on the wall," replied Mrs. Brigham.

Rebecca sat with her face hidden: Caroline dipped her pen in the inkstand.

"Why don't you turn around and look?" asked Mrs. Brigham in a wondering and somewhat aggrieved way.

"I am in a hurry to finish this letter, if Mrs. Wilson Ebbit is going to get word in time to come to the funeral," replied Caroline shortly.

Mrs. Brigham rose, her work slipping to the floor, and she began walking around the room, moving various articles of furniture, with her eyes on the shadow.

Then suddenly she shrieked out:

"Look at this awful shadow! What is it? Caroline, look, look! Rebecca, look! WHAT IS IT?"

All Mrs. Brigham's triumphant placidity was gone. Her handsome face was livid with horror. She stood stiffly pointing at the shadow.

"Look!" said she, pointing her finger at it. "Look! What is it?"

Then Rebecca burst out in a wild wail after a shuddering glance at the wall:

"Oh, Caroline, there it is again! There it is again!"

"Caroline Glynn, you look!" said Mrs. Brigham. "Look! What is that dreadful shadow?"

Caroline rose, turned, and stood confronting the wall.

"How should I know?" she said.

"It has been there every night since he died," cried Rebecca.

"Every night?"

"Yes. He died Thursday and this is Saturday; that makes three nights," said Caroline rigidly. She stood as if holding herself calm with a vise of concentrated will.

"It – it looks like – like – " stammered Mrs. Brigham in a tone of intense horror.

"I know what it looks like well enough," said Caroline. "I've got eyes in my head."

"It looks like Edward," burst out Rebecca in a sort of frenzy of fear. "Only – "

"Yes, it does," assented Mrs. Brigham, whose horror-stricken tone matched her sister's, "only – Oh, it is awful! What is it, Caroline?"

"I ask you again, how should I know?" replied Caroline. "I see it there like you. How should I know any more than you?"

"It MUST be something in the room," said Mrs. Brigham, staring wildly around.

"We moved everything in the room the first night it came," said Rebecca; "it is not anything in the room."

Caroline turned upon her with a sort of fury. "Of course it is something in the room," said she. "How you act! What do you mean by talking so? Of course it is something in the room."

"Of course, it is," agreed Mrs. Brigham, looking at Caroline suspiciously. "Of course it must be. It is only a coincidence. It just happens so. Perhaps it is that fold of the window curtain that makes it. It must be something in the room."

"It is not anything in the room," repeated Rebecca with obstinate horror.

The door opened suddenly and Henry Glynn entered. He began to speak, then his eyes followed the direction of the others'. He stood stock still staring at the shadow on the wall. It was life size and stretched across the white parallelogram of a door, half across the wall space on which the picture hung.

"What is that?" he demanded in a strange voice.

"It must be due to something in the room, Mrs. Brigham said faintly.

"It is not due to anything in the room," said Rebecca again with the shrill insistency of terror.

"How you act, Rebecca Glynn," said Caroline.

Henry Glynn stood and stared a moment longer. His face showed a gamut of emotions – horror, conviction, then furious incredulity. Suddenly he began hastening hither and thither about the room. He moved the furniture with fierce jerks, turning ever to see the effect upon the shadow on the wall. Not a line of its terrible outlines wavered.

"It must be something in the room!" he declared in a voice which seemed to snap like a lash.

His face changed. The inmost secrecy of his nature seemed evident until one almost lost sight of his lineaments. Rebecca stood close to her sofa, regarding him with woeful, fascinated eyes. Mrs. Brigham clutched Caroline's hand. They both stood in a corner out of his way. For a few moments he raged about the room like a caged wild animal. He moved every piece of furniture; when the moving of a piece did not affect the shadow, he flung it to the floor, his sisters watching.

Then suddenly he desisted. He laughed and began straightening the furniture which he had flung down.

"What an absurdity," he said easily. "Such a to-do about a shadow."

"That's so," assented Mrs. Brigham, in a scared voice which she tried to make natural. As she spoke she lifted a chair near her.

"I think you have broken the chair that Edward was so fond of," said Caroline.

Terror and wrath were struggling for expression on her face. Her mouth was set, her eyes shrinking. Henry lifted the chair with a show of anxiety.

"Just as good as ever," he said pleasantly. He laughed again, looking at his sisters. "Did I scare you?" he said. "I should think you might be used to me by this time. You know my way of wanting to leap to the bottom of a mystery, and that shadow does look - queer, like - and I thought if there was any way of accounting for it I would like to without any delay."

"You don't seem to have succeeded," remarked Caroline dryly, with a slight glance at the wall.

Henry's eyes followed hers and he quivered perceptibly.

"Oh, there is no accounting for shadows," he said, and he

laughed again. "A man is a fool to try to account for shadows."

Then the supper bell rang, and they all left the room, but Henry kept his back to the wall, as did, indeed, the others.

Mrs. Brigham pressed close to Caroline as she crossed the hall. "He looked like a demon!" she breathed in her ear.

Henry led the way with an alert motion like a boy; Rebecca brought up the rear; she could scarcely walk, her knees trembled so.

"I can't sit in that room again this evening," she whispered to Caroline after supper.

"Very well, we will sit in the south room," replied Caroline. "I think we will sit in the south parlor," she said aloud; "it isn't as damp as the study, and I have a cold."

So they all sat in the south room with their sewing. Henry read the newspaper, his chair drawn close to the lamp on the table. About nine o'clock he rose abruptly and crossed the hall to the study. The three sisters looked at one another. Mrs. Brigham rose, folded her rustling skirts compactly around her, and began tiptoeing toward the door.

"What are you going to do?" inquired Rebecca agitatedly.

"I am going to see what he is about," replied Mrs. Brigham cautiously.

She pointed as she spoke to the study door across the hall; it was ajar. Henry had striven to pull it together behind him, but it had somehow swollen beyond the limit with curious speed. It was still ajar and a streak of light showed from top to bottom. The hall lamp was not lit.

"You had better stay where you are," said Caroline with guarded sharpness.

"I am going to see," repeated Mrs. Brigham firmly.

Then she folded her skirts so tightly that her bulk with its swelling curves was revealed in a black silk sheath, and she went with a slow toddle across the hall to the study door. She stood there, her eye at the crack.

In the south room Rebecca stopped sewing and sat watching with dilated eyes. Caroline sewed steadily. What Mrs. Brigham, standing at the crack in the study door, saw was this:

Henry Glynn, evidently reasoning that the source of the strange shadow must be between the table on which the lamp stood and the wall, was making systematic passes and thrusts all over and through the intervening space with an old sword which had belonged to his father. Not an inch was left unpierced. He seemed to have divided the space into mathematical sections. He brandished the sword with a sort of cold fury and calculation; the blade gave out flashes of light, the shadow remained unmoved. Mrs. Brigham, watching, felt herself cold with horror.

Finally Henry ceased and stood with the sword in hand and raised as if to strike, surveying the shadow on the wall threateningly. Mrs. Brigham toddled back across the hall and shut the south room door behind her before she related what she had seen.

"He looked like a demon!" she said again. "Have you got any of that old wine in the house, Caroline? I don't feel as if I could stand much more."

Indeed, she looked overcome. Her handsome placid face was worn and strained and pale.

"Yes, there's plenty," said Caroline; "you can have some when you go to bed."

"I think we had all better take some," said Mrs. Brigham. "Oh, my God, Caroline, what – "

"Don't ask and don't speak," said Caroline.

"No, I am not going to," replied Mrs. Brigham; "but – "

Rebecca moaned aloud.

"What are you doing that for?" asked Caroline harshly.

"Poor Edward," returned Rebecca.

"That is all you have to groan for," said Caroline. "There is nothing else."

"I am going to bed," said Mrs. Brigham. "I sha'n't be able to be at the funeral if I don't."

Soon the three sisters went to their chambers and the south parlor was deserted. Caroline called to Henry in the study to put out the light before he came upstairs. They had been gone about an hour when he came into the room bringing the lamp which had stood in the study. He set it on the table and waited a few minutes, pacing up and down. His face was terrible, his fair complexion showed livid; his blue eyes seemed dark blanks of awful reflections.

Then he took the lamp up and returned to the library. He set the lamp on the centre table, and the shadow sprang out on the wall. Again he studied the furniture and moved it about, but deliberately, with none of his former frenzy. Nothing affected the shadow. Then he returned to the south room with the lamp and again waited. Again he returned to the study and placed the lamp on the table, and the shadow sprang out upon the wall. It was midnight before he went upstairs. Mrs. Brigham and the other sisters, who could not sleep, heard him.

The next day was the funeral. That evening the family sat in the south room. Some relatives were with them. Nobody entered the study until Henry carried a lamp in there after the others had retired for the night. He saw again the shadow on the wall leap to an awful life before the light.

The next morning at breakfast Henry Glynn announced that he had to go to the city for three days. The sisters looked at him with surprise. He very seldom left home, and just now his practice had been neglected on account of Edward's death. He was a physician.

"How can you leave your patients now?" asked Mrs. Brigham wonderingly.

"I don't know how to, but there is no other way," replied Henry easily. "I have had a telegram from Doctor Mitford."

"Consultation?" inquired Mrs. Brigham.

"I have business," replied Henry.

Doctor Mitford was an old classmate of his who lived in a neighboring city and who occasionally called upon him in the case of a consultation.

After he had gone Mrs. Brigham said to Caroline that after all Henry had not said that he was going to consult with Doctor Mitford, and she thought it very strange.

"Everything is very strange," said Rebecca with a shudder.

"What do you mean?" inquired Caroline sharply.

"Nothing," replied Rebecca.

Nobody entered the library that day, nor the next, nor the next. The third day Henry was expected home, but he did not arrive and the last train from the city had come.

"I call it pretty queer work," said Mrs. Brigham. "The idea of a doctor leaving his patients for three days anyhow, at such a time as this, and I know he has some very sick ones; he said so. And the idea of a consultation lasting three days! There is no sense in it, and NOW he has not come. I don't understand it, for my part."

"I don't either," said Rebecca.

They were all in the south parlor. There was no light in the study opposite, and the door was ajar.

Presently Mrs. Brigham rose – she could not have told why; something seemed to impel her, some will outside her own. She went out of the room, again wrapping her rustling skirts around that she might pass noiselessly, and began pushing at the swollen door of the study.

"She has not got any lamp," said Rebecca in a shaking voice.

Caroline, who was writing letters, rose again, took a lamp

(there were two in the room) and followed her sister. Rebecca had risen, but she stood trembling, not venturing to follow.

The doorbell rang, but the others did not hear it; it was on the south door on the other side of the house from the study. Rebecca, after hesitating until the bell rang the second time, went to the door; she remembered that the servant was out.

Caroline and her sister Emma entered the study. Caroline set the lamp on the table. They looked at the wall. "Oh, my God," gasped Mrs. Brigham, "there are – there are TWO – shadows." The sisters stood clutching each other, staring at the awful things on the wall. Then Rebecca came in, staggering, with a telegram in her hand. "Here is – a telegram," she gasped. "Henry is – dead."

From "The Wind in the Rosebush," by Mary E. Wilkins Freeman.

Melville Davisson Post

Introduction to The Corpus Delicti

The high ground of the field of crime has not been explored; it has not even been entered. The book stalls have been filled to weariness with tales based upon plans whereby the DETECTIVE, or FERRETING power of the State might be baffled. But, prodigious marvel! no writer has attempted to construct tales based upon plans whereby the PUNISHING power of the State might be baffled.

The distinction, if one pauses for a moment to consider it, is striking. It is possible, even easy, deliberately to plan crimes so that the criminal agent and the criminal agency cannot be detected. Is it possible to plan and execute wrongs in such a manner that they will have all the effect and all the resulting profit of desperate crimes and yet not be crimes before the law?

We are prone to forget that the law is no perfect structure, that it is simply the result of human labor and human genius, and that whatever laws human ingenuity can create for the protection of men, those same laws human ingenuity can evade. The Spirit of Evil is no dwarf; he has developed equally with the Spirit of Good.

All wrongs are not crimes. Indeed only those wrongs are crimes in which certain technical elements are present. The law provides a Procrustean standard for all crimes. Thus a wrong, to become criminal, must fit exactly into the measure laid down by the law, else it is no crime; if it varies never so little from the legal measure, the law must, and will, refuse to regard it as criminal, no matter how injurious a wrong it may be. There is no measure of morality, or equity, or common right that can be applied to the individual case. The gauge of the law is iron-bound. The wrong measured by this gauge is either a crime or it is not. There is no middle ground.

Hence is it, that if one knows well the technicalities of the law, one may commit horrible wrongs that will yield all the gain and all the resulting effect of the highest crimes, and yet the wrongs perpetrated will constitute no one of the crimes described by the law. Thus the highest crimes, even murder, may be committed in such manner that although the criminal is known and the law holds him in custody, yet it cannot punish him. So it happens that in this year of our Lord of the nineteenth century, the skillful attorney marvels at the stupidity of the rogue who, committing crimes by the ordinary methods, subjects himself to unnecessary peril, when the result which he seeks can easily be attained by other methods, equally expeditious and without danger of liability in any criminal tribunal. This is the field into which the author has ventured, and he believes it to be new and full of interest.

It may be objected that the writer has prepared here a textbook for the shrewd knave. To this it is answered that, if he instructs the enemies, he also warns the friends of law and order; and that Evil has never yet been stronger because the sun shone on it.

[See Lord Hale's Rule, Russell on Crimes. For the law in New York see 18th N. Y. Reports, 179; also N. Y. Reports, 49, page 137. The doctrine there laid down obtains in almost every State, with the possible exception of a few Western States, where the decisions are muddy.]

The Corpus Delicti

I

"That man Mason," said Samuel Walcott, "is the mysterious member of this club. He is more than that; he is the mysterious man of New York."

"I was much surprised to see him," answered his companion, Marshall St. Clair, of the great law firm of Seward, St. Clair & De Muth. "I had lost track of him since he went to Paris as counsel for the American stockholders of the Canal Company. When did he come back to the States?"

"He turned up suddenly in his ancient haunts about four months ago," said Walcott, "as grand, gloomy, and peculiar as Napoleon ever was in his palmiest days. The younger members of the club call him 'Zanona Redivivus.' He wanders through the house usually late at night, apparently without noticing anything or anybody. His mind seems to be deeply and busily at work, leaving his bodily self to wander as it may happen. Naturally, strange stories are told of him; indeed, his individuality and his habit of doing some unexpected thing, and doing it in such a marvelously original manner that men who are experts at it look on in wonder, cannot fail to make him an object of interest.

"He has never been known to play at any game whatever, and yet one night he sat down to the chess table with old Admiral Du Brey. You know the Admiral is the great champion since he beat the French and English officers in the tournament last winter. Well, you also know that the conventional openings at chess are scientifically and accurately determined. To the utter disgust of Du Brey, Mason opened the game with an unheard-of attack from the extremes of the board. The old Admiral stopped and, in a kindly patronizing way, pointed out the weak and absurd folly of his move and asked him to begin again with some one of the safe openings. Mason smiled and answered that if one had a head that he could trust he should use it; if not, then it was the part of wisdom to follow blindly the dead forms of some man who had a head. Du Brey was naturally angry and set himself to demolish Mason as quickly as possible. The game was rapid for a few moments. Mason lost piece after piece. His opening was broken and destroyed and its utter folly apparent to the lookers-on. The Admiral smiled and the game seemed all one- sided, when, suddenly, to his utter horror, Du Brey found that his king was in a trap. The foolish opening had been only a piece of shrewd strategy. The old Admiral fought and cursed and sacrificed his pieces, but it was of no use. He was gone. Mason checkmated him in two moves and arose wearily.

"'Where in Heaven's name, man,' said the old Admiral, thunderstruck, 'did you learn that masterpiece?'

"'Just here,' replied Mason. 'To play chess, one should know his opponent. How could the dead masters lay down rules by which you could be beaten, sir? They had never seen you'; and thereupon he turned and left the room. Of course, St. Clair, such a strange man would soon become an object of all kinds of mysterious rumors. Some are true and some are not. At any rate, I know that Mason is an unusual man with a gigantic intellect. Of late he seems to have taken a strange fancy to me. In fact, I seem to be the only member of the club that he will talk with, and I confess that he startles and fascinates me. He is an original genius, St. Clair, of an unusual order."

"I recall vividly," said the younger man, "that before Mason went to Paris he was considered one of the greatest lawyers of this city and he was feared and hated by the bar at large. He came here, I believe, from Virginia and began with the high-grade criminal practice. He soon became famous for his powerful and ingenious defenses. He found holes in the law through which his clients escaped, holes that by the profession at large were not suspected to exist, and that frequently astonished the judges. His ability caught the attention of the great corporations. They tested him and found in him learning and unlimited resources. He pointed out methods by which they could evade obnoxious statutes, by which they could comply with the apparent letter of the law and yet violate its spirit, and advised them well in that most important of all things, just how far they could bend the law without breaking it. At the time he left for Paris he had a vast clientage and was in the midst of a brilliant career. The day he took passage from New York, the bar lost sight of him. No matter how great a man may be, the wave soon closes over him in a city like this. In a few years Mason was forgotten. Now only the older practitioners would recall him, and they would do so with hatred and bitterness. He was a tireless, savage, uncompromising fighter, always a recluse."

"Well," said Walcott, "he reminds me of a great world-weary cynic, transplanted from some ancient mysterious empire. When I come into the man's presence I feel instinctively the grip of his intellect. I tell you, St. Clair, Randolph Mason is the mysterious man of New York."

At this moment a messenger boy came into the room and handed Mr. Walcott a telegram. "St. Clair," said that gentleman, rising, "the directors of the Elevated are in session, and we must hurry." The two men put on their coats and left the house.

Samuel Walcott was not a club man after the manner of the Smart Set, and yet he was in fact a club man. He was a bachelor in the latter thirties, and resided in a great silent house on the avenue. On the street he was a man of substance, shrewd and progressive, backed by great wealth. He had various corporate interests in the larger syndicates, but the basis and foundation of his fortune was real estate. His houses on the avenue were the best possible property, and his elevator row in the importers' quarter was indeed a literal gold mine. It was known that, many years before, his grandfather had died and left him the property, which, at that time, was of no great value. Young Walcott had gone out into the gold-fields and had been lost sight of and forgotten. Ten years afterwards he had turned up suddenly in New York and taken possession of his property, then vastly increased in value. His speculations were almost phenomenally successful, and, backed by the now enormous value of his real property, he was soon on a level with the merchant princes. His judgment was considered sound, and he had the full confidence of his business associates for safety and caution. Fortune heaped up riches around him with a lavish hand. He was unmarried and the halo of his wealth caught the keen eye of the matron with marriageable daughters. He was invited out, caught by the whirl of society, and tossed into its maelstrom. In a measure he reciprocated. He kept horses and a yacht. His dinners at Delmonico's and the club were above reproach. But with all he was a silent man with a shadow deep in his eyes, and seemed to court the society of his fellows, not because he loved them, but because he either hated or feared solitude. For years the strategy of the match-maker had gone gracefully afield, but Fate is relentless. If she shields the victim from the traps of men, it is not because she wishes him to escape, but because she is pleased to reserve him for her own trap. So it happened that, when Virginia St. Clair assisted Mrs. Miriam Steuvisant at her midwinter reception, this same Samuel Walcott fell deeply and hopelessly and utterly in love, and it was so apparent to the beaten generals present, that Mrs. Miriam Steuvisant applauded herself, so to speak, with encore after encore. It was good to see this courteous, silent man literally at the feet of the young debutante. He was there of right. Even the mothers of marriageable daughters admitted that. The young girl was brown-haired, brown-eyed, and tall enough, said the experts, and of the blue blood royal, with all the grace, courtesy, and inbred genius of such princely heritage.

Perhaps it was objected by the censors of the Smart Set that Miss St. Clair's frankness and honesty were a trifle old-fashioned, and that she was a shadowy bit of a Puritan; and perhaps it was of these same qualities that Samuel Walcott received his hurt. At any rate the hurt was there and deep, and the new actor stepped up into the old time-worn, semi-tragic drama, and began his role with a tireless, utter sincerity that was deadly dangerous if he lost.

II

Perhaps a week after the conversation between St. Clair and Walcott, Randolph Mason stood in the private waiting-room of the club with his hands behind his back.

He was a man apparently in the middle forties; tall and reasonably broad across the shoulders; muscular without being either stout or lean. His hair was thin and of a brown color, with erratic streaks of gray. His forehead was broad and high and of a faint reddish color. His eyes were restless inky black, and not over-large. The nose was big and muscular and bowed. The eyebrows were black and heavy, almost bushy. There were heavy furrows, running from the nose downward and outward to the corners of the mouth. The mouth was straight and the jaw was heavy, and square.

Looking at the face of Randolph Mason from above, the expression in repose was crafty and cynical; viewed from below upward, it was savage and vindictive, almost brutal; while from the front, if looked squarely in the face, the stranger was fascinated by the animation of the man and at once concluded that his expression was fearless and sneering. He was evidently of Southern extraction and a man of unusual power.

A fire smoldered on the hearth. It was a crisp evening in the early fall, and with that far-off touch of melancholy which ever heralds the coming winter, even in the midst of a city. The man's face looked tired and ugly. His long white hands were clasped tight together. His entire figure and face wore every mark of weakness and physical exhaustion; but his eyes contradicted. They were red and restless.

In the private dining-room the dinner party was in the best of spirits. Samuel Walcott was happy. Across the table from him was Miss Virginia St. Clair, radiant, a tinge of color in her cheeks. On either side, Mrs. Miriam Steuvisant and Marshall St. Clair were brilliant and lighthearted. Walcott looked at the young girl and the measure of his worship was full. He wondered for the thousandth time how she could possibly love him and by what earthly miracle she had come to accept him, and how it would be always to have her across the table from him, his own table in his own house.

They were about to rise from the table when one of the waiters entered the room and handed Walcott an envelope. He thrust it quickly into his pocket. In the confusion of rising the others did not notice him, but his face was ash white and his hands trembled violently as he placed the wraps around the bewitching shoulders of Miss St. Clair.

"Marshall," he said, and despite the powerful effort his voice was hollow, "you will see the ladies safely cared for, I am called to attend a grave matter."

"All right, Walcott," answered the young man, with cheery good nature, "you are too serious, old man, trot along."

"The poor dear," murmured Mrs. Steuvisant, after Walcott had helped them to the carriage and turned to go up the steps of the club, – "The poor dear is hard hit, and men are such funny creatures when they are hard hit."

Samuel Walcott, as his fate would, went direct to the private writing-room and opened the door. The lights were not turned on and in the dark he did not see Mason motionless by the mantel-shelf. He went quickly across the room to the writing-table, turned on one of the lights, and, taking the envelope from his pocket, tore it open. Then he bent down by the light to read the contents. As his eyes ran over the paper, his jaw fell. The skin drew away from his cheekbones and his face seemed literally to sink in. His knees gave way under him and he would have gone down in a heap had it not been for Mason's long arms that closed around him and held him up. The human economy is ever mysterious. The moment the new danger threatened, the latent power of the man as an animal, hidden away in the centers of intelligence, asserted itself. His hand clutched the paper and, with a half slide, he turned in Mason's arms. For a moment he stared up at the ugly man whose thin arms felt like wire ropes.

"You are under the dead-fall, aye," said Mason. "The cunning of my enemy is sublime."

"Your enemy?" gasped Walcott. "When did you come into it? How in God's name did you know it? How your enemy?"

Mason looked down at the wide bulging eyes of the man.

"Who should know better than I?" he said. "Haven't I broken through all the traps and plots that she could set?"

"She? She trap you?" The man's voice was full of horror.

"The old schemer," muttered Mason. "The cowardly old schemer, to strike in the back; but we can beat her. She did not count on my helping you – I, who know her so well."

Mason's face was red, and his eyes burned. In the midst of it all he dropped his hands and went over to the fire. Samuel Walcott arose, panting, and stood looking at Mason, with his hands behind him on the table. The naturally strong nature and the rigid school in which the man had been trained presently began to tell. His composure in part returned and he thought rapidly. What did this strange man know? Was he simply making shrewd guesses, or had he some mysterious knowledge of this matter? Walcott could not know that Mason meant only Fate, that he believed her to be his great enemy. Walcott had never before doubted his own ability to meet any emergency. This mighty jerk had carried him off his feet. He was unstrung and panic-stricken. At any rate this man had promised help. He would take it. He put the paper and envelope carefully into his pocket, smoothed out his rumpled coat, and going over to Mason touched him on the shoulder.

"Come," he said, "if you are to help me we must go."

The man turned and followed him without a word. In the hall Mason put on his hat and overcoat, and the two went out into the street. Walcott hailed a cab, and the two were driven to his house on the avenue. Walcott took out his latchkey, opened the door, and led the way into the library. He turned on the light and motioned Mason to seat himself at the table. Then he went into another room and presently returned with a bundle of papers and a decanter of brandy. He poured out a glass of the liquor and offered it to Mason. The man shook his head. Walcott poured the contents of the glass down his own throat. Then he set the decanter down and drew up a chair on the side of the table opposite Mason.

"Sir," said Walcott, in a voice deliberate, indeed, but as hollow as a sepulcher, "I am done for. God has finally gathered up the ends of the net, and it is knotted tight."

"Am I not here to help you?" said Mason, turning savagely. "I can beat Fate. Give me the details of her trap."

He bent forward and rested his arms on the table. His streaked gray hair was rumpled and on end, and his face was ugly. For a moment Walcott did not answer. He moved a little into the shadow; then he spread the bundle of old yellow papers out before him.

"To begin with," he said, "I am a living lie, a gilded crime-made sham, every bit of me. There is not an honest piece anywhere. It is all lie. I am a liar and a thief before men. The property which I possess is not mine, but stolen from a dead man. The very name which I bear is not my own, but is the bastard child of a crime. I am more than all that – I am a murderer; a murderer before the law; a murderer before God; and worse than a murderer before the pure woman whom I love more than anything that God could make."

He paused for a moment and wiped the perspiration from his face.

"Sir," said Mason, "this is all drivel, infantile drivel. What you are is of no importance. How to get out is the problem, how to get out."

Samuel Walcott leaned forward, poured out a glass of brandy and swallowed it.

"Well," he said, speaking slowly, "my right name is Richard Warren. In the spring of 1879 I came to New York and fell in with the real Samuel Walcott, a young man with a little money and some property which his grandfather had left him. We became friends, and concluded to go to the far west together. Accordingly we scraped together what money we could lay our hands on, and landed in the gold-mining regions of California. We were young and inexperienced, and our money went rapidly. One April morning we drifted into a little shack camp, away up in the Sierra Nevadas, called Hell's Elbow. Here we struggled and starved for perhaps a year. Finally, in utter desperation, Walcott married the daughter of a Mexican gambler, who ran an eating house and a poker joint. With them we lived from hand to mouth in a wild God-forsaken way for several years. After a time the woman began to take a strange fancy to me. Walcott finally noticed it, and grew jealous.

"One night, in a drunken brawl, we quarreled, and I killed him. It was late at night, and, beside the woman, there were four of us in the poker room, – the Mexican gambler, a half-breed devil called Cherubim Pete, Walcott, and myself. When Walcott fell, the half- breed whipped out his weapon, and fired at me across the table; but the woman, Nina San Croix, struck his arm, and, instead of killing me, as he intended, the bullet mortally wounded her father, the Mexican gambler. I shot the half-breed through the forehead, and turned round, expecting the woman to attack me. On the contrary, she pointed to the window, and bade me wait for her on the cross trail below.

"It was fully three hours later before the woman joined me at the place indicated. She had a bag of gold dust, a few jewels that belonged to her father, and a package of papers. I asked her why she had stayed behind so long, and she replied that the men were not killed outright, and that she had brought a priest to them and waited until they had died. This was the truth, but not all the truth. Moved by superstition or foresight, the woman had induced the priest to take down the sworn statements of the two dying men, seal it, and give it to her. This paper she brought with her. All this I learned afterwards. At the time I knew nothing of this damning evidence.

"We struck out together for the Pacific coast. The country was lawless. The privations we endured were almost past belief. At times the woman exhibited cunning and ability that were almost genius; and through it all, often in the very fingers of death, her devotion to me never wavered. It was doglike, and seemed to be her only object on earth. When we reached San Francisco, the woman put these papers into my hands." Walcott took up the yellow package, and pushed it across the table to Mason.

"She proposed that I assume Walcott's name, and that we come boldly to New York and claim the property. I examined the papers, found a copy of the will by which Walcott inherited the property, a bundle of correspondence, and sufficient documentary evidence to establish his identity beyond the shadow of a doubt. Desperate gambler as I now was, I quailed before the daring plan of Nina San Croix. I urged that I, Richard Warren, would be known, that the attempted fraud would be detected and would result in investigation, and perhaps unearth the whole horrible matter.

"The woman pointed out how much I resembled Walcott, what vast changes ten years of such life as we had led would naturally be expected to make in men, how utterly impossible it would be to trace back the fraud to Walcott's murder at Hell's Elbow, in the wild passes of the Sierra Nevadas. She bade me remember that we were both outcasts, both crime-branded, both enemies of man's law and God's; that we had nothing to lose; we were both sunk to the bottom. Then she laughed, and said that she had not found me a coward until now, but that if I had turned chicken-hearted, that was the end of it, of course. The result was, we sold the gold dust and jewels in San Francisco, took on such evidences of civilization as possible, and purchased passage to New York on the best steamer we could find.

"I was growing to depend on the bold gambler spirit of this woman, Nina San Croix; I felt the need of her strong, profligate nature. She was of a queer breed and a queerer school. Her mother was the daughter of a Spanish engineer, and had been stolen by the Mexican, her father. She herself had been raised and educated as best might be in one of the monasteries along the Rio Grande, and had there grown to womanhood before her father, fleeing into the mountains of California, carried her with him.

"When we landed in New York I offered to announce her as my wife, but she refused, saying that her presence would excite comment and perhaps attract the attention of Walcott's relatives. We therefore arranged that I should go alone into the city, claim the property, and announce myself as Samuel Walcott, and that she should remain under cover until such time as we would feel the ground safe under us.

"Every detail of the plan was fatally successful. I established my identity without difficulty and secured the property. It had increased vastly in value, and I, as Samuel Walcott, soon found myself a rich man. I went to Nina San Croix in hiding and gave her a large sum of money, with which she purchased a residence in a retired part of the city, far up in the northern suburb. Here she lived secluded and unknown while I remained in the city, living here as a wealthy bachelor.

"I did not attempt to abandon the woman, but went to her from time to time in disguise and under cover of the greatest secrecy. For a time everything ran smooth, the woman was still devoted to me above everything else, and thought always of my welfare first and seemed content to wait so long as I thought best. My business expanded. I was sought after and consulted and drawn into the higher life of New York, and more and more felt that the woman was an albatross on my neck. I put her off with one excuse after another. Finally she began to suspect me and demanded that I should recognize her as my wife. I attempted to point out the difficulties. She met them all by saying that we should both go to Spain, there I could marry her and we could return to America and drop into my place in society without causing more than a passing comment.

"I concluded to meet the matter squarely once for all. I said that I would convert half of the property into money and give it to her, but that I would not marry her. She did not fly into a storming rage as I had expected, but went quietly out of the room and presently returned with two papers, which she read. One was the certificate of her marriage to Walcott duly authenticated; the other was the dying statement of her father, the Mexican gambler, and of Samuel Walcott, charging me with murder. It was in proper form and certified by the Jesuit priest.

"'Now,' she said, sweetly, when she had finished, 'which do you prefer, to recognize your wife, or to turn all the property over to Samuel Walcott's widow and hang for his murder?'

"I was dumfounded and horrified. I saw the trap that I was in and I consented to do anything she should say if she would only destroy the papers. This she refused to do. I pleaded with her and implored her to destroy them. Finally she gave them to me with a great show of returning confidence, and I tore them into bits and threw them into the fire.

"That was three months ago. We arranged to go to Spain and do as she said. She was to sail this morning and I was to follow. Of course I never intended to go. I congratulated myself on the fact that all trace of evidence against me was destroyed and that her grip was now broken. My plan was to induce her to sail, believing that I would follow. When she was gone I would marry Miss St. Clair, and if Nina San Croix should return I would defy her and lock her up as a lunatic. But I was reckoning like an infernal ass, to imagine for a moment that I could thus hoodwink such a woman as Nina San Croix.

"To-night I received this." Walcott took the envelope from his pocket and gave it to Mason. "You saw the effect of it; read it and you will understand why. I felt the death hand when I saw her writing on the envelope."

Mason took the paper from the envelope. It was written in Spanish, and ran:

"Greeting to RICHARD WARREN.

"The great Senor does his little Nina injustice to think she would go away to Spain and leave him to the beautiful American. She is not so thoughtless. Before she goes, she shall be, Oh so very rich! and the dear Senor shall be, Oh so very safe! The Archbishop and the kind Church hate murderers.

"NINA SAN CROIX.

"Of course, fool, the papers you destroyed were copies.

"N. SAN C."

To this was pinned a line in a delicate aristocratic hand saying that the Archbishop would willingly listen to Madam San Croix's statement if she would come to him on Friday morning at eleven.

"You see," said Walcott, desperately, "there is no possible way out. I know the woman – when she decides to do a thing that is the end of it. She has decided to do this."

Mason turned around from the table, stretched out his long legs, and thrust his hands deep into his pockets. Walcott sat with his head down, watching Mason hopelessly, almost indifferently, his face blank and sunken. The ticking of the bronze clock on the mantel shelf was loud, painfully loud. Suddenly Mason drew his knees in and bent over, put both his bony hands on the table, and looked at Walcott.

"Sir," he said, "this matter is in such shape that there is only one thing to do. This growth must be cut out at the roots, and cut out quickly. This is the first fact to be determined, and a fool would know it. The second fact is that you must do it yourself. Hired killers are like the grave and the daughters of the horse leech, – they cry always, 'Give, Give.' They are only palliatives, not cures. By using them you swap perils. You simply take a stay of execution at best. The common criminal would know this. These are the facts of your problem. The master plotters of crime would see here but two difficulties to meet:

"A practical method for accomplishing the body of the crime.

"A cover for the criminal agent.

"They would see no farther, and attempt to guard no farther. After they had provided a plan for the killing, and a means by which the killer could cover his trail and escape from the theater of the homicide, they would believe all the requirements of the problems met, and would stop. The greatest, the very giants among them, have stopped here and have been in great error.

"In every crime, especially in the great ones, there exists a third element, preeminently vital. This third element the master plotters have either overlooked or else have not had the genius to construct. They plan with rare cunning to baffle the victim. They plan with vast wisdom, almost genius, to baffle the trailer. But they fail utterly to provide any plan for baffling the punisher. Ergo, their plots are fatally defective and often result in ruin.

Hence the vital necessity for providing the third element – the escape ipso jure."

Mason arose, walked around the table, and put his hand firmly on Samuel Walcott's shoulder. "This must be done to-morrow night," he continued; "you must arrange your business matters to-morrow and announce that you are going on a yacht cruise, by order of your physician, and may not return for some weeks. You must prepare your yacht for a voyage, instruct your men to touch at a certain point on Staten Island, and wait until six o'clock day after tomorrow morning. If you do not come aboard by that time, they are to go to one of the South American ports and remain until further orders. By this means your absence for an indefinite period will be explained. You will go to Nina San Croix in the disguise which you have always used, and from her to the yacht, and by this means step out of your real status and back into it without leaving traces. I will come here to-morrow evening and furnish you with everything that you shall need and give you full and exact instructions in every particular. These details you must execute with the greatest care, as they will be vitally essential to the success of my plan."

Through it all Walcott had been silent and motionless. Now he arose, and in his face there must have been some premonition of protest, for Mason stepped back and put out his hand. "Sir," he said, with brutal emphasis, "not a word. Remember that you are only the hand, and the hand does not think." Then he turned around abruptly and went out of the house.

III

The place which Samuel Walcott had selected for the residence of Nina San Croix was far up in the northern suburb of New York. The place was very old. The lawn was large and ill kept; the house, a square old-fashioned brick, was set far back from the street, and partly hidden by trees. Around it all was a rusty iron fence. The place had the air of genteel ruin, such as one finds in the Virginias.

On a Thursday of November, about three o'clock in the afternoon, a little man, driving a dray, stopped in the alley at the rear of the house. As he opened the back gate an old negro woman came down the steps from the kitchen and demanded to know what he wanted. The drayman asked if the lady of the house was in. The old negro answered that she was asleep at this hour and could not be seen.

"That is good," said the little man, "now there won't be any row. I brought up some cases of wine which she ordered from our house last week and which the Boss told me to deliver at once, but I forgot it until to-day. Just let me put it in the cellar now, Auntie, and don't say a word to the lady about it and she won't ever know that it was not brought up on time."

The drayman stopped, fished a silver dollar out of his pocket, and gave it to the old negro. "There now, Auntie," he said, "my job depends upon the lady not knowing about this wine; keep it mum."

"Dat's all right, honey," said the old servant, beaming like a May morning. "De cellar door is open, carry it all in and put it in de back part and nobody ain't never going to know how long it has been in dar."

The old negro went back into the kitchen and the little man began to unload the dray. He carried in five wine cases and stowed them away in the back part of the cellar as the old woman had directed. Then, after having satisfied himself that no one was watching, he took from the dray two heavy paper sacks, presumably filled with flour, and a little bundle wrapped in an old newspaper; these he carefully hid behind the wine cases in the cellar. After awhile he closed the door, climbed on his dray, and drove off down the alley.

About eight o'clock in the evening of the same day, a Mexican sailor dodged in the front gate and slipped down to the side of the house. He stopped by the window and tapped on it with his finger. In a moment a woman opened the door. She was tall, lithe, and splendidly proportioned, with a dark Spanish face and straight hair. The man stepped inside. The woman bolted the door and turned round.

"Ah," she said, smiling, "it is you, Senor? How good of you!"

The man started. "Whom else did you expect?" he said quickly.

"Oh!" laughed the woman, "perhaps the Archbishop."

"Nina!" said the man, in a broken voice that expressed love, humility, and reproach. His face was white under the black sunburn.

For a moment the woman wavered. A shadow flitted over her eyes, then she stepped back. "No," she said, "not yet."

The man walked across to the fire, sank down in a chair, and covered his face with his hands. The woman stepped up noiselessly behind him and leaned over the chair. The man was either in great agony or else he was a superb actor, for the muscles of his neck twitched violently and his shoulders trembled.

"Oh," he muttered, as though echoing his thoughts, "I can't do it, I can't!"

The woman caught the words and leaped up as though some one had struck her in the face. She threw back her head. Her nostrils dilated and her eyes flashed.

"You can't do it!" she cried. "Then you do love her! You shall do it! Do you hear me? You shall do it! You killed him! You got rid of him! but you shall not get rid of me. I have the evidence, all of it. The Archbishop will have it to-morrow. They shall hang you! Do you hear me? They shall hang you!"

The woman's voice rose, it was loud and shrill. The man turned slowly round without looking up, and stretched out his arms toward the woman. She stopped and looked down at him. The fire glittered for a moment and then died out of her eyes, her bosom heaved and her lips began to tremble. With a cry she flung herself into his arms, caught him around the neck, and pressed his face up close against her cheek.

"Oh! Dick, Dick," she sobbed, "I do love you so! I can't live without you! Not another hour, Dick! I do want you so much, so much, Dick!"

The man shifted his right arm quickly, slipped a great Mexican knife out of his sleeve, and passed his fingers slowly up the woman's side until he felt the heart beat under his hand, then he raised the knife, gripped the handle tight, and drove the keen blade into the woman's bosom. The hot blood gushed out over his arm, and down on his leg. The body, warm and limp, slipped down in his arms. The man got up, pulled out the knife, and thrust it into a sheath at his belt, unbuttoned the dress, and slipped it off of the body. As he did this a bundle of papers dropped upon the floor; these he glanced at hastily and put into his pocket. Then he took the dead woman up in his arms, went out into the hall, and started to go up the stairway. The body was relaxed and heavy, and for that reason difficult to carry. He doubled it up into an awful heap, with the knees against the chin, and walked slowly and heavily up the stairs and out into the bathroom. There he laid the corpse down on the tiled floor. Then he opened the window, closed the shutters, and lighted the gas. The bathroom was small and contained an ordinary steel tub, porcelain lined, standing near the window and raised about six inches above the floor. The sailor went over to the tub, pried up the metal rim of the outlet with his knife, removed it, and fitted into its place a porcelain disk which he took from his pocket; to this disk was attached a long platinum wire, the end of which he fastened on the outside of the tub. After he had done this he went back to the body, stripped off its clothing, put it down in the tub and began to dismember it with the great Mexican knife. The blade was strong and sharp as a razor. The man worked rapidly and with the greatest care.

When he had finally cut the body into as small pieces as possible, he replaced the knife in its sheath, washed his hands, and went out of the bathroom and downstairs to the lower hall. The sailor seemed perfectly familiar with the house. By a side door he passed into the cellar. There he lighted the gas, opened one of the wine cases, and, taking up all the bottles that he could conveniently carry, returned to the bathroom. There he poured the contents into the tub on the dismembered body, and then returned to the cellar with the empty bottles, which he replaced in the wine cases. This he continued to do until all the cases but one were emptied and the bath tub was more than half full of liquid. This liquid was sulphuric acid.

When the sailor returned to the cellar with the last empty wine bottles, he opened the fifth case, which really contained wine, took some of it out, and poured a little into each of the empty bottles in order to remove any possible odor of the sulphuric acid. Then he turned out the gas and brought up to the bathroom with him the two paper flour sacks and the little heavy bundle. These sacks were filled with nitrate of soda. He set them down by the door, opened the little bundle, and took out two long rubber tubes, each attached to a heavy gas burner, not unlike the ordinary burners of a small gas stove. He fastened the tubes to two of the gas jets, put the burners under the tub, turned the gas on full, and lighted it. Then he threw into the tub the woman's clothing and the papers which he had found on her body, after which he took up the two heavy sacks of nitrate of soda and dropped them carefully into the sulphuric acid. When he had done this he went quickly out of the bathroom and closed the door.

The deadly acids at once attacked the body and began to destroy it; as the heat increased, the acids boiled and the destructive process was rapid and awful. From time to time the sailor opened the door of the bathroom cautiously, and, holding a wet towel over his mouth and nose, looked in at his horrible work. At the end of a few hours there was only a swimming mass in the tub. When the man looked at four o'clock, it was all a thick murky liquid. He turned off the gas quickly and stepped back out of the room. For perhaps half an hour he waited in the hall; finally, when the acids had cooled so that they no longer gave off fumes, he opened the door and went in, took hold of the platinum wire and, pulling the porcelain disk from the stopcock, allowed the awful contents of the tub to run out. Then he turned on the hot water, rinsed the tub clean, and replaced the metal outlet. Removing the rubber tubes, he cut them into pieces, broke the porcelain disk, and, rolling up the platinum wire, washed it all down the sewer pipe.

The fumes had escaped through the open window; this he now closed and set himself to putting the bathroom in order, and effectually removing every trace of his night's work. The sailor moved around with the very greatest degree of care. Finally, when he had arranged everything to his complete satisfaction, he picked up the two burners, turned out the gas, and left the bathroom, closing the door after him. From the bathroom he went directly to the attic, concealed the two rusty burners under a heap of rubbish, and then walked carefully and noiselessly down the stairs and through the lower hall. As he opened the door and stepped into the room where he had killed the woman, two police officers sprang out and seized him. The man screamed like a wild beast taken in a trap and sank down.

"Oh! oh!" he cried, "it was no use! it was no use to do it!" Then he recovered himself in a manner and was silent. The officers handcuffed him, summoned the patrol, and took him at once to the station house. There he said he was a Mexican sailor and that his name was Victor Ancona; but he would say nothing further. The following morning he sent for Randolph Mason and the two were long together.

IV

The obscure defendant charged with murder has little reason to complain of the law's delays. The morning following the arrest of Victor Ancona, the newspapers published long sensational articles, denounced him as a fiend, and convicted him. The grand jury, as it happened, was in session. The preliminaries were soon arranged and the case was railroaded into trial. The indictment contained a great many counts, and charged the prisoner with the murder of Nina San Croix by striking, stabbing, choking, poisoning, and so forth.

The trial had continued for three days and had appeared so overwhelmingly one-sided that the spectators who were crowded in the court room had grown to be violent and bitter partisans, to such an extent that the police watched them closely. The attorneys for the People were dramatic and denunciatory, and forced their case with arrogant confidence. Mason, as counsel for the prisoner, was indifferent and listless. Throughout the entire trial he had sat almost motionless at the table, his gaunt form bent over, his long legs drawn up under his chair, and his weary, heavy-muscled face, with its restless eyes, fixed and staring out over the heads of the jury, was like a tragic mask. The bar, and even the judge, believed that the prisoner's counsel had abandoned his case.

The evidence was all in and the People rested. It had been shown that Nina San Croix had resided for many years in the house in which the prisoner was arrested; that she had lived by herself, with no other companion than an old negro servant; that her past was unknown, and that she received no visitors, save the Mexican sailor, who came to her house at long intervals. Nothing whatever was shown tending to explain who the prisoner was or whence he had come. It was shown that on Tuesday preceding the killing the Archbishop had received a communication from Nina San Croix, in which she said she desired to make a statement of the greatest import, and asking for an audience. To this the Archbishop replied that he would willingly grant her a hearing if she would come to him at eleven o'clock on Friday morning. Two policemen testified that about eight o'clock on the night of Thursday they had noticed the prisoner slip into the gate of Nina San Croix's residence and go down to the side of the house, where he was admitted; that his appearance and seeming haste had attracted their attention; that they had concluded that it was some clandestine amour, and out of curiosity had both slipped down to the house and endeavored to find a position from which they could see into the room, but were unable to do so, and were about to go back to the street when they heard a woman's voice cry out in, great anger: "I know that you love her and that you want to get rid of me, but you shall not do it! You murdered him, but you shall not murder me! I have all the evidence to convict you of murdering him! The Archbishop will have it to- morrow! They shall hang you! Do you hear me? They shall hang you for this murder!" that thereupon one of the policemen proposed that they should break into the house and see what was wrong, but the other had urged that it was only the usual lovers' quarrel and if they should interfere they would find nothing upon which a charge could be based and would only be laughed at by the chief; that they had waited and listened for a time, but hearing nothing further had gone back to the street and contented themselves with keeping a strict watch on the house.

The People proved further, that on Thursday evening Nina San Croix had given the old negro domestic a sum of money and dismissed her, with the instruction that she was not to return until sent for. The old woman testified that she had gone directly to the house of her son, and later had discovered that she had forgotten some articles of clothing which she needed; that thereupon she had returned to the house and had gone up the back way to her room, – this was about eight o'clock; that while there she had heard Nina San Croix's voice in great passion and remembered that she had used the words stated by the policemen; that these sudden, violent cries had frightened her greatly and she had bolted the door and been afraid to leave the room; shortly thereafter, she had heard heavy footsteps ascending the stairs, slowly and with great difficulty, as though some one were carrying a heavy burden; that therefore her fear had increased and that she had put out the light and hidden under the bed. She remembered hearing the footsteps moving about upstairs for many hours, how long she could not tell. Finally, about half-past four in the morning, she crept out, opened the door, slipped downstairs, and ran out into the street. There she had found the policemen and requested them to search the house.

The two officers had gone to the house with the woman. She had opened the door and they had had just time to step back into the shadow when the prisoner entered. When arrested, Victor Ancona had screamed with terror, and cried out, "It was no use! it was no use to do it!"

The Chief of Police had come to the house and instituted a careful search. In the room below, from which the cries had come, he found a dress which was identified as belonging to Nina San Croix and which she was wearing when last seen by the domestic, about six o'clock that evening. This dress was covered with blood, and had a slit about two inches long in the left side of the bosom, into which the Mexican knife, found on the prisoner, fitted perfectly. These articles were introduced in evidence, and it was shown that the slit would be exactly over the heart of the wearer, and that such a wound would certainly result in death. There was much blood on one of the chairs and on the floor. There was also blood on the prisoner's coat and the leg of his trousers, and the heavy Mexican knife was also bloody. The blood was shown by the experts to be human blood.

The body of the woman was not found, and the most rigid and tireless search failed to develop the slightest trace of the corpse, or the manner of its disposal. The body of the woman had disappeared as completely as though it had vanished into the air.

When counsel announced that he had closed for the People, the judge turned and looked gravely down at Mason. "Sir," he said, "the evidence for the defense may now be introduced."

Randolph Mason arose slowly and faced the judge.

"If your Honor please," he said, speaking slowly and distinctly, "the defendant has no evidence to offer." He paused while a murmur of astonishment ran over the court room. "But, if your Honor please," he continued, "I move that the jury be directed to find the prisoner not guilty."

The crowd stirred. The counsel for the People smiled. The judge looked sharply at the speaker over his glasses. "On what ground?" he said curtly.

"On the ground," replied Mason, "that the corpus delicti has not been proven."

"Ah!" said the judge, for once losing his judicial gravity. Mason sat down abruptly. The senior counsel for the prosecution was on his feet in a moment.

"What!" he said, "the gentleman bases his motion on a failure to establish the corpus delicti? Does he jest, or has he forgotten the evidence? The term 'corpus delicti' is technical, and means the body of the crime, or the substantial fact that a crime has been committed. Does anyone doubt it in this case? It is true that no one actually saw the prisoner kill the decedent, and that he has so successfully hidden the body that it has not been found, but the powerful chain of circumstances, clear and close-linked, proving motive, the criminal agency, and the criminal act, is overwhelming.

"The victim in this case is on the eve of making a statement that would prove fatal to the prisoner. The night before the statement is to be made he goes to her residence. They quarrel. Her voice is heard, raised high in the greatest passion, denouncing him, and charging that he is a murderer, that she has the evidence and will reveal it, that he shall be hanged, and that he shall not be rid of her. Here is the motive for the crime, clear as light. Are not the bloody knife, the bloody dress, the bloody clothes of the prisoner, unimpeachable witnesses to the criminal act? The criminal agency of the prisoner has not the shadow of a possibility to obscure it. His motive is gigantic. The blood on him, and his despair when arrested, cry 'Murder! murder!' with a thousand tongues.

"Men may lie, but circumstances cannot. The thousand hopes and fears and passions of men may delude, or bias the witness. Yet it is beyond the human mind to conceive that a clear, complete chain of concatenated circumstances can be in error. Hence it is that the greatest jurists have declared that such evidence, being rarely liable to delusion or fraud, is safest and most powerful. The machinery of human justice cannot guard against the remote and improbable doubt. The inference is persistent in the affairs of men. It is the only means by which the human mind reaches the truth. If you forbid the jury to exercise it, you bid them work after first striking off their hands. Rule out the irresistible inference, and the end of justice is come in this land; and you may as well leave the spider to weave his web through the abandoned court room."

The attorney stopped, looked down at Mason with a pompous sneer, and retired to his place at the table. The judge sat thoughtful and motionless. The jurymen leaned forward in their seats.

"If your Honor please," said Mason, rising, "this is a matter of law, plain, clear, and so well settled in the State of New York that even counsel for the People should know it. The question before your Honor is simple. If the corpus delicti, the body of the crime, has been proven, as required by the laws of the commonwealth, then this case should go to the jury. If not, then it is the duty of this Court to direct the jury to find the prisoner not guilty. There is here no room for judicial discretion. Your Honor has but to recall and apply the rigid rule announced by our courts prescribing distinctly how the corpus delicti in murder must be proven.

"The prisoner here stands charged with the highest crime. The law demands, first, that the crime, as a fact, be established. The fact that the victim is indeed dead must first be made certain before anyone can be convicted for her killing, because, so long as there remains the remotest doubt as to the death, there can be no certainty as to the criminal agent, although the circumstantial evidence indicating the guilt of the accused may be positive, complete, and utterly irresistible. In murder, the corpus delicti, or body of the crime, is composed of two elements:

"Death, as a result.

"The criminal agency of another as the means.

It is the fixed and immutable law of this State, laid down in the leading case of Ruloff v. The People, and binding upon this Court, that both components of the corpus delicti shall not be established by circumstantial evidence. There must be direct proof of one or the other of these two component elements of the corpus delicti. If one is proven by direct evidence, the other may be presumed; but both shall not be presumed from circumstances, no matter how powerful, how cogent, or how completely overwhelming the circumstances may be. In other words, no man can be convicted of murder in the State of New York, unless the body of the victim be found and identified, or there be direct proof that the prisoner did some act adequate to produce death, and did it in such a manner as to account for the disappearance of the body."

The face of the judge cleared and grew hard. The members of

the bar were attentive and alert; they were beginning to see the legal escape open up. The audience were puzzled; they did not yet understand. Mason turned to the counsel for the People. His ugly face was bitter with contempt.

"For three days," he said," I have been tortured by this useless and expensive farce. If counsel for the People had been other than play-actors, they would have known in the beginning that Victor Ancona could not be convicted for murder, unless he were confronted in this court room with a living witness, who had looked into the dead face of Nina San Croix; or, if not that, a living witness who had seen him drive the dagger into her bosom.

"I care not if the circumstantial evidence in this case were so strong and irresistible as to be overpowering; if the judge on the bench, if the jury, if every man within sound of my voice, were convinced of the guilt of the prisoner to the degree of certainty that is absolute; if the circumstantial evidence left in the mind no shadow of the remotest improbable doubt; yet, in the absence of the eyewitness, this prisoner cannot be punished, and this Court must compel the jury to acquit him."

The audience now understood, and they were dumfounded. Surely this was not the law. They had been taught that the law was common sense, and this, – this was anything else.

Mason saw it all, and grinned. "In its tenderness," he sneered, "the law shields the innocent. The good law of New York reaches out its hand and lifts the prisoner out of the clutches of the fierce jury that would hang him."

Mason sat down. The room was silent. The jurymen looked at each other in amazement. The counsel for the People arose. His face was white with anger, and incredulous.

"Your Honor," he said, "this doctrine is monstrous. Can it be said that, in order to evade punishment, the murderer has only to hide or destroy the body of the victim, or sink it into the sea? Then, if he is not seen to kill, the law is powerless and the murderer can snap his finger in the face of retributive justice. If this is the law, then the law for the highest crime is a dead letter. The great commonwealth winks at murder and invites every man to kill his enemy, provided he kill him in secret and hide him. I repeat, your Honor," – the man's voice was now loud and angry and rang through the court room – "that this doctrine is monstrous!"

"So said Best, and Story, and many another," muttered Mason, "and the law remained."

"The Court," said the judge, abruptly, "desires no further argument."

The counsel for the People resumed his seat. His face lighted up with triumph. The Court was going to sustain him.

The judge turned and looked down at the jury. He was grave, and spoke with deliberate emphasis.

"Gentlemen of the jury," he said, "the rule of Lord Hale obtains in this State and is binding upon me. It is the law as stated by counsel for the prisoner: that to warrant conviction of murder there must be direct proof either of the death, as of the finding and identification of the corpse, or of criminal violence adequate to produce death, and exerted in such a manner as to account for the disappearance of the body; and it is only when there is direct proof of the one that the other can be established by circumstantial evidence. This is the law, and cannot now be departed from. I do not presume to explain its wisdom. Chief- Justice Johnson has observed, in the leading case, that it may have its probable foundation in the idea that where direct proof is absent as to both the fact of the death and of criminal violence capable of producing death, no evidence can rise to the degree of moral certainty that the individual is dead by criminal intervention, or even lead by direct inference to this result; and that, where the fact of death is not certainly ascertained, all inculpatory circumstantial evidence wants the key necessary for its satisfactory interpretation, and cannot be depended on to furnish more than probable results. It may be, also, that such a rule has some reference to the dangerous possibility that a general preconception of guilt, or a general excitement of popular feeling, may creep in to supply the place of evidence, if, upon other than direct proof of death or a cause of death, a jury are permitted to pronounce a prisoner guilty.

"In this case the body has not been found and there is no direct proof of criminal agency on the part of the prisoner, although the chain of circumstantial evidence is complete and irresistible in the highest degree. Nevertheless, it is all circumstantial evidence, and under the laws of New York the prisoner cannot be punished. I have no right of discretion. The law does not permit a conviction in this case, although every one of us may be morally certain of the prisoner's guilt. I am, therefore, gentlemen of the jury, compelled to direct you to find the prisoner not guilty."

"Judge," interrupted the foreman, jumping up in the box, "we cannot find that verdict under our oath; we know that this man is guilty."

"Sir," said the judge, "this is a matter of law in which the wishes of the jury cannot be considered. The clerk will write a verdict of not guilty, which you, as foreman, will sign."

The spectators broke out into a threatening murmur that began to grow and gather volume. The judge rapped on his desk and ordered the bailiffs promptly to suppress any demonstration on the part of the audience. Then he directed the foreman to sign the verdict prepared by the clerk. When this was done he turned to Victor Ancona; his face was hard and there was a cold glitter in his eyes.

"Prisoner at the bar," he said, "you have been put to trial before this tribunal on a charge of cold-blooded and atrocious murder. The evidence produced against you was of such powerful and overwhelming character that it seems to have left no doubt in the minds of the jury, nor indeed in the mind of any person present in this court room.

"Had the question of your guilt been submitted to these twelve arbiters, a conviction would certainly have resulted and the death penalty would have been imposed. But the law, rigid, passionless, even-eyed, has thrust in between you and the wrath of your fellows and saved you from it. I do not cry out against the impotency of the law; it is perhaps as wise as imperfect humanity could make it. I deplore, rather, the genius of evil men who, by cunning design, are enabled to slip through the fingers of this law. I have no word of censure or admonition for you, Victor Ancona. The law of New York compels me to acquit you. I am only its mouthpiece, with my individual wishes throttled. I speak only those things which the law directs I shall speak.

"You are now at liberty to leave this court room, not guiltless of the crime of murder, perhaps, but at least rid of its punishment. The eyes of men may see Cain's mark on your brow, but the eyes of the Law are blind to it."

When the audience fully realized what the judge had said they were amazed and silent. They knew as well as men could know, that Victor Ancona was guilty of murder, and yet he was now going out of the court room free. Could it happen that the law protected only against the blundering rogue? They had heard always of the boasted completeness of the law which magistrates from time immemorial had labored to perfect, and now when the skillful villain sought to evade it, they saw how weak a thing it was.

V

The wedding march of Lohengrin floated out from the Episcopal Church of St. Mark, clear and sweet, and perhaps heavy with its paradox of warning. The theater of this coming contract before high heaven was a wilderness of roses worth the taxes of a county. The high caste of Manhattan, by the grace of the check book, were present, clothed in Parisian purple and fine linen, cunningly and marvelously wrought.

Over in her private pew, ablaze with jewels, and decked with fabrics from the deft hand of many a weaver, sat Mrs. Miriam Steuvisant as imperious and self-complacent as a queen. To her it was all a kind of triumphal procession, proclaiming her ability as a general. With her were a choice few of the genus homo, which obtains at the five-o'clock teas, instituted, say the sages, for the purpose of sprinkling the holy water of Lethe.

"Czarina," whispered Reggie Du Puyster, leaning forward, "I

salute you. The ceremony sub jugum is superb."

"Walcott is an excellent fellow," answered Mrs. Steuvisant; "not a vice, you know, Reggie."

"Aye, Empress," put in the others, "a purist taken in the net. The clean-skirted one has come to the altar. Vive la vertu!"

Samuel Walcott, still sunburned from his cruise, stood before the chancel with the only daughter of the blue blooded St. Clairs. His face was clear and honest and his voice firm. This was life and not romance. The lid of the sepulcher had closed and he had slipped from under it. And now, and ever after, the hand red with murder was clean as any.

The minister raised his voice, proclaiming the holy union before God, and this twain, half pure, half foul, now by divine ordinance one flesh, bowed down before it. No blood cried from the ground. The sunlight of high noon streamed down through the window panes like a benediction.

Back in the pew of Mrs. Miriam Steuvisant, Reggie Du Puyster turned down his thumb. "Habet!" he said.

From "The Strange Schemes of Randolph Mason," by Melville Davisson Post.

Ambrose Bierce

An Heiress from Redhorse

CORONADO, *June 20th.*

I find myself more and more interested in him. It is not, I am sure, his – do you know any noun corresponding to the adjective "handsome"? One does not like to say "beauty" when speaking of a man. He is handsome enough, heaven knows; I should not even care to trust you with him – faithful of all possible wives that you are – when he looks his best, as he always does. Nor do I think the fascination of his manner has much to do with it. You recollect that the charm of art inheres in that which is undefinable, and to you and me, my dear Irene, I fancy there is rather less of that in the branch of art under consideration than to girls in their first season. I fancy I know how my fine gentleman produces many of his effects, and could, perhaps, give him a pointer on heightening them. Nevertheless, his manner is something truly delightful. I suppose what interests me chiefly is the man's brains. His conversation is the best I have ever heard, and altogether unlike anyone's else. He seems to know everything, as, indeed, he ought, for he has been everywhere, read everything, seen all there is to see – sometimes I think rather more than is good for him – and had acquaintance with the QUEEREST people. And then his voice – Irene, when I hear it I actually feel as if I ought to have PAID AT THE DOOR, though, of course, it is my own door.

July 3d.

I fear my remarks about Dr. Barritz must have been, being thoughtless, very silly, or you would not have written of him with such levity, not to say disrespect. Believe me, dearest, he has more dignity and seriousness (of the kind, I mean, which is not inconsistent with a manner sometimes playful and always charming) than any of the men that you and I ever met. And young Raynor – you knew Raynor at Monterey – tells me that the men all like him, and that he is treated with something like deference everywhere. There is a mystery, too – something about his connection with the Blavatsky people in Northern India. Raynor either would not or could not tell me the particulars. I infer that Dr. Barritz is thought – don't you dare to laugh at me – a magician! Could anything be finer than that? An ordinary mystery is not, of course, as good as a scandal, but when it relates to dark and dreadful practices – to the exercise of unearthly powers – could anything be more piquant? It explains, too, the singular influence the man has upon me. It is the undefinable in his art – black art. Seriously, dear, I quite tremble when he looks me full in the eyes with those unfathomable orbs of his, which I have already vainly attempted to describe to you. How dreadful if we have the power to make one fall in love! Do you know if the Blavatsky crowd have that power – outside of Sepoy?

July 1

The strangest thing! Last evening while Auntie was attending one of the hotel hops (I hate them) Dr. Barritz called. It was scandalously late – I actually believe he had talked with Auntie in the ballroom, and learned from her that I was alone. I had been all the evening contriving how to worm out of him the truth about his connection with the Thugs in Sepoy, and all of that black business, but the moment he fixed his eyes on me (for I admitted him, I'm ashamed to say) I was helpless, I trembled, I blushed, I – O Irene, Irene, I love the man beyond expression, and you know how it is yourself!

Fancy! I, an ugly duckling from Redhorse – daughter (they say) of old Calamity Jim – certainly his heiress, with no living relation but an absurd old aunt, who spoils me a thousand and fifty ways – absolutely destitute of everything but a million dollars and a hope in Paris – I daring to love a god like him! My dear, if I had you here, I could tear your hair out with mortification.

I am convinced that he is aware of my feeling, for he stayed but a few moments, said nothing but what another man might have said half as well, and pretending that he had an engagement went away. I learned to-day (a little bird told me – the bell bird) that he went straight to bed. How does that strike you as evidence of exemplary habits?

July 17th.

That little wretch, Raynor, called yesterday, and his babble set me almost wild. He never runs down – that is to say, when he exterminates a score of reputations, more or less, he does not pause between one reputation and the next. (By the way, he inquired about you, and his manifestations of interest in you had, I confess, a good deal of vraisemblance.)

Mr. Raynor observes no game laws; like Death (which he would inflict if slander were fatal) he has all seasons for his own. But I like him, for we knew one another at Redhorse when we were young and true-hearted and barefooted. He was known in those far fair days as "Giggles," and I – O Irene, can you ever forgive me? – I was called "Gunny." God knows why; perhaps in allusion to the material of my pinafores; perhaps because the name is in alliteration with "Giggles," for Gig and I were inseparable playmates, and the miners may have thought it a delicate compliment to recognize some kind of relationship between us.

Later, we took in a third – another of Adversity's brood, who, like Garrick between Tragedy and Comedy, had a chronic inability to adjudicate the rival claims (to himself) of Frost and Famine. Between him and the grave there was seldom anything more than a single suspender and the hope of a meal which would at the same time support life and make it insupportable. He literally picked up a precarious living for himself and an aged mother by "chloriding the dumps," that is to say, the miners permitted him to search the heaps of waste rock for such pieces of "pay ore" as had been overlooked; and these he sacked up and sold at the Syndicate Mill. He became a member of our firm – "Gunny, Giggles, and Dumps," thenceforth – through my favor; for I could not then, nor can I now, be indifferent to his courage and prowess in defending against Giggles the immemorial right of his sex to insult a strange and unprotected female – myself. After old Jim struck it in the Calamity, and I began to wear shoes and go to school, and in emulation Giggles took to washing his face, and became Jack Raynor, of Wells, Fargo & Co., and old Mrs. Barts was herself chlorided to her fathers, Dumps drifted over to San Juan Smith and turned stage driver, and was killed by road agents, and so forth.

Why do I tell you all this, dear? Because it is heavy on my heart. Because I walk the Valley of Humility. Because I am subduing myself to permanent consciousness of my unworthiness to unloose the latchet of Dr. Barritz's shoe. Because-oh, dear, oh, dear – there's a cousin of Dumps at this hotel! I haven't spoken to him. I never had any acquaintance with him, but – do you suppose he has recognized me? Do, please, give me in your next your candid, sure- enough opinion about it, and say you don't think so. Do you think He knows about me already and that is why He left me last evening when He saw that I blushed and trembled like a fool under His eyes? You know I can't bribe ALL the newspapers, and I can't go back on anybody who was good to Gunny at Redhorse – not if I'm pitched out of society into the sea. So the skeleton sometimes rattles behind the door. I never cared much before, as you know, but now – NOW it is not the same. Jack Raynor I am sure of – he will not tell him. He seems, indeed, to hold him in such respect as hardly to dare speak to him at all, and I'm a good deal that way myself. Dear, dear! I wish I had something besides a million dollars! If Jack were three inches taller I'd marry him alive and go back to Redhorse and wear sackcloth again to the end of my miserable days.

July 25th.

We had a perfectly splendid sunset last evening, and I must tell you all about it. I ran away from Auntie and everybody, and was walking alone on the beach. I expect you to believe, you infidel! that I had not looked out of my window on the seaward side of the hotel and seen him walking alone on the beach. If you are not lost to every feeling of womanly delicacy you will accept my statement without question. I soon established myself under my sunshade and had for some time been gazing out dreamily over the sea, when he approached, walking close to the edge of the water – it was ebb tide. I assure you the wet sand actually brightened about his feet! As he approached me, he lifted his hat, saying: "Miss Dement, may I sit with you? – or will you walk with me?"

The possibility that neither might be agreeable seems not to have occurred to him. Did you ever know such assurance? Assurance? My dear, it was gall, downright GALL! Well, I didn't find it wormwood, and replied, with my untutored Redhorse heart in my throat: "I – I shall be pleased to do ANYTHING." Could words have been more stupid? There are depths of fatuity in me, friend o' my soul, which are simply bottomless!

He extended his hand, smiling, and I delivered mine into it without a moment's hesitation, and when his fingers closed about it to assist me to my feet, the consciousness that it trembled made me blush worse than the red west. I got up, however, and after a while, observing that he had not let go my hand, I pulled on it a little, but unsuccessfully. He simply held on, saying nothing, but looking down into my face with some kind of a smile – I didn't know – how could I? – whether it was affectionate, derisive, or what, for I did not look at him. How beautiful he was! – with the red fires of the sunset burning in the depths of his eyes. Do you know, dear, if the Thugs and Experts of the Blavatsky region have any special kind of eyes? Ah, you should have seen his superb attitude, the godlike inclination of his head as he stood over me after I had got upon my feet! It was a noble picture, but I soon destroyed it, for I began at once to sink again to the earth. There was only one thing for him to do, and he did it; he supported me with an arm about my waist.

"Miss Dement, are you ill?" he said.

It was not an exclamation; there was neither alarm nor solicitude in it. If he had added: "I suppose that is about what I am expected to say," he would hardly have expressed his sense of the situation more clearly. His manner filled me with shame and indignation, for I was suffering acutely. I wrenched my hand out of his, grasped the arm supporting me, and, pushing myself free, fell plump into the sand and sat helpless. My hat had fallen off in the struggle, and my hair tumbled about my face and shoulders in the most mortifying way.

"Go away from me," I cried, half choking. "Oh, PLEASE go away, you – you Thug! How dare you think THAT when my leg is asleep?"

I actually said those identical words! And then I broke down and sobbed. Irene, I BLUBBERED!

His manner altered in an instant – I could see that much through my fingers and hair. He dropped on one knee beside me, parted the tangle of hair, and said, in the tenderest way: My poor girl, God knows I have not intended to pain you. How should I? – I who love you – I who have loved you for – for years and years!"

He had pulled my wet hands away from my face and was covering them with kisses. My cheeks were like two coals, my whole face was flaming and, I think, steaming. What could I do? I hid it on his shoulder – there was no other place. And, oh, my dear friend, how my leg tingled and thrilled, and how I wanted to kick!

We sat so for a long time. He had released one of my hands to pass his arm about me again, and I possessed myself of my handkerchief and was drying my eyes and my nose. I would not look up until that was done; he tried in vain to push me a little away and gaze into my eyes. Presently, when it was all right, and it had grown a bit dark, I lifted my head, looked him straight in the eyes, and smiled my best – my level best, dear.

"What do you mean," I said, "by 'years and years'?"

"Dearest," he replied, very gravely, very earnestly, "in the absence of the sunken cheeks, the hollow eyes, the lank hair, the slouching gait, the rags, dirt, and youth, can you not – will you not understand? Gunny, I'm Dumps!"

In a moment I was upon my feet and he upon his. I seized him by the lapels of his coat and peered into his handsome face in the deepening darkness. I was breathless with excitement.

"And you are not dead?" I asked, hardly knowing what I said.

"Only dead in love, dear. I recovered from the road agent's bullet, but this, I fear, is fatal."

"But about Jack – Mr. Raynor? Don't you know – "

"I am ashamed to say, darling, that it was through that unworthy person's invitation that I came here from Vienna."

Irene, they have played it upon your affectionate friend,

MARY JANE DEMENT.

P.S. – The worst of it is that there is no mystery. That was an invention of Jack to arouse my curiosity and interest. James is not a Thug. He solemnly assures me that in all his wanderings he has never set foot in Sepoy.

The Man and the Snake

I

It is of veritabyll report, and attested of so many that there be nowe of wyse and learned none to gaynsaye it, that ye serpente hys eye hath a magnetick propertie that whosoe falleth into its svasion is drawn forwards in despyte of his wille, and perisheth miserabyll by ye creature hys byte.

Stretched at ease upon a sofa, in gown and slippers, Harker Brayton smiled as he read the foregoing sentence in old Morryster's "Marvells of Science." "The only marvel in the matter," he said to himself, "is that the wise and learned in Morryster's day should have believed such nonsense as is rejected by most of even the ignorant in ours."

A train of reflections followed – for Brayton was a man of thought – and he unconsciously lowered his book without altering the direction of his eyes. As soon as the volume had gone below the line of sight, something in an obscure corner of the room recalled his attention to his surroundings. What he saw, in the shadow under his bed, were two small points of light, apparently about an inch apart. They might have been reflections of the gas jet above him, in metal nail heads; he gave them but little thought and resumed his reading. A moment later something – some impulse which it did not occur to him to analyze – impelled him to lower the book again and seek for what he saw before. The points of light were still there. They seemed to have become brighter than before, shining with a greenish luster which he had not at first observed. He thought, too, that they might have moved a trifle – were somewhat nearer. They were still too much in the shadow, however, to reveal their nature and origin to an indolent attention, and he resumed his reading. Suddenly something in the text suggested a thought which made him start and drop the book for the third time to the side of the sofa, whence, escaping from his hand, it fell sprawling to the floor, back upward. Brayton, half-risen, was staring intently into the obscurity beneath the bed, where the points of light shone with, it seemed to him, an added fire. His attention was now fully aroused, his gaze eager and imperative. It disclosed, almost directly beneath the foot rail of the bed, the coils of a large serpent – the points of light were its eyes! Its horrible head, thrust flatly forth from the innermost coil and resting upon the outermost, was directed straight toward him, the definition of the wide, brutal jaw and the idiotlike forehead serving to show the direction of its malevolent gaze. The eyes were no longer merely luminous points; they looked into his own with a meaning, a malign significance.

II

A snake in a bedroom of a modern city dwelling of the better sort is, happily, not so common a phenomenon as to make explanation altogether needless. Harker Brayton, a bachelor of thirty-five, a scholar, idler, and something of an athlete, rich, popular, and of sound health, had returned to San Francisco from all manner of remote and unfamiliar countries. His tastes, always a trifle luxurious, had taken on an added exuberance from long privation; and the resources of even the Castle Hotel being inadequate for their perfect gratification, he had gladly accepted the hospitality of his friend, Dr. Druring, the distinguished scientist. Dr. Druring's house, a large, old-fashioned one in what was now an obscure quarter of the city, had an outer and visible aspect of reserve. It plainly would not associate with the contiguous elements of its altered environment, and appeared to have developed some of the eccentricities which come of isolation. One of these was a "wing," conspicuously irrelevant in point of architecture, and no less rebellious in the matter of purpose; for it was a combination of laboratory, menagerie, and museum. It was here that the doctor indulged the scientific side of his nature in the study of such forms of animal life as engaged his interest and comforted his taste – which, it must be confessed, ran rather to the lower forms. For one of the higher types nimbly and sweetly to recommend itself unto his gentle senses, it had at least to retain certain rudimentary characteristics allying it to such "dragons of the prime" as toads and snakes. His scientific sympathies were distinctly reptilian; he loved nature's vulgarians and described himself as the Zola of zoology. His wife and daughters, not having the advantage to share his enlightened curiosity regarding the works and ways of our ill-starred fellow-creatures, were, with needless austerity, excluded from what he called the Snakery, and doomed to companionship with their own kind; though, to soften the rigors of their lot, he had permitted them, out of his great wealth, to outdo the reptiles in the gorgeousness of their surroundings and to shine with a superior splendor.

Architecturally, and in point of "furnishing," the Snakery had a severe simplicity befitting the humble circumstances of its occupants, many of whom, indeed, could not safely have been intrusted with the liberty which is necessary to the full enjoyment of luxury, for they had the troublesome peculiarity of being alive. In their own apartments, however, they were under as little personal restraint as was compatible with their protection from the baneful habit of swallowing one another; and, as Brayton had thoughtfully been apprised, it was more than a tradition that some of them had at divers times been found in parts of the premises where it would have embarrassed them to explain their presence. Despite the Snakery and its uncanny associations – to which, indeed, he gave little attention – Brayton found life at the Druring mansion very much to his mind.

III

Beyond a smart shock of surprise and a shudder of mere loathing, Mr. Brayton was not greatly affected. His first thought was to ring the call bell and bring a servant; but, although the bell cord dangled within easy reach, he made no movement toward it; it had occurred to his mind that the act might subject him to the suspicion of fear, which he certainly did not feel. He was more keenly conscious of the incongruous nature of the situation than affected by its perils; it was revolting, but absurd.

The reptile was of a species with which Brayton was unfamiliar. Its length he could only conjecture; the body at the largest visible part seemed about as thick as his forearm. In what way was it dangerous, if in any way? Was it venomous? Was it a constrictor? His knowledge of nature's danger signals did not enable him to say; he had never deciphered the code.

If not dangerous, the creature was at least offensive. It was de trop – "matter out of place" – an impertinence. The gem was unworthy of the setting. Even the barbarous taste of our time and country, which had loaded the walls of the room with pictures, the floor with furniture, and the furniture with bric-a-brac, had not quite fitted the place for this bit of the savage life of the jungle. Besides – insupportable thought! – the exhalations of its breath mingled with the atmosphere which he himself was breathing!

These thoughts shaped themselves with greater or less definition in Brayton's mind, and begot action. The process is what we call consideration and decision. It is thus that we are wise and unwise. It is thus that the withered leaf in an autumn breeze shows greater or less intelligence than its fellows, falling upon the land or upon the lake. The secret of human action is an open one – something contracts our muscles. Does it matter if we give to the preparatory molecular changes the name of will?

Brayton rose to his feet and prepared to back softly away from the snake, without disturbing it, if possible, and through the door. People retire so from the presence of the great, for greatness is power, and power is a menace. He knew that he could walk backward without obstruction, and find the door without error. Should the monster follow, the taste which had plastered the walls with paintings had consistently supplied a rack of murderous Oriental weapons from which he could snatch one to suit the occasion. In the meantime the snake's eyes burned with a more pitiless malevolence than ever.

Brayton lifted his right foot free of the floor to step backward. That moment he felt a strong aversion to doing so.

"I am accounted brave," he murmured; "is bravery, then, no more than pride? Because there are none to witness the shame shall I retreat?"

He was steadying himself with his right hand upon the back of a chair, his foot suspended.

"Nonsense!" he said aloud; "I am not so great a coward as to fear to seem to myself afraid."

He lifted the foot a little higher by slightly bending the knee, and thrust it sharply to the floor – an inch in front of the other! He could not think how that occurred. A trial with the left foot had the same result; it was again in advance of the right. The hand upon the chair back was grasping it; the arm was straight, reaching somewhat backward. One might have seen that he was reluctant to lose his hold. The snake's malignant head was still thrust forth from the inner coil as before, the neck level. It had not moved, but its eyes were now electric sparks, radiating an infinity of luminous needles.

The man had an ashy pallor. Again he took a step forward, and another, partly dragging the chair, which, when finally released, fell upon the floor with a crash. The man groaned; the snake made neither sound nor motion, but its eyes were two dazzling suns. The reptile itself was wholly concealed by them. They gave off enlarging rings of rich and vivid colors, which at their greatest expansion successively vanished like soap bubbles; they seemed to approach his very face, and anon were an immeasurable distance away. He heard, somewhere, the continual throbbing of a great drum, with desultory bursts of far music, inconceivably sweet, like the tones of an aeolian harp. He knew it for the sunrise melody of Memnon's statue, and thought he stood in the Nileside reeds, hearing, with exalted sense, that immortal anthem through the silence of the centuries.

The music ceased; rather, it became by insensible degrees the distant roll of a retreating thunderstorm. A landscape, glittering with sun and rain, stretched before him, arched with a vivid rainbow, framing in its giant curve a hundred visible cities. In the middle distance a vast serpent, wearing a crown, reared its head out of its voluminous convolutions and looked at him with his dead mother's eyes. Suddenly this enchanting landscape seemed to rise swiftly upward, like the drop scene at a theater, and vanished in a blank. Something struck him a hard blow upon the face and breast. He had fallen to the floor; the blood ran from his broken nose and his bruised lips. For a moment he was dazed and stunned, and lay with closed eyes, his face against the door. In a few moments he had recovered, and then realized that his fall, by withdrawing his eyes, had broken the spell which held him. He felt that now, by keeping his gaze averted, he would be able to retreat. But the thought of the serpent within a few feet of his head, yet unseen – perhaps in the very act of springing upon him and throwing its coils about his throat – was too horrible. He lifted his head, stared again into those baleful eyes, and was again in bondage.

The snake had not moved, and appeared somewhat to have lost its power upon the imagination; the gorgeous illusions of a few moments before were not repeated. Beneath that flat and brainless brow its black, beady eyes simply glittered, as at first, with an expression unspeakably malignant. It was as if the creature, knowing its triumph assured, had determined to practice no more alluring wiles.

Now ensued a fearful scene. The man, prone upon the floor, within a yard of his enemy, raised the upper part of his body upon his elbows, his head thrown back, his legs extended to their full length. His face was white between its gouts of blood; his eyes were strained open to their uttermost expansion. There was froth upon his lips; it dropped off in flakes. Strong convulsions ran through his body, making almost serpentine undulations. He bent himself at the waist, shifting his legs from side to side. And every movement left him a little nearer to the snake. He thrust his hands forward to brace himself back, yet constantly advanced upon his elbows.

IV

Dr. Druring and his wife sat in the library. The scientist was in rare good humor.

"I have just obtained, by exchange with another collector," he said, "a splendid specimen of the Ophiophagus."

"And what may that be?" the lady inquired with a somewhat languid interest.

"Why, bless my soul, what profound ignorance! My dear, a

man who ascertains after marriage that his wife does not know Greek, is entitled to a divorce. The Ophiophagus is a snake which eats other snakes."

"I hope it will eat all yours," she said, absently shifting the lamp. "But how does it get the other snakes? By charming them, I suppose."

"That is just like you, dear," said the doctor, with an affectation of petulance. "You know how irritating to me is any allusion to that vulgar superstition about the snake's power of fascination."

The conversation was interrupted by a mighty cry which rang through the silent house like the voice of a demon shouting in a tomb. Again and yet again it sounded, with terrible distinctness. They sprang to their feet, the man confused, the lady pale and speechless with fright. Almost before the echoes of the last cry had died away the doctor was out of the room, springing up the staircase two steps at a time. In the corridor, in front of Brayton's chamber, he met some servants who had come from the upper floor. Together they rushed at the door without knocking. It was unfastened, and gave way. Brayton lay upon his stomach on the floor, dead. His head and arms were partly concealed under the foot rail of the bed. They pulled the body away, turning it upon the back. The face was daubed with blood and froth, the eyes were wide open, staring – a dreadful sight!

"Died in a fit," said the scientist, bending his knee and placing his hand upon the heart. While in that position he happened to glance under the bed. "Good God!" he added; "how did this thing get in here?"

He reached under the bed, pulled out the snake, and flung it, still coiled, to the center of the room, whence, with a harsh, shuffling sound, it slid across the polished floor till stopped by the wall, where it lay without motion. It was a stuffed snake; its eyes were two shoe buttons.

From "Tales of Soldiers and Civilians," by Ambrose Bierce.

Edgar Allan Poe

The Oblong Box

Some years ago, I engaged passage from Charleston, S. C, to the city of New York, in the fine packet-ship "Independence," Captain Hardy. We were to sail on the fifteenth of the month (June), weather permitting; and on the fourteenth, I went on board to arrange some matters in my stateroom.

I found that we were to have a great many passengers, including a more than usual number of ladies. On the list were several of my acquaintances, and among other names, I was rejoiced to see that of Mr. Cornelius Wyatt, a young artist, for whom I entertained feelings of warm friendship. He had been with me a fellow-student at C – – University, where we were very much together. He had the ordinary temperament of genius, and was a compound of misanthropy, sensibility, and enthusiasm. To these qualities he united the warmest and truest heart which ever beat in a human bosom.

I observed that his name was carded upon THREE state-rooms; and, upon again referring to the list of passengers, I found that he had engaged passage for himself, wife, and two sisters – his own. The state-rooms were sufficiently roomy, and each had two berths, one above the other. These berths, to be sure, were so exceedingly narrow as to be insufficient for more than one person; still, I could not comprehend why there were THREE state-rooms for these four persons. I was, just at that epoch, in one of those moody frames of mind which make a man abnormally inquisitive about trifles: and I confess, with shame, that I busied myself in a variety of ill- bred and preposterous conjectures about this matter of the supernumerary stateroom. It was no business of mine, to be sure, but with none the less pertinacity did I occupy myself in attempts to resolve the enigma. At last I reached a conclusion which wrought in me great wonder why I had not arrived at it before. "It is a servant of course," I said; "what a fool I am, not sooner to have thought of so obvious a solution!" And then I again repaired to the list – but here I saw distinctly that NO servant was to come with the party, although, in fact, it had been the original design to bring one – for the words "and servant" had been first written and then over-scored. "Oh, extra baggage, to be sure," I now said to myself – "something he wishes not to be put in the hold – something to be kept under his own eye – ah, I have it – a painting or so – and this is what he has been bargaining about with Nicolino, the Italian Jew." This idea satisfied me, and I dismissed my curiosity for the nonce.

Wyatt's two sisters I knew very well, and most amiable and clever girls they were. His wife he had newly married, and I had never yet seen her. He had often talked about her in my presence, however, and in his usual style of enthusiasm. He described her as of surpassing beauty, wit, and accomplishment. I was, therefore, quite anxious to make her acquaintance.

On the day in which I visited the ship (the fourteenth), Wyatt and party were also to visit it – so the captain informed me – and I waited on board an hour longer than I had designed, in hope of being presented to the bride, but then an apology came. "Mrs. W. was a little indisposed, and would decline coming on board until to-morrow, at the hour of sailing."

The morrow having arrived, I was going from my hotel to the wharf, when Captain Hardy met me and said that, "owing to circumstances" (a stupid but convenient phrase), "he rather thought the 'Independence' would not sail for a day or two, and that when all was ready, he would send up and let me know." This I thought strange, for there was a stiff southerly breeze; but as "the circumstances" were not forthcoming, although I pumped for them with much perseverance, I had nothing to do but to return home and digest my impatience at leisure.

I did not receive the expected message from the captain for nearly a week. It came at length, however, and I immediately went on board. The ship was crowded with passengers, and every thing was in the bustle attendant upon making sail. Wyatt's party arrived in about ten minutes after myself. There were the two sisters, the bride, and the artist – the latter in one of his customary fits of moody misanthropy. I was too well used to these, however, to pay them any special attention. He did not even introduce me to his wife; – this courtesy devolving, per force, upon his sister Marian – a very sweet and intelligent girl, who, in a few hurried words, made us acquainted.

Mrs. Wyatt had been closely veiled; and when she raised her veil, in acknowledging my bow, I confess that I was very profoundly astonished. I should have been much more so, however, had not long experience advised me not to trust, with too implicit a reliance, the enthusiastic descriptions of my friend, the artist, when indulging in comments upon the loveliness of woman. When beauty was the theme, I well knew with what facility he soared into the regions of the purely ideal.

The truth is, I could not help regarding Mrs. Wyatt as a decidedly plain-looking woman. If not positively ugly, she was not, I think, very far from it. She was dressed, however, in exquisite taste – and then I had no doubt that she had captivated my friend's heart by the more enduring graces of the intellect and soul. She said very few words, and passed at once into her state-room with Mr. W.

My old inquisitiveness now returned. There was NO servant – THAT was a settled point. I looked, therefore, for the extra baggage. After some delay, a cart arrived at the wharf, with an oblong pine box, which was every thing that seemed to be expected. Immediately upon its arrival we made sail, and in a short time were safely over the bar and standing out to sea.

The box in question was, as I say, oblong. It was about six feet in length by two and a half in breadth; I observed it attentively, and like to be precise. Now this shape was PECULIAR; and no sooner had I seen it, than I took credit to myself for the accuracy of my guessing. I had reached the conclusion, it will be remembered, that the extra baggage of my friend, the artist, would prove to be pictures, or at least a picture; for I knew he had been for several weeks in conference with Nicolino: – and now here was a box, which, from its shape, COULD possibly contain nothing in the world but a copy of Leonardo's "Last Supper;" and a copy of this very "Last Supper," done by Rubini the younger, at Florence, I had known, for some time, to be in the possession of

Nicolino. This point, therefore, I considered as sufficiently settled. I chuckled excessively when I thought of my acumen. It was the first time I had ever known Wyatt to keep from me any of his artistical secrets; but here he evidently intended to steal a march upon me, and smuggle a fine picture to New York, under my very nose; expecting me to know nothing of the matter. I resolved to quiz him WELL, now and hereafter.

One thing, however, annoyed me not a little. The box did NOT go into the extra stateroom. It was deposited in Wyatt's own; and there, too, it remained, occupying very nearly the whole of the floor – no doubt to the exceeding discomfort of the artist and his wife; – this the more especially as the tar or paint with which it was lettered in sprawling capitals, emitted a strong, disagreeable, and, to my fancy, a peculiarly disgusting odor. On the lid were painted the words – "Mrs. Adelaide Curtis, Albany, New York. Charge of Cornelius Wyatt, Esq. This side up. To be handled with care."

Now, I was aware that Mrs. Adelaide Curtis, of Albany, was the artist's wife's mother, – but then I looked upon the whole address as a mystification, intended especially for myself. I made up my mind, of course, that the box and contents would never get farther north than the studio of my misanthropic friend, in Chambers Street, New York.

For the first three or four days we had fine weather, although the wind was dead ahead; having chopped round to the northward, immediately upon our losing sight of the coast. The passengers were, consequently, in high spirits and disposed to be social. I MUST except, however, Wyatt and his sisters, who behaved stiffly, and, I could not help thinking, uncourteously to the rest of the party. Wyatt's conduct I did not so much regard. He was gloomy, even beyond his usual habit – in fact he was MOROSE – but in him I was prepared for eccentricity. For the sisters, however, I could make no excuse. They secluded themselves in their staterooms during the greater part of the passage, and absolutely refused, although I repeatedly urged them, to hold communication with any person on board.

Mrs. Wyatt herself was far more agreeable. That is to say, she was CHATTY; and to be chatty is no slight recommendation at sea. She became EXCESSIVELY intimate with most of the ladies; and, to my profound astonishment, evinced no equivocal disposition to coquet with the men. She amused us all very much. I say "amused" – and scarcely know how to explain myself. The truth is, I soon found that Mrs. W. was far oftener laughed AT than WITH. The gentlemen said little about her; but the ladies, in a little while, pronounced her "a good-hearted thing, rather indifferent looking, totally uneducated, and decidedly vulgar." The great wonder was, how Wyatt had been entrapped into such a match. Wealth was the general solution – but this I knew to be no solution at all; for Wyatt had told me that she neither brought him a dollar nor had any expectations from any source whatever. "He had married," he said, "for love, and for love only; and his bride was far more than worthy of his love." When I thought of these expressions, on the part of my friend, I confess that I felt indescribably puzzled. Could it be possible that he was taking leave of his senses? What else could I think? HE, so refined, so intellectual, so fastidious, with so exquisite a perception of the faulty, and so keen an appreciation of the beautiful! To be sure, the lady seemed especially fond of HIM – particularly so in his absence – when she made herself ridiculous by frequent quotations of what had been said by her "beloved husband, Mr. Wyatt." The word "husband" seemed forever – to use one of her own delicate expressions – forever "on the tip of her tongue." In the meantime, it was observed by all on board, that he avoided HER in the most pointed manner, and, for the most part, shut himself up alone in his state-room, where, in fact, he might have been said to live altogether, leaving his wife at full liberty to amuse herself as she thought best, in the public society of the main cabin.

My conclusion, from what I saw and heard, was, that, the artist, by some unaccountable freak of fate, or perhaps in some fit of enthusiastic and fanciful passion, had been induced to unite himself with a person altogether beneath him, and that the natural result, entire and speedy disgust, had ensued. I pitied him from the bottom of my heart – but could not, for that reason, quite forgive his incommunicativeness in the matter of the "Last Supper." For this I resolved to have my revenge.

One day he came upon deck, and, taking his arm as had been my wont, I sauntered with him backward and forward. His gloom, however (which I considered quite natural under the circumstances), seemed entirely unabated. He said little, and that moodily, and with evident effort. I ventured a jest or two, and he made a sickening attempt at a smile. Poor fellow! – as I thought of HIS WIFE, I wondered that he could have heart to put on even the semblance of mirth. At last I ventured a home thrust. I determined to commence a series of covert insinuations, or innuendoes, about the oblong box – just to let him perceive, gradually, that I was NOT altogether the butt, or victim, of his little bit of pleasant mystification. My first observation was by way of opening a masked battery. I said something about the "peculiar shape of THAT box – ,"and, as I spoke the words, I smiled knowingly, winked, and touched him gently with my forefinger in the ribs.

The manner in which Wyatt received this harmless pleasantry convinced me, at once, that he was mad. At first he stared at me as if he found it impossible to comprehend the witticism of my remark; but as its point seemed slowly to make its way into his brain, his eyes, in the same proportion, seemed protruding from their sockets. Then he grew very red – then hideously pale – then, as if highly amused with what I had insinuated, he began a loud and boisterous laugh, which, to my astonishment, he kept up, with gradually increasing vigor, for ten minutes or more. In conclusion, he fell flat and heavily upon the deck. When I ran to uplift him, to all appearance he was DEAD.

I called assistance, and, with much difficulty, we brought him to himself. Upon reviving he spoke incoherently for some time. At length we bled him and put him to bed. The next morning he was quite recovered, so far as regarded his mere bodily health. Of his mind I say nothing, of course. I avoided him during the rest of the passage, by advice of the captain, who seemed to coincide with me altogether in my views of his insanity, but cautioned me to say nothing on this head to any person on board.

Several circumstances occurred immediately after this fit of

Wyatt which contributed to heighten the curiosity with which I was already possessed. Among other things, this: I had been nervous – drank too much strong green tea, and slept ill at night – in fact, for two nights I could not be properly said to sleep at all. Now, my state-room opened into the main cabin, or dining-room, as did those of all the single men on board. Wyatt's three rooms were in the after-cabin, which was separated from the main one by a slight sliding door, never locked even at night. As we were almost constantly on a wind, and the breeze was not a little stiff, the ship heeled to leeward very considerably; and whenever her starboard side was to leeward, the sliding door between the cabins slid open, and so remained, nobody taking the trouble to get up and shut it. But my berth was in such a position, that when my own state-room door was open, as well as the sliding door in question (and my own door was ALWAYS open on account of the heat,) I could see into the after-cabin quite distinctly, and just at that portion of it, too, where were situated the state-rooms of Mr. Wyatt. Well, during two nights (NOT consecutive) while I lay awake, I clearly saw Mrs. W., about eleven o'clock upon each night, steal cautiously from the state-room of Mr. W., and enter the extra room, where she remained until daybreak, when she was called by her husband and went back. That they were virtually separated was clear. They had separate apartments – no doubt in contemplation of a more permanent divorce; and here, after all I thought was the mystery of the extra stateroom.

There was another circumstance, too, which interested me much. During the two wakeful nights in question, and immediately after the disappearance of Mrs. Wyatt into the extra stateroom, I was attracted by certain singular cautious, subdued noises in that of her husband. After listening to them for some time, with thoughtful attention, I at length succeeded perfectly in translating their import. They were sounds occasioned by the artist in prying open the oblong box, by means of a chisel and mallet – the latter being apparently muffled, or deadened, by some soft woollen or cotton substance in which its head was enveloped.

In this manner I fancied I could distinguish the precise moment when he fairly disengaged the lid – also, that I could determine when he removed it altogether, and when he deposited it upon the lower berth in his room; this latter point I knew, for example, by certain slight taps which the lid made in striking against the wooden edges of the berth, as he endeavored to lay it down VERY gently – there being no room for it on the floor. After this there was a dead stillness, and I heard nothing more, upon either occasion, until nearly daybreak; unless, perhaps, I may mention a low sobbing, or murmuring sound, so very much suppressed as to be nearly inaudible – if, indeed, the whole of this latter noise were not rather produced by my own imagination. I say it seemed to RESEMBLE sobbing or sighing – but, of course, it could not have been either. I rather think it was a ringing in my own ears. Mr. Wyatt, no doubt, according to custom, was merely giving the rein to one of his hobbies – indulging in one of his fits of artistic enthusiasm. He had opened his oblong box, in order to feast his eyes on the pictorial treasure within. There was nothing in this, however, to make him SOB. I repeat, therefore, that it must have been simply a freak of my own fancy, distempered by good Captain Hardy's green tea. just before dawn, on each of the two nights of which I speak, I distinctly heard Mr. Wyatt replace the lid upon the oblong box, and force the nails into their old places by means of the muffled mallet. Having done this, he issued from his state- room, fully dressed, and proceeded to call Mrs. W. from hers.

We had been at sea seven days, and were now off Cape Hatteras, when there came a tremendously heavy blow from the southwest. We were, in a measure, prepared for it, however, as the weather had been holding out threats for some time. Every thing was made snug, alow and aloft; and as the wind steadily freshened, we lay to, at length, under spanker and foretopsail, both double-reefed.

In this trim we rode safely enough for forty-eight hours – the ship proving herself an excellent sea-boat in many respects, and shipping no water of any consequence. At the end of this period, however, the gale had freshened into a hurricane, and our after – sail split into ribbons, bringing us so much in the trough of the water that we shipped several prodigious seas, one immediately after the other. By this accident we lost three men overboard with the caboose, and nearly the whole of the larboard bulwarks. Scarcely had we recovered our senses, before the foretopsail went into shreds, when we got up a storm staysail and with this did pretty well for some hours, the ship heading the sea much more steadily than before.

The gale still held on, however, and we saw no signs of its abating. The rigging was found to be ill-fitted, and greatly strained; and on the third day of the blow, about five in the afternoon, our mizzen-mast, in a heavy lurch to windward, went by the board. For an hour or more, we tried in vain to get rid of it, on account of the prodigious rolling of the ship; and, before we had succeeded, the carpenter came aft and announced four feet of water in the hold. To add to our dilemma, we found the pumps choked and nearly useless.

All was now confusion and despair – but an effort was made to lighten the ship by throwing overboard as much of her cargo as could be reached, and by cutting away the two masts that remained. This we at last accomplished – but we were still unable to do any thing at the pumps; and, in the meantime, the leak gained on us very fast.

At sundown, the gale had sensibly diminished in violence, and as the sea went down with it, we still entertained faint hopes of saving ourselves in the boats. At eight P. M., the clouds broke away to windward, and we had the advantage of a full moon – a piece of good fortune which served wonderfully to cheer our drooping spirits.

After incredible labor we succeeded, at length, in getting the longboat over the side without material accident, and into this we crowded the whole of the crew and most of the passengers. This party made off immediately, and, after undergoing much suffering, finally arrived, in safety, at Ocracoke Inlet, on the third day after the wreck.

Fourteen passengers, with the captain, remained on board, resolving to trust their fortunes to the jolly-boat at the stern. We lowered it without difficulty, although it was only by a miracle that we prevented it from swamping as it touched the water. It contained, when afloat, the captain and his wife, Mr. Wyatt and party, a Mexican officer, wife, four children, and myself, with a negro valet.

We had no room, of course, for any thing except a few positively necessary instruments, some provisions, and the clothes upon our backs. No one had thought of even attempting to save any thing more. What must have been the astonishment of all, then, when having proceeded a few fathoms from the ship, Mr. Wyatt stood up in the stern-sheets, and coolly demanded of Captain Hardy that the boat should be put back for the purpose of taking in his oblong box!

"Sit down, Mr. Wyatt," replied the captain, somewhat sternly, "you will capsize us if you do not sit quite still. Our gunwhale is almost in the water now."

"The box!" vociferated Mr. Wyatt, still standing – "the box, I say! Captain Hardy, you cannot, you will not refuse me. Its weight will be but a trifle – it is nothing – mere nothing. By the mother who bore you – for the love of Heaven – by your hope of salvation, I implore you to put back for the box!"

The captain, for a moment, seemed touched by the earnest appeal of the artist, but he regained his stern composure, and merely said:

"Mr. Wyatt, you are mad. I cannot listen to you. Sit down, I say, or you will swamp the boat. Stay – hold him – seize him! – he is about to spring overboard! There – I knew it – he is over!"

As the captain said this, Mr. Wyatt, in fact, sprang from the boat, and, as we were yet in the lee of the wreck, succeeded, by almost superhuman exertion, in getting hold of a rope which hung from the fore-chains. In another moment he was on board, and rushing frantically down into the cabin.

In the meantime, we had been swept astern of the ship, and being quite out of her lee, were at the mercy of the tremendous sea which was still running. We made a determined effort to put back, but our little boat was like a feather in the breath of the tempest. We saw at a glance that the doom of the unfortunate artist was sealed.

As our distance from the wreck rapidly increased, the madman (for as such only could we regard him) was seen to emerge from the companion – way, up which by dint of strength that appeared gigantic, he dragged, bodily, the oblong box. While we gazed in the extremity of astonishment, he passed, rapidly, several turns of a three-inch rope, first around the box and then around his body. In another instant both body and box were in the sea – disappearing suddenly, at once and forever.

We lingered awhile sadly upon our oars, with our eyes riveted upon the spot. At length we pulled away. The silence remained unbroken for an hour. Finally, I hazarded a remark.

"Did you observe, captain, how suddenly they sank? Was not that an exceedingly singular thing? I confess that I entertained some feeble hope of his final deliverance, when I saw him lash himself to the box, and commit himself to the sea."

"They sank as a matter of course," replied the captain, "and that like a shot. They will soon rise again, however – BUT NOT TILL THE SALT MELTS."

"The salt!" I ejaculated.

"Hush!" said the captain, pointing to the wife and sisters of the deceased. "We must talk of these things at some more appropriate time."

We suffered much, and made a narrow escape, but fortune befriended us, as well as our mates in the long-boat. We landed, in fine, more dead than alive, after four days of intense distress, upon the beach opposite Roanoke Island. We remained here a week, were not ill-treated by the wreckers, and at length obtained a passage to New York.

About a month after the loss of the "Independence," I happened to meet Captain Hardy in Broadway. Our conversation turned, naturally, upon the disaster, and especially upon the sad fate of poor Wyatt. I thus learned the following particulars.

The artist had engaged passage for himself, wife, two sisters and a servant. His wife was, indeed, as she had been represented, a most lovely, and most accomplished woman. On the morning of the fourteenth of June (the day in which I first visited the ship), the lady suddenly sickened and died. The young husband was frantic with grief – but circumstances imperatively forbade the deferring his voyage to New York. It was necessary to take to her mother the corpse of his adored wife, and, on the other hand, the universal prejudice which would prevent his doing so openly was well known. Nine-tenths of the passengers would have abandoned the ship rather than take passage with a dead body.

In this dilemma, Captain Hardy arranged that the corpse, being first partially embalmed, and packed, with a large quantity of salt, in a box of suitable dimensions, should be conveyed on board as merchandise. Nothing was to be said of the lady's decease; and, as it was well understood that Mr. Wyatt had engaged passage for his wife, it became necessary that some person should personate her during the voyage. This the deceased lady's-maid was easily prevailed on to do. The extra state-room, originally engaged for this girl during her mistress' life, was now merely retained. In this state-room the pseudo-wife, slept, of course, every night. In the daytime she performed, to the best of her ability, the part of her mistress – whose person, it had been carefully ascertained, was unknown to any of the passengers on board.

My own mistake arose, naturally enough, through too careless, too inquisitive, and too impulsive a temperament. But of late, it is a rare thing that I sleep soundly at night. There is a countenance which haunts me, turn as I will. There is an hysterical laugh which will forever ring within my ears.

The Gold-Bug

What ho! what ho! this fellow is dancing mad!
He hath been bitten by the Tarantula.
– All in the Wrong.

Many years ago, I contracted an intimacy with a Mr. William Legrand. He was of an ancient Huguenot family, and had once been wealthy: but a series of misfortunes had reduced him to want. To avoid the mortification consequent upon his disasters, he left New Orleans, the city of his forefathers, and took up his residence at Sullivan's Island, near Charleston, South Carolina.

This island is a very singular one. It consists of little else than the sea sand, and is about three miles long. Its breadth at no point exceeds a quarter of a mile. It is separated from the mainland by a scarcely perceptible creek, oozing its way through a wilderness of reeds and slime, a favorite resort of the marsh hen. The vegetation, as might be supposed, is scant, or at least dwarfish. No trees of any magnitude are to be seen. Near the western extremity, where Fort Moultrie stands, and where are some miserable frame buildings, tenanted, during summer, by the fugitives from Charleston dust and fever, may be found, indeed, the bristly palmetto; but the whole island, with the exception of this western point, and a line of hard, white beach on the seacoast, is covered with a dense undergrowth of the sweet myrtle so much prized by the horticulturists of England. The shrub here often attains the height of fifteen or twenty feet, and forms an almost impenetrable coppice, burdening the air with its fragrance.

In the inmost recesses of this coppice, not far from the eastern or more remote end of the island, Legrand had built himself a small hut, which he occupied when I first, by mere accident, made his acquaintance. This soon ripened into friendship – for there was much in the recluse to excite interest and esteem. I found him well educated, with unusual powers of mind, but infected with misanthropy, and subject to perverse moods of alternate enthusiasm and melancholy. He had with him many books, but rarely employed them. His chief amusements were gunning and fishing, or sauntering along the beach and through the myrtles, in quest of shells or entomological specimens – his collection of the latter might have been envied by a Swammerdamm. In these excursions he was usually accompanied by an old negro, called Jupiter, who had been manumitted before the reverses of the family, but who could be induced, neither by threats nor by promises, to abandon what he considered his right of attendance upon the footsteps of his young "Massa Will." It is not improbable that the relatives of Legrand, conceiving him to be somewhat unsettled in intellect, had contrived to instill this obstinacy into Jupiter, with a view to the supervision and guardianship of the wanderer.

The winters in the latitude of Sullivan's Island are seldom very severe, and in the fall of the year it is a rare event indeed when a fire is considered necessary. About the middle of October, 18 – , there occurred, however, a day of remarkable chilliness. Just before sunset I scrambled my way through the evergreens to the hut of my friend, whom I had not visited for several weeks – my residence being, at that time, in Charleston, a distance of nine miles from the island, while the facilities of passage and repassage were very far behind those of the present day. Upon reaching the hut I rapped, as was my custom, and getting no reply, sought for the key where I knew it was secreted, unlocked the door, and went in. A fine fire was blazing upon the hearth. It was a novelty, and by no means an ungrateful one. I threw off an overcoat, took an armchair by the crackling logs, and awaited patiently the arrival of my hosts.

Soon after dark they arrived, and gave me a most cordial welcome. Jupiter, grinning from ear to ear, bustled about to prepare some marsh hens for supper. Legrand was in one of his fits – how else shall I term them? – of enthusiasm. He had found an unknown bivalve, forming a new genus, and, more than this, he had hunted down and secured, with Jupiter's assistance, a scarabaeus which he believed to be totally new, but in respect to which he wished to have my opinion on the morrow.

"And why not to-night?" I asked, rubbing my hands over the blaze, and wishing the whole tribe of scarabaei at the devil.

"Ah, if I had only known you were here!" said Legrand, "but it's so long since I saw you; and how could I foresee that you would pay me a visit this very night of all others? As I was coming home I met Lieutenant G – – , from the fort, and, very foolishly, I lent him the bug; so it will be impossible for you to see it until the morning. Stay here to-night, and I will send Jup down for it at sunrise. It is the loveliest thing in creation!"

"What? – sunrise?"

"Nonsense! no! – the bug. It is of a brilliant gold color – about the size of a large hickory nut – with two jet black spots near one extremity of the back, and another, somewhat longer, at the other. The antennae are – "

"Dey ain't NO tin in him, Massa Will, I keep a tellin' on you," here interrupted Jupiter; "de bug is a goole-bug, solid, ebery bit of him, inside and all, sep him wing – neber feel half so hebby a bug in my life."

"Well, suppose it is, Jup," replied Legrand, somewhat more earnestly, it seemed to me, than the case demanded; "is that any reason for your letting the birds burn? The color" – here he turned to me – "is really almost enough to warrant Jupiter's idea. You never saw a more brilliant metallic luster than the scales emit – but of this you cannot judge till to-morrow. In the meantime I can give you some idea of the shape." Saying this, he seated himself at a small table, on which were a pen and ink, but no paper. He looked for some in a drawer, but found none.

"Never mind," he said at length, "this will answer;" and he drew from his waistcoat pocket a scrap of what I took to be very dirty foolscap, and made upon it a rough drawing with the pen. While he did this, I retained my seat by the fire, for I was still chilly. When the design was complete, he handed it to me without rising. As I received it, a loud growl was heard, succeeded by a scratching at the door. Jupiter opened it, and a large Newfoundland, belonging to Legrand, rushed in, leaped upon my shoulders, and loaded me with caresses; for I had shown him much attention during previous visits. When his gambols were over, I looked at the paper, and, to speak the truth, found myself not a little puzzled at what my friend had depicted.

"Well!" I said, after contemplating it for some minutes, "this IS a strange scarabaeus, I must confess; new to me; never saw anything like it before – unless it was a skull, or a death's head, which it more nearly resembles than anything else that has come under MY observation."

"A death's head!" echoed Legrand. "Oh – yes – well, it has something of that appearance upon paper, no doubt. The two upper black spots look like eyes, eh? and the longer one at the bottom like a mouth – and then the shape of the whole is oval."

"Perhaps so," said I; "but, Legrand, I fear you are no artist. I must wait until I see the beetle itself, if I am to form any idea of its personal appearance."

"Well, I don't know," said he, a little nettled, "I draw tolerably – SHOULD do it at least – have had good masters, and flatter myself that I am not quite a blockhead."

"But, my dear fellow, you are joking then," said I, "this is a very passable SKULL – indeed, I may say that it is a very EXCELLENT skull, according to the vulgar notions about such specimens of physiology – and your scarabaeus must be the queerest scarabaeus in the world if it resembles it. Why, we may get up a very thrilling bit of superstition upon this hint. I presume you will call the bug Scarabaeus caput hominis, or something of that kind – there many similar titles in the Natural Histories. But where are the antennae you spoke of?"

"The antennae!" said Legrand, who seemed to be getting unaccountably warm upon the subject; "I am sure you must see the antennae. I made them as distinct as they are in the original insect, and I presume that is sufficient."

"Well, well," I said, "perhaps you have – still I don't see them;" and I handed him the paper without additional remark, not wishing to ruffle his temper; but I was much surprised at the turn affairs had taken; his ill humor puzzled me – and, as for the drawing of the beetle, there were positively NO antennae visible, and the whole DID bear a very close resemblance to the ordinary cuts of a death's head.

He received the paper very peevishly, and was about to crumple it, apparently to throw it in the fire, when a casual glance at the design seemed suddenly to rivet his attention. In an instant his face grew violently red – in another excessively pale. For some minutes he continued to scrutinize the drawing minutely where he sat. At length he arose, took a candle from the table, and proceeded to seat himself upon a sea chest in the farthest corner of the room. Here again he made an anxious examination of the paper, turning it in all directions. He said nothing, however, and his conduct greatly astonished me; yet I thought it prudent not to exacerbate the growing moodiness of his temper by any comment. Presently he took from his coat pocket a wallet, placed the paper carefully in it, and deposited both in a writing desk, which he locked. He now grew more composed in his demeanor; but his original air of enthusiasm had quite disappeared. Yet he seemed not so much sulky as abstracted. As the evening wore away he became more and more absorbed in reverie, from which no sallies of mine could arouse him. It had been my intention to pass the night at the hut, as I had frequently done before, but, seeing my host in this mood, I deemed it proper to take leave. He did not press me to remain, but, as I departed, he shook my hand with even more than his usual cordiality.

It was about a month after this (and during the interval I had seen nothing of Legrand) when I received a visit, at Charleston, from his man, Jupiter. I had never seen the good old negro look so dispirited, and I feared that some serious disaster had befallen my friend.

"Well, Jup," said I, "what is the matter now? – how is your master?"

"Why, to speak the troof, massa, him not so berry well as mought be."

"Not well! I am truly sorry to hear it. What does he complain of?"

"Dar! dot's it! – him neber 'plain of notin' – but him berry sick for all dat."

"VERY sick, Jupiter! – why didn't you say so at once? Is he confined to bed?"

"No, dat he aint! – he aint 'fin'd nowhar – dat's just whar de shoe pinch – my mind is got to be berry hebby 'bout poor Massa Will."

"Jupiter, I should like to understand what it is you are talking about. You say your master is sick. Hasn't he told you what ails him?"

"Why, massa, 'taint worf while for to git mad about de matter – Massa Will say noffin at all aint de matter wid him – but den what make him go about looking dis here way, wid he head down and he soldiers up, and as white as a goose? And den he keep a syphon all de time – "

"Keeps a what, Jupiter?"

"Keeps a syphon wid de figgurs on de slate – de queerest figgurs I ebber did see. Ise gittin' to be skeered, I tell you. Hab for to keep mighty tight eye 'pon him 'noovers. Todder day he gib me slip 'fore de sun up and was gone de whole ob de blessed day. I had a big stick ready cut for to gib him deuced good beating when he did come – but Ise sich a fool dat I hadn't de heart arter all – he looked so berry poorly."

"Eh? – what? – ah yes! – upon the whole I think you had better not be too severe with the poor fellow – don't flog him, Jupiter – he can't very well stand it – but can you form no idea of what has occasioned this illness, or rather this change of conduct? Has anything unpleasant happened since I saw you?"

"No, massa, dey aint bin noffin onpleasant SINCE den – 'twas 'FORE den I'm feared – 'twas de berry day you was dare."

"How? what do you mean."

"Why, massa, I mean de bug – dare now."

"The what?"

"De bug – I'm berry sartin dat Massa Will bin bit somewhere 'bout de head by dat goole-bug."

"And what cause have you, Jupiter, for such a supposition?"

"Claws enuff, massa, and mouff, too. I nebber did see sich a deuced bug – he kick and he bite eberyting what cum near him. Massa Will cotch him fuss, but had for to let him go 'gin mighty quick, I tell you – den was de time he must ha' got de bite. I didn't like de look ob de bug mouff, myself, nohow, so I wouldn't take hold oh him wid my finger, but I cotch him wid a piece oh paper dat I found. I rap him up in de paper and stuff a piece of it in he mouff – dat was de way."

"And you think, then, that your master was really bitten by the beetle, and that the bite made him sick?"

"I don't think noffin about it – I nose it. What make him dream 'bout de goole so much, if 'taint cause he bit by the goole-bug? Ise heered 'bout dem goole-bugs 'fore dis."

"But how do you know he dreams about gold?"

"How I know? why, 'cause he talk about it in he sleep – dat's how I nose."

"Well, Jup, perhaps you are right; but to what fortunate circumstance am I to attribute the honor of a visit from you to- day?"

"What de matter, massa?"

"Did you bring any message from Mr. Legrand?"

"No, massa, I bring dis here pissel;" and here Jupiter handed me a note which ran thus:

"MY DEAR – –

"Why have I not seen you for so long a time? I hope you have not been so foolish as to take offense at any little brusquerie of mine; but no, that is improbable.

"Since I saw you I have had great cause for anxiety. I have something to tell you, yet scarcely know how to tell it, or whether I should tell it at all.

"I have not been quite well for some days past, and poor old Jup annoys me, almost beyond endurance, by his well-meant attentions. Would you believe it? – he had prepared a huge stick, the other day, with which to chastise me for giving him the slip, and spending the day, solus, among the hills on the mainland. I verily believe that my ill looks alone saved me a flogging.

"I have made no addition to my cabinet since we met. "If you can, in any way, make it convenient, come over with Jupiter. DO come. I wish to see you TO-NIGHT, upon business of importance. I assure you that it is of the HIGHEST importance.

"Ever yours,

"WILLIAM LEGRAND."

There was something in the tone of this note which gave me great uneasiness. Its whole style differed materially from that of Legrand. What could he be dreaming of? What new crotchet possessed his excitable brain? What "business of the highest importance" could HE possibly have to transact? Jupiter's account of him boded no good. I dreaded lest the continued pressure of misfortune had, at length, fairly unsettled the reason of my friend. Without a moment's hesitation, therefore, I prepared to accompany the negro.

Upon reaching the wharf, I noticed a scythe and three spades, all apparently new, lying in the bottom of the boat in which we were to embark.

"What is the meaning of all this, Jup?" I inquired.

"Him syfe, massa, and spade."

"Very true; but what are they doing here?"

"Him de syfe and de spade what Massa Will sis 'pon my buying for him in de town, and de debbil's own lot of money I had to gib for em."

"But what, in the name of all that is mysterious, is your 'Massa Will' going to do with scythes and spades?"

"Dat's more dan I know, and debbil take me if I don't b'lieve 'tis more dan he know too. But it's all cum ob de bug."

Finding that no satisfaction was to be obtained of Jupiter, whose whole intellect seemed to be absorbed by "de bug," I now stepped into the boat, and made sail. With a fair and strong breeze we soon ran into the little cove to the northward of Fort Moultrie, and a walk of some two miles brought us to the hut. It was about three in the afternoon when we arrived. Legrand had been awaiting us in eager expectation. He grasped my hand with a nervous empressement which alarmed me and strengthened the suspicions already entertained. His countenance was pale even to ghastliness, and his deep-set eyes glared with unnatural luster. After some inquiries respecting his health, I asked him, not knowing what better to say, if he had yet obtained the scarabaeus from Lieutenant G – – .

"Oh, yes," he replied, coloring violently, "I got it from him the next morning. Nothing should tempt me to part with that scarabaeus. Do you know that Jupiter is quite right about it?"

"In what way?" I asked, with a sad foreboding at heart.

"In supposing it to be a bug of REAL GOLD." He said this with an air of profound seriousness, and I felt inexpressibly shocked.

"This bug is to make my fortune," he continued, with a triumphant smile; "to reinstate me in my family possessions. Is it any wonder, then, that I prize it? Since Fortune has thought fit to bestow it upon me, I have only to use it properly, and I shall arrive at the gold of which it is the index. Jupiter, bring me that scarabaeus!"

"What! de bug, massa? I'd rudder not go fer trubble dat bug; you mus' git him for your own self." Hereupon Legrand arose, with a grave and stately air, and brought me the beetle from a glass case in which it was enclosed. It was a beautiful scarabaeus, and, at that time, unknown to naturalists – of course a great prize in a scientific point of view. There were two round black spots near one extremity of the back, and a long one near the other. The scales were exceedingly hard and glossy, with all the appearance of burnished gold. The weight of the insect was very remarkable, and, taking all things into consideration, I could hardly blame Jupiter for his opinion respecting it; but what to make of Legrand's concordance with that opinion, I could not, for the life of me, tell.

"I sent for you," said he, in a grandiloquent tone, when I had completed my examination of the beetle, "I sent for you that I might have your counsel and assistance in furthering the views of Fate and of the bug – "

"My dear Legrand," I cried, interrupting him, "you are certainly unwell, and had better use some little precautions. You shall go to bed, and I will remain with you a few days, until you get over this. You are feverish and – "

"Feel my pulse," said he.

I felt it, and, to say the truth, found not the slightest indication of fever.

"But you may be ill and yet have no fever. Allow me this once to prescribe for you. In the first place go to bed. In the next – "

"You are mistaken," he interposed, "I am as well as I can expect to be under the excitement which I suffer. If you really wish me well, you will relieve this excitement."

"And how is this to be done?"

"Very easily. Jupiter and myself are going upon an expedition into the hills, upon the mainland, and, in this expedition, we shall need the aid of some person in whom we can confide. You are the only one we can trust. Whether we succeed or fail, the excitement which you now perceive in me will be equally allayed."

"I am anxious to oblige you in any way," I replied; "but do you mean to say that this infernal beetle has any connection with your expedition into the hills?"

"It has."

"Then, Legrand, I can become a party to no such absurd proceeding."

"I am sorry – very sorry – for we shall have to try it by ourselves."

"Try it by yourselves! The man is surely mad! – but stay! – how long do you propose to be absent?"

"Probably all night. We shall start immediately, and be back, at all events, by sunrise."

"And will you promise me, upon your honor, that when this freak of yours is over, and the bug business (good God!) settled to your satisfaction, you will then return home and follow my advice implicitly, as that of your physician?"

"Yes; I promise; and now let us be off, for we have no time to lose."

With a heavy heart I accompanied my friend. We started about four o'clock – Legrand, Jupiter, the dog, and myself. Jupiter had with him the scythe and spades – the whole of which he insisted upon carrying – more through fear, it seemed to me, of trusting either of the implements within reach of his master, than from any excess of industry or complaisance. His demeanor was dogged in the extreme, and "dat deuced bug" were the sole words which escaped his lips during the journey. For my own part, I had charge of a couple of dark lanterns, while Legrand contented himself with the scarabaeus, which he carried attached to the end of a bit of whipcord; twirling it to and fro, with the air of a conjurer, as he went. When I observed this last, plain evidence of my friend's aberration of mind, I could scarcely refrain from tears. I thought it best, however, to humor his fancy, at least for the present, or until I could adopt some more energetic measures with a chance of success. In the meantime I endeavored, but all in vain, to sound him in regard to the object of the expedition. Having succeeded in inducing me to accompany him, he seemed unwilling to hold conversation upon any topic of minor importance, and to all my questions vouchsafed no other reply than "we shall see!"

We crossed the creek at the head of the island by means of a skiff, and, ascending the high grounds on the shore of the mainland, proceeded in a northwesterly direction, through a tract of country excessively wild and desolate, where no trace of a human footstep was to be seen. Legrand led the way with decision; pausing only for an instant, here and there, to consult what appeared to be certain landmarks of his own contrivance upon a former occasion.

In this manner we journeyed for about two hours, and the sun was just setting when we entered a region infinitely more dreary than any yet seen. It was a species of table-land, near the summit of an almost inaccessible hill, densely wooded from base to pinnacle, and interspersed with huge crags that appeared to lie loosely upon the soil, and in many cases were prevented from precipitating themselves into the valleys below, merely by the support of the trees against which they reclined. Deep ravines, in various directions, gave an air of still sterner solemnity to the scene.

The natural platform to which we had clambered was thickly overgrown with brambles, through which we soon discovered that it would have been impossible to force our way but for the scythe; and Jupiter, by direction of his master, proceeded to clear for us a path to the foot of an enormously tall tulip tree, which stood, with some eight or ten oaks, upon the level, and far surpassed them all, and all other trees which I had then ever seen, in the beauty of its foliage and form, in the wide spread of its branches, and in the general majesty of its appearance. When we reached this tree, Legrand turned to Jupiter, and asked him if he thought he could climb it. The old man seemed a little staggered by the question, and for some moments made no reply. At length he approached the huge trunk, walked slowly around it, and examined it with minute attention. When he had completed his scrutiny, he merely said:

"Yes, massa, Jup climb any tree he ebber see in he life."

"Then up with you as soon as possible, for it will soon be too dark to see what we are about."

"How far mus' go up, massa?" inquired Jupiter.

"Get up the main trunk first, and then I will tell you which way to go – and here – stop! take this beetle with you."

"De bug, Massa Will! – de goole-bug!" cried the negro, drawing back in dismay – "what for mus' tote de bug way up de tree? – d – n if I do!"

"If you are afraid, Jup, a great big negro like you, to take hold of a harmless little dead beetle, why you can carry it up by this string – but, if you do not take it up with you in some way, I shall be under the necessity of breaking your head with this shovel."

"What de matter now, massa?" said Jup, evidently shamed into compliance; "always want for to raise fuss wid old nigger. Was only funnin anyhow. ME feered de bug! what I keer for de bug?" Here he took cautiously hold of the extreme end of the string, and, maintaining the insect as far from his person as circumstances would permit, prepared to ascend the tree.

In youth, the tulip tree, or Liriodendron tulipiferum, the most magnificent of American foresters, has a trunk peculiarly smooth, and often rises to a great height without lateral branches; but, in its riper age, the bark becomes gnarled and uneven, while many short limbs make their appearance on the stem. Thus the difficulty of ascension, in the present case, lay more in semblance than in reality. Embracing the huge cylinder, as closely as possible, with his arms and knees, seizing with his hands some projections, and resting his naked toes upon others, Jupiter, after one or two narrow escapes from falling, at length wriggled himself into the first great fork, and seemed to consider the whole business as virtually accomplished. The RISK of the achievement was, in fact, now over, although the climber was some sixty or seventy feet from the ground.

"Which way mus' go now, Massa Will?" he asked.

"Keep up the largest branch – the one on this side," said Legrand. The negro obeyed him promptly, and apparently with but little trouble; ascending higher and higher, until no glimpse of his squat figure could be obtained through the dense foliage which enveloped it. Presently his voice was heard in a sort of halloo.

"How much fudder is got to go?"

"How high up are you?" asked Legrand.

"Ebber so fur," replied the negro; "can see de sky fru de top oh de tree."

"Never mind the sky, but attend to what I say. Look down the trunk and count the limbs below you on this side. How many limbs have you passed?"

"One, two, tree, four, fibe – I done pass fibe big limb, massa, 'pon dis side."

"Then go one limb higher."

In a few minutes the voice was heard again, announcing that the seventh limb was attained.

"Now, Jup," cried Legrand, evidently much excited, "I want you to work your way out upon that limb as far as you can. If you see anything strange let me know."

By this time what little doubt I might have entertained of my poor friend's insanity was put finally at rest. I had no alternative but to conclude him stricken with lunacy, and I became seriously anxious about getting him home. While I was pondering upon what was best to be done, Jupiter's voice was again heard.

"Mos feered for to ventur pon dis limb berry far – 'tis dead limb putty much all de way."

"Did you say it was a DEAD limb, Jupiter?" cried Legrand in a quavering voice.

"Yes, massa, him dead as de door-nail – done up for sartin – done departed dis here life."

"What in the name of heaven shall I do?" asked Legrand, seemingly in the greatest distress.

"Do!" said I, glad of an opportunity to interpose a word, "why come home and go to bed. Come now! – that's a fine fellow.

It's getting late, and, besides, you remember your promise."

"Jupiter," cried he, without heeding me in the least, "do you hear me?"

"Yes, Massa Will, hear you ebber so plain."

"Try the wood well, then, with your knife, and see if you think it VERY rotten."

"Him rotten, massa, sure nuff," replied the negro in a few moments, "but not so berry rotten as mought be. Mought venture out leetle way pon de limb by myself, dat's true."

"By yourself! – what do you mean?"

"Why, I mean de bug. 'Tis BERRY hebby bug. Spose I drop him down fuss, an den de limb won't break wid just de weight of one nigger."

"You infernal scoundrel!" cried Legrand, apparently much relieved, "what do you mean by telling me such nonsense as that? As sure as you drop that beetle I'll break your neck. Look here, Jupiter, do you hear me?"

"Yes, massa, needn't hollo at poor nigger dat style."

"Well! now listen! – if you will venture out on the limb as far as you think safe, and not let go the beetle, I'll make you a present of a silver dollar as soon as you get down."

"I'm gwine, Massa Will – deed I is," replied the negro very promptly – "mos out to the eend now."

"OUT TO THE END!" here fairly screamed Legrand; "do you say you are out to the end of that limb?"

"Soon be to de eend, massa – o-o-o-o-oh! Lor-gol-a-marcy! what IS dis here pon de tree?"

"Well!" cried Legrand, highly delighted, "what is it?"

"Why 'taint noffin but a skull – somebody bin lef him head up de tree, and de crows done gobble ebery bit ob de meat off."

"A skull, you say! – very well, – how is it fastened to the

limb? – what holds it on?"

"Sure nuff, massa; mus look. Why dis berry curious sarcumstance, pon my word – dare's a great big nail in de skull, what fastens ob it on to de tree."

"Well now, Jupiter, do exactly as I tell you – do you hear?"

"Yes, massa."

"Pay attention, then – find the left eye of the skull."

"Hum! hoo! dat's good! why dey ain't no eye lef at all."

"Curse your stupidity! do you know your right hand from your left?"

"Yes, I knows dat – knows all about dat – 'tis my lef hand what I chops de wood wid."

"To be sure! you are left-handed; and your left eye is on the same side as your left hand. Now, I suppose, you can find the left eye of the skull, or the place where the left eye has been. Have you found it?"

Here was a long pause. At length the negro asked:

"Is de lef eye of de skull pon de same side as de lef hand of de skull too? – cause de skull aint got not a bit oh a hand at all – nebber mind! I got de lef eye now – here de lef eye! what mus do wid it?"

Let the beetle drop through it, as far as the string will reach – but be careful and not let go your hold of the string."

"All dat done, Massa Will; mighty easy ting for to put de bug fru de hole – look out for him dare below!"

During this colloquy no portion of Jupiter's person could be seen; but the beetle, which he had suffered to descend, was now visible at the end of the string, and glistened, like a globe of burnished gold, in the last rays of the setting sun, some of which still faintly illumined the eminence upon which we stood. The scarabaeus hung quite clear of any branches, and, if allowed to fall, would have fallen at our feet. Legrand immediately took the scythe, and cleared with it a circular space, three or four yards in diameter, just beneath the insect, and, having accomplished this, ordered Jupiter to let go the string and come down from the tree.

Driving a peg, with great nicety, into the ground, at the precise spot where the beetle fell, my friend now produced from his pocket a tape measure. Fastening one end of this at that point of the trunk of the tree which was nearest the peg, he unrolled it till it reached the peg and thence further unrolled it, in the direction already established by the two points of the tree and the peg, for the distance of fifty feet – Jupiter clearing away the brambles with the scythe. At the spot thus attained a second peg was driven, and about this, as a center, a rude circle, about four feet in diameter, described. Taking now a spade himself, and giving one to Jupiter and one to me, Legrand begged us to set about digging as quickly as possible.

To speak the truth, I had no especial relish for such amusement at any time, and, at that particular moment, would willingly have declined it; for the night was coming on, and I felt much fatigued with the exercise already taken; but I saw no mode of escape, and was fearful of disturbing my poor friend's equanimity by a refusal. Could I have depended, indeed, upon Jupiter's aid, I would have had no hesitation in attempting to get the lunatic home by force; but I was too well assured of the old negro's disposition, to hope that he would assist me, under any circumstances, in a personal contest with his master. I made no doubt that the latter had been infected with some of the innumerable Southern superstitions about money buried, and that his fantasy had received confirmation by the finding of the scarabaeus, or, perhaps, by Jupiter's obstinacy in maintaining it to be "a bug of real gold." A mind disposed to lunacy would readily be led away by such suggestions – especially if chiming in with favorite preconceived ideas – and then I called to mind the poor fellow's speech about the beetle's being "the index of his fortune." Upon the whole, I was sadly vexed and puzzled, but, at length, I concluded to make a virtue of necessity – to dig with a good will, and thus the sooner to convince the visionary, by ocular demonstration, of the fallacy of the opinion he entertained.

The lanterns having been lit, we all fell to work with a zeal worthy a more rational cause; and, as the glare fell upon our persons and implements, I could not help thinking how picturesque a group we composed, and how strange and suspicious our labors must have appeared to any interloper who, by chance, might have stumbled upon our whereabouts.

We dug very steadily for two hours. Little was said; and our chief embarrassment lay in the yelpings of the dog, who took exceeding interest in our proceedings. He, at length, became so obstreperous that we grew fearful of his giving the alarm to some stragglers in the vicinity, – or, rather, this was the apprehension of Legrand; – for myself, I should have rejoiced at any interruption which might have enabled me to get the wanderer home. The noise was, at length, very effectually silenced by Jupiter, who, getting out of the hole with a dogged air of deliberation, tied the brute's mouth up with one of his suspenders, and then returned, with a grave chuckle, to his task.

When the time mentioned had expired, we had reached a depth of five feet, and yet no signs of any treasure became manifest. A general pause ensued, and I began to hope that the farce was at an end. Legrand, however, although evidently much disconcerted, wiped his brow thoughtfully and recommenced. We had excavated the entire circle of four feet diameter, and now we slightly enlarged the limit, and went to the farther depth of two feet. Still nothing appeared. The gold-seeker, whom I sincerely pitied, at length clambered from the pit, with the bitterest disappointment imprinted upon every feature, and proceeded, slowly and reluctantly, to put on his coat, which he had thrown off at the beginning of his labor. In the meantime I made no remark. Jupiter, at a signal from his master, began to gather up his tools. This done, and the dog having been unmuzzled, we turned in profound silence toward home.

We had taken, perhaps, a dozen steps in this direction, when, with a loud oath, Legrand strode up to Jupiter, and seized him by the collar. The astonished negro opened his eyes and mouth to the fullest extent, let fall the spades, and fell upon his knees.

"You scoundrel!" said Legrand, hissing out the syllables from between his clenched teeth – "you infernal black villain! – speak, I tell you! – answer me this instant, without prevarication! – which – which is your left eye?"

"Oh, my golly, Massa Will! aint dis here my lef eye for sartain?" roared the terrified Jupiter, placing his hand upon his RIGHT organ of vision, and holding it there with a desperate pertinacity, as if in immediate, dread of his master's attempt at a gouge.

"I thought so! – I knew it! hurrah!" vociferated Legrand, letting the negro go and executing a series of curvets and caracols, much to the astonishment of his valet, who, arising from his knees, looked, mutely, from his master to myself, and then from myself to his master.

"Come! we must go back," said the latter, "the game's not up yet;" and he again led the way to the tulip tree.

"Jupiter," said he, when we reached its foot, "come here! was the skull nailed to the limb with the face outward, or with the face to the limb?"

"De face was out, massa, so dat de crows could get at de eyes good, widout any trouble."

"Well, then, was it this eye or that through which you dropped the beetle?" here Legrand touched each of Jupiter's eyes.

"'Twas dis eye, massa – de lef eye – jis as you tell me," and here it was his right eye that the negro indicated.

"That will do – we must try it again."

Here my friend, about whose madness I now saw, or fancied that I saw, certain indications of method, removed the peg which marked the spot where the beetle fell, to a spot about three inches to the westward of its former position. Taking, now, the tape measure from the nearest point of the trunk to the peg, as before, and continuing the extension in a straight line to the distance of fifty feet, a spot was indicated, removed, by several yards, from the point at which we had been digging.

Around the new position a circle, somewhat larger than in the former instance, was now described, and we again set to work with the spade. I was dreadfully weary, but, scarcely understanding what had occasioned the change in my thoughts, I felt no longer any great aversion from the labor imposed. I had become most unaccountably interested – nay, even excited. Perhaps there was something, amid all the extravagant demeanor of Legrand – some air of forethought, or of deliberation, which impressed me. I dug eagerly, and now and then caught myself actually looking, with something that very much resembled expectation, for the fancied treasure, the vision of which had demented my unfortunate companion. At a period when such vagaries of thought most fully possessed me, and when we had been at work perhaps an hour and a half, we were again interrupted by the violent howlings of the dog. His uneasiness, in the first instance, had been, evidently, but the result of playfulness or caprice, but he now assumed a bitter and serious tone. Upon Jupiter's again attempting to muzzle him, he made furious resistance, and, leaping into the hole, tore up the mold frantically with his claws. In a few seconds he had uncovered a mass of human bones, forming two complete skeletons, intermingled with several buttons of metal, and what appeared to be the dust of decayed woolen. One or two strokes of a spade upturned the blade of a large Spanish knife, and, as we dug farther, three or four loose pieces of gold and silver coin came to light.

At sight of these the joy of Jupiter could scarcely be restrained, but the countenance of his master wore an air of extreme disappointment. He urged us, however, to continue our exertions, and the words were hardly uttered when I stumbled and fell forward, having caught the toe of my boot in a large ring of iron that lay half buried in the loose earth.

We now worked in earnest, and never did I pass ten minutes of more intense excitement. During this interval we had fairly unearthed an oblong chest of wood, which, from its perfect preservation and wonderful hardness, had plainly been subjected to some mineralizing process – perhaps that of the bichloride of mercury. This box was three feet and a half long, three feet broad, and two and a half feet deep. It was firmly secured by bands of wrought iron, riveted, and forming a kind of open trelliswork over the whole. On each side of the chest, near the top, were three rings of iron – six in all – by means of which a firm hold could be obtained by six persons. Our utmost united endeavors served only to disturb the coffer very slightly in its bed. We at once saw the impossibility of removing so great a weight. Luckily, the sole fastenings of the lid consisted of two sliding bolts. These we drew back – trembling and panting with anxiety. In an instant, a treasure of incalculable value lay gleaming before us. As the rays of the lanterns fell within the pit, there flashed upward a glow and a glare, from a confused heap of gold and of jewels, that absolutely dazzled our eyes.

I shall not pretend to describe the feelings with which I gazed. Amazement was, of course, predominant. Legrand appeared exhausted with excitement, and spoke very few words. Jupiter's countenance wore, for some minutes, as deadly a pallor as it is possible, in the nature of things, for any negro's visage to assume. He seemed stupefied – thunderstricken. Presently he fell upon his knees in the pit, and burying his naked arms up to the elbows in gold, let them there remain, as if enjoying the luxury of a bath. At length, with a deep sigh, he exclaimed, as if in a soliloquy:

"And dis all cum of de goole-bug! de putty goole-bug! de poor little goole-bug, what I boosed in that sabage kind oh style! Ain't you shamed oh yourself, nigger? – answer me dat!"

It became necessary, at last, that I should arouse both master and valet to the expediency of removing the treasure. It was growing late, and it behooved us to make exertion, that we might get everything housed before daylight. It was difficult to say what should he done, and much time was spent in deliberation – so confused were the ideas of all. We, finally, lightened the box by removing two thirds of its contents, when we were enabled, with some trouble, to raise it from the hole. The articles taken out were deposited among the brambles, and the dog left to guard them, with strict orders from Jupiter neither, upon any pretense, to stir from the spot, nor to open his mouth until our return. We then hurriedly made for home with the chest; reaching the hut in safety, but after excessive toil, at one o'clock in the morning. Worn out as we were, it was not in human nature to do more immediately. We rested until two, and had supper; starting for the hills immediately afterwards, armed with three stout sacks, which, by good luck, were upon the premises. A little before four we arrived at the pit, divided the remainder of the booty, as equally as might be, among us, and, leaving the holes unfilled, again set out for the hut, at which, for the second time, we deposited our golden burdens, just as the first faint streaks of the dawn gleamed from over the treetops in the east.

We were now thoroughly broken down; but the intense excitement of the time denied us repose. After an unquiet slumber of some three or four hours' duration, we arose, as if by preconcert, to make examination of our treasure.

The chest had been full to the brim, and we spent the whole day, and the greater part of the next night, in a scrutiny of its contents. There had been nothing like order or arrangement. Everything had been heaped in promiscuously. Having assorted all with care, we found ourselves possessed of even vaster wealth than we had at first supposed. In coin there was rather more than four hundred and fifty thousand dollars – estimating the value of the pieces, as accurately as we could, by the tables of the period. There was not a particle of silver. All was gold of antique date and of great variety – French, Spanish, and German money, with a few English guineas, and some counters, of which we had never seen specimens before. There were several very large and heavy coins, so worn that we could make nothing of their inscriptions. There was no American money. The value of the jewels we found more difficulty in estimating. There were diamonds – some of them exceedingly large and fine – a hundred and ten in all, and not one of them small; eighteen rubies of remarkable brilliancy; – three hundred and ten emeralds, all very beautiful; and twenty-one sapphires, with an opal. These stones had all been broken from their settings and thrown loose in the chest. The settings themselves, which we picked out from among the other gold, appeared to have been beaten up with hammers, as if to prevent identification. Besides all this, there was a vast quantity of solid gold ornaments; nearly two hundred massive finger and ears rings; rich chains – thirty of these, if I remember; eighty-three very large and heavy crucifixes; five gold censers of great value; a prodigious golden punch bowl, ornamented with richly chased vine leaves and Bacchanalian figures; with two sword handles exquisitely embossed, and many other smaller articles which I cannot recollect. The weight of these valuables exceeded three hundred and fifty pounds avoirdupois; and in this estimate I have not included one hundred and ninety-seven superb gold watches; three of the number being worth each five hundred dollars, if one. Many of them were very old, and as timekeepers valueless; the works having suffered, more or less, from corrosion – but all were richly jeweled and in cases of great worth. We estimated the entire contents of the chest, that night, at a million and a half of dollars; and upon the subsequent disposal of the trinkets and jewels (a few being retained for our own use), it was found that we had greatly undervalued the treasure.

When, at length, we had concluded our examination, and the intense excitement of the time had, in some measure, subsided, Legrand, who saw that I was dying with impatience for a solution of this most extraordinary riddle, entered into a full detail of all the circumstances connected with it.

"You remember," said he, "the night when I handed you the rough sketch I had made of the scarabaeus. You recollect, also, that I became quite vexed at you for insisting that my drawing resembled a death's head. When you first made this assertion I thought you were jesting; but afterwards I called to mind the peculiar spots on the back of the insect, and admitted to myself that your remark had some little foundation in fact. Still, the sneer at my graphic powers irritated me – for I am considered a good artist – and, therefore, when you handed me the scrap of parchment, I was about to crumple it up and throw it angrily into the fire."

"The scrap of paper, you mean," said I.

"No; it had much of the appearance of paper, and at first I

supposed it to be such, but when I came to draw upon it, I discovered it at once to be a piece of very thin parchment. It was quite dirty, you remember. Well, as I was in the very act of crumpling it up, my glance fell upon the sketch at which you had been looking, and you may imagine my astonishment when I perceived, in fact, the figure of a death's head just where, it seemed to me, I had made the drawing of the beetle. For a moment I was too much amazed to think with accuracy. I knew that my design was very different in detail from this – although there was a certain similarity in general outline. Presently I took a candle, and seating myself at the other end of the room, proceeded to scrutinize the parchment more closely. Upon turning it over, I saw my own sketch upon the reverse, just as I had made it. My first idea, now, was mere surprise at the really remarkable similarity of outline – at the singular coincidence involved in the fact that, unknown to me, there should have been a skull upon the other side of the parchment, immediately beneath my figure of the scarabaeus, and that this skull, not only in outline, but in size, should so closely resemble my drawing. I say the singularity of this coincidence absolutely stupefied me for a time. This is the usual effect of such coincidences. The mind struggles to establish a connection – a sequence of cause and effect – and, being unable to do so, suffers a species of temporary paralysis. But, when I recovered from this stupor, there dawned upon me gradually a conviction which startled me even far more than the coincidence. I began distinctly, positively, to remember that there had been NO drawing upon the parchment, when I made my sketch of the scarabaeus. I became perfectly certain of this; for I recollected turning up first one side and then the other, in search of the cleanest spot. Had the skull been then there, of course I could not have failed to notice it. Here was indeed a mystery which I felt it impossible to explain; but, even at that early moment, there seemed to glimmer, faintly, within the most remote and secret chambers of my intellect, a glow-wormlike conception of that truth which last night's adventure brought to so magnificent a demonstration. I arose at once, and putting the parchment securely away, dismissed all further reflection until I should be alone.

"When you had gone, and when Jupiter was fast asleep, I betook myself to a more methodical investigation of the affair. In the first place I considered the manner in which the parchment had come into my possession. The spot where we discovered the scarabaeus was on the coast of the mainland, about a mile eastward of the island, and but a short distance above high-water mark. Upon my taking hold of it, it gave me a sharp bite, which caused me to let it drop. Jupiter, with his accustomed caution, before seizing the insect, which had flown toward him, looked about him for a leaf, or something of that nature, by which to take hold of it. It was at this moment that his eyes, and mine also, fell upon the scrap of parchment, which I then supposed to be paper. It was lying half buried in the sand, a corner sticking up. Near the spot where we found it, I observed the remnants of the hull of what appeared to have been a ship's longboat. The wreck seemed to have been there for a very great while, for the resemblance to boat timbers could scarcely be traced.

"Well, Jupiter picked up the parchment, wrapped the beetle in it, and gave it to me. Soon afterwards we turned to go home, and on the way met Lieutenant G – – . I showed him the insect, and he begged me to let him take it to the fort. Upon my consenting, he thrust it forthwith into his waistcoat pocket, without the parchment in which it had been wrapped, and which I had continued to hold in my hand during his inspection. Perhaps he dreaded my changing my mind, and thought it best to make sure of the prize at once – you know how enthusiastic he is on all subjects connected with Natural History. At the same time, without being conscious of it, I must have deposited the parchment in my own pocket.

"You remember that when I went to the table, for the purpose of making a sketch of the beetle, I found no paper where it was usually kept. I looked in the drawer, and found none there. I searched my pockets, hoping to find an old letter, when my hand fell upon the parchment. I thus detail the precise mode in which it came into my possession, for the circumstances impressed me with peculiar force.

"No doubt you will think me fanciful – but I had already established a kind of CONNECTION. I had put together two links of a great chain. There was a boat lying upon a seacoast, and not far from the boat was a parchment – NOT A PAPER – with a skull depicted upon it. You will, of course, ask 'where is the connection?' I reply that the skull, or death's head, is the well-known emblem of the pirate. The flag of the death's head is hoisted in all engagements.

"I have said that the scrap was parchment, and not paper. Parchment is durable – almost imperishable. Matters of little moment are rarely consigned to parchment; since, for the mere ordinary purposes of drawing or writing, it is not nearly so well adapted as paper. This reflection suggested some meaning – some relevancy – in the death's head. I did not fail to observe, also, the FORM of the parchment. Although one of its corners had been, by some accident, destroyed, it could be seen that the original form was oblong. It was just such a slip, indeed, as might have been chosen for a memorandum – for a record of something to be long remembered, and carefully preserved."

"But," I interposed, "you say that the skull was NOT upon the parchment when you made the drawing of the beetle. How then do you trace any connection between the boat and the skull – since this latter, according to your own admission, must have been designed (God only knows how or by whom) at some period subsequent to your sketching the scarabaeus?"

"Ah, hereupon turns the whole mystery; although the secret, at this point, I had comparatively little difficulty in solving. My steps were sure, and could afford but a single result. I reasoned, for example, thus: When I drew the scarabaeus, there was no skull apparent upon the parchment. When I had completed the drawing I gave it to you, and observed you narrowly until you returned it. YOU, therefore, did not design the skull, and no one else was present to do it. Then it was not done by human agency. And nevertheless it was done.

"At this stage of my reflections I endeavored to remember, and DID remember, with entire distinctness, every incident which occurred about the period in question. The weather was chilly (oh, rare and happy accident!), and a fire was blazing upon the hearth. I was heated with exercise and sat near the table. You, however, had drawn a chair close to the chimney. Just as I placed the parchment in your hand, and as you were in the act of inspecting it, Wolf, the Newfoundland, entered, and leaped upon your shoulders. With your left hand you caressed him and kept him off, while your right, holding the parchment, was permitted to fall listlessly between your knees, and in close proximity to the fire. At one moment I thought the blaze had caught it, and was about to caution you, but, before I could speak, you had withdrawn it, and were engaged in its examination. When I considered all these particulars, I doubted not for a moment that HEAT had been the agent in bringing to light, upon the parchment, the skull which I saw designed upon it. You are well aware that chemical preparations exist, and have existed time out of mind, by means of which it is possible to write upon either paper or vellum, so that the characters shall become visible only when subjected to the action of fire. Zaffre, digested in aqua regia, and diluted with four times its weight of water, is sometimes employed; a green tint results. The regulus of cobalt, dissolved in spirit of niter, gives a red. These colors disappear at longer or shorter intervals after the material written upon cools, but again become apparent upon the reapplication of heat.

"I now scrutinized the death's head with care. Its outer edges – the edges of the drawing nearest the edge of the vellum – were far more DISTINCT than the others. It was clear that the action of the caloric had been imperfect or unequal. I immediately kindled a fire, and subjected every portion of the parchment to a glowing heat. At first, the only effect was the strengthening of the faint lines in the skull; but, upon persevering in the experiment, there became visible, at the corner of the slip, diagonally opposite to the spot in which the death's head was delineated, the figure of what I at first supposed to be a goat. A closer scrutiny, however, satisfied me that it was intended for a kid."

"Ha! ha!" said I, "to be sure I have no right to laugh at you – a million and a half of money is too serious a matter for mirth – but you are not about to establish a third link in your chain – you will not find any especial connection between your pirates and a goat – pirates, you know, have nothing to do with goats; they appertain to the farming interest."

"But I have just said that the figure was NOT that of a goat."

"Well, a kid then – pretty much the same thing."

"Pretty much, but not altogether," said Legrand. "You may have heard of one CAPTAIN Kidd. I at once looked upon the figure of the animal as a kind of punning or hieroglyphical signature. I say signature; because its position upon the vellum suggested this idea. The death's head at the corner diagonally opposite, had, in the same manner, the air of a stamp, or seal. But I was sorely put out by the absence of all else – of the body to my imagined instrument – of the text for my context."

"I presume you expected to find a letter between the stamp and the signature."

"Something of that kind. The fact is, I felt irresistibly impressed with a presentiment of some vast good fortune impending. I can scarcely say why. Perhaps, after all, it was rather a desire than an actual belief; – but do you know that Jupiter's silly words, about the bug being of solid gold, had a remarkable effect upon my fancy? And then the series of accidents and coincidents – these were so VERY extraordinary. Do you observe how mere an accident it was that these events should have occurred upon the SOLE day of all the year in which it has been, or may be sufficiently cool for fire, and that without the fire, or without the intervention of the dog at the precise moment in which he appeared, I should never have become aware of the death's head, and so never the possessor of the treasure?"

"But proceed – I am all impatience."

"Well; you have heard, of course, the many stories current – the thousand vague rumors afloat about money buried, somewhere upon the Atlantic coast, by Kidd and his associates. These rumors must have had some foundation in fact. And that the rumors have existed so long and so continuous, could have resulted, it appeared to me, only from the circumstance of the buried treasures still REMAINING entombed. Had Kidd concealed his plunder for a time, and afterwards reclaimed it, the rumors would scarcely have reached us in their present unvarying form. You will observe that the stories told are all about money-seekers, not about money-finders. Had the pirate recovered his money, there the affair would have dropped. It seemed to me that some accident – say the loss of a memorandum indicating its locality – had deprived him of the means of recovering it, and that this accident had become known to his followers, who otherwise might never have heard that the treasure had been concealed at all, and who, busying themselves in vain, because unguided, attempts to regain it, had given first birth, and then universal currency, to the reports which are now so common. Have you ever heard of any important treasure being unearthed along the coast?"

"Never."

"But that Kidd's accumulations were immense, is well known. I took it for granted, therefore, that the earth still held them; and you will scarcely be surprised when I tell you that I felt a hope, nearly amounting to certainty, that the parchment so strangely found involved a lost record of the place of deposit."

"But how did you proceed?"

"I held the vellum again to the fire, after increasing the heat, but nothing appeared. I now thought it possible that the coating of dirt might have something to do with the failure: so I carefully rinsed the parchment by pouring warm water over it, and, having done this, I placed it in a tin pan, with the skull downward, and put the pan upon a furnace of lighted charcoal. In a few minutes, the pan having become thoroughly heated, I removed the slip, and, to my inexpressible joy, found it spotted, in several places, with what appeared to be figures arranged in lines. Again I placed it in the pan, and suffered it to remain another minute. Upon taking it off, the whole was just as you see it now."

Here Legrand, having reheated the parchment, submitted it to my inspection. The following characters were rudely traced, in a red tint, between the death's head and the goat:

"53++!305))6*;4826)4+)4+).;806*;48!8]60))85;1+8*:+(;:+*8!83(88)5*!;
46(;88*96*?;8)*+(;485);5*!2:*+(;4956*2(5*-4)8]8*;4069285);)6!8)4++;
1(+9;48081;8:8+1;48!85;4)485!528806*81(+9;48;(88;4(+?34;48)4+;161;
: 188;+?;"

"But," said I, returning him the slip, "I am as much in the dark as ever. Were all the jewels of Golconda awaiting me upon my solution of this enigma, I am quite sure that I should be unable to earn them."

"And yet," said Legrand, "the solution is by no means so difficult as you might be led to imagine from the first hasty inspection of the characters. These characters, as anyone might readily guess, form a cipher – that is to say, they convey a meaning; but then from what is known of Kidd, I could not suppose him capable of constructing any of the more abstruse cryptographs. I made up my mind, at once, that this was of a simple species – such, however, as would appear, to the crude intellect of the sailor, absolutely insoluble without the key."

"And you really solved it?"

"Readily; I have solved others of an abstruseness ten thousand times greater. Circumstances, and a certain bias of mind, have led me to take interest in such riddles, and it may well be doubted whether human ingenuity can construct an enigma of the kind which human ingenuity may not, by proper application, resolve. In fact, having once established connected and legible characters, I scarcely gave a thought to the mere difficulty of developing their import.

"In the present case – indeed in all cases of secret writing – the first question regards the LANGUAGE of the cipher; for the principles of solution, so far, especially, as the more simple ciphers are concerned, depend upon, and are varied by, the genius of the particular idiom. In general, there is no alternative but experiment (directed by probabilities) of every tongue known to him who attempts the solution, until the true one be attained. But, with the cipher now before us, all difficulty was removed by the signature. The pun upon the word 'Kidd' is appreciable in no other language than the English. But for this consideration I should have begun my attempts with the Spanish and French, as the tongues in which a secret of this kind would most naturally have been written by a pirate of the Spanish main. As it was, I assumed the cryptograph to be English.

"You observe there are no divisions between the words. Had there been divisions the task would have been comparatively easy. In such cases I should have commenced with a collation and analysis of the shorter words, and, had a word of a single letter occurred, as is most likely, (a or I, for example,) I should have considered the solution as assured. But, there being no division, my first step was to ascertain the predominant letters, as well as the least frequent. Counting all, I constructed a table thus:

Of the character 8 there are 33.
; " 26.
4 " 19.
+) " 16.
* " 13.
5 " 12.
6 " 11.
!1 " 8.
0 " 6.
92 " 5.
:3 " 4.
? " 3.
] " 2.
-. " 1.

"Now, in English, the letter which most frequently occurs is e. Afterwards, the succession runs thus: a o i d h n r s t u y c f g l m w b k p q x z. E predominates so remarkably, that an individual sentence of any length is rarely seen, in which it is not the prevailing character.

"Here, then, we have, in the very beginning, the groundwork for something more than a mere guess. The general use which may be made of the table is obvious – but, in this particular cipher, we shall only very partially require its aid. As our predominant character is 8, we will commence by assuming it as the

142

e of the natural alphabet. To verify the supposition, let us observe if the 8 be seen often in couples – for e is doubled with great frequency in English – in such words, for example, as 'meet,' 'fleet,' 'speed,' 'seen,' 'been,' 'agree,' etc. In the present instance we see it doubled no less than five times, although the cryptograph is brief.

"Let us assume 8, then, as e. Now, of all WORDS in the language, 'the' is most usual; let us see, therefore, whether there are not repetitions of any three characters, in the same order of collocation, the last of them being 8. If we discover repetitions of such letters, so arranged, they will most probably represent the word 'the.' Upon inspection, we find no less than seven such arrangements, the characters being ;48. We may, therefore, assume that ; represents t, 4 represents h, and 8 represents e – the last being now well confirmed. Thus a great step has been taken.

"But, having established a single word, we are enabled to establish a vastly important point; that is to say, several commencements and terminations of other words. Let us refer, for example, to the last instance but one, in which the combination ;48 occurs – not far from the end of the cipher. We know that the ; immediately ensuing is the commencement of a word, and, of the six characters succeeding this 'the,' we are cognizant of no less than five. Let us set these characters down, thus, by the letters we know them to represent, leaving a space for the unknown –

t eeth.

"Here we are enabled, at once, to discard the 'th,' as forming no portion of the word commencing with the first t; since, by experiment of the entire alphabet for a letter adapted to the vacancy, we perceive that no word can be formed of which this th can be a part. We are thus narrowed into

t ee,

and, going through the alphabet, if necessary, as before, we arrive at the word 'tree,' as the sole possible reading. We thus gain another letter, r, represented by (, with the words 'the tree' in juxtaposition.

"Looking beyond these words, for a short distance, we again

see the combination ;48, and employ it by way of TERMINA-
TION to what immediately precedes. We have thus this arrangement:

the tree ;4(4+?34 the,

or, substituting the natural letters, where known, it reads thus:

the tree thr+?3h the.

"Now, if, in place of the unknown characters, we leave blank spaces, or substitute dots, we read thus:

the tree thr...h the,

when the word 'through' makes itself evident at once. But this discovery gives us three new letters, o, u, and g, represented by +, ?, and 3.

"Looking now, narrowly, through the cipher for combinations of known characters, we find, not very far from the beginning, this arrangement,

83(88, or egree,

which plainly, is the conclusion of the word 'degree,' and gives us another letter, d, represented by !.

"Four letters beyond the word 'degree,' we perceive the combination

;46(;88.

"Translating the known characters, and representing the unknown by dots, as before, we read thus:

th.rtee,

an arrangement immediately suggestive of the word thirteen,' and again furnishing us with two new characters, i and n, represented by 6 and *.

"Referring, now, to the beginning of the cryptograph, we find the combination,

53++!.

"Translating as before, we obtain

.good,

which assures us that the first letter is A, and that the first two words are 'A good.'

"It is now time that we arrange our key, as far as discovered, in a tabular form, to avoid confusion. It will stand thus:

5 represents a ! " d 8 " e 3 " g 4 " h 6 " i * " n + " o (" r ; " t ? " u

"We have, therefore, no less than eleven of the most important letters represented, and it will be unnecessary to proceed with the details of the solution. I have said enough to convince you that ciphers of this nature are readily soluble, and to give you some insight into the rationale of their development. But be assured that the specimen before us appertains to the very simplest species of cryptograph. It now only remains to give you the full translation of the characters upon the parchment, as unriddled. Here it is:

"'A good glass in the bishop's hostel in the devil's seat forty-one degrees and thirteen minutes northeast and by north main branch seventh limb east side shoot from the left eye of the death's head a bee-line from the tree through the shot fifty feet out.'"

"But," said I, "the enigma seems still in as bad a condition as ever. How is it possible to extort a meaning from all this jargon about 'devil's seats,' 'death's heads,' and 'bishop's hostels'?"

"I confess," replied Legrand, "that the matter still wears a serious aspect, when regarded with a casual glance. My first endeavor was to divide the sentence into the natural division intended by the cryptographist."

"You mean, to punctuate it?"

"Something of that kind."

"But how was it possible to effect this?"

"I reflected that it had been a POINT with the writer to run his words together without division, so as to increase the difficulty of solution. Now, a not overacute man, in pursuing such an object, would be nearly certain to overdo the matter. When, in the course of his composition, he arrived at a break in his subject which would naturally require a pause, or a point, he would be exceedingly apt to run his characters, at this place, more than usually close together. If you will observe the MS., in the present instance, you will easily detect five such cases of unusual crowding. Acting upon this hint I made the division thus:

"'A good glass in the bishop's hostel in the devil's seat – forty- one degrees and thirteen minutes – northeast and by north – main branch seventh limb east side – shoot from the left eye of the death's head – a bee-line from the tree through the shot fifty feet out.'"

"Even this division," said I, "leaves me still in the dark."

"It left me also in the dark," replied Legrand, "for a few days; during which I made diligent inquiry in the neighborhood of Sullivan's Island, for any building which went by name of the 'Bishop's Hotel'; for, of course, I dropped the obsolete word 'hostel.' Gaining no information on the subject, I was on the point of extending my sphere of search, and proceeding in a more systematic manner, when, one morning, it entered into my head, quite suddenly, that this 'Bishop's Hostel' might have some reference to an old family, of the name of Bessop, which, time out of mind, had held possession of an ancient manor house, about four miles to the northward of the island. I accordingly went over to the plantation, and reinstituted my inquiries among the older negroes of the place. At length one of the most aged of the women said that she had heard of such a place as Bessop's Castle, and thought that she could guide me to it, but that it was not a castle, nor a tavern, but a high rock.

"I offered to pay her well for her trouble, and, after some demur, she consented to accompany me to the spot. We found it without much difficulty, when, dismissing her, I proceeded to examine the place. The 'castle' consisted of an irregular assemblage of cliffs and rocks – one of the latter being quite remarkable for its height as well as for its insulated and artificial appearance. I clambered to its apex, and then felt much at a loss as to what should be next done.

"While I was busied in reflection, my eyes fell upon a narrow ledge in the eastern face of the rock, perhaps a yard below the summit upon which I stood. This ledge projected about eighteen inches, and was not more than a foot wide, while a niche in the cliff just above it gave it a rude resemblance to one of the hollow-backed chairs used by our ancestors. I made no doubt that here was the 'devil's seat' alluded to in the MS., and now I seemed to grasp the full secret of the riddle.

"The 'good glass,' I knew, could have reference to nothing but a telescope; for the word 'glass' is rarely employed in any other sense by seamen. Now here, I at once saw, was a telescope to be used, and a definite point of view, ADMITTING NO VARIATION, from which to use it. Nor did I hesitate to believe that the phrases, 'forty-one degrees and thirteen minutes,' and 'northeast and by north,' were intended as directions for the leveling of the glass. Greatly excited by these discoveries, I hurried home, procured a telescope, and returned to the rock.

"I let myself down to the ledge, and found that it was impossible to retain a seat upon it except in one particular position. This fact confirmed my preconceived idea. I proceeded to use the glass. Of course, the 'forty-one degrees and thirteen minutes' could allude to nothing but elevation above the visible horizon, since the horizontal direction was clearly indicated by the words, 'northeast and by north.' This latter direction I at once established by means of a pocket compass; then, pointing the glass as nearly at an angle of forty-one degrees of elevation as I could do it by guess, I moved it cautiously up or down, until my attention was arrested by a circular rift or opening in the foliage of a large tree that overtopped its fellows in the distance. In the center of this rift I perceived a white spot, but could not, at first, distinguish what it was. Adjusting the focus of the telescope, I again looked, and now made it out to be a human skull.

"Upon this discovery I was so sanguine as to consider the

enigma solved; for the phrase 'main branch, seventh limb, east side,' could refer only to the position of the skull upon the tree, while 'shoot from the left eye of the death's head' admitted, also, of but one interpretation, in regard to a search for buried treasure. I perceived that the design was to drop a bullet from the left eye of the skull, and that a bee-line, or, in other words, a straight line, drawn from the nearest point of the trunk 'through the shot' (or the spot where the bullet fell), and thence extended to a distance of fifty feet, would indicate a definite point – and beneath this point I thought it at least POSSIBLE that a deposit of value lay concealed."

"All this," I said, "is exceedingly clear, and, although ingenious, still simple and explicit. When you left the Bishop's Hotel, what then?"

"Why, having carefully taken the bearings of the tree, I turned homeward. The instant that I left 'the devil's seat,' however, the circular rift vanished; nor could I get a glimpse of it afterwards, turn as I would. What seems to me the chief ingenuity in this whole business, is the fact (for repeated experiment has convinced me it IS a fact) that the circular opening in question is visible from no other attainable point of view than that afforded by the narrow ledge upon the face of the rock.

"In this expedition to the 'Bishop's Hotel' I had been attended by Jupiter, who had, no doubt, observed, for some weeks past, the abstraction of my demeanor, and took especial care not to leave me alone. But, on the next day, getting up very early, I contrived to give him the slip, and went into the hills in search of the tree. After much toil I found it. When I came home at night my valet proposed to give me a flogging. With the rest of the adventure I believe you are as well acquainted as myself."

"I suppose," said I, "you missed the spot, in the first attempt at digging, through Jupiter's stupidity in letting the bug fall through the right instead of through the left eye of the skull."

"Precisely. This mistake made a difference of about two inches and a half in the 'shot' – that is to say, in the position of the peg nearest the tree; and had the treasure been BENEATH the 'shot,' the error would have been of little moment; but 'the shot,' together with the nearest point of the tree, were merely two points for the establishment of a line of direction; of course the error, however trivial in the beginning, increased as we proceeded with the line, and by the time we had gone fifty feet threw us quite off the scent. But for my deep-seated impressions that treasure was here somewhere actually buried, we might have had all our labor in vain."

"But your grandiloquence, and your conduct in swinging the beetle – how excessively odd! I was sure you were mad. And why did you insist upon letting fall the bug, instead of a bullet, from the skull?"

"Why, to be frank, I felt somewhat annoyed by your evident suspicions touching my sanity, and so resolved to punish you quietly, in my own way, by a little bit of sober mystification. For this reason I swung the beetle, and for this reason I let it fall from the tree. An observation of yours about its great weight suggested the latter idea."

"Yes, I perceive; and now there is only one point which puzzles me. What are we to make of the skeletons found in the hole?"

"That is a question I am no more able to answer than yourself. There seems, however, only one plausible way of accounting for them – and yet it is dreadful to believe in such atrocity as my suggestion would imply. It is clear that Kidd – if Kidd indeed secreted this treasure, which I doubt not – it is clear that he must have had assistance in the labor. But this labor concluded, he may have thought it expedient to remove all participants in his secret. Perhaps a couple of blows with a mattock were sufficient, while his coadjutors were busy in the pit; perhaps it required a dozen – who shall tell?"

Washington Irving

Wolfert Webber, or Golden Dreams

In the year of grace one thousand seven hundred and – blank – for I do not remember the precise date; however, it was somewhere in the early part of the last century, – there lived in the ancient city of the Manhattoes a worthy burgher, Wolfert Webber by name. He was descended from old Cobus Webber of the Brill [1] in Holland, one of the original settlers, famous for introducing the cultivation of cabbages, and who came over to the province during the protectorship of Oloffe Van Kortlandt, otherwise called "the Dreamer."

[1] The Brill is a fortified seaport of Holland, on the Meuse River, near Rotterdam.

The field in which Cobus Webber first planted himself and his cabbages had remained ever since in the family, who continued in the same line of husbandry with that praiseworthy perseverance for which our Dutch burghers are noted. The whole family genius, during several generations, was devoted to the study and development of this one noble vegetable, and to this concentration of intellect may doubtless be ascribed the prodigious renown to which the Webber cabbages attained.

The Webber dynasty continued in uninterrupted succession, and never did a line give more unquestionable proofs of legitimacy. The eldest son succeeded to the looks as well as the territory of his sire, and had the portraits of this line of tranquil potentates been taken, they would have presented a row of heads marvelously resembling, in shape and magnitude, the vegetables over which they reigned.

The seat of government continued unchanged in the family mansion, – a Dutch-built house, with a front, or rather gable end, of yellow brick, tapering to a point, with the customary iron weathercock at the top. Everything about the building bore the air of long- settled ease and security. Flights of martins peopled the little coops nailed against its walls, and swallows built their nests under the eaves, and everyone knows that these house-loving birds bring good luck to the dwelling where they take up their abode. In a bright summer morning in early summer, it was delectable to hear their cheerful notes as they sported about in the pure, sweet air, chirping forth, as it were, the greatness and prosperity of the Webbers.

Thus quietly and comfortably did this excellent family vegetate under the shade of a mighty buttonwood tree, which by little and little grew so great as entirely to overshadow their palace. The city gradually spread its suburbs round their domain. Houses sprang up to interrupt their prospects. The rural lanes in the vicinity began to grow into the bustle and populousness of streets; in short, with all the habits of rustic life they began to find themselves the inhabitants of a city. Still, however, they maintained their hereditary character and hereditary possessions, with all the tenacity of petty German princes in the midst of the empire. Wolfert was the last of the line, and succeeded to the patriarchal bench at the door, under the family tree, and swayed the scepter of his fathers, – a kind of rural potentate in the midst of the metropolis.

To share the cares and sweets of sovereignty he had taken unto himself a helpmate, one of that excellent kind called "stirring women"; that is to say, she was one of those notable little housewives who are always busy where there is nothing to do. Her activity, however, took one particular direction, – her whole life seemed devoted to intense knitting; whether at home or abroad, walking or sitting, her needles were continually in motion, and it is even affirmed that by her unwearied industry she very nearly supplied her household with stockings throughout the year. This worthy couple were blessed with one daughter who was brought up with great tenderness and care; uncommon pains had been taken with her education, so that she could stitch in every variety of way, make all kinds of pickles and preserves, and mark her own name on a sampler. The influence of her taste was seen also in the family garden, where the ornamental began to mingle with the useful; whole rows of fiery marigolds and splendid hollyhocks bordered the cabbage beds, and gigantic sunflowers lolled their broad, jolly faces over the fences, seeming to ogle most affectionately the passers-by.

Thus reigned and vegetated Wolfert Webber over his paternal acres, peacefully and contentedly. Not but that, like all other sovereigns, he had his occasional cares and vexations. The growth of his native city sometimes caused him annoyance. His little territory gradually became hemmed in by streets and houses, which intercepted air and sunshine. He was now and then subjected to the eruptions of the border population that infest the streets of a metropolis, who would make midnight forays into his dominions, and carry off captive whole platoons of his noblest subjects. Vagrant swine would make a descent, too, now and then, when the gate was left open, and lay all waste before them; and mischievous urchins would decapitate the illustrious sunflowers, the glory of the garden, as they lolled their heads so fondly over the walls. Still all these were petty grievances, which might now and then ruffle the surface of his mind, as a summer breeze will ruffle the surface of a mill pond, but they could not disturb the deep-seated quiet of his soul. He would but seize a trusty staff that stood behind the door, issue suddenly out, and anoint the back of the aggressor, whether pig or urchin, and then return within doors, marvelously refreshed and tranquilized.

The chief cause of anxiety to honest Wolfert, however, was the growing prosperity of the city. The expenses of living doubled and trebled, but he could not double and treble the magnitude of his cabbages, and the number of competitors prevented the increase of price; thus, therefore, while everyone around him grew richer, Wolfert grew poorer, and he could not, for the life of him, perceive how the evil was to be remedied.

This growing care, which increased from day to day, had its gradual effect upon our worthy burgher, insomuch that it at length implanted two or three wrinkles in his brow, things unknown before in the family of the Webbers, and it seemed to pinch up the corners of his cocked hat into an expression of anxiety totally opposite to the tranquil, broad-brimmed, low-crowned beavers of his illustrious progenitors.

Perhaps even this would not have materially disturbed the serenity of his mind had he had only himself and his wife to care for; but there was his daughter gradually growing to maturity, and all the world knows that when daughters begin to ripen, no fruit nor flower requires so much looking after. I have no talent at describing female charms, else fain would I depict the progress of this little Dutch beauty: how her blue eyes grew deeper and deeper, and her cherry lips redder and redder, and how she ripened and ripened, and rounded and rounded, in the opening breath of sixteen summers, until, in her seventeenth spring, she seemed ready to burst out of her bodice, like a half-blown rosebud.

Ah, well-a-day! Could I but show her as she was then, tricked out on a Sunday morning in the hereditary finery of the old Dutch clothespress, of which her mother had confided to her the key! The wedding dress of her grandmother, modernized for use, with sundry ornaments, handed down as heirlooms in the family. Her pale brown hair smoothed with buttermilk in flat, waving lines on each side of her fair forehead. The chain of yellow, virgin gold that encircled her neck; the little cross that just rested at the entrance of a soft valley of happiness, as if it would sanctify the place. The – but pooh! it is not for an old man like me to be prosing about female beauty; suffice it to say, Amy had attained her seventeenth year. Long since had her sampler exhibited hearts in couples desperately transfixed with arrows, and true lovers' knots worked in deep blue silk, and it was evident she began to languish for some more interesting occupation than the rearing of sunflowers or pickling of cucumbers.

At this critical period of female existence, when the heart within a damsel's bosom, like its emblem, the miniature which hangs without, is apt to be engrossed by a single image, a new visitor began to make his appearance under the roof of Wolfert Webber. This was Dirk Waldron, the only son of a poor widow, but who could boast of more fathers than any lad in the province, for his mother had had four husbands, and this only child, so that, though born in her last wedlock, he might fairly claim to be the tardy fruit of a long course of cultivation. This son of four fathers united the merits and the vigor of all his sires. If he had not had a great family before him he seemed likely to have a great one after him, for you had only to look at the fresh, buxom youth to see that he was formed to be the founder of a mighty race.

This youngster gradually became an intimate visitor of the family. He talked little, but he sat long. He filled the father's pipe when it was empty, gathered up the mother's knitting needle, or ball of worsted, when it fell to the ground, stroked the sleek coat of the tortoise-shell cat, and replenished the teapot for the daughter from the bright copper kettle that sang before the fire. All these quiet little offices may seem of trifling import, but when true love is translated into Low Dutch it is in this way that it eloquently expresses itself. They were not lost upon the Webber family. The winning youngster found marvelous favor in the eyes of the mother; the tortoise-shell cat, albeit the most staid and demure of her kind, gave indubitable signs of approbation of his visits; the teakettle seemed to sing out a cheering note of welcome at his approach; and if the sly glances of the daughter might be rightly read, as she sat bridling and dimpling, and sewing by her mother's side, she was not a whit behind Dame Webber, or grimalkin, or the teakettle, in good will.

Wolfert alone saw nothing of what was going on. Profoundly wrapt up in meditation on the growth of the city and his cabbages, he sat looking in the fire, and puffing his pipe in silence. One night, however, as the gentle Amy, according to custom, lighted her lover to the outer door, and he, according to custom, took his parting salute, the smack resounded so vigorously through the long, silent entry as to startle even the dull ear of Wolfert. He was slowly roused to a new source of anxiety. It had never entered into his head that this mere child, who, as it seemed, but the other day had been climbing about his knees and playing with dolls and baby houses, could all at once be thinking of lovers and matrimony. He rubbed his eyes, examined into the fact, and really found that while he had been dreaming of other matters, she had actually grown to be a woman, and, what was worse, had fallen in love. Here arose new cares for Wolfert. He was a kind father, but he was a prudent man. The young man was a lively, stirring lad, but then he had neither money nor land. Wolfert's ideas all ran in one channel, and he saw no alternative in case of a marriage but to portion off the young couple with a corner of his cabbage garden, the whole of which was barely sufficient for the support of his family.

Like a prudent father, therefore, he determined to nip this passion in the bud, and forbade the youngster the house, though sorely did it go against his fatherly heart, and many a silent tear did it cause in the bright eye of his daughter. She showed herself, however, a pattern of filial piety and obedience. She never pouted and sulked; she never flew in the face of parental authority; she never flew into a passion, nor fell into hysterics, as many romantic, novel-read young ladies would do. Not she, indeed. She was none such heroical, rebellious trumpery, I'll warrant ye. On the contrary, she acquiesced like an obedient daughter, shut the street door in her lover's face, and if ever she did grant him an interview, it was either out of the kitchen window or over the garden fence.

Wolfert was deeply cogitating these matters in his mind, and his brow wrinkled with unusual care, as he wended his way one Saturday afternoon to a rural inn, about two miles from the city. It was a favorite resort of the Dutch part of the community, from being always held by a Dutch line of landlords, and retaining an air and relish of the good old times. It was a Dutch-built house, that had probably been a country seat of some opulent burgher in the early time of the settlement. It stood near a point of land called Corlear's Hook, [1] which stretches out into the Sound, and against which the tide, at its flux and reflux, sets with extraordinary rapidity. The venerable and somewhat crazy mansion was distinguished from afar by a grove of elms and sycamores that seemed to wave a hospitable invitation, while a few weeping willows, with their dank, drooping foliage, resembling falling waters, gave an idea of coolness that rendered it an attractive spot during the heats of summer.

[1] A point of land at the bend of the East River below Grand Street, New York City.

Here, therefore, as I said, resorted many of the old inhabitants of the Manhattoes, where, while some played at shuffle-board [1] and quoits, [2] and ninepins, others smoked a deliberate pipe, and talked over public affairs.

[1] A game played by pushing or shaking pieces of money or metal so as to make them reach certain marks on a board.

[2] A game played by pitching a flattened, ring-shaped piece of iron, called a quoit, at a fixed object.

It was on a blustering autumnal afternoon that Wolfert made his visit to the inn. The grove of elms and willows was stripped of its leaves, which whirled in rustling eddies about the fields. The ninepin alley was deserted, for the premature chilliness of the day had driven the company within doors. As it was Saturday afternoon the habitual club was in session, composed principally of regular Dutch burghers, though mingled occasionally with persons of various character and country, as is natural in a place of such motley population.

Beside the fireplace, in a huge, leather-bottomed armchair, sat the dictator of this little world, the venerable Rem, or, as it was pronounced, "Ramm" Rapelye. He was a man of Walloon [1] race, and illustrious for the antiquity of his line, his great-grandmother having been the first white child born in the province. But he was still more illustrious for his wealth and dignity. He had long filled the noble office of alderman, and was a man to whom the governor himself took off his hat. He had maintained possession of the leather-bottomed chair from time immemorial, and had gradually waxed in bulk as he sat in his seat of government, until in the course of years he filled its whole magnitude. His word was decisive with his subjects, for he was so rich a man that he was never expected to support any opinion by argument. The landlord waited on him with peculiar officiousness, – not that he paid better than his neighbors, but then the coin of a rich man seems always to be so much more acceptable. The landlord had ever a pleasant word and a joke to insinuate in the ear of the august Ramm. It is true Ramm never laughed, and, indeed, ever maintained a mastiff-like gravity and even surliness of aspect; yet he now and then rewarded mine host with a token of approbation, which, though nothing more nor less than a kind of grunt, still delighted the landlord more than a broad laugh from a poorer man.

[1] A people of French origin, inhabiting the frontiers between France and Flanders. A colony of one hundred and ten Walloons came to New York in 1624.

"This will be a rough night for the money diggers," said mine host, as a gust of wind bowled round the house and rattled at the windows.

"What! are they at their works again?" said an English half-pay captain, with one eye, who was a very frequent attendant at the inn.

"Aye are they," said the landlord, "and well may they be. They've had luck of late. They say a great pot of money has been dug up in the fields just behind Stuyvesant's orchard. Folks think it must have been buried there in old times by Peter Stuyvesant, the Dutch governor."

"Fudge!" said the one-eyed man of war, as he added a small portion of water to a bottom of brandy.

"Well, you may believe it or not, as you please," said mine host, somewhat nettled, "but everybody knows that the old governor buried a great deal of his money at the time of the Dutch troubles, when the English redcoats seized on the province. They say, too, the old gentleman walks, aye, and in the very same dress that he wears in the picture that hangs up in the family house."

"Fudge!" said the half-pay officer.

"Fudge, if you please! But didn't Corney Van Zandt see him at midnight, stalking about in the meadow with his wooden leg, and a drawn sword in his hand, that flashed like fire? And what can he be walking for but because people have been troubling the place where he buried his money in old times?"

Here the landlord was interrupted by several guttural sounds from Ramm Rapelye, betokening that he was laboring with the unusual production of an idea. As he was too great a man to be slighted by a prudent publican, mine host respectfully paused until he should deliver himself. The corpulent frame of this mighty burgher now gave all the symptoms of a volcanic mountain on the point of an eruption. First there was a certain heaving of the abdomen, not unlike an earthquake; then was emitted a cloud of tobacco smoke from that crater, his mouth; then there was a kind of rattle in the throat, as if the idea were working its way up through a region of phlegm; then there were several disjointed members of a sentence thrown out, ending in a cough; at length his voice forced its way into a slow, but absolute tone of a man who feels the weight of his purse, if not of his ideas, every portion of his speech being marked by a testy puff of tobacco smoke.

"Who talks of old Peter Stuyvesant's walking? (puff). Have people no respect for persons? (puff – puff). Peter Stuyvesant knew better what to do with his money than to bury it (puff). I know the Stuyvesant family (puff), every one of them (puff); not a more respectable family in the province (puff) – old standards (puff) – warm householders (puff) – none of your upstarts (puff – puff – puff). Don't talk to me of Peter Stuyvesant's walking (puff – puff – puff – puff)."

Here the redoubtable Ramm contracted his brow, clasped up his mouth till it wrinkled at each corner, and redoubled his smoking with such vehemence that the cloudy volumes soon wreathed round his head, as the smoke envelops the awful summit of Mount Aetna.

A general silence followed the sudden rebuke of this very rich man. The subject, however, was too interesting to be readily abandoned. The conversation soon broke forth again from the lips of Peechy Prauw Van Hook, the chronicler of the club, one of those prosing, narrative old men who seem to be troubled with an incontinence of words as they grow old.

Peechy could, at any time, tell as many stories in an evening as his hearers could digest in a month. He now resumed the conversation by affirming that, to his knowledge, money had, at different times, been digged up in various parts of the island. The lucky persons who had discovered them had always dreamed of them three times beforehand, and, what was worthy of remark, those treasures had never been found but by some descendant of the good old Dutch families, which clearly proved that they had been buried by Dutchmen in the olden time.

"Fiddlestick with your Dutchmen!" cried the half-pay officer. "The Dutch had nothing to do with them. They were all buried by

Kidd the pirate, and his crew."

Here a keynote was touched that roused the whole company. The name of Captain Kidd was like a talisman in those times, and was associated with a thousand marvelous stories.

The half-pay officer took the lead, and in his narrations fathered upon Kidd all the plunderings and exploits of Morgan, [1] Blackbeard, [2] and the whole list of bloody buccaneers.

[1] Sir Henry Morgan (1637-90), a noted Welsh buccaneer. He was captured and sent to England for trial, but Charles II., instead of punishing him, knighted him, and subsequently appointed him governor of Jamaica.

[2] Edward Teach, one of the most cruel of the pirates, took command of a pirate ship in 1717, and thereafter committed all sorts of atrocities until he was slain by Lieutenant Maynard in 1718. His nickname of "Blackbeard" was given him because of his black beard.

The officer was a man of great weight among the peaceable members of the club, by reason of his warlike character and gunpowder tales. All his golden stories of Kidd, however, and of the booty he had buried, were obstinately rivaled by the tales of Peechy Prauw, who, rather than suffer his Dutch progenitors to be eclipsed by a foreign freebooter, enriched every field and shore in the neighborhood with the hidden wealth of Peter Stuyvesant and his contemporaries.

Not a word of this conversation was lost upon Wolfert Webber. He returned pensively home, full of magnificent ideas. The soil of his native island seemed to be turned into gold dust, and every field to teem with treasure. His head almost reeled at the thought how often he must have heedlessly rambled over places where countless sums lay, scarcely covered by the turf beneath his feet. His mind was in an uproar with this whirl of new ideas. As he came in sight of the venerable mansion of his forefathers, and the little realm where the Webbers had so long and so contentedly flourished, his gorge rose at the narrowness of his destiny.

"Unlucky Wolfert!" exclaimed he; "others can go to bed and dream themselves into whole mines of wealth; they have but to seize a spade in the morning, and turn up doubloons [1] like potatoes; but thou must dream of hardships, and rise to poverty, must dig thy field from year's end to year's end, and yet raise nothing but cabbages!"

[1] Spanish gold coins, equivalent to $15.60.

Wolfert Webber went to bed with a heavy heart, and it was long before the golden visions that disturbed his brain permitted him to sink into repose. The same visions, however, extended into his sleeping thoughts, and assumed a more definite form. He dreamed that he had discovered an immense treasure in the center of his garden. At every stroke of the spade he laid bare a golden ingot; diamond crosses sparkled out of the dust; bags of money turned up their bellies, corpulent with pieces-of-eight [1] or venerable doubloons; and chests wedged close with moidores, [2] ducats, [3] and pistareens, [4] yawned before his ravished eyes, and vomited forth their glittering contents.

[1] Spanish coins, worth about $1 each. [2] Portuguese gold coins, valued at $6.50. [3] Coins of gold and silver, valued at $2 and $1 respectively. [4] Spanish silver coins, worth about $.20.

Wolfert awoke a poorer man than ever. He had no heart to go about his daily concerns, which appeared so paltry and profitless, but sat all day long in the chimney corner, picturing to himself ingots and heaps of gold in the fire. The next night his dream was repeated. He was again in his garden digging, and laying open stores of hidden wealth. There was something very singular in this repetition. He passed another day of reverie, and though it was cleaning day, and the house, as usual in Dutch households, completely topsy-turvy, yet he sat unmoved amidst the general uproar.

The third night he went to bed with a palpitating heart. He put on his red nightcap wrong side outward, for good luck. It was deep midnight before his anxious mind could settle itself into sleep. Again the golden dream was repeated, and again he saw his garden teeming with ingots and money bags.

Wolfert rose the next morning in complete bewilderment. A dream, three times repeated, was never known to lie, and if so, his fortune was made.

160

In his agitation he put on his waistcoat with the hind part before, and this was a corroboration of good luck. [1] He no longer doubted that a huge store of money lay buried somewhere in his cabbage field, coyly waiting to be sought for, and he repined at having so long been scratching about the surface of the soil instead of digging to the center.

[1] It is an old superstition that to put on one's clothes wrong side out forebodes good luck.

He took his seat at the breakfast table, full of these speculations, asked his daughter to put a lump of gold into his tea, and on handing his wife a plate of slapjacks, begged her to help herself to a doubloon.

His grand care now was how to secure this immense treasure without its being known. Instead of his working regularly in his grounds in the daytime, he now stole from his bed at night, and with spade and pickax went to work to rip up and dig about his paternal acres, from one end to the other. In a little time the whole garden, which had presented such a goodly and regular appearance, with its phalanx of cabbages, like a vegetable army in battle array, was reduced to a scene of devastation, while the relentless Wolfert, with nightcap on head and lantern and spade in hand, stalked through the slaughtered ranks, the destroying angel of his own vegetable world.

Every morning bore testimony to the ravages of the preceding night in cabbages of all ages and conditions, from the tender sprout to the full-grown head, piteously rooted from their quiet beds like worthless weeds, and left to wither in the sunshine. In vain Wolfert's wife remonstrated; in vain his darling daughter wept over the destruction of some favorite marigold. "Thou shalt have gold of another-guess [1] sort," he would cry, chucking her under the chin; "thou shalt have a string of crooked ducats for thy wedding necklace, my child." His family began really to fear that the poor man's wits were diseased. He muttered in his sleep at night about mines of wealth, about pearls and diamonds, and bars of gold. In the daytime he was moody and abstracted, and walked about as if in a trance. Dame Webber held frequent councils with all the old women of the neighborhood; scarce an hour in the day but a knot of them might be seen wagging their white caps together round her door, while the poor woman made some piteous recital. The daughter, too, was fain to seek for more frequent consolation from the stolen interviews of her favored swain, Dirk Waldron. The delectable little Dutch songs with which she used to dulcify the house grew less and less frequent, and she would forget her sewing, and look wistfully in her father's face as he sat pondering by the fireside. Wolfert caught her eye one day fixed on him thus anxiously, and for a moment was roused from his golden reveries. "Cheer up, my girl," said he exultingly; "why dost thou droop? Thou shalt hold up thy head one day with the Brinckerhoffs, and the Schermerhorns, the Van Hornes, and the Van Dams. [2] By St. Nicholas, but the patroon [3] himself shall be glad to get thee for his son!"

[1] A corruption of the old expression "another-gates," or "of another gate," meaning "of another way or manner"; hence, "of another kind."

[2] Names of rich and influential Dutch families in the old Dutch colony of New Amsterdam.

[3] The patroons were members of the Dutch West India Company, who purchased land in New Netherlands of the Indians, and after fulfilling certain conditions imposed with a view to colonizing their territory, enjoyed feudal rights similar to those of the barons of the Middle Ages.

Amy shook her head at his vainglorious boast, and was more than ever in doubt of the soundness of the good man's intellect.

In the meantime Wolfert went on digging and digging; but the field was extensive, and as his dream had indicated no precise spot, he had to dig at random. The winter set in before one tenth of the scene of promise had been explored.

The ground became frozen hard, and the nights too cold for the labors of the spade.

No sooner, however, did the returning warmth of spring loosen the soil, and the small frogs begin to pipe in the meadows, but Wolfert resumed his labors with renovated zeal. Still, however, the hours of industry were reversed.

Instead of working cheerily all day, planting and setting out his vegetables, he remained thoughtfully idle, until the shades of night summoned him to his secret labors. In this way he continued to dig from night to night, and week to week, and month to month, but not a stiver [1] did he find. On the contrary, the more he digged the poorer he grew. The rich soil of his garden was digged away, and the sand and gravel from beneath was thrown to the surface, until the whole field presented an aspect of sandy barrenness.

[1] A Dutch coin, worth about two cents; hence, anything of little worth.

In the meantime, the seasons gradually rolled on. The little frogs which had piped in the meadows in early spring croaked as bullfrogs during the summer heats, and then sank into silence. The peach tree budded, blossomed, and bore its fruit. The swallows and martins came, twittered about the roof, built their nests, reared their young, held their congress along the eaves, and then winged their flight in search of another spring. The caterpillar spun its winding sheet, dangled in it from the great buttonwood tree before the house, turned into a moth, fluttered with the last sunshine of summer, and disappeared; and finally the leaves of the buttonwood tree turned yellow, then brown, then rustled one by one to the ground, and whirling about in little eddies of wind and dust, whispered that winter was at hand.

Wolfert gradually woke from his dream of wealth as the year declined. He had reared no crop for the supply of his household during the sterility of winter. The season was long and severe, and for the first time the family was really straitened in its comforts. By degrees a revulsion of thought took place in Wolfert's mind, common to those whose golden dreams have been disturbed by pinching realities. The idea gradually stole upon him that he should come to want. He already considered himself one of the most unfortunate men in the province, having lost such an incalculable amount of undiscovered treasure, and now, when thousands of pounds had eluded his search, to be perplexed for shillings and pence was cruel in the extreme.

Haggard care gathered about his brow; he went about with a money- seeking air, his eyes bent downward into the dust, and carrying his hands in his pockets, as men are apt to do when they have nothing else to put into them. He could not even pass the city almshouse without giving it a rueful glance, as if destined to be his future abode.

The strangeness of his conduct and of his looks occasioned much speculation and remark. For a long time he was suspected of being crazy, and then everybody pitied him; and at length it began to be suspected that he was poor, and then everybody avoided him.

The rich old burghers of his acquaintance met him outside the door when he called, entertained him hospitably on the threshold, pressed him warmly by the hand at parting, shook their heads as he walked away, with the kindhearted expression of "poor Wolfert," and turned a corner nimbly if by chance they saw him approaching as they walked the streets. Even the barber and the cobbler of the neighborhood, and a tattered tailor in an alley hard by, three of the poorest and merriest rogues in the world, eyed him with that abundant sympathy which usually attends a lack of means, and there is not a doubt but their pockets would have been at his command, only that they happened to be empty.

Thus everybody deserted the Webber mansion, as if poverty were contagious, like the plague – everybody but honest Dirk Waldron, who still kept up his stolen visits to the daughter, and indeed seemed to wax more affectionate as the fortunes of his mistress were on the wane.

Many months had elapsed since Wolfert had frequented his old resort, the rural inn. He was taking a long, lonely walk one Saturday afternoon, musing over his wants and disappointments, when his feet took instinctively their wonted direction, and on awaking out of a reverie, he found himself before the door of the inn. For some moments he hesitated whether to enter, but his heart yearned for companionship, and where can a ruined man find better companionship than at a tavern, where there is neither sober example nor sober advice to put him out of countenance?

Wolfert found several of the old frequenters of the inn at their usual posts and seated in their usual places; but one was missing, the great Ramm Rapelye, who for many years had filled the leather- bottomed chair of state. His place was supplied by a stranger, who seemed, however, completely at home in the chair and the tavern. He was rather under size, but deep-chested, square, and muscular. His broad shoulders, double joints, and bow knees gave tokens of prodigious strength. His face was dark and weather-beaten; a deep scar, as if from the slash of a cutlass, had almost divided his nose, and made a gash in his upper lip, through which his teeth shone like a bulldog's. A mop of iron-gray hair gave a grisly finish to this hard-favored visage. His dress was of an amphibious character. He wore an old hat edged with tarnished lace, and cocked in martial style on one side of his head; a rusty [1] blue military coat with brass buttons; and a wide pair of short petticoat trousers, – or rather breeches, for they were gathered up at the knees. He ordered everybody about him with an authoritative air, talking in a brattling [2] voice that sounded like the crackling of thorns under a pot, d – d the landlord and servants with perfect impunity, and was waited upon with greater obsequiousness than had ever been shown to the mighty Ramm himself.

[1] Shabby.

[2] Noisy.

 Wolfert's curiosity was awakened to know who and what was this stranger who had thus usurped absolute sway in this ancient domain. Peechy Prauw took him aside into a remote corner of the hall, and there, in an under voice and with great caution, imparted to him all that he knew on the subject. The inn had been aroused several months before, on a dark, stormy night, by repeated long shouts that seemed like the howlings of a wolf. They came from the water side, and at length were distinguished to be hailing the house in the seafaring manner, "House ahoy!" The landlord turned out with his head waiter, tapster, hostler, and errand boy – that is to say, with his old negro Cuff. On approaching the place whence the voice proceeded, they found this amphibious-looking personage at the water's edge, quite alone, and seated on a great oaken sea chest. How he came there, – whether he had been set on shore from some boat, or had floated to land on his chest, – nobody could tell, for he did not seem disposed to answer questions, and there was something in his looks and manners that put a stop to all questioning. Suffice it to say, he took possession of a corner room of the inn, to which his chest was removed with great difficulty. Here he had remained ever since, keeping about the inn and its vicinity. Sometimes, it is true, he disappeared for one, two, or three days at a time, going and returning without giving any notice or account of his movements. He always appeared to have plenty of money, though often of very strange, outlandish coinage, and he regularly paid his bill every evening before turning in.

He had fitted up his room to his own fancy, having slung a hammock from the ceiling instead of a bed, and decorated the walls with rusty pistols and cutlasses of foreign workmanship. A greater part of his time was passed in this room, seated by the window, which commanded a wide view of the Sound, a short, old-fashioned pipe in his mouth, a glass of rum toddy [1] at his elbow, and a pocket telescope in his hand, with which he reconnoitered every boat that moved upon the water. Large square-rigged vessels seemed to excite but little attention; but the moment he descried anything with a shoulder-of-mutton [2] sail, or that a barge or yawl or jolly-boat hove in sight, up went the telescope, and he examined it with the most scrupulous attention.

[1] A mixture of rum and hot water sweetened.
[2] Triangular.

All this might have passed without much notice, for in those times the province was so much the resort of adventurers of all characters and climes that any oddity in dress or behavior attracted but small attention. In a little while, however, this strange sea monster, thus strangely cast upon dry land, began to encroach upon the long established customs and customers of the place, and to interfere in a dictatorial manner in the affairs of the ninepin alley and the barroom, until in the end he usurped an absolute command over the whole inn. It was all in vain to attempt to withstand his authority. He was not exactly quarrelsome, but boisterous and peremptory, like one accustomed to tyrannize on a quarter-deck; and there was a dare-devil [1] air about everything he said and did that inspired wariness in all bystanders.

Even the half-pay officer, so long the hero of the club, was soon silenced by him, and the quiet burghers stared with wonder at seeing their inflammable man of war so readily and quietly extinguished.

[1] Reckless.

And then the tales that he would tell were enough to make a peaceable man's hair stand on end. There was not a sea fight, nor marauding nor freebooting adventure that had happened within the last twenty years, but he seemed perfectly versed in it. He delighted to talk of the exploits of the buccaneers in the West Indies and on the Spanish Main. [1] How his eyes would glisten as he described the waylaying of treasure ships; the desperate fights, yardarm and yardarm, [2] broadside and broadside; [3] the boarding and capturing huge Spanish galleons! With what chuckling relish would he describe the descent upon some rich Spanish colony, the rifling of a church, the sacking of a convent! You would have thought you heard some gormandizer dilating upon the roasting of a savory goose at Michaelmas, [4] as he described the roasting of some Spanish don to make him discover his treasure, – a detail given with a minuteness that made every rich old burgher present turn uncomfortably in his chair. All this would be told with infinite glee, as if he considered it an excellent joke, and then he would give such a tyrannical leer in the face of his next neighbor that the poor man would be fain to laugh out of sheer faint-heartedness. If anyone, however, pretended to contradict him in any of his stories, he was on fire in an instant. His very cocked hat assumed a momentary fierceness, and seemed to resent the contradiction. "How the devil should you know as well as I? I tell you it was as I say;" and he would at the same time let slip a broadside of thundering oaths [5] and tremendous sea phrases, such as had never been heard before within these peaceful walls.

[1] The coast of the northern part of South America along the Caribbean Sea, the route formerly traversed by the Spanish treasure ships between the Old and New Worlds.

[2] Ships are said to be yardarm and yardarm when so near as to touch or interlock their yards, which are the long pieces of timber designed to support and extend the square sails.

[3] "Broadside and broadside," i.e., with the side of one ship touching that of another.

[4] The Feast of the Archangel Michael, a church festival celebrated on September 29th.

[5] "Broadside of thundering oaths," i.e., a volley of abuse.

Indeed, the worthy burghers began to surmise that he knew more of those stories than mere hearsay. Day after day their conjectures concerning him grew more and more wild and fearful. The strangeness of his arrival, the strangeness of his manners, the mystery that surrounded him, – all made him something incomprehensible in their eyes. He was a kind of monster of the deep to them; he was a merman, he was a behemoth, he was a leviathan, – in short, they knew not what he was.

The domineering spirit of this boisterous sea urchin at length grew quite intolerable. He was no respecter of persons; he contradicted the richest burghers without hesitation; he took possession of the sacred elbow chair, which time out of mind had been the seat of sovereignty of the illustrious Ramm Rapelye. Nay, he even went so far, in one of his rough, jocular moods, as to slap that mighty burgher on the back, drink his toddy, and wink in his face, – a thing scarcely to be believed. From this time Ramm Rapelye appeared no more at the inn. His example was followed by several of the most eminent customers, who were too rich to tolerate being bullied out of their opinions or being obliged to laugh at another man's jokes. The landlord was almost in despair; but he knew not how to get rid of this sea monster and his sea chest, who seemed both to have grown like fixtures, or excrescences on his establishment.

Such was the account whispered cautiously in Wolfert's ear by the narrator, Peechy Prauw, as he held him by the button in a corner of the hall, casting a wary glance now and then toward the door of the barroom, lest he should be overheard by the terrible hero of his tale.

Wolfert took his seat in a remote part of the room in silence, impressed with profound awe of this unknown, so versed in freebooting history. It was to him a wonderful instance of the revolutions of mighty empires, to find the venerable Ramm Rapelye thus ousted from the throne, and a rugged tarpaulin [1] dictating from his elbow chair, hectoring the patriarchs, and filling this tranquil little realm with brawl and bravado.

[1] A kind of canvas used about a ship; hence, a sailor.

The stranger was, on this evening, in a more than usually communicative mood, and was narrating a number of astounding stories of plunderings and burnings on the high seas. He dwelt upon them with peculiar relish, heightening the frightful particulars in proportion to their effect on his peaceful auditors. He gave a swaggering detail of the capture of a Spanish merchantman. She was lying becalmed during a long summer's day, just off from the island which was one of the lurking places of the pirates. They had reconnoitered her with their spyglasses from the shore, and ascertained her character and force. At night a picked crew of daring fellows set off for her in a whaleboat. They approached with muffled oars, as she lay rocking idly with the undulations of the sea, and her sails flapping against the masts. They were close under the stern before the guard on deck was aware of their approach. The alarm was given; the pirates threw hand grenades [1] on deck, and sprang up the main chains, [2] sword in hand.

[1] "Hand grenades," i.e., small shells of iron or glass filled with gunpowder and thrown by hand.

[2] "Main chains," i.e., strong bars of iron bolted at the lower end to the side of a vessel, and secured at the upper end to the iron straps of the blocks by which the shrouds supporting the masts are extended.

The crew flew to arms, but in great confusion; some were shot down, others took refuge in the tops, others were driven overboard and drowned, while others fought hand to hand from the main deck to the quarter-deck, disputing gallantly every inch of ground. There were three Spanish gentlemen on board, with their ladies, who made the most desperate resistance. They defended the companion way, [1] cut down several of their assailants, and fought like very devils, for they were maddened by the shrieks of the ladies from the cabin. One of the dons was old, and soon dispatched. The other two kept their ground vigorously, even though the captain of the pirates was among their assailants.

Just then there was a shout of victory from the main deck. "The ship is ours!" cried the pirates.

[1] The companion way is a staircase leading to the cabin of a ship.

One of the dons immediately dropped his sword and surrendered; the other, who was a hot-headed youngster, and just married, gave the captain a slash in the face that laid all open. The captain just made out to articulate the words, "No quarter."

"And what did they do with their prisoners?" said Peechy Prauw eagerly.

"Threw them all overboard," was the answer. A dead pause followed the reply. Peechy Prauw sank quietly back, like a man who had unwarily stolen upon the lair of a sleeping lion. The honest burghers cast fearful glances at the deep scar slashed across the visage of the stranger, and moved their chairs a little farther off. The seaman, however, smoked on without moving a muscle, as though he either did not perceive, or did not regard, the unfavorable effect he had produced upon his hearers.

The half-pay officer was the first to break the silence, for he was continually tempted to make ineffectual head against this tyrant of the seas, and to regain his lost consequence in the eyes of his ancient companions. He now tried to match the gunpowder tales of the stranger by others equally tremendous. Kidd, as usual, was his hero, concerning whom he seemed to have picked up many of the floating traditions of the province. The seaman had always evinced a settled pique against the one-eyed warrior. On this occasion he listened with peculiar impatience. He sat with one arm akimbo, the other elbow on the table, the hand holding on to the small pipe he was pettishly puffing, his legs crossed, drumming with one foot on the ground, and casting every now and then the side glance of a basilisk at the prosing captain. At length the latter spoke of Kidd's having ascended the Hudson with some of his crew, to land his plunder in secrecy.

Kidd up the Hudson!" burst forth the seaman, with a tremendous oath; "Kidd never was up the Hudson!"

"I tell you he was," said the other. "Aye, and they say he buried a quantity of treasure on the little flat that runs out into the river, called the Devil's Dans Kammer." [1]

[1] A huge, flat rock, projecting into the Hudson River above the Highlands.

"The Devil's Dans Kammer in your teeth!" [1] cried the seaman. "I tell you Kidd never was up the Hudson. What a plague do you know of Kidd and his haunts?"

[1] "In your teeth," a phrase to denote direct opposition or defiance.

"What do I know?" echoed the half-pay officer. "Why, I was in London at the time of his trial; aye, and I had the pleasure of seeing him hanged at Execution Dock."

"Then, sir, let me tell you that you saw as pretty a fellow hanged as ever trod shoe leather. Aye!" putting his face nearer to that of the officer, "and there was many a landlubber [1] looked on that might much better have swung in his stead."

[1] A term of contempt used by seamen for those who pass their lives on land.

The half-pay officer was silenced; but the indignation thus pent up in his bosom glowed with intense vehemence in his single eye, which kindled like a coal.

Peechy Prauw, who never could remain silent, observed that the gentleman certainly was in the right. Kidd never did bury money up the Hudson, nor indeed in any of those parts, though many affirmed such to be the fact. It was Bradish [1] and others of the buccaneers who had buried money, some said in Turtle Bay, [2] others on Long Island, others in the neighborhood of Hell Gate. "Indeed," added he, "I recollect an adventure of Sam, the negro fisherman, many years ago, which some think had something to do with the buccaneers. As we are all friends here, and as it will go no further, I'll tell it to you.

[1] Bradish was a pirate whose actions were blended in the popular mind with those of Kidd. He was boatswain of a ship which sailed from England in 1697, and which, like Kidd's, bore the name of the Adventure. In the absence of the captain on shore, he seized the ship and set out on a piratical cruise. After amassing a fortune, he sailed for America and deposited a large amount of his wealth with a confederate on Long Island. He was apprehended in Rhode Island, sent to England, and executed.

[2] A small cove in the East River two miles north of Corlear's Hook.

"Upon a dark night many years ago, as Black Sam was returning from fishing in Hell Gate – "

Here the story was nipped in the bud by a sudden movement from the unknown, who, laying his iron fist on the table, knuckles downward, with a quiet force that indented the very boards, and looking grimly over his shoulder, with the grin of an angry bear, – "Hearkee, neighbor," said he, with significant nodding of the head, "you'd better let the buccaneers and their money alone; they're not for old men and old women to meddle with. They fought hard for their money – they gave body and soul for it; and wherever it lies buried, depend upon it he must have a tug with the devil who gets it!

This sudden explosion was succeeded by a blank silence throughout the room. Peechy Prauw shrunk within himself, and even the one-eyed officer turned pale. Wolfert, who from a dark corner of the room had listened with intense eagerness to all this talk about buried treasure, looked with mingled awe and reverence at this bold buccaneer, for such he really suspected him to be. There was a chinking of gold and a sparkling of jewels in all his stories about the Spanish Main that gave a value to every period, and Wolfert would have given anything for the rummaging of the ponderous sea chest, which his imagination crammed full of golden chalices, crucifixes, and jolly round bags of doubloons.

The dead stillness that had fallen upon the company was at length interrupted by the stranger, who pulled out a prodigious watch of curious and ancient workmanship, and which in Wolfert's eyes had a decidedly Spanish look. On touching a spring, it struck ten o'clock, upon which the sailor called for his reckoning, and having paid it out of a handful of outlandish coin, he drank off the remainder of his beverage, and without taking leave of anyone, rolled out of the room, muttering to himself as he stamped upstairs to his chamber.

It was some time before the company could recover from the silence into which they had been thrown. The very footsteps of the stranger, which were heard now and then as he traversed his chamber, inspired awe.

Still the conversation in which they had been engaged was too interesting not to be resumed. A heavy thunder gust had gathered up unnoticed while they were lost in talk, and the torrents of rain that fell forbade all thoughts of setting off for home until the storm should subside. They drew nearer together, therefore, and entreated the worthy Peechy Prauw to continue the tale which had been so discourteously interrupted. He readily complied, whispering, however, in a tone scarcely above his breath, and drowned occasionally by the rolling of the thunder; and he would pause every now and then and listen, with evident awe, as he heard the heavy footsteps of the stranger pacing overhead. The following is the purport of his story:

Adventure of the Black Fisherman

Everybody knows Black Sam, the old negro fisherman, or, as he is commonly called, "Mud Sam," who has fished about the Sound for the last half century. It is now many years since Sam, who was then as active a young negro as any in the province, and worked on the farm of Killian Suydam on Long Island, having finished his day's work at an early hour, was fishing, one still summer evening, just about the neighborhood of Hell Gate.

He was in a light skiff, and being well acquainted with the currents and eddies, had shifted his station, according to the shifting of the tide, from the Hen and Chickens to the Hog's Back, from the Hog's Back to the Pot, and from the Pot to the Frying Pan; but in the eagerness of his sport he did not see that the tide was rapidly ebbing, until the roaring of the whirlpools and eddies warned him of his danger, and he had some difficulty in shooting his skiff from among the rocks and breakers, and getting to the point of Blackwell's Island. [1] Here he cast anchor for some time, waiting the turn of the tide to enable him to return homeward. As the night set in, it grew blustering and gusty. Dark clouds came bundling up in the west, and now and then a growl of thunder or a flash of lightning told that a summer storm was at hand. Sam pulled over, therefore, under the lee of Manhattan Island, and, coasting along, came to a snug nook, just under a steep, beetling rock, where he fastened his skiff to the root of a tree that shot out from a cleft, and spread its broad branches like a canopy over the water. The gust came scouring along, the wind threw up the river in white surges, the rain rattled among the leaves, the thunder bellowed worse than that which is now bellowing, the lightning seemed to lick up the surges of the stream; but Sam, snugly sheltered under rock and tree, lay crouching in his skiff, rocking upon the billows until he fell asleep.

[1] A long, narrow island in the East River, between New York and Long Island City.

When he woke all was quiet. The gust had passed away, and only now and then a faint gleam of lightning in the east showed which way it had gone. The night was dark and moonless, and from the state of the tide Sam concluded it was near midnight. He was on the point of making loose his skiff to return homeward when he saw a light gleaming along the water from a distance, which seemed rapidly approaching. As it drew near he perceived it came from a lantern in the bow of a boat gliding along under shadow of the land. It pulled up in a small cove close to where he was. A man jumped on shore, and searching about with the lantern, exclaimed, "This is the place – here's the iron ring." The boat was then made fast, and the man, returning on board, assisted his comrades in conveying something heavy on shore. As the light gleamed among them, Sam saw that they were five stout, desperate-looking fellows, in red woolen caps, with a leader in a three-cornered hat, and that some of them were armed with dirks, or long knives, and pistols. They talked low to one another, and occasionally in some outlandish tongue which he could not understand.

On landing they made their way among the bushes, taking turns to relieve each other in lugging their burden up the rocky bank. Sam's curiosity was now fully aroused, so leaving his skiff he clambered silently up a ridge that overlooked their path. They had stopped to rest for a moment, and the leader was looking about among the bushes with his lantern. "Have you brought the spades?" said one. "They are here," replied another, who had them on his shoulder. "We must dig deep, where there will be no risk of discovery," said a third.

A cold chill ran through Sam's veins. He fancied he saw before him a gang of murderers, about to bury their victim. His knees smote together. In his agitation he shook the branch of a tree with which he was supporting himself as he looked over the edge of the cliff.

"What's that?" cried one of the gang. "Some one stirs among the bushes!"

The lantern was held up in the direction of the noise. One of the red-caps cocked a pistol, and pointed it toward the very place where Sam was standing. He stood motionless, breathless, expecting the next moment to be his last. Fortunately his dingy complexion was in his favor, and made no glare among the leaves.

"'Tis no one," said the man with the lantern. "What a plague! you would not fire off your pistol and alarm the country!"

The pistol was uncocked, the burden was resumed, and the party slowly toiled along the bank. Sam watched them as they went, the light sending back fitful gleams through the dripping bushes, and it was not till they were fairly out of sight that he ventured to draw breath freely. He now thought of getting back to his boat, and making his escape out of the reach of such dangerous neighbors; but curiosity was all-powerful. He hesitated, and lingered, and listened. By and by he heard the strokes of spades. "They are digging the grave!" said he to himself, and the cold sweat started upon his forehead. Every stroke of a spade, as it sounded through the silent groves, went to his heart. It was evident there was as little noise made as possible; everything had an air of terrible mystery and secrecy. Sam had a great relish for the horrible; a tale of murder was a treat for him, and he was a constant attendant at executions. He could not resist an impulse, in spite of every danger, to steal nearer to the scene of mystery, and overlook the midnight fellows at their work. He crawled along cautiously, therefore, inch by inch, stepping with the utmost care among the dry leaves, lest their rustling should betray him. He came at length to where a steep rock intervened between him and the gang, for he saw the light of their lantern shining up against the branches of the trees on the other side. Sam slowly and silently clambered up the surface of the rock, and raising his head above its naked edge, beheld the villains immediately below him, and so near that though he dreaded discovery he dared not withdraw lest the least movement should be heard. In this way he remained, with his round black face peering above the edge of the rock, like the sun just emerging above the edge of the horizon, or the round- cheeked moon on the dial of a clock.

The red-caps had nearly finished their work, the grave was filled up, and they were carefully replacing the turf. This done they scattered dry leaves over the place. "And now," said the leader, "I defy the devil himself to find it out."

"The murderers!" exclaimed Sam involuntarily.

The whole gang started, and looking up beheld the round black head of Sam just above them, his white eyes strained half out of their orbits, his white teeth chattering, and his whole visage shining with cold perspiration.

"We're discovered!" cried one.

"Down with him!" cried another.

Sam heard the cocking of a pistol, but did not pause for the report. He scrambled over rock and stone, through brush and brier, rolled down banks like a hedgehog, scrambled up others like a catamount. In every direction he heard some one or other of the gang hemming him in. At length he reached the rocky ridge along the river; one of the red-caps was hard behind him. A steep rock like a wall rose directly in his way; it seemed to cut off all retreat, when fortunately he espied the strong, cord-like branch of a grapevine reaching half way down it. He sprang at it with the force of a desperate man, seized it with both hands, and, being young and agile, succeeded in swinging himself to the summit of the cliff. Here he stood in full relief against the sky, when the red-cap cocked his pistol and fired. The ball whistled by Sam's head. With the lucky thought of a man in an emergency, he uttered a yell, fell to the ground, and detached at the same time a fragment of the rock, which tumbled with a loud splash into the river.

"I've done his business," said the red-cap to one or two of his comrades as they arrived panting. "He'll tell no tales, except to the fishes in the river."

His pursuers now turned to meet their companions. Sam, sliding silently down the surface of the rock, let himself quietly into his skiff, cast loose the fastening, and abandoned himself to the rapid current, which in that place runs like a mill stream, and soon swept him off from the neighborhood. It was not, however, until he had drifted a great distance that he ventured to ply his oars, when he made his skiff dart like an arrow through the strait of Hell Gate, never heeding the danger of Pot, Frying Pan, nor Hog's Back itself, nor did he feel himself thoroughly secure until safely nestled in bed in the cockloft of the ancient farmhouse of the Suydams.

Here the worthy Peechy Prauw paused to take breath, and to take a sip of the gossip tankard that stood at his elbow. His auditors remained with open mouths and outstretched necks, gaping like a nest of swallows for an additional mouthful.

"And is that all?" exclaimed the half-pay officer.

"That's all that belongs to the story," said Peechy Prauw.

"And did Sam never find out what was buried by the red-caps?" said Wolfert eagerly, whose mind was haunted by nothing but ingots and doubloons.

"Not that I know of," said Peechy; "he had no time to spare from his work, and, to tell the truth, he did not like to run the risk of another race among the rocks. Besides, how should he recollect the spot where the grave had been digged? everything would look so different by daylight. And then, where was the use of looking for a dead body when there was no chance of hanging the murderers?"

"Aye, but are you sure it was a dead body they buried?" said Wolfert.

"To be sure," cried Peechy Prauw exultingly. "Does it not haunt in the neighborhood to this very day?"

"Haunts!" exclaimed several of the party, opening their eyes still wider, and edging their chairs still closer.

"Aye, haunts," repeated Peechy; "have none of you heard of Father Red-cap, who haunts the old burned farmhouse in the woods, on the border of the Sound, near Hell Gate?"

"Oh, to be sure, I've heard tell of something of the kind, but then I took it for some old wives' fable."

"Old wives' fable or not," said Peechy Prauw, "that farmhouse stands hard by the very spot. It's been unoccupied time out of mind, and stands in a lonely part of the coast, but those who fish in the neighborhood have often heard strange noises there, and lights have been seen about the wood at night, and an old fellow in a red cap has been seen at the windows more than once, which people take to be the ghost of the body buried there. Once upon a time three soldiers took shelter in the building for the night, and rummaged it from top to bottom, when they found old Father Red-cap astride of a cider barrel in the cellar, with a jug in one hand and a goblet in the other. He offered them a drink out of his goblet, but just as one of the soldiers was putting it to his mouth – whew!- -a flash of fire blazed through the cellar, blinded every mother's son of them for several minutes, and when they recovered their eyesight, jug, goblet, and Red-cap had vanished, and nothing but the empty cider barrel remained."

Here the half-pay officer, who was growing very muzzy and sleepy, and nodding over his liquor, with half-extinguished eye, suddenly gleamed up like an expiring rush-light.

"That's all fudge!" said he, as Peechy finished his last story.

"Well, I don't vouch for the truth of it myself," said Peechy Prauw, "though all the world knows that there's something strange about that house and grounds; but as to the story of Mud Sam, I believe it just as well as if it had happened to myself."

The deep interest taken in this conversation by the company had made them unconscious of the uproar abroad among the elements, when suddenly they were electrified by a tremendous clap of thunder. A lumbering crash followed instantaneously, shaking the building to its very foundation. All started from their seats, imagining it the shock of an earthquake, or that old Father Red-cap was coming among them in all his terrors. They listened for a moment, but only heard the rain pelting against the windows and the wind howling among the trees. The explosion was soon explained by the apparition of an old negro's bald head thrust in at the door, his white goggle eyes contrasting with his jetty poll, which was wet with rain, and shone like a bottle. In a jargon but half intelligible he announced that the kitchen chimney had been struck with lightning.

A sullen pause of the storm, which now rose and sank in gusts, produced a momentary stillness. In this interval the report of a musket was heard, and a long shout, almost like a yell, resounded from the shores. Everyone crowded to the window; another musket shot was heard, and another long shout, mingled wildly with a rising blast of wind. It seemed as if the cry came up from the bosom of the waters, for though incessant flashes of lightning spread a light about the shore, no one was to be seen.

Suddenly the window of the room overhead was opened, and a loud halloo uttered by the mysterious stranger. Several hailings passed from one party to the other, but in a language which none of the company in the barroom could understand, and presently they heard the window closed, and a great noise overhead, as if all the furniture were pulled and hauled about the room. The negro servant was summoned, and shortly afterwards was seen assisting the veteran to lug the ponderous sea chest downstairs.

The landlord was in amazement. "What, you are not going on the water in such a storm?"

"Storm!" said the other scornfully, "do you call such a sputter of weather a storm?"

"You'll get drenched to the skin; you'll catch your death!" said Peechy Prauw affectionately.

"Thunder and lightning!" exclaimed the veteran; "don't preach about weather to a man that has cruised in whirlwinds and tornadoes."

The obsequious Peechy was again struck dumb. The voice from the water was heard once more in a tone of impatience; the bystanders stared with redoubled awe at this man of storms, who seemed to have come up out of the deep, and to be summoned back to it again. As, with the assistance of the negro, he slowly bore his ponderous sea chest toward the shore, they eyed it with a superstitious feeling, half doubting whether he were not really about to embark upon it and launch forth upon the wild waves. They followed him at a distance with a lantern.

"Dowse [1] the light!" roared the hoarse voice from the water. "No one wants light here!"

[1] Extinguish.

"Thunder and lightning!" exclaimed the veteran, turning short upon them; "back to the house with you!"

Wolfert and his companions shrank back in dismay. Still their curiosity would not allow them entirely to withdraw. A long sheet of lightning now flickered across the waves, and discovered a boat, filled with men, just under a rocky point, rising and sinking with the heaving surges, and swashing the waters at every heave. It was with difficulty held to the rocks by a boat hook, for the current rushed furiously round the point. The veteran hoisted one end of the lumbering sea chest on the gunwale of the boat, and seized the handle at the other end to lift it in, when the motion propelled the boat from the shore, the chest slipped off from the gunwale, and, sinking into the waves, pulled the veteran headlong after it. A loud shriek was uttered by all on shore, and a volley of execrations by those on board, but boat and man were hurried away by the rushing swiftness of the tide. A pitchy darkness succeeded. Wolfert Webber, indeed, fancied that he distinguished a cry for help, and that he beheld the drowning man beckoning for assistance; but when the lightning again gleamed along the water all was void; neither man nor boat was to be seen, – nothing but the dashing and weltering of the waves as they hurried past.

The company returned to the tavern to await the subsiding

of the storm. They resumed their seats and gazed on each other with dismay. The whole transaction had not occupied five minutes, and not a dozen words had been spoken. When they looked at the oaken chair they could scarcely realize the fact that the strange being who had so lately tenanted it, full of life and Herculean vigor, should already be a corpse. There was the very glass he had just drunk from; there lay the ashes from the pipe which he had smoked, as it were, with his last breath. As the worthy burghers pondered on these things, they felt a terrible conviction of the uncertainty of existence, and each felt as if the ground on which he stood was rendered less stable by his awful example.

As, however, the most of the company were possessed of that valuable philosophy which enables a man to bear up with fortitude against the misfortunes of his neighbors, they soon managed to console themselves for the tragic end of the veteran. The landlord was particularly happy that the poor dear man had paid his reckoning before he went, and made a kind of farewell speech on the occasion.

"He came," said he, "in a storm, and he went in a storm; he came in the night, and he went in the night; he came nobody knows whence, and he has gone nobody knows where. For aught I know he has gone to sea once more on his chest, and may land to bother some people on the other side of the world; though it's a thousand pities," added he, "if he has gone to Davy Jones's [1] locker, that he had not left his own locker [2] behind him."

[1] Davy Jones is the spirit of the sea, or the sea devil, and Davy Jones's locker is the bottom of the ocean; hence, "gone to Davy Jones's locker" signifies "dead and buried in the sea."

[2] Chest.

"His locker! St. Nicholas preserve us!" cried Peechy Prauw. "I'd not have had that sea chest in the house for any money; I'll warrant he'd come racketing after it at nights, and making a haunted house of the inn. And as to his going to sea in his chest, I recollect what happened to Skipper Onderdonk's ship on his voyage from Amsterdam.

"The boatswain died during a storm, so they wrapped him

up in a sheet, and put him in his own sea chest, and threw him overboard; but they neglected, in their hurry-skurry, to say prayers over him, and the storm raged and roared louder than ever, and they saw the dead man seated in his chest, with his shroud for a sail, coming hard after the ship, and the sea breaking before him in great sprays like fire; and there they kept scudding day after day and night after night, expecting every moment to go to wreck; and every night they saw the dead boatswain in his sea chest trying to get up with them, and they heard his whistle above the blasts of wind, and he seemed to send great seas, mountain high, after them that would have swamped the ship if they had not put up the deadlights. And so it went on till they lost sight of him in the fogs off Newfoundland, and supposed he had veered ship and stood for Dead Man's Isle. [1] So much for burying a man at sea without saying prayers over him."

[1] Probably Deadman's Point, a small island near Deadman's Bay, off the eastern coast of Newfoundland.

The thunder gust which had hitherto detained the company was now at an end. The cuckoo clock in the hall told midnight; everyone pressed to depart, for seldom was such a late hour of the night trespassed on by these quiet burghers. As they sallied forth they found the heavens once more serene. The storm which had lately obscured them had rolled away, and lay piled up in fleecy masses on the horizon, lighted up by the bright crescent of the moon, which looked like a little silver lamp hung up in a palace of clouds.

The dismal occurrence of the night, and the dismal narrations they had made, had left a superstitious feeling in every mind. They cast a fearful glance at the spot where the buccaneer had disappeared, almost expecting to see him sailing on his chest in the cool moonshine. The trembling rays glittered along the waters, but all was placid, and the current dimpled over the spot where he had gone down. The party huddled together in a little crowd as they repaired homeward, particularly when they passed a lonely field where a man had been murdered, and even the sexton, who had to complete his journey alone, though accustomed, one would think, to ghosts and goblins, went a long way round rather than pass by his own churchyard.

Wolfert Webber had now carried home a fresh stock of stories and notions to ruminate upon. These accounts of pots of money and Spanish treasures, buried here and there and everywhere about the rocks and bays of these wild shores, made him almost dizzy. "Blessed St. Nicholas!" ejaculated he, half aloud, "is it not possible to come upon one of these golden hoards, and to make oneself rich in a twinkling? How hard that I must go on, delving and delving, day in and day out, merely to make a morsel of bread, when one lucky stroke of a spade might enable me to ride in my carriage for the rest of my life!"

As he turned over in his thoughts all that had been told of the singular adventure of the negro fisherman, his imagination gave a totally different complexion [1] to the tale. He saw in the gang of red-caps nothing but a crew of pirates burying their spoils, and his cupidity was once more awakened by the possibility of at length getting on the traces of some of this lurking wealth. Indeed, his infected fancy tinged everything with gold. He felt like the greedy inhabitant of Bagdad when his eyes had been greased with the magic ointment of the dervish, that gave him to see all the treasures of the earth. [2] Caskets of buried jewels, chests of ingots, and barrels of outlandish coins seemed to court him from their concealments, and supplicate him to relieve them from their untimely graves.

[1] Aspect.

[2] See Story of the Blind Man, Baba Abdalla, in Arabian Nights' Entertainment. An inhabitant of Bagdad, Asiatic Turkey, meets with a dervish, or Turkish monk, who presents him with a vast treasure and with a box of magic ointment, which, applied to the left eye, enables one to see the treasures in the bosom of the earth, but on touching the right eye, causes blindness. Having applied it to the left eye with the result predicted, he uses it on his right eye, in the hope that still greater treasures may be revealed, and immediately becomes blind.

On making private inquiries about the grounds said to be haunted by Feather Red-cap, he was more and more confirmed in his surmise. He learned that the place had several times been visited by experienced money diggers who had heard Black Sam's story, though none of them had met with success. On the contrary, they had always been dogged with ill luck of some kind or other, in consequence, as Wolfert concluded, of not going to work at the proper time and with the proper ceremonials. The last attempt had been made by Cobus Quackenbos, who dug for a whole night, and met with incredible difficulty, for as fast as he threw one shovelful of earth out of the hole, two were thrown in by invisible hands. He succeeded so far, however, as to uncover an iron chest, when there was a terrible roaring, ramping, and raging of uncouth figures about the hole, and at length a shower of blows, dealt by invisible cudgels, fairly belabored him off of the forbidden ground. This Cobus Quackenbos had declared on his deathbed, so that there could not be any doubt of it. He was a man that had devoted many years of his life to money digging, and it was thought would have ultimately succeeded had he not died recently of a brain fever in the almshouse.

Wolfert Webber was now in a worry of trepidation and impatience, fearful lest some rival adventurer should get a scent of the buried gold. He determined privately to seek out the black fisherman, and get him to serve as guide to the place where he had witnessed the mysterious scene of interment. Sam was easily found, for he was one of those old habitual beings that live about a neighborhood until they wear themselves a place in the public mind, and become, in a manner, public characters. There was not an unlucky urchin about town that did not know Sam the fisherman, and think that he had a right to play his tricks upon the old negro. Sam had led an amphibious life for more than half a century, about the shores of the bay and the fishing grounds of the Sound. He passed the greater part of his time on and in the water, particularly about Hell Gate, and might have been taken, in bad weather, for one of the hobgoblins that used to haunt that strait. There would he be seen, at all times and in all weathers, sometimes in his skiff, anchored among the eddies, or prowling like a shark about some wreck, where the fish are supposed to be most abundant; sometimes seated on a rock from hour to hour, looking, in the mist and drizzle, like a solitary heron watching for its prey. He was well acquainted with every hole and corner of the Sound, from the Wallabout [1] to Hell Gate, and from Hell Gate unto the Devil's Stepping-Stones; and it was even affirmed that he knew all the fish in the river by their Christian names.

[1] A bay of the East River, on which the Brooklyn Navy Yard is situated.

Wolfert found him at his cabin, which was not much larger than a tolerable dog house. It was rudely constructed of fragments of wrecks and driftwood, and built on the rocky shore at the foot of the old fort, just about what at present forms the point of the Battery. [1] A "very ancient and fishlike smell" [2] pervaded the place. Oars, paddles, and fishing rods were leaning against the wall of the fort, a net was spread on the sand to dry, a skiff was drawn up on the beach, and at the door of his cabin was Mud Sam himself, indulging in the true negro luxury of sleeping in the sunshine.

[1] The southern extremity of New York City.

[2] See Shakespeare's The Tempest, act ii., sc. 2.

Many years had passed away since the time of Sam's youthful adventure, and the snows of many a winter had grizzled the knotty wool upon his head. He perfectly recollected the circumstances, however, for he had often been called upon to relate them, though in his version of the story he differed in many points from Peechy Prauw, as is not infrequently the case with authentic historians. As to the subsequent researches of money diggers, Sam knew nothing about them; they were matters quite out of his line; neither did the cautious Wolfert care to disturb his thoughts on that point. His only wish was to secure the old fisherman as a pilot to the spot, and this was readily effected. The long time that had intervened since his nocturnal adventure had effaced all Sam's awe of the place, and the promise of a trifling reward roused him at once from his sleep and his sunshine.

The tide was adverse to making the expedition by water, and Wolfert was too impatient to get to the land of promise to wait for its turning; they set off, therefore, by land. A walk of four or five miles brought them to the edge of a wood, which at that time covered the greater part of the eastern side of the island. It was just beyond the pleasant region of Bloomen-dael. [1] Here they struck into a long lane, straggling among trees and bushes very much overgrown with weeds and mullein stalks, as if but seldom used, and so completely overshadowed as to enjoy but a kind of twilight. Wild vines entangled the trees and flaunted in their faces; brambles and briers caught their clothes as they passed; the garter snake glided across their path; the spotted toad hopped and waddled before them; and the restless catbird mewed at them from every thicket. Had Wolfert Webber been deeply read in romantic legend he might have fancied himself entering upon forbidden, enchanted ground, or that these were some of the guardians set to keep watch upon buried treasure. As it was, the loneliness of the place, and the wild stories connected with it, had their effect upon his mind.

[1] At the time this story was written Bloomen-dael (Flowery Valley) was a village four miles from New York. It is now that part of New York known as Bloomingdale, on the west side, between about Seventieth and One Hundredth Streets.

On reaching the lower end of the lane they found themselves near the shore of the Sound, in a kind of amphitheater surrounded by forest trees. The area had once been a grass plot, but was now shagged with briers and rank weeds. At one end, and just on the river bank, was a ruined building, little better than a heap of rubbish, with a stack of chimneys rising like a solitary tower out of the center. The current of the Sound rushed along just below it, with wildly grown trees drooping their branches into its waves.

Wolfert had not a doubt that this was the haunted house of Father Red-cap, and called to mind the story of Peechy Prauw. The evening was approaching, and the light, falling dubiously among the woody places, gave a melancholy tone to the scene well calculated to foster any lurking feeling of awe or superstition. The night hawk, wheeling about in the highest regions of the air, emitted his peevish, boding cry. The woodpecker gave a lonely tap now and then on some hollow tree, and the firebird [1] streamed by them with his deep red plumage.

[1] Orchard oriole.

They now came to an inclosure that had once been a garden. It extended along the foot of a rocky ridge, but was little better than a wilderness of weeds, with here and there a matted rosebush, or a peach or plum tree, grown wild and ragged, and covered with moss. At the lower end of the garden they passed a kind of vault in the side of a bank, facing the water. It had the look of a root house. [1] The door, though decayed, was still strong, and appeared to have been recently patched up. Wolfert pushed it open. It gave a harsh grating upon its hinges, and striking against something like a box, a rattling sound ensued, and a skull rolled on the floor. Wolfert drew back shuddering, but was reassured on being informed by the negro that this was a family vault, belonging to one of the old Dutch families that owned this estate, an assertion corroborated by the sight of coffins of various sizes piled within. Sam had been familiar with all these scenes when a boy, and now knew that he could not be far from the place of which they were in quest.

[1] "Root house," i.e., a house for storing up potatoes, turnips, or other roots for the winter feed of cattle.

They now made their way to the water's edge, scrambling along ledges of rocks that overhung the waves, and obliged often to hold by shrubs and grapevines to avoid slipping into the deep and hurried stream. At length they came to a small cove, or rather indent of the shore. It was protected by steep rocks, and overshadowed by a thick copse of oaks and chestnuts, so as to be sheltered and almost concealed. The beach shelved gradually within the cove, but, the current swept deep and black and rapid along its jutting points. The negro paused, raised his remnant of a hat, and scratched his grizzled poll for a moment, as he regarded this nook; then suddenly clapping his hands, he stepped exultingly forward, and pointed to a large iron ring, stapled firmly in the rock, just where a broad shelf of stone furnished a commodious landing place. It was the very spot where the red-caps had landed. Years had changed the more perishable features of the scene; but rock and iron yield slowly to the influence of time. On looking more closely Wolfert remarked three crosses cut in the rock just above the ring, which had no doubt some mysterious signification. Old Sam now readily recognized the overhanging rock under which his skiff had been sheltered during the thunder gust. To follow up the course which the midnight gang had taken, however, was a harder task. His mind had been so much taken up on that eventful occasion by the persons of the drama as to pay but little attention to the scenes, and these places looked so different by night and day. After wandering about for some time, however, they came to an opening among the trees which Sam thought resembled the place. There was a ledge of rock of moderate height, like a wall, on one side, which he thought might be the very ridge whence he had overlooked the diggers. Wolfert examined it narrowly, and at length discovered three crosses similar to those on the above ring, cut deeply into the face of the rock, but nearly obliterated by moss that had grown over them. His heart leaped with joy, for he doubted not they were the private marks of the buccaneers. All now that remained was to ascertain the precise spot where the treasure lay buried, for otherwise he might dig at random in the neighborhood of the crosses, without coming upon the spoils, and he had already had enough of such profitless labor. Here, however, the old negro was perfectly at a loss, and indeed perplexed him by a variety of opinions, for his recollections were all confused. Sometimes he declared it must have been at the foot of a mulberry tree hard by; then beside a great white stone; then under a small green knoll, a short distance from the ledge of rocks, until at length Wolfert became as bewildered as himself.

The shadows of evening were now spreading themselves over the woods, and rock and tree began to mingle together. It was evidently too late to attempt anything further at present, and, indeed, Wolfert had come unprovided with implements to prosecute his researches. Satisfied, therefore, with having ascertained the place, he took note of all its landmarks, that he might recognize it again, and set out on his return homeward, resolved to prosecute this golden enterprise without delay.

The leading anxiety which had hitherto absorbed every feeling being now in some measure appeased, fancy began to wander, and to conjure up a thousand shapes and chimeras as he returned through this haunted region. Pirates hanging in chains seemed to swing from every tree, and he almost expected to see some Spanish don, with his throat cut from ear to ear, rising slowly out of the ground, and shaking the ghost of a money bag.

Their way back lay through the desolate garden, and Wolfert's nerves had arrived at so sensitive a state that the flitting of a bird, the rustling of a leaf, or the falling of a nut was enough to startle him. As they entered the confines of the garden, they caught sight of a figure at a distance advancing slowly up one of the walks, and bending under the weight of a burden. They paused and regarded him attentively. He wore what appeared to be a woolen cap, and, still more alarming, of a most sanguinary red.

The figure moved slowly on, ascended the bank, and stopped at the very door of the sepulchral vault. Just before entering it he looked around. What was the affright of Wolfert when he recognized the grisly visage of the drowned buccaneer! He uttered an ejaculation of horror. The figure slowly raised his iron fist and shook it with a terrible menace. Wolfert did not pause to see any more, but hurried off as fast as his legs could carry him, nor was Sam slow in following at his heels, having all his ancient terrors revived. Away, then, did they scramble through bush and brake, horribly frightened at every bramble that tugged at their skirts, nor did they pause to breathe until they had blundered their way through this perilous wood, and fairly reached the highroad to the city.

Several days elapsed before Wolfert could summon courage enough to prosecute the enterprise, so much had he been dismayed by the apparition, whether living or dead, of the grisly buccaneer. In the meantime, what a conflict of mind did he suffer! He neglected all his concerns, was moody and restless all day, lost his appetite, wandered in his thoughts and words, and committed a thousand blunders. His rest was broken, and when he fell asleep the nightmare, in shape of a huge money bag, sat squatted upon his breast. He babbled about incalculable sums, fancied himself engaged in money digging, threw the bedclothes right and left, in the idea that he was shoveling away the dirt, groped under the bed in quest of the treasure, and lugged forth, as he supposed, an inestimable pot of gold.

Dame Webber and her daughter were in despair at what they conceived a returning touch of insanity. There are two family oracles, one or other of which Dutch housewives consult in all cases of great doubt and perplexity, – the dominie and the doctor. In the present instance they repaired to the doctor. There was at that time a little dark, moldy man of medicine, famous among the old wives of the Manhattoes for his skill, not only in the healing art, but in all matters of strange and mysterious nature. His name was Dr. Knipperhausen, but he was more commonly known by the appellation of the "High German Doctor." [1] To him did the poor women repair for counsel and assistance touching the mental vagaries of Wolfert Webber.

[1] The same, no doubt, of whom mention is made in the history of Dolph Heyliger.

They found the doctor seated in his little study, clad in his dark camlet [1] robe of knowledge, with his black velvet cap, after the manner of Boerhaave, [2] Van Helmont, [3] and other medical sages, a pair of green spectacles set in black horn upon his clubbed nose, and poring over a German folio that reflected back the darkness of his physiognomy. The doctor listened to their statement of the symptoms of Wolfert's malady with profound attention, but when they came to mention his raving about buried money the little man pricked up his ears. Alas, poor women! they little knew the aid they had called in.

[1] A fabric made of goat's hair and silk, or wool and cotton.

[2] Hermann Boerhaave (1668-1738), a celebrated Dutch physician and philosopher.

[3] Jan Baptista Van Helmont (1577-1644), a celebrated Flemish physician and chemist.

Dr. Knipperhausen had been half his life engaged in seeking the short cuts to fortune, in quest of which so many a long lifetime is wasted. He had passed some years of his youth among the Harz [1] mountains of Germany, and had derived much valuable instruction from the miners touching the mode of seeking treasure buried in the earth. He had prosecuted his studies, also, under a traveling sage who united the mysteries of medicine with magic and legerdemain. His mind, therefore, had become stored with all kinds of mystic lore; he had dabbled a little in astrology, alchemy, divination; [2] knew how to detect stolen money, and to tell where springs of water lay hidden; in a word, by the dark nature of his knowledge he had acquired the name of the "High German Doctor," which is pretty nearly equivalent to that of necromancer. The doctor had often heard rumors of treasure being buried in various parts of the island, and had long been anxious to get on the traces of it. No sooner were Wolfert's waking and sleeping vagaries confided to him than he beheld in them the confirmed symptoms of a case of money digging, and lost no time in probing it to the bottom. Wolfert had long been sorely oppressed in mind by the golden secret, and as a family physician is a kind of father confessor, he was glad of any opportunity of unburdening himself. So far from curing, the doctor caught the malady from his patient. The circumstances unfolded to him awakened all his cupidity; he had not a doubt of money being buried somewhere in the neighborhood of the mysterious crosses, and offered to join Wolfert in the search. He informed him that much secrecy and caution must be observed in enterprises of the kind; that money is only to be dug for at night, with certain forms and ceremonies and burning of drugs, the repeating of mystic words, and, above all, that the seekers must first be provided with a divining rod, [3] which had the wonderful property of pointing to the very spot on the surface of the earth under which treasure lay hidden. As the doctor had given much of his mind to these matters he charged himself with all the necessary preparations, and, as the quarter of the moon was propitious, he undertook to have the divining rod ready by a certain night.

[1] A mountain chain in northwestern Germany, between the Elbe and the Weser.

[2] Astrology, alchemy, and divination were three imaginary arts. The first pretended to judge of the influence of the stars on human affairs, and to foretell events by their positions and aspects; the second aimed to transmute the baser metals into gold, and to find a universal remedy for diseases; while the third dealt with the discovery of secret or future events by preternatural means.

[3] A divining rod is a rod used by those who pretend to discover water or metals underground. It is commonly made of witch hazel, with forked branches.

Wolfert's heart leaped with joy at having met with so learned and able a coadjutor. Everything went on secretly but swimmingly. The doctor had many consultations with his patient, and the good women of the household lauded the comforting effect of his visits. In the meantime the wonderful divining rod, that great key to nature's secrets, was duly prepared. The doctor had thumbed over all his books of knowledge for the occasion, and the black fisherman was engaged to take them in his skiff to the scene of enterprise, to work with spade and pickax in unearthing the treasure, and to freight his bark with the weighty spoils they were certain of finding.

At length the appointed night arrived for this perilous undertaking. Before Wolfert left his home he counseled his wife and daughter to go to bed, and feel no alarm if he should not return during the night. Like reasonable women, on being told not to feel alarm they fell immediately into a panic. They saw at once by his manner that something unusual was in agitation; all their fears about the unsettled state of his mind were revived with tenfold force; they hung about him, entreating him not to expose himself to the night air, but all in vain. When once Wolfert was mounted on his hobby, [1] it was no easy manner to get him out of the saddle. It was a clear, starlight night when he issued out of the portal of the Webber palace. He wore a large flapped hat, tied under the chin with a handkerchief of his daughter's, to secure him from the night damp, while Dame Webber threw her long red cloak about his shoulders, and fastened it round his neck.

[1] Hobby, or hobbyhorse, a favorite theme of thought; hence, "to mount a hobby" is to follow a favorite pursuit.

The doctor had been no less carefully armed and accoutered by his housekeeper, the vigilant Frau Ilsy, and sallied forth in his camlet robe by way of surcoat, [1] his black velvet cap under his cocked hat, a thick clasped book under his arm, a basket of drugs and dried herbs in one hand, and in the other the miraculous rod of divination.

[1] Overcoat.

The great church clock struck ten as Wolfert and the doctor passed by the churchyard, and the watchman bawled in hoarse voice a long and doleful "All's well!" A deep sleep had already fallen upon this primitive little burgh; nothing disturbed this awful silence excepting now and then the bark of some profligate, night-walking dog, or the serenade of some romantic cat. It is true

Wolfert fancied more than once that he heard the sound of a stealthy footfall at a distance behind them; but it might have been merely the echo of their own steps along the quiet streets. He thought also at one time that he saw a tall figure skulking after them, stopping when they stopped and moving on as they proceeded; but the dim and uncertain lamplight threw such vague gleams and shadows that this might all have been mere fancy.

They found the old fisherman waiting for them, smoking his pipe in the stern of the skiff, which was moored just in front of his little cabin. A pickax and spade were lying in the bottom of the boat, with a dark lantern, and a stone bottle of good Dutch courage, [1] in which honest Sam no doubt put even more faith than Dr. Knipperhausen in his drugs.

[1] Dutch courage is courage that results from indulgence in Dutch gin or Hollands; here applied to the gin itself.

Thus, then, did these three worthies embark in their cockleshell of a skiff upon this nocturnal expedition, with a wisdom and valor equaled only by the three wise men of Gotham,[1] who adventured to sea in a bowl. The tide was rising and running rapidly up the Sound. The current bore them along, almost without the aid of an oar. The profile of the town lay all in shadow. Here and there a light feebly glimmered from some sick chamber, or from the cabin window of some vessel at anchor in the stream. Not a cloud obscured the deep, starry firmament, the lights of which wavered on the surface of the placid river, and a shooting meteor, streaking its pale course in the very direction they were taking, was interpreted by the doctor into a most propitious omen.

[1] "Three wise men of Gotham,
   They went to sea in a bowl –
   And if the bowl had been stronger,
   My tale had been longer."
   Mother Goose Melody.

[1] Gotham was a village proverbial for the blundering simplicity of its inhabitants. At first the name referred to an English village. Irving applied it to New York City.

In a little while they glided by the point of Corlear's Hook, with the rural inn which had been the scene of such night adventures. The family had retired to rest, and the house was dark and still. Wolfert felt a chill pass over him as they passed the point where the buccaneer had disappeared. He pointed it out to Dr. Knipperhausen. While regarding it they thought they saw a boat actually lurking at the very place; but the shore cast such a shadow over the border of the water that they could discern nothing distinctly. They had not proceeded far when they heard the low sounds of distant oars, as if cautiously pulled. Sam plied his oars with redoubled vigor, and knowing all the eddies and currents of the stream, soon left their followers, if such they were, far astern. In a little while they stretched across Turtle Bay and Kip's Bay, [1] then shrouded themselves in the deep shadows of the Manhattan shore, and glided swiftly along, secure from observation. At length the negro shot his skiff into a little cove, darkly embowered by trees, and made it fast to the well-known iron ring. They now landed, and lighting the lantern gathered their various implements and proceeded slowly through the bushes. Every sound startled them, even that of their own footsteps among the dry leaves, and the hooting of a screech owl, from the shattered chimney of the neighboring ruin, made their blood run cold.

[1] A small bay in the East River below Corlear's Hook.

In spite of all Wolfert's caution in taking note of the landmarks, it was some time before they could find the open place among the trees, where the treasure was supposed to be buried. At length they came to the ledge of rock, and on examining its surface by the aid of the lantern, Wolfert recognized the three mystic crosses. Their hearts beat quick, for the momentous trial was at hand that was to determine their hopes.

The lantern was now held by Wolfert Webber, while the doctor produced the divining rod. It was a forked twig, one end of which was grasped firmly in each hand, while the center, forming the stem, pointed perpendicularly upward. The doctor moved his wand about, within a certain distance of the earth, from place to place, but for some time without any effect, while Wolfert kept the light of the lantern turned full upon it, and watched it with the most breathless interest. At length the rod began slowly to turn. The doctor grasped it with greater earnestness, his hands trembling with the agitation of his mind. The wand continued to turn gradually, until at length the stem had reversed its position, and pointed perpendicularly downward, and remained pointing to one spot as fixedly as the needle to the pole.

"This is the spot!" said the doctor, in an almost inaudible tone.

Wolfert's heart was in his throat.

"Shall I dig?" said the negro, grasping the spade.

"Pots tausend, [1] no!" replied the little doctor hastily. He now ordered his companions to keep close by him, and to maintain the most inflexible silence; that certain precautions must be taken and ceremonies used to prevent the evil spirits which kept about buried treasure from doing them any harm. He then drew a circle about the place, enough to include the whole party. He next gathered dry twigs and leaves and made a fire, upon which he threw certain drugs and dried herbs which he had brought in his basket. A thick smoke rose, diffusing a potent odor savoring marvelously of brimstone and asafetida, which, however grateful it might be to the olfactory nerves of spirits, nearly strangled poor Wolfert, and produced a fit of coughing and wheezing that made the whole grove resound. Dr. Knipperhausen then unclasped the volume which he had brought under his arm, which was printed in red and black characters in German text. While Wolfert held the lantern, the doctor, by the aid of his spectacles, read off several forms of conjuration in Latin and German. He then ordered Sam to seize the pickax and proceed to work. The close-bound soil gave obstinate signs of not having been disturbed for many a year. After having picked his way through the surface, Sam came to a bed of sand and gravel, which he threw briskly to right and left with the spade.

[1] A German exclamation of anger, equivalent to the English "zounds!"

"Hark!" said Wolfert, who fancied he heard a trampling among the dry leaves and a rustling through the bushes. Sam paused for a moment, and they listened. No footstep was near. The bat flitted by them in silence; a bird, roused from its roost by the light which glared up among the trees, flew circling about the flame. In the profound stillness of the woodland they could distinguish the current rippling along the rocky shore, and the distant murmuring and roaring of Hell Gate.

The negro continued his labors, and had already digged a considerable hole. The doctor stood on the edge, reading formulae every now and then from his black-letter volume, or throwing more drugs and herbs upon the fire, while Wolfert bent anxiously over the pit, watching every stroke of the spade. Anyone witnessing the scene thus lighted up by fire, lantern, and the reflection of Wolfert's red mantle, might have mistaken the little doctor for some foul magician, busied in his incantations, and the grizzly-headed negro for some swart goblin obedient to his commands.

At length the spade of the fisherman struck upon something that sounded hollow. The sound vibrated to Wolfert's heart. He struck his spade again.

"'Tis a chest," said Sam.

"Full of gold, I'll warrant it!" cried Wolfert, clasping his hands with rapture.

Scarcely had he uttered the words when a sound from above caught his ear. He cast up his eyes, and lo! by the expiring light of the fire he beheld, just over the disk of the rock, what appeared to be the grim visage of the drowned buccaneer, grinning hideously down upon him.

Wolfert gave a loud cry and let fall the lantern. His panic communicated itself to his companions. The negro leaped out of the hole, the doctor dropped his book and basket, and began to pray in German. All was horror and confusion. The fire was scattered about, the lantern extinguished. In their hurry-scurry [1] they ran against and confounded one another. They fancied a legion of hobgoblins let loose upon them, and that they saw, by the fitful gleams of the scattered embers, strange figures, in red caps, gibbering and ramping around them. The doctor ran one way, the negro another, and Wolfert made for the water side. As he plunged struggling onward through brush and brake, he heard the tread of some one in pursuit. He scrambled frantically forward. The footsteps gained upon him. He felt himself grasped by his cloak, when suddenly his pursuer was attacked in turn; a fierce fight and struggle ensued, a pistol was discharged that lit up rock and bush for a second, and showed two figures grappling together; all was then darker than ever. The contest continued, the combatants clinched each other, and panted and groaned, and rolled among the rocks. There was snarling and growling as of a cur, mingled with curses, in which Wolfert fancied he could recognize the voice of the buccaneer. He would fain have fled, but he was on the brink of a precipice, and could go no farther.

[1] A swift, disorderly movement.

Again the parties were on their feet, again there was a tugging and struggling, as if strength alone could decide the combat, until one was precipitated from the brow of the cliff, and sent headlong into the deep stream that whirled below. Wolfert heard the plunge, and a kind of strangling, bubbling murmur, but the darkness of the night hid everything from him, and the swiftness of the current swept everything instantly out of hearing. One of the combatants was disposed of, but whether friend or foe Wolfert could not tell, nor whether they might not both be foes. He heard the survivor approach, and his terror revived. He saw, where the profile of the rocks rose against the horizon, a human form advancing. He could not be mistaken; it must be the buccaneer. Whither should he fly?- -a precipice was on one side, a murderer on the other. The enemy approached – he was close at hand. Wolfert attempted to let himself down the face of the cliff. His cloak caught in a thorn that grew on the edge. He was jerked from off his feet, and held dangling in the air, half choked by the string with which his careful wife had fastened the garment around his neck. Wolfert thought his last moment was arrived; already had he committed his soul to St. Nicholas, when the string broke, and he tumbled down the bank, bumping from rock to rock and bush to bush, and leaving the red cloak fluttering like a bloody banner in the air.

It was a long while before Wolfert came to himself. When he opened his eyes, the ruddy streaks of morning were already shooting up the sky. He found himself grievously battered, and lying in the bottom of a boat. He attempted to sit up, but was too sore and stiff to move. A voice requested him in a friendly accents to lie still. He turned his eyes toward the speaker; it was Dirk Waldron. He had dogged the party, at the earnest request of Dame Webber and her daughter, who, with the laudable curiosity of their sex, had pried into the secret consultations of Wolfert and the doctor. Dirk had been completely distanced in following the light skiff of the fisherman, and had just come in time to rescue the poor money digger from his pursuer.

Thus ended this perilous enterprise. The doctor and Black Sam severally found their way back to the Manhattoes, each having some dreadful tale of peril to relate. As to poor Wolfert, instead of returning in triumph, laden with bags of gold, he was borne home on a shutter, followed by a rabble-rout [1] of curious urchins. His wife and daughter saw the dismal pageant from a distance, and alarmed the neighborhood with their cries; they thought the poor man had suddenly settled the great debt of nature in one of his wayward moods. Finding him, however, still living, they had him speedily to bed, and a jury of old matrons of the neighborhood assembled to determine how he should be doctored. The whole town was in a buzz with the story of the money diggers. Many repaired to the scene of the previous night's adventures; but though they found the very place of the digging, they discovered nothing that compensated them for their trouble. Some say they found the fragments of an oaken chest, and an iron pot lid, which savored strongly of hidden money, and that in the old family vault there were traces of bales and boxes; but this is all very dubious.

[1] A noisy throng.

In fact, the secret of all this story has never to this day been discovered. Whether any treasure were ever actually buried at that place; whether, if so, it were carried off at night by those who had buried it; or whether it still remains there under the guardianship of gnomes and spirits until it shall be properly sought for, is all matter of conjecture. For my part, I incline to the latter opinion, and make no doubt that great sums lie buried, both there and in other parts of this island and its neighborhood, ever since the times of the buccaneers and the Dutch colonists; and I would earnestly recommend the search after them to such of my fellow citizens as are not engaged in any other speculations.

There were many conjectures formed, also, as to who and what was the strange man of the seas, who had domineered over the little fraternity at Corlear's Hook for a time, disappeared so strangely, and reappeared so fearfully. Some supposed him a smuggler stationed at that place to assist his comrades in landing their goods among the rocky coves of the island. Others, that he was one of the ancient comrades of Kidd or Bradish, returned to convey away treasures formerly hidden in the vicinity. The only circumstance that throws anything like a vague light on this mysterious matter is a report which prevailed of a strange, foreign-built shallop, with much the look of a picaroon, [1] having been seen hovering about the Sound for several days without landing or reporting herself, though boats were seen going to and from her at night; and that she was seen standing out of the mouth of the harbor, in the gray of the dawn, after the catastrophe of the money diggers.

[1] A piratical vessel.

I must not omit to mention another report, also, which I confess is rather apocryphal, of the buccaneer who is supposed to have been drowned, being seen before daybreak, with a lantern in his hand, seated astride of his great sea chest, and sailing through Hell Gate, which just then began to roar and bellow with redoubled fury.

While all the gossip world was thus filled with talk and rumor, poor Wolfert lay sick and sorrowfully in his bed, bruised in body and sorely beaten down in mind. His wife and daughter did all they could to bind up his wounds, both corporal and spiritual. The good old dame never stirred from his bedside, where she sat knitting from morning till night, while his daughter busied herself about him with the fondest care. Nor did they lack assistance from abroad. Whatever may be said of the desertion of friends in distress, they had no complaint of the kind to make. Not an old wife of the neighborhood but abandoned her work to crowd to the mansion of Wolfert Webber, to inquire after his health and the particulars of his story. Not one came, moreover, without her little pipkin of pennyroyal, sage, balm, or other herb tea, delighted at an opportunity of signalizing her kindness and her doctorship. What drenchings did not the poor Wolfert undergo, and all in vain! It was a moving sight to behold him wasting away day by day, growing thinner and thinner and ghastlier and ghastlier, and staring with rueful visage from under an old patchwork counterpane, upon the jury of matrons kindly assembled to sigh and groan and look unhappy around him.

Dirk Waldron was the only being that seemed to shed a ray of sunshine into this house of mourning. He came in with cheery look and manly spirit, and tried to reanimate the expiring heart of the poor money digger, but it was all in vain. Wolfert was completely done over. [1] If anything was wanting to complete his despair, it was a notice, served upon him in the midst of his distress, that the corporation was about to run a new street through the very center of his cabbage garden. He now saw nothing before him but poverty and ruin; his last reliance, the garden of his forefathers, was to be laid waste, and what then was to become of his poor wife and child?

[1] Exhausted.

His eyes filled with tears as they followed the dutiful Amy out of the room one morning. Dirk Waldron was seated beside him; Wolfert grasped his hand, pointed after his daughter, and for the first time since his illness broke the silence he had maintained.

"I am going!" said he, shaking his head feebly, "and when I am gone, my poor daughter – "

"Leave her to me, father!" said Dirk manfully; "I'll take care of her!"

Wolfert looked up in the face of the cheery, strapping youngster, and saw there was none better able to take care of a woman.

"Enough," said he, "she is yours! And now fetch me a lawyer – let me make my will and die."

The lawyer was brought, – a dapper, bustling, round-headed little man, Roorback (or Rollebuck, as it was pronounced) by name. At the sight of him the women broke into loud lamentations, for they looked upon the signing of a will as the signing of a death warrant. Wolfert made a feeble motion for them to be silent. Poor Amy buried her face and her grief in the bed curtain. Dame Webber resumed her knitting to hide her distress, which betrayed itself, however, in a pellucid tear, which trickled silently down, and hung at the end of her peaked nose; while the cat, the only unconcerned member of the family, played with the good dame's ball of worsted as it rolled about the floor.

Wolfert lay on his back, his nightcap drawn over his forehead, his eyes closed, his whole visage the picture of death. He begged the lawyer to be brief, for he felt his end approaching, and that he had no time to lose. The lawyer nibbed [1] his pen, spread out his paper, and prepared to write.

[1] In Irving's time, quills were made into pens by pointing or "nibbing" their ends.

"I give and bequeath," said Wolfert faintly, "my small farm –"

"What! all?" exclaimed the lawyer.

Wolfert half opened his eyes and looked upon the lawyer.

"Yes, all," said he.

"What! all that great patch of land with cabbages and sunflowers, which the corporation is just going to run a main street through?"

"The same," said Wolfert, with a heavy sigh, and sinking back upon his pillow.

"I wish him joy that inherits it!" said the little lawyer, chuckling and rubbing his hands involuntarily.

"What do you mean?" said Wolfert, again opening his eyes.

"That he'll be one of the richest men in the place," cried little

Rollebuck.

The expiring Wolfert seemed to step back from the threshold of existence; his eyes again lighted up; he raised himself in his bed, shoved back his red worsted nightcap, and stared broadly at the lawyer.

"You don't say so!" exclaimed he.

"Faith but I do!" rejoined the other. "Why, when that great field and that huge meadow come to be laid out in streets and cut up into snug building lots, – why, whoever owns it need not pull off his hat to the patroon!"

"Say you so?" cried Wolfert, half thrusting one leg out of bed; "why, then, I think I'll not make my will yet."

To the surprise of everybody the dying man actually recovered. The vital spark, which had glimmered faintly in the socket, received fresh fuel from the oil of gladness which the little lawyer poured into his soul. It once more burned up into a flame.

Give physic to the heart, ye who would revive the body of a spirit-broken man! In a few days Wolfert left his room; in a few days more his table was covered with deeds, plans of streets and building lots. Little Rollebuck was constantly with him, his right hand man and adviser, and instead of making his will assisted in the more agreeable task of making his fortune. In fact Wolfert Webber was one of those worthy Dutch burghers of the Manhattoes whose fortunes have been made, in a manner, in spite of themselves; who have tenaciously held on to their hereditary acres, raising turnips and cabbages about the skirts of the city, hardly able to make both ends meet, until the corporation has cruelly driven streets through their abodes, and they have suddenly awakened out of their lethargy, and, to their astonishment, found themselves rich men.

Before many months had elapsed a great, bustling street passed through the very center of the Webber garden, just where Wolfert had dreamed of finding a treasure. His golden dream was accomplished; he did, indeed, find an unlooked-for source of wealth, for, when his paternal lands were distributed into building lots and rented out to safe tenants, instead of producing a paltry crop of cabbages they returned him an abundant crop of rent, insomuch that on quarter day it was a goodly sight to see his tenants knocking at the door from morning till night, each with a little round-bellied bag of money, a golden produce of the soil.

The ancient mansion of his forefathers was still kept up, but, instead of being a little yellow-fronted Dutch house in a garden, it now stood boldly in the midst of a street, the grand home of the neighborhood; for Wolfert enlarged it with a wing on each side, and a cupola or tea room on top, where he might climb up and smoke his pipe in hot weather, and in the course of time the whole mansion was overrun by the chubby-faced progeny of Amy Webber and Dirk Waldron.

As Wolfert waxed old and rich and corpulent he also set up a great gingerbread-colored carriage, drawn by a pair of black Flanders mares with tails that swept the ground; and to commemorate the origin of his greatness he had for his crest a full-blown cabbage painted on the panels, with the pithy motto, ALLES KOPF, that is to say, ALL HEAD, meaning thereby that he had risen by sheer head work.

To fill the measure of his greatness, in the fullness of time the renowned Ramm Rapelye slept with his fathers, and Wolfert Webber succeeded to the leather-bottomed armchair in the inn parlor at Corlear's Hook; where he long reigned, greatly honored and respected, insomuch that he was never known to tell a story without its being believed, nor to utter a joke without its being laughed at.

Introduction to "Wieland's Madness," from "Wieland, or The Transformation."

> From Virtue's blissful paths away
> The double-tongued are sure to stray;
> Good is a forth-right journey still.
> And mazy paths but lead to ill.

"WIELAND" is the first American novel. It appeared in 1798; its author was soon recognized as the earliest American novelist; and he remained the greatest, until Fenimore Cooper brought forth his Leather-stocking Tales, a quarter of a century later.

Although modern sophistication easily points out flaws in Charles Brockden Brown's story-structure, and reproves him for improbability, morbidness, and a style often too elevated, yet his work lives. His downright originality is worthy of Cooper himself, and his weird imaginations and horribly sustained scenes of terror have been surpassed by few writers save Edgar Allan Poe.

Charles Brockden Brown

Wieland's Madness

FIRST PART

I

[As the story opens, the narratress, Clara Wieland, is entering upon the happy realization of her love for Henry Pleyel, closest friend of her brother "Wieland."

Their woodland home, Mettingen, on the banks of the then remote Schuylkill, is the abode of music, letters and thorough culture. The peace of high thinking and simple outdoor life hovers over all.]

One sunny afternoon I was standing in the door of my house, when I marked a person passing close to the edge of the bank that was in front. His pace was a careless and lingering one, and had none of that gracefulness and ease which distinguish a person with certain advantages of education from a clown. His gait was rustic and awkward. His form was ungainly and disproportioned. Shoulders broad and square, breast sunken, his head drooping, his body of uniform breadth, supported by long and lank legs, were the ingredients of his frame. His garb was not ill adapted to such a figure. A slouched hat, tarnished by the weather, a coat of thick gray cloth, cut and wrought, as it seemed, by a country tailor, blue worsted stockings, and shoes fastened by thongs and deeply discolored by dust, which brush had never disturbed, constituted his dress.

There was nothing remarkable in these appearances: they were frequently to be met with on the road and in the harvest-field. I cannot tell why I gazed upon them, on this occasion, with more than ordinary attention, unless it were that such figures were seldom seen by me except on the road or field. This lawn was only traversed by men whose views were directed to the pleasures of the walk or the grandeur of the scenery.

He passed slowly along, frequently pausing, as if to examine the prospect more deliberately, but never turning his eye toward the house, so as to allow me a view of his countenance. Presently he entered a copse at a small distance, and disappeared. My eye followed him while he remained in sight. If his image remained for any duration in my fancy after his departure, it was because no other object occurred sufficient to expel it.

I continued in the same spot for half an hour, vaguely, and by fits, contemplating the image of this wanderer, and drawing from outward appearances those inferences, with respect to the intellectual history of this person, which experience affords us. I reflected on the alliance which commonly subsists between ignorance and the practice of agriculture, and indulged myself in airy speculations as to the influence of progressive knowledge in dissolving this alliance and embodying the dreams of the poets. I asked why the plow and the hoe might not become the trade of every human being, and how this trade might be made conducive to, or at least consistent with, the acquisition of wisdom and eloquence.

Weary with these reflections, I returned to the kitchen to perform some household office. I had usually but one servant, and she was a girl about my own age. I was busy near the chimney, and she was employed near the door of the apartment, when some one knocked. The door was opened by her, and she was immediately addressed with, "Prythee, good girl, canst thou supply a thirsty man with a glass of buttermilk?" She answered that there was none in the house. "Aye, but there is some in the dairy yonder. Thou knowest as well as I, though Hermes never taught thee, that, though every dairy be a house, every house is not a dairy." To this speech, though she understood only a part of it, she replied by repeating her assurances that she had none to give. "Well, then," rejoined the stranger, "for charity's sweet sake, hand me forth a cup of cold water." The girl said she would go to the spring and fetch it. "Nay, give me the cup, and suffer me to help myself. Neither manacled nor lame, I should merit burial in the maw of carrion crows if I laid this task upon thee." She gave him the cup, and he turned to go to the spring.

I listened to this dialogue in silence. The words uttered by the person without affected me as somewhat singular; but what chiefly rendered them remarkable was the tone that accompanied them. It was wholly new. My brother's voice and Pleyel's were musical and energetic. I had fondly imagined that, in this respect, they were surpassed by none. Now my mistake was detected. I cannot pretend to communicate the impression that was made upon me by these accents, or to depict the degree in which force and sweetness were blended in them. They were articulated with a distinctness that was unexampled in my experience. But this was not all. The voice was not only mellifluent and clear, but the emphasis was so just, and the modulation so impassioned, that it seemed as if a heart of stone could not fail of being moved by it. It imparted to me an emotion altogether involuntary and uncontrollable. When he uttered the words, "for charity's sweet sake," I dropped the cloth that I held in my hand; my heart overflowed with sympathy and my eyes with unbidden tears.

This description will appear to you trifling or incredible. The importance of these circumstances will be manifested in the sequel. The manner in which I was affected on this occasion was, to my own apprehension, a subject of astonishment. The tones were indeed such as I never heard before; but that they should in an instant, as it were, dissolve me in tears, will not easily be believed by others, and can scarcely be comprehended by myself.

It will be readily supposed that I was somewhat inquisitive as to the person and demeanor of our visitant. After a moment's pause, I stepped to the door and looked after him. Judge my surprise when I beheld the selfsame figure that had appeared a half-hour before upon the bank. My fancy had conjured up a very different image. A form and attitude and garb were instantly created worthy to accompany such elocution; but this person was, in all visible respects, the reverse of this phantom. Strange as it may seem, I could not speedily reconcile myself to this disappointment. Instead of returning to my employment, I threw myself in a chair that was placed opposite the door, and sunk into a fit of musing.

My attention was in a few minutes recalled by the stranger, who returned with the empty cup in his hand. I had not thought of the circumstance, or should certainly have chosen a different seat. He no sooner showed himself, than a confused sense of impropriety, added to the suddenness of the interview, for which, not having foreseen it, I had made no preparation, threw me into a state of the most painful embarrassment. He brought with him a placid brow; but no sooner had he cast his eyes upon me than his face was as glowingly suffused as my own. He placed the cup upon the bench, stammered out thanks, and retired.

It was some time before I could recover my wonted composure. I had snatched a view of the stranger's countenance. The impression that it made was vivid and indelible. His cheeks were pallid and lank, his eyes sunken, his forehead overshadowed by coarse straggling hairs, his teeth large and irregular, though sound and brilliantly white, and his chin discolored by a tetter. His skin was of coarse grain and sallow hue. Every feature was wide of beauty, and the outline of his face reminded you of an inverted cone.

And yet his forehead, so far as shaggy locks would allow it to be seen, his eyes lustrously black, and possessing, in the midst of haggardness, a radiance inexpressibly serene and potent, and something in the rest of his features which it would be in vain to describe, but which served to betoken a mind of the highest order, were essential ingredients in the portrait. This, in the effects which immediately flowed from it, I count among the most extraordinary incidents of my life. This face, seen for a moment, continued for hours to occupy my fancy, to the exclusion of almost every other image. I had proposed to spend the evening with my brother; but I could not resist the inclination of forming a sketch upon paper of this memorable visage. Whether my hand was aided by any peculiar inspiration, or I was deceived by my own fond conceptions, this portrait, though hastily executed, appeared unexceptionable to my own taste.

I placed it at all distances and in all lights; my eyes were riveted upon it. Half the night passed away in wakefulness and in contemplation of this picture. So flexible, and yet so stubborn, is the human mind! So obedient to impulses the most transient and brief, and yet so unalterably observant of the direction which is given to it! How little did I then foresee the termination of that chain of which this may be regarded as the first link!

Next day arose in darkness and storm. Torrents of rain fell during the whole day, attended with incessant thunder, which reverberated in stunning echoes from the opposite declivity. The inclemency of the air would not allow me to walk out. I had, indeed, no inclination to leave my apartment. I betook myself to the contemplation of this portrait, whose attractions time had rather enhanced than diminished. I laid aside my usual occupations, and, seating myself at a window, consumed the day in alternately looking out upon the storm and gazing at the picture which lay upon a table before me. You will perhaps deem this conduct somewhat singular, and ascribe it to certain peculiarities of temper. I am not aware of any such peculiarities. I can account for my devotion to this image no otherwise than by supposing that its properties were rare and prodigious. Perhaps you will suspect that such were the first inroads of a passion incident to every female heart, and which frequently gains a footing by means even more slight and more improbable than these. I shall not controvert the reasonableness of the suspicion, but leave you at liberty to draw from my narrative what conclusions you please.

Night at length returned, and the storm ceased. The air was once more clear and calm, and bore an affecting contrast to that uproar of the elements by which it had been preceded. I spent the darksome hours, as I spent the day, contemplative and seated at the window. Why was my mind absorbed in thoughts ominous and dreary? Why did my bosom heave with sighs and my eyes overflow with tears? Was the tempest that had just passed a signal of the ruin which impended over me? My soul fondly dwelt upon the images of my brother and his children; yet they only increased the mournfulness of my contemplations. The smiles of the charming babes were as bland as formerly. The same dignity sat on the brow of their father, and yet I thought of them with anguish. Something whispered that the happiness we at present enjoyed was set on mutable foundations. Death must happen to all. Whether our felicity was to be subverted by it to-morrow, or whether it was ordained that we should lay down our heads full of years and of honor, was a question that no human being could solve. At other times these ideas seldom intruded. I either forbore to reflect upon the destiny that is reserved for all men, or the reflection was mixed up with images that disrobed it of terror; but now the uncertainty of life occurred to me without any of its usual and alleviating accompaniments. I said to myself, We must die. Sooner or later, we must disappear forever from the face of the earth. Whatever be the links that hold us to life, they must be broken. This scene of existence is, in all its parts, calamitous. The greater number is oppressed with immediate evils, and those the tide of whose fortunes is full, how small is their portion of enjoyment, since they know that it will terminate!

For some time I indulged myself, without reluctance, in these gloomy thoughts; but at length the delection which they produced became insupportably painful. I endeavored to dissipate it with music. I had all my grandfather's melody as well as poetry by rote. I now lighted by chance on a ballad which commemorated the fate of a German cavalier who fell at the siege of Nice under Godfrey of Bouillon. My choice was unfortunate; for the scenes of violence and carnage which were here wildly but forcibly portrayed only suggested to my thoughts a new topic in the horrors of war.

I sought refuge, but ineffectually, in sleep. My mind was thronged by vivid but confused images, and no effort that I made was sufficient to drive them away. In this situation I heard the clock, which hung in the room, give the signal for twelve. It was the same instrument which formerly hung in my father's chamber, and which, on account of its being his workmanship, was regarded by everyone of our family with veneration. It had fallen to me in the division of his property, and was placed in this asylum. The sound awakened a series of reflections respecting his death. I was not allowed to pursue them; for scarcely had the vibrations ceased, when my attention was attracted by a whisper, which, at first, appeared to proceed from lips that were laid close to my ear.

No wonder that a circumstance like this startled me. In the first impulse of my terror, I uttered a slight scream and shrunk to the opposite side of the bed. In a moment, however, I recovered from my trepidation. I was habitually indifferent to all the causes of fear by which the majority are afflicted. I entertained no apprehension of either ghosts or robbers. Our security had never been molested by either, and I made use of no means to prevent or counterwork their machinations. My tranquillity on this occasion was quickly retrieved. The whisper evidently proceeded from one who was posted at my bedside. The first idea that suggested itself was that it was uttered by the girl who lived with me as a servant. Perhaps somewhat had alarmed her, or she was sick, and had come to request my assistance. By whispering in my ear she intended to rouse without alarming me.

Full of this persuasion, I called, "Judith, is it you? What do you want? Is there anything the matter with you?" No answer was returned. I repeated my inquiry, but equally in vain. Cloudy as was the atmosphere, and curtained as my bed was, nothing was visible. I withdrew the curtain, and, leaning my head on my elbow, I listened with the deepest attention to catch some new sound. Meanwhile, I ran over in my thoughts every circumstance that could assist my conjectures.

My habitation was a wooden edifice, consisting of two stories. In each story were two rooms, separated by an entry, or middle passage, with which they communicated by opposite doors. The passage on the lower story had doors at the two ends, and a staircase. Windows answered to the doors on the upper story. Annexed to this, on the eastern side, were wings, divided in like manner into an upper and lower room; one of them comprised a kitchen, and chamber above it for the servant, and communicated on both stories with the parlor adjoining it below and the chamber adjoining it above. The opposite wing is of smaller dimensions, the rooms not being above eight feet square. The lower of these was used as a depository of household implements; the upper was a closet in which I deposited my books and papers. They had but one inlet, which was from the room adjoining. There was no window in the lower one, and in the upper a small aperture which communicated light and air, but would scarcely admit the body. The door which led into this was close to my bed head, and was always locked but when I myself was within. The avenues below were accustomed to be closed and bolted at nights.

The maid was my only companion; and she could not reach my chamber without previously passing through the opposite chamber and the middle passage, of which, however, the doors were usually unfastened. If she had occasioned this noise, she would have answered my repeated calls. No other conclusion, therefore, was left me, but that I had mistaken the sounds, and that my imagination had transformed some casual noise into the voice of a human creature. Satisfied with this solution, I was preparing to relinquish my listening attitude, when my ear was again saluted with a new and yet louder whispering. It appeared, as before, to issue from lips that touched my pillow. A second effort of attention, however, clearly showed me that the sounds issued from within the closet, the door of which was not more than eight inches from my pillow.

This second interruption occasioned a shock less vehement than the former. I started, but gave no audible token of alarm. I was so much mistress of my feelings as to continue listening to what should be said. The whisper was distinct, hoarse, and uttered so as to show that the speaker was desirous of being heard by some one near, but, at the same time, studious to avoid being overheard by any other: –

"Stop! stop, I say, madman as you are! there are better means than that. Curse upon your rashness! There is no need to shoot."

Such were the words uttered, in a tone of eagerness and anger, within so small a distance of my pillow. What construction could I put upon them? My heart began to palpitate with dread of some unknown danger. Presently, another voice, but equally near me, was heard whispering in answer, "Why not? I will draw a trigger in this business; but perdition be my lot if I do more!" To this the first voice returned, in a tone which rage had heightened in a small degree above a whisper, "Coward! stand aside, and see me do it. I will grasp her throat; I will do her business in an instant; she shall not have time so much as to groan." What wonder that I was petrified by sounds so dreadful! Murderers lurked in my closet. They were planning the means of my destruction. One resolved to shoot, and the other menaced suffocation. Their means being chosen, they would forthwith break the door. Flight instantly suggested itself as most eligible in circumstances so perilous. I deliberated not a moment; but, fear adding wings to my speed, I leaped out of bed, and, scantily robed as I was, rushed out of the chamber, downstairs, and into the open air. I can hardly recollect the process of turning keys and withdrawing bolts. My terrors urged me forward with almost a mechanical impulse. I stopped not till I reached my brother's door. I had not gained the threshold, when, exhausted by the violence of my emotions and by my speed, I sunk down in a fit.

How long I remained in this situation I know not. When I recovered, I found myself stretched on a bed, surrounded by my sister and her female servants. I was astonished at the scene before me, but gradually recovered the recollection of what had happened. I answered their importunate inquiries as well as I was able. My brother and Pleyel, whom the storm of the preceding day chanced to detain here, informing themselves of every particular, proceeded with lights and weapons to my deserted habitation. They entered my chamber and my closet, and found everything in its proper place and customary order. The door of the closet was locked, and appeared not to have been opened in my absence. They went to Judith's apartment. They found her asleep and in safety. Pleyel's caution induced him to forbear alarming the girl; and, finding her wholly ignorant of what had passed, they directed her to return to her chamber. They then fastened the doors and returned.

My friends were disposed to regard this transaction as a dream. That persons should be actually immured in this closet, to which, in the circumstances of the time, access from without or within was apparently impossible, they could not seriously believe. That any human beings had intended murder, unless it were to cover a scheme of pillage, was incredible; but that no such design had been formed was evident from the security in which the furniture of the house and the closet remained.

I revolved every incident and expression that had occurred. My senses assured me of the truth of them; and yet their abruptness and improbability made me, in my turn, somewhat incredulous. The adventure had made a deep impression on my fancy; and it was not till after a week's abode at my brother's that I resolved to resume the possession of my own dwelling.

There was another circumstance that enhanced the mysteriousness of this event. After my recovery, it was obvious to inquire by what means the attention of the family had been drawn to my situation. I had fallen before I had reached the threshold or was able to give any signal. My brother related that, while this was transacting in my chamber, he himself was awake, in consequence of some slight indisposition, and lay, according to his custom, musing on some favorite topic. Suddenly the silence, which was remarkably profound, was broken by a voice of most piercing shrillness, that seemed to be uttered by one in the hall below his chamber. "Awake! arise!" it exclaimed; "hasten to succor one that is dying at your door!"

This summons was effectual. There was no one in the house who was not roused by it. Pleyel was the first to obey, and my brother overtook him before he reached the hall. What was the general astonishment when your friend was discovered stretched upon the grass before the door, pale, ghastly, and with every mark of death!

But how was I to regard this midnight conversation? Hoarse and manlike voices conferring on the means of death, so near my bed, and at such an hour! How had my ancient security vanished! That dwelling which had hitherto been an inviolate asylum was now beset with danger to my life. That solitude formerly so dear to me could no longer be endured. Pleyel, who had consented to reside with us during the months of spring, lodged in the vacant chamber, in order to quiet my alarms. He treated my fears with ridicule, and in a short time very slight traces of them remained; but, as it was wholly indifferent to him whether his nights were passed at my house or at my brother's, this arrangement gave general satisfaction.

II

I will enumerate the various inquiries and conjectures which these incidents occasioned. After all our efforts, we came no nearer to dispelling the mist in which they were involved; and time, instead of facilitating a solution, only accumulated our doubts.

In the midst of thoughts excited by these events, I was not unmindful of my interview with the stranger. I related the particulars, and showed the portrait to my friends. Pleyel recollected to have met with a figure resembling my description in the city; but neither his face or garb made the same impression upon him that it made upon me. It was a hint to rally me upon my prepossessions, and to amuse us with a thousand ludicrous anecdotes which he had collected in his travels. He made no scruple to charge me with being in love; and threatened to inform the swain, when he met him, of his good fortune.

Pleyel's temper made him susceptible of no durable impressions. His conversation was occasionally visited by gleams of his ancient vivacity; but, though his impetuosity was sometimes inconvenient, there was nothing to dread from his malice. I had no fear that my character or dignity would suffer in his hands, and was not heartily displeased when he declared his intention of profiting by his first meeting with the stranger to introduce him to our acquaintance.

Some weeks after this I had spent a toilsome day, and, as the sun declined, found myself disposed to seek relief in a walk. The river bank is, at this part of it and for some considerable space upward, so rugged and steep as not to be easily descended. In a recess of this declivity, near the southern verge of my little demesne, was placed a slight building, with seats and lattices. From a crevice of the rock to which this edifice was attached there burst forth a stream of the purest water, which, leaping from ledge to ledge for the space of sixty feet, produced a freshness in the air, and a murmur, the most delicious and soothing imaginable. These, added to the odors of the cedars which embowered it, and of the honeysuckle which clustered among the lattices, rendered this my favorite retreat in summer.

On this occasion I repaired hither. My spirits drooped through the fatigue of long attention, and I threw myself upon a bench, in a state, both mentally and personally, of the utmost supineness. The lulling sounds of the waterfall, the fragrance, and the dusk, combined to becalm my spirits, and, in a short time, to sink me into sleep. Either the uneasiness of my posture, or some slight indisposition, molested my repose with dreams of no cheerful hue. After various incoherences had taken their turn to occupy my fancy, I at length imagined myself walking, in the evening twilight, to my brother's habitation. A pit, methought, had been dug in the path I had taken, of which I was not aware. As I carelessly pursued my walk, I thought I saw my brother standing at some distance before me, beckoning and calling me to make haste. He stood on the opposite edge of the gulf. I mended my pace, and one step more would have plunged me into this abyss, had not some one from behind caught suddenly my arm, and exclaimed, in a voice of eagerness and terror, "Hold! hold!"

The sound broke my sleep, and I found myself, at the next moment, standing on my feet, and surrounded by the deepest darkness. Images so terrific and forcible disabled me for a time from distinguishing between sleep and wakefulness, and withheld from me the knowledge of my actual condition. My first panic was succeeded by the perturbations of surprise to find myself alone in the open air and immersed in so deep a gloom. I slowly recollected the incidents of the afternoon, and how I came hither. I could not estimate the time, but saw the propriety of returning with speed to the house. My faculties were still too confused, and the darkness too intense, to allow me immediately to find my way up the steep. I sat down, therefore, to recover myself, and to reflect upon my situation.

This was no sooner done, than a low voice was heard from behind the lattice, on the side where I sat. Between the rock and the lattice was a chasm not wide enough to admit a human body; yet in this chasm he that spoke appeared to be stationed. "Attend! attend! but be not terrified."

I started, and exclaimed, "Good heavens! what is that? Who are you?"

"A friend; one come not to injure but to save you: fear nothing."

This voice was immediately recognized to be the same with one of those which I had heard in the closet; it was the voice of him who had proposed to shoot rather than to strangle his victim. My terror made me at once mute and motionless. He continued, "I leagued to murder you. I repent. Mark my bidding, and be safe. Avoid this spot. The snares of death encompass it. Elsewhere danger will be distant; but this spot, shun it as you value your life. Mark me further: profit by this warning, but divulge it not. If a syllable of what has passed escape you, your doom is sealed. Remember your father, and be faithful."

Here the accents ceased, and left me overwhelmed with dismay. I was fraught with the persuasion that during every moment I remained here my life was endangered; but I could not take a step without hazard of falling to the bottom of the precipice. The path leading to the summit was short, but rugged and intricate. Even starlight was excluded by the umbrage, and not the faintest gleam was afforded to guide my steps. What should I do? To depart or remain was equally and eminently perilous.

In this state of uncertainty, I perceived a ray flit across the gloom and disappear. Another succeeded, which was stronger, and remained for a passing moment. It glittered on the shrubs that were scattered at the entrance, and gleam continued to succeed gleam for a few seconds, till they finally gave place to unintermitted darkness.

The first visitings of this light called up a train of horrors in my mind; destruction impended over this spot; the voice which I had lately heard had warned me to retire, and had menaced me with the fate of my father if I refused. I was desirous, but unable to obey; these gleams were such as preluded the stroke by which he fell; the hour, perhaps, was the same. I shuddered as if I had beheld suspended over me the exterminating sword.

Presently a new and stronger illumination burst through the lattice on the right hand, and a voice from the edge of the precipice above called out my name. It was Pleyel. Joyfully did I recognize his accents; but such was the tumult of my thoughts that I had not power to answer him till he had frequently repeated his summons. I hurried at length from the fatal spot, and, directed by the lantern which he bore, ascended the hill.

Pale and breathless, it was with difficulty I could support myself. He anxiously inquired into the cause of my affright and the motive of my unusual absence. He had returned from my brother's at a late hour, and was informed by Judith that I had walked out before sunset and had not yet returned. This intelligence was somewhat alarming. He waited some time; but, my absence continuing, he had set out in search of me. He had explored the neighborhood with the utmost care, but, receiving no tidings of me, he was preparing to acquaint my brother with this circumstance, when he recollected the summer-house on the bank, and conceived it possible that some accident had detained me there. He again inquired into the cause of this detention, and of that confusion and dismay which my looks testified.

I told him that I had strolled hither in the afternoon, that sleep had overtaken me as I sat, and that I had awakened a few minutes before his arrival. I could tell him no more. In the present impetuosity of my thoughts, I was almost dubious whether the pit into which my brother had endeavored to entice me, and the voice that talked through the lattice, were not parts of the same dream. I remembered, likewise, the charge of secrecy, and the penalty denounced if I should rashly divulge what I had heard. For these reasons I was silent on that subject, and, shutting myself in my chamber, delivered myself up to contemplation.

What I have related will, no doubt, appear to you a fable. You will believe that calamity has subverted my reason, and that I am amusing you with the chimeras of my brain instead of facts that have really happened. I shall not be surprised or offended if these be your suspicions. I know not, indeed, how you can deny them admission. For, if to me, the immediate witness, they were fertile of perplexity and doubt, how must they affect another to whom they are recommended only by my testimony? It was only by subsequent events that I was fully and incontestably assured of the veracity of my senses.

Meanwhile, what was I to think? I had been assured that a design had been formed against my life. The ruffians had leagued to murder me. Whom had I offended? Who was there, with whom I had ever maintained intercourse, who was capable of harboring such atrocious purposes?

My temper was the reverse of cruel and imperious. My heart was touched with sympathy for the children of misfortune. But this sympathy was not a barren sentiment. My purse, scanty as it was, was ever open, and my hands ever active, to relieve distress. Many were the wretches whom my personal exertions had extricated from want and disease, and who rewarded me with their gratitude. There was no face which lowered at my approach, and no lips which uttered imprecations in my hearing. On the contrary, there was none, over whose fate I had exerted any influence or to whom I was known by reputation, who did not greet me with smiles and dismiss me with proofs of veneration: yet did not my senses assure me that a plot was laid against my life?

I am not destitute of courage. I have shown myself deliberative and calm in the midst of peril. I have hazarded my own life for the preservation of another; but now was I confused and panic- struck. I have not lived so as to fear death; yet to perish by an unseen and secret stroke, to be mangled by the knife of an assassin, was a thought at which I shuddered: what had I done to deserve to be made the victim of malignant passions?

But soft! was I not assured that my life was safe in all places but one? And why was the treason limited to take effect in this spot? I was everywhere equally defenseless. My house and chamber were at all times accessible. Danger still impended over me; the bloody purpose was still entertained, but the hand that was to execute it was powerless in all places but one!

Here I had remained for the last four or five hours, without the means of resistance or defense; yet I had not been attacked. A human being was at hand, who was conscious of my presence, and warned me hereafter to avoid this retreat. His voice was not absolutely new, but had I never heard it but once before? But why did he prohibit me from relating this incident to others, and what species of death will be awarded if I disobey?

Such were the reflections that haunted me during the night, and which effectually deprived me of sleep. Next morning, at breakfast, Pleyel related an event which my disappearance had hindered him from mentioning the night before. Early the preceding morning, his occasions called him to the city: he had stepped into a coffee-house to while away an hour; here he had met a person whose appearance instantly bespoke him to be the same whose hasty visit I have mentioned, and whose extraordinary visage and tones had so powerfully affected me. On an attentive survey, however, he proved, likewise, to be one with whom my friend had had some intercourse in Europe. This authorized the liberty of accosting him, and after some conversation, mindful, as Pleyel said, of the footing which this stranger had gained in my heart, he had ventured to invite him to Mettingen. The invitation had been cheerfully accepted, and a visit promised on the afternoon of the next day.

This information excited no sober emotions in my breast. I was, of course, eager to be informed as to the circumstances of their ancient intercourse. When and where had they met? What knew he of the life and character of this man?

In answer to my inquiries, he informed me that, three years before, he was a traveler in Spain. He had made an excursion from Valencia to Murviedro, with a view to inspect the remains of Roman magnificence scattered in the environs of that town. While traversing the site of the theater of old Saguntum, he alighted upon this man, seated on a stone, and deeply engaged in perusing the work of the deacon Marti. A short conversation ensued, which proved the stranger to be English. They returned to Valencia together.

His garb, aspect, and deportment were wholly Spanish. A residence of three years in the country, indefatigable attention to the language, and a studious conformity with the customs of the people, had made him indistinguishable from a native when he chose to assume that character. Pleyel found him to be connected, on the footing of friendship and respect, with many eminent merchants in that city. He had embraced the Catholic religion, and adopted a Spanish name instead of his own, which was CARWIN, and devoted himself to the literature and religion of his new country. He pursued no profession, but subsisted on remittances from England.

While Pleyel remained in Valencia, Carwin betrayed no aversion to intercourse, and the former found no small attractions in the society of this new acquaintance, On general topics he was highly intelligent and communicative. He had visited every corner of Spain, and could furnish the most accurate details respecting its ancient and present state. On topics of religion and of his own history, previous to his TRANSFORMATION into a Spaniard, he was invariably silent. You could merely gather from his discourse that he was English, and that he was well acquainted with the neighboring countries.

His character excited considerable curiosity in the observer. It was not easy to reconcile his conversion to the Romish faith with those proofs of knowledge and capacity that were exhibited by him on different occasions. A suspicion was sometimes admitted that his belief was counterfeited for some political purpose. The most careful observation, however, produced no discovery. His manners were at all times harmless and inartificial, and his habits those of a lover of contemplation and seclusion. He appeared to have contracted an affection for Pleyel, who was not slow to return it.

My friend, after a month's residence in this city, returned into France, and, since that period, had heard nothing concerning Carwin till his appearance at Mettingen.

On this occasion Carwin had received Pleyel's greeting with a certain distance and solemnity to which the latter had not been accustomed. He had waived noticing the inquiries of Pleyel respecting his desertion of Spain, in which he had formerly declared that it was his purpose to spend his life. He had assiduously diverted the attention of the latter to indifferent topics, but was still, on every theme, as eloquent and judicious as formerly. Why he had assumed the garb of a rustic Pleyel was unable to conjecture. Perhaps it might be poverty; perhaps he was swayed by motives which it was his interest to conceal, but which were connected with consequences of the utmost moment.

Such was the sum of my friend's information. I was not sorry to be left alone during the greater part of this day. Every employment was irksome which did not leave me at liberty to meditate. I had now a new subject on which to exercise my thoughts. Before evening I should be ushered into his presence, and listen to those tones whose magical and thrilling power I had already experienced. But with what new images would he then be accompanied?

Carwin was an adherent to the Romish faith, yet was an Englishman by birth, and, perhaps, a Protestant by education. He had adopted Spain for his country, and had intimated a design to spend his days there, yet now was an inhabitant of this district, and disguised by the habiliments of a clown! What could have obliterated the impressions of his youth and made him abjure his religion and his country? What subsequent events had introduced so total a change in his plans? In withdrawing from Spain, had he reverted to the religion of his ancestors? or was it true that his former conversion was deceitful, and that his conduct had been swayed by motives which it was prudent to conceal?

Hours were consumed in revolving these ideas. My meditations were intense; and, when the series was broken, I began to reflect with astonishment on my situation. From the death of my parents till the commencement of this year my life had been serene and blissful beyond the ordinary portion of humanity; but now my bosom was corroded by anxiety. I was visited by dread of unknown dangers, and the future was a scene over which clouds rolled and thunders muttered. I compared the cause with the effect, and they seemed disproportioned to each other. All unaware, and in a manner which I had no power to explain, I was pushed from my immovable and lofty station and cast upon a sea of troubles.

I determined to be my brother's visitant on this evening; yet my resolves were not unattended with wavering and reluctance. Pleyel's insinuations that I was in love affected in no degree my belief; yet the consciousness that this was the opinion of one who would probably be present at our introduction to each other would excite all that confusion which the passion itself is apt to produce. This would confirm him in his error and call forth new railleries. His mirth, when exerted upon this topic, was the source of the bitterest vexation. Had he been aware of its influence upon my happiness, his temper would not have allowed him to persist; but this influence it was my chief endeavor to conceal. That the belief of my having bestowed my heart upon another produced in my friend none but ludicrous sensations was the true cause of my distress; but if this had been discovered by him my distress would have been unspeakably aggravated.

III

As soon as evening arrived, I performed my visit. Carwin made one of the company into which I was ushered. Appearances were the same as when I before beheld him. His garb was equally negligent and rustic. I gazed upon his countenance with new curiosity. My situation was such as to enable me to bestow upon it a deliberate examination. Viewed at more leisure, it lost none of its wonderful properties. I could not deny my homage to the intelligence expressed in it, but was wholly uncertain whether he were an object to be dreaded or adored, and whether his powers had been exerted to evil or to good.

He was sparing in discourse; but whatever he said was pregnant with meaning, and uttered with rectitude of articulation and force of emphasis of which I had entertained no conception previously to my knowledge of him. Notwithstanding the uncouthness of his garb, his manners were not unpolished. All topics were handled by him with skill, and without pedantry or affectation. He uttered no sentiment calculated to produce a disadvantageous impression; on the contrary, his observations denoted a mind alive to every generous and heroic feeling. They were introduced without parade, and accompanied with that degree of earnestness which indicates sincerity.

He parted from us not till late, refusing an invitation to spend the night here, but readily consented to repeat his visit. His visits were frequently repeated. Each day introduced us to a more intimate acquaintance with his sentiments, but left us wholly in the dark concerning that about which we were most inquisitive. He studiously avoided all mention of his past or present situation. Even the place of his abode in the city he concealed from us.

Our sphere in this respect being somewhat limited, and the intellectual endowments of this man being indisputably great, his deportment was more diligently marked and copiously commented on by us than you, perhaps, will think the circumstances warranted. Not a gesture, or glance, or accent, that was not, in our private assemblies, discussed, and inferences deduced from it. It may well be thought that he modeled his behavior by an uncommon standard, when, with all our opportunities and accuracy of observation, we were able for a long time to gather no satisfactory information. He afforded us no ground on which to build even a plausible conjecture.

There is a degree of familiarity which takes place between constant associates, that justifies the negligence of many rules of which, in an earlier period of their intercourse, politeness requires the exact observance. Inquiries into our condition are allowable when they are prompted by a disinterested concern for our welfare; and this solicitude is not only pardonable, but may justly be demanded from those who choose us for their companions. This state of things was more slow to arrive at on this occasion than on most others, on account of the gravity and loftiness of this man's behavior.

Pleyel, however, began at length to employ regular means for this end. He occasionally alluded to the circumstances in which they had formerly met, and remarked the incongruousness between the religion and habits of a Spaniard with those of a native of Britain. He expressed his astonishment at meeting our guest in this corner of the globe, especially as, when they parted in Spain, he was taught to believe that Carwin should never leave that country. He insinuated that a change so great must have been prompted by motives of a singular and momentous kind.

No answer, or an answer wide of the purpose, was generally made to these insinuations. Britons and Spaniards, he said, are votaries of the same Deity, and square their faith by the same precepts; their ideas are drawn from the same fountains of literature, and they speak dialects of the same tongue; their government and laws have more resemblances than differences; they were formerly provinces of the same civil, and, till lately, of the same religious, empire.

As to the motives which induce men to change the place of their abode, these must unavoidably be fleeting and mutable. If not bound to one spot by conjugal or parental ties, or by the nature of that employment to which we are indebted for subsistence, the inducements to change are far more numerous and powerful than opposite inducements.

He spoke as if desirous of showing that he was not aware of the tendency of Pleyel's remarks; yet certain tokens were apparent that proved him by no means wanting in penetration. These tokens were to be read in his countenance, and not in his words. When anything was said indicating curiosity in us, the gloom of his countenance was deepened, his eyes sunk to the ground, and his wonted air was not resumed without visible struggle. Hence, it was obvious to infer that some incidents of his life were reflected on by him with regret; and that, since these incidents were carefully concealed, and even that regret which flowed from them laboriously stifled, they had not been merely disastrous. The secrecy that was observed appeared not designed to provoke or baffle the inquisitive, but was prompted by the shame or by the prudence of guilt.

These ideas, which were adopted by Pleyel and my brother as well as myself, hindered us from employing more direct means for accomplishing our wishes. Questions might have been put in such terms that no room should be left for the pretense of misapprehension; and, if modesty merely had been the obstacle, such questions would not have been wanting; but we considered that, if the disclosure were productive of pain or disgrace, it was inhuman to extort it.

Amidst the various topics that were discussed in his presence, allusions were, of course, made to the inexplicable events that had lately happened. At those times the words and looks of this man were objects of my particular attention. The subject was extraordinary; and anyone whose experience or reflections could throw any light upon it was entitled to my gratitude. As this man was enlightened by reading and travel, I listened with eagerness to the remarks which he should make.

At first I entertained a kind of apprehension that the tale would be heard by him with incredulity and secret ridicule. I had formerly heard stories that resembled this in some of their mysterious circumstances; but they were commonly heard by me with contempt. I was doubtful whether the same impression would not now be made on the mind of our guest; but I was mistaken in my fears.

He heard them with seriousness, and without any marks either of surprise or incredulity. He pursued with visible pleasure that kind of disquisition which was naturally suggested by them. His fancy was eminently vigorous and prolific; and, if he did not persuade us that human beings are sometimes admitted to a sensible intercourse with the Author of nature, he at least won over our inclination to the cause. He merely deduced, from his own reasonings, that such intercourse was probable, but confessed that, though he was acquainted with many instances somewhat similar to those which had been related by us, none of them were perfectly exempted from the suspicion of human agency.

On being requested to relate these instances, he amused us with many curious details. His narratives were constructed with so much skill, and rehearsed with so much energy, that all the effects of a dramatic exhibition were frequently produced by them. Those that were most coherent and most minute, and, of consequence, least entitled to credit, were yet rendered probable by the exquisite art of this rhetorician. For every difficulty that was suggested a ready and plausible solution was furnished.

Mysterious voices had always a share in producing the catastrophe; but they were always to be explained on some known principles, either as reflected into a focus or communicated through a tube. I could not but remark that his narratives, however complex or marvelous, contained no instance sufficiently parallel to those that had befallen ourselves, and in which the solution was applicable to our own case.

My brother was a much more sanguine reasoner than our guest. Even in some of the facts which were related by Carwin, he maintained the probability of celestial interference, when the latter was disposed to deny it, and had found, as he imagined, footsteps of a human agent. Pleyel was by no means equally credulous. He scrupled not to deny faith to any testimony but that of his senses, and allowed the facts which had lately been supported by this testimony not to mold his belief, but merely to give birth to doubts.

It was soon observed that Carwin adopted, in some degree, a similar distinction. A tale of this kind, related by others, he would believe, provided it was explicable upon known principles; but that such notices were actually communicated by beings of a higher order he would believe only when his own ears were assailed in a manner which could not be otherwise accounted for. Civility forbade him to contradict my brother or myself, but his understanding refused to acquiesce in our testimony. Besides, he was disposed to question whether the voices were not really uttered by human organs. On this supposition he was desired to explain how the effect was produced.

He answered that the cry for help, heard in the hall on the night of my adventure, was to be ascribed to a human creature, who actually stood in the hall when he uttered it. It was of no moment, he said, that we could not explain by what motives he that made the signal was led hither. How imperfectly acquainted were we with the condition and designs of the beings that surrounded us! The city was near at hand, and thousands might there exist whose powers and purposes might easily explain whatever was mysterious in this transaction. As to the closet dialogue, he was obliged to adopt one of two suppositions, and affirm either that it was fashioned in my own fancy, or that it actually took place between two persons in the closet.

Such was Carwin's mode of explaining these appearances. It is such, perhaps, as would commend itself as most plausible to the most sagacious minds; but it was insufficient to impart conviction to us. As to the treason that was meditated against me, it was doubtless just to conclude that it was either real or imaginary; but that it was real was attested by the mysterious warning in the summer-house, the secret of which I had hitherto locked up in my own breast.

A month passed away in this kind of intercourse. As to Carwin, our ignorance was in no degree enlightened respecting his genuine character and views. Appearances were uniform. No man possessed a larger store of knowledge, or a greater degree of skill in the communication of it to others; hence he was regarded as an inestimable addition to our society. Considering the distance of my brother's house from the city, he was frequently prevailed upon to pass the night where he spent the evening. Two days seldom elapsed without a visit from him; hence he was regarded as a kind of inmate of the house. He entered and departed without ceremony. When he arrived he received an unaffected welcome, and when he chose to retire no importunities were used to induce him to remain.

Carwin never parted with his gravity. The inscrutableness of his character, and the uncertainty whether his fellowship tended to good or to evil, were seldom absent from our minds. This circumstance powerfully contributed to sadden us.

My heart was the seat of growing disquietudes. This change in one who had formerly been characterized by all the exuberances of soul could not fail to be remarked by my friends. My brother was always a pattern of solemnity. My sister was clay, molded by the circumstances in which she happened to be placed. There was but one whose deportment remains to be described as being of importance to our happiness. Had Pleyel likewise dismissed his vivacity?

He was as whimsical and jestful as ever, but he was not

happy. The truth in this respect was of too much importance to me not to make me a vigilant observer. His mirth was easily perceived to be the fruit of exertion. When his thoughts wandered from the company, an air of dissatisfaction and impatience stole across his features. Even the punctuality and frequency of his visits were somewhat lessened. It may be supposed that my own uneasiness was heightened by these tokens; but, strange as it may seem, I found, in the present state of my mind, no relief but in the persuasion that Pleyel was unhappy.

That unhappiness, indeed, depended for its value in my eyes on the cause that produced it. There was but one source whence it could flow. A nameless ecstasy thrilled through my frame when any new proof occurred that the ambiguousness of my behavior was the cause.

IV

My brother had received a new book from Germany. It was a tragedy, and the first attempt of a Saxon poet of whom my brother had been taught to entertain the highest expectations. The exploits of Zisca, the Bohemian hero, were woven into a dramatic series and connection. According to German custom, it was minute and diffuse, and dictated by an adventurous and lawless fancy. It was a chain of audacious acts and unheard-of disasters. The moated fortress and the thicket, the ambush and the battle, and the conflict of headlong passions, were portrayed in wild numbers and with terrific energy. An afternoon was set apart to rehearse this performance. The language was familiar to all of us but Carwin, whose company, therefore, was tacitly dispensed with.

The morning previous to this intended rehearsal I spent at home. My mind was occupied with reflections relative to my own situation. The sentiment which lived with chief energy in my heart was connected with the image of Pleyel. In the midst of my anguish, I had not been destitute of consolation. His late deportment had given spring to my hopes. Was not the hour at hand which should render me the happiest of human creatures? He suspected that I looked with favorable eyes upon Carwin. Hence arose disquietudes which he struggled in vain to conceal. He loved me, but was hopeless that his love would be compensated. Is it not time, said I, to rectify this error? But by what means is this to be effected? It can only be done by a change of deportment in me; but how must I demean myself for this purpose?

I must not speak. Neither eyes nor lips must impart the information. He must not be assured that my heart is his, previous to the tender of his own; but he must be convinced that it has not been given to another; he must be supplied with space whereon to build a doubt as to the true state of my affections; he must be prompted to avow himself. The line of delicate propriety, – how hard it is not to fall short, and not to overleap it!

This afternoon we shall meet. . . . We shall not separate till late. It will be his province to accompany me home. The airy expanse is without a speck. This breeze is usually steadfast, and its promise of a bland and cloudless evening may be trusted. The moon will rise at eleven, and at that hour we shall wind along this bank. Possibly that hour may decide my fate. If suitable encouragement be given, Pleyel will reveal his soul to me; and I, ere I reach this threshold, will be made the happiest of beings.

And is this good to be mine? Add wings to thy speed, sweet evening; and thou, moon, I charge thee, shroud thy beams at the moment when my Pleyel whispers love. I would not for the world that the burning blushes and the mounting raptures of that moment should be visible.

But what encouragement is wanting? I must be regardful of insurmountable limits. Yet, when minds are imbued with a genuine sympathy, are not words and looks superfluous? Are not motion and touch sufficient to impart feelings such as mine? Has he not eyed me at moments when the pressure of his hand has thrown me into tumults, and was it impossible that he mistook the impetuosities of love for the eloquence of indignation?

But the hastening evening will decide. Would it were come! And yet I shudder at its near approach. An interview that must thus terminate is surely to be wished for by me; and yet it is not without its terrors. Would to heaven it were come and gone!

I feel no reluctance, my friends, to be thus explicit. Time was, when these emotions would be hidden with immeasurable solicitude from every human eye. Alas! these airy and fleeting impulses of shame are gone. My scruples were preposterous and criminal. They are bred in all hearts by a perverse and vicious education, and they would still have maintained their place in my heart, had not my portion been set in misery. My errors have taught me thus much wisdom: – that those sentiments which we ought not to disclose it is criminal to harbor.

It was proposed to begin the rehearsal at four o'clock. I counted the minutes as they passed; their flight was at once too rapid and too slow: my sensations were of an excruciating kind; I could taste no food, nor apply to any task, nor enjoy a moment's repose; when the hour arrived I hastened to my brother's.

Pleyel was not there. He had not yet come. On ordinary occasions he was eminent for punctuality. He had testified great eagerness to share in the pleasures of this rehearsal. He was to divide the task with my brother, and in tasks like these he always engaged with peculiar zeal. His elocution was less sweet than sonorous, and, therefore, better adapted than the mellifluences of his friend to the outrageous vehemence of this drama.

What could detain him? Perhaps he lingered through forgetfulness. Yet this was incredible. Never had his memory been known to fail upon even more trivial occasions. Not less impossible was it that the scheme had lost its attractions, and that he stayed because his coming would afford him no gratification. But why should we expect him to adhere to the minute?

A half-hour elapsed, but Pleyel was still at a distance. Perhaps he had misunderstood the hour which had been proposed. Perhaps he had conceived that to-morrow, and not to-day, had been selected for this purpose; but no. A review of preceding circumstances demonstrated that such misapprehension was impossible; for he had himself proposed this day, and this hour. This day his attention would not otherwise be occupied; but to-morrow an indispensable engagement was foreseen, by which all his time would be engrossed; his detention, therefore, must be owing to some unforeseen and extraordinary event. Our conjectures were vague, tumultuous, and sometimes fearful. His sickness and his death might possibly have detained him.

Tortured with suspense, we sat gazing at each other, and at the path which led from the road. Every horseman that passed was, for a moment, imagined to be him. Hour succeeded hour, and the sun, gradually declining, at length disappeared. Every signal of his coming proved fallacious, and our hopes were at length dismissed. His absence affected my friends in no insupportable degree. They should be obliged, they said, to defer this undertaking till the morrow; and perhaps their impatient curiosity would compel them to dispense entirely with his presence. No doubt some harmless occurrence had diverted him from his purpose; and they trusted that they should receive a satisfactory account of him in the morning.

It may be supposed that this disappointment affected me in a very different manner. I turned aside my head to conceal my tears. I fled into solitude, to give vent to my reproaches without interruption or restraint. My heart was ready to burst with indignation and grief. Pleyel was not the only object of my keen but unjust upbraiding. Deeply did I execrate my own folly. Thus fallen into ruins was the gay fabric which I had reared! Thus had my golden vision melted into air!

How fondly did I dream that Pleyel was a lover! If he were, would he have suffered any obstacle to hinder his coming? "Blind and infatuated man!" I exclaimed. "Thou sportest with happiness. The good that is offered thee thou hast the insolence and folly to refuse. Well, I will henceforth intrust my felicity to no one's keeping but my own."

The first agonies of this disappointment would not allow me to be reasonable or just. Every ground on which I had built the persuasion that Pleyel was not unimpressed in my favor appeared to vanish. It seemed as if I had been misled into this opinion by the most palpable illusions.

I made some trifling excuse, and returned, much earlier than I expected, to my own house. I retired early to my chamber, without designing to sleep. I placed myself at a window, and gave the reins to reflection.

The hateful and degrading impulses which had lately controlled me were, in some degree, removed. New dejection succeeded, but was now produced by contemplating my late behavior. Surely that passion is worthy to be abhorred which obscures our understanding and urges us to the commission of injustice. What right had I to expect his attendance? Had I not demeaned myself like one indifferent to his happiness, and as having bestowed my regards upon another? His absence might be prompted by the love which I considered his absence as a proof that he wanted. He came not because the sight of me, the spectacle of my coldness or aversion, contributed to his despair. Why should I prolong, by hypocrisy or silence, his misery as well as my own? Why not deal with him explicitly, and assure him of the truth?

You will hardly believe that, in obedience to this suggestion, I rose for the purpose of ordering a light, that I might instantly make this confession in a letter. A second thought showed me the rashness of this scheme, and I wondered by what infirmity of mind I could be betrayed into a momentary approbation of it. I saw with the utmost clearness that a confession like that would be the most remediless and unpardonable outrage upon the dignity of my sex, and utterly unworthy of that passion which controlled me.

I resumed my seat and my musing. To account for the absence of Pleyel became once more the scope of my conjectures. How many incidents might occur to raise an insuperable impediment in his way! When I was a child, a scheme of pleasure, in which he and his sister were parties, had been in like manner frustrated by his absence; but his absence, in that instance, had been occasioned by his falling from a boat into the river, in consequence of which he had run the most imminent hazard of being drowned. Here was a second disappointment endured by the same persons, and produced by his failure. Might it not originate in the same cause? Had he not designed to cross the river that morning to make some necessary purchases in New Jersey? He had preconcerted to return to his own house to dinner but perhaps some disaster had befallen him. Experience had taught me the insecurity of a canoe, and that was the only kind of boat which Pleyel used; I was, likewise, actuated by an hereditary dread of water. These circumstances combined to bestow considerable plausibility on this conjecture; but the consternation with which I began to be seized was allayed by reflecting that, if this disaster had happened, my brother would have received the speediest information of it. The consolation which this idea imparted was ravished from me by a new thought. This disaster might have happened, and his family not be apprised of it. The first intelligence of his fate may be communicated by the livid corpse which the tide may cast, many days hence, upon the shore.

Thus was I distressed by opposite conjectures; thus was I tormented by phantoms of my own creation. It was not always thus. I can ascertain the date when my mind became the victim of this imbecility; perhaps it was coeval with the inroad of a fatal passion, – a passion that will never rank me in the number of its eulogists; it was alone sufficient to the extermination of my peace; it was itself a plenteous source of calamity, and needed not the concurrence of other evils to take away the attractions of existence and dig for me an untimely grave.

The state of my mind naturally introduced a train of reflections upon the dangers and cares which inevitably beset a human being. By no violent transition was I led to ponder on the turbulent life and mysterious end of my father. I cherished with the utmost veneration the memory of this man, and every relic connected with his fate was preserved with the most scrupulous care. Among these was to be numbered a manuscript containing memoirs of his own life. The narrative was by no means recommended by its eloquence; but neither did all its value flow from my relationship to the author. Its style had an unaffected and picturesque simplicity. The great variety and circumstantial display of the incidents, together with their intrinsic importance as descriptive of human manners and passions, made it the most useful book in my collection. It was late: but, being sensible of no inclination to sleep, I resolved to betake myself to the perusal of it.

To do this, it was requisite to procure a light. The girl had long since retired to her chamber: it was therefore proper to wait upon myself. A lamp, and the means of lighting it, were only to be found in the kitchen. Thither I resolved forthwith to repair; but the light was of use merely to enable me to read the book. I knew the shelf and the spot where it stood. Whether I took down the book, or prepared the lamp in the first place, appeared to be a matter of no moment. The latter was preferred, and, leaving my seat, I approached the closet in which, as I mentioned formerly, my books and papers were deposited.

Suddenly the remembrance of what had lately passed in this closet occurred. Whether midnight was approaching, or had passed, I knew not. I was, as then, alone and defenseless. The wind was in that direction in which, aided by the deathlike repose of nature, it brought to me the murmur of the waterfall. This was mingled with that solemn and enchanting sound which a breeze produces among the leaves of pines. The words of that mysterious dialogue, their fearful import, and the wild excess to which I was transported by my terrors, filled my imagination anew. My steps faltered, and I stood a moment to recover myself.

I prevailed on myself at length to move toward the closet. I touched the lock, but my fingers were powerless; I was visited afresh by unconquerable apprehensions. A sort of belief darted into my mind that some being was concealed within whose purposes were evil. I began to contend with those fears, when it occurred to me that I might, without impropriety, go for a lamp previously to opening the closet. I receded a few steps; but before I reached the chamber door my thoughts took a new direction. Motion seemed to produce a mechanical influence upon me. I was ashamed of my weakness. Besides, what aid could be afforded me by a lamp?

My fears had pictured to themselves no precise object. It would be difficult to depict in words the ingredients and hues of that phantom which haunted me. A hand invisible and of preternatural strength, lifted by human passions, and selecting my life for its aim, were parts of this terrific image. All places were alike accessible to this foe; or, if his empire were restricted by local bounds, those bounds were utterly inscrutable by me. But had I not been told, by some one in league with this enemy, that every place but the recess in the bank was exempt from danger?

I returned to the closet, and once more put my hand upon the lock. Oh, may my ears lose their sensibility ere they be again assailed by a shriek so terrible! Not merely my understanding was subdued by the sound; it acted on my nerves like an edge of steel. It appeared to cut asunder the fibers of my brain and rack every joint with agony.

The cry, loud and piercing as it was, was nevertheless human. No articulation was ever more distinct. The breath which accompanied it did not fan my hair, yet did every circumstance combine to persuade me that the lips which uttered it touched my very shoulder.

"Hold! hold!" were the words of this tremendous prohibition, in whose tone the whole soul seemed to be wrapped up, and every energy converted into eagerness and terror.

Shuddering, I dashed myself against the wall, and, by the same involuntary impulse, turned my face backward to examine the mysterious monitor. The moonlight streamed into each window, and every corner of the room was conspicuous, and yet I beheld nothing!

The interval was too brief to be artificially measured, between the utterance of these words and my scrutiny directed to the quarter whence they came. Yet, if a human being had been there, could he fail to have been visible? Which of my senses was the prey of a fatal illusion? The shock which the sound produced was still felt in every part of my frame. The sound, therefore, could not but be a genuine commotion. But that I had heard it was not more true than that the being who uttered it was stationed at my right ear; yet my attendant was invisible.

I cannot describe the state of my thoughts at that moment. Surprise had mastered my faculties. My frame shook, and the vital current was congealed. I was conscious only of the vehemence of my sensations. This condition could not be lasting. Like a tide, which suddenly mounts to an overwhelming height and then gradually subsides, my confusion slowly gave place to order, and my tumults to a calm. I was able to deliberate and move. I resumed my feet, and advanced into the midst of the room. Upward, and behind, and on each side, I threw penetrating glances. I was not satisfied with one examination. He that hitherto refused to be seen might change his purpose, and on the next survey be clearly distinguishable.

Solitude imposes least restraint upon the fancy. Dark is less fertile of images than the feeble luster of the moon. I was alone, and the walls were checkered by shadowy forms. As the moon passed behind a cloud and emerged, these shadows seemed to be endowed with life, and to move. The apartment was open to the breeze, and the curtain was occasionally blown from its ordinary position. This motion was not unaccompanied with sound. I failed not to snatch a look and to listen when this motion and this sound occurred. My belief that my monitor was posted near was strong, and instantly converted these appearances to tokens of his presence; and yet I could discern nothing.

When my thoughts were at length permitted to revert to the past, the first idea that occurred was the resemblance between the words of the voice which I had just heard and those which had terminated my dream in the summer-house. There are means by which we are able to distinguish a substance from a shadow, a reality from the phantom of a dream. The pit, my brother beckoning me forward, the seizure of my arm, and the voice behind, were surely imaginary. That these incidents were fashioned in my sleep is supported by the same indubitable evidence that compels me to believe myself awake at present; yet the words and the voice were the same. Then, by some inexplicable contrivance, I was aware of the danger, while my actions and sensations were those of one wholly unacquainted with it. Now, was it not equally true that my actions and persuasions were at war? Had not the belief that evil lurked in the closet gained admittance, and had not my actions betokened an unwarrantable security? To obviate the effects of my infatuation, the same means had been used.

In my dream, he that tempted me to my destruction was my brother. Death was ambushed in my path. From what evil was I now rescued? What minister or implement of ill was shut up in this recess? Who was it whose suffocating grasp I was to feel should I dare to enter it? What monstrous conception is this? My brother?

No; protection, and not injury, is his province. Strange and terrible chimera! Yet it would not be suddenly dismissed. It was surely no vulgar agency that gave this form to my fears. He to whom all parts of time are equally present, whom no contingency approaches, was the author of that spell which now seized upon me. Life was dear to me. No consideration was present that enjoined me to relinquish it. Sacred duty combined with every spontaneous sentiment to endear to me my being. Should I not shudder when my being was endangered? But what emotion should possess me when the arm lifted against me was Wieland's?

Ideas exist in our minds that can be accounted for by no established laws. Why did I dream that my brother was my foe? Why but because an omen of my fate was ordained to be communicated? Yet what salutary end did it serve? Did it arm me with caution to elude or fortitude to bear the evils to which I was reserved? My present thoughts were, no doubt, indebted for their hue to the similitude existing between these incidents and those of my dream. Surely it was frenzy that dictated my deed. That a ruffian was hidden in the closet was an idea the genuine tendency of which was to urge me to flight. Such had been the effect formerly produced. Had my mind been simply occupied with this thought at present, no doubt the same impulse would have been experienced; but now it was my brother whom I was irresistibly persuaded to regard as the contriver of that ill of which I had been forewarned. This persuasion did not extenuate my fears or my danger. Why then did I again approach the closet and withdraw the bolt? My resolution was instantly conceived, and executed without faltering.

The door was formed of light materials. The lock, of simple structure, easily forewent its hold. It opened into the room, and commonly moved upon its hinges, after being unfastened, without any effort of mine. This effort, however, was bestowed upon the present occasion. It was my purpose to open it with quickness; but the exertion which I made was ineffectual. It refused to open.

At another time, this circumstance would not have looked with a face of mystery. I should have supposed some casual obstruction and repeated my efforts to surmount it. But now my mind was accessible to no conjecture but one. The door was hindered from opening by human force. Surely, here was a new cause for affright. This was confirmation proper to decide my conduct. Now was all ground of hesitation taken away. What could be supposed but that I deserted the chamber and the house? that I at least endeavored no longer to withdraw the door?

Have I not said that my actions were dictated by frenzy? My reason had forborne, for a time, to suggest or to sway my resolves. I reiterated my endeavors. I exerted all my force to overcome the obstacle, but in vain. The strength that was exerted to keep it shut was superior to mine.

A casual observer might, perhaps, applaud the audaciousness of this conduct. Whence, but from a habitual defiance of danger, could my perseverance arise? I have already assigned, as distinctly as I am able, the cause of it. The frantic conception that my brother was within, that the resistance made to my design was exerted by him, had rooted itself in my mind. You will comprehend the height of this infatuation, when I tell you that, finding all my exertions vain, I betook myself to exclamations. Surely I was utterly bereft of understanding.

Now I had arrived at the crisis of my fate. "Oh, hinder not the door to open," I exclaimed, in a tone that had less of fear than of grief in it. "I know you well. Come forth, but harm me not. I beseech you, come forth."

I had taken my hand from the lock and removed to a small distance from the door. I had scarcely uttered these words, when the door swung upon its hinges and displayed to my view the interior of the closet. Whoever was within was shrouded in darkness. A few seconds passed without interruption of the silence. I knew not what to expect or to fear. My eyes would not stray from the recess. Presently, a deep sigh was heard. The quarter from which it came heightened the eagerness of my gaze. Some one approached from the farther end. I quickly perceived the outlines of a human figure. Its steps were irresolute and slow. I recoiled as it advanced.

By coming at length within the verge of the room, his form was clearly distinguishable. I had prefigured to myself a very different personage. The face that presented itself was the last that I should desire to meet at an hour and in a place like this. My wonder was stifled by my fears. Assassins had lurked in this recess. Some divine voice warned me of danger that at this moment awaited me. I had spurned the intimation, and challenged my adversary.

I recalled the mysterious countenance and dubious character of Carwin. What motive but atrocious ones could guide his steps hither? I was alone. My habit suited the hour, and the place, and the warmth of the season. All succor was remote. He had placed himself between me and the door. My frame shook with the vehemence of my apprehensions.

Yet I was not wholly lost to myself; I vigilantly marked his demeanor. His looks were grave, but not without perturbation. What species of inquietude it betrayed the light was not strong enough to enable me to discover. He stood still; but his eyes wandered from one object to another. When these powerful organs were fixed upon me, I shrunk into myself. At length he broke silence. Earnestness, and not embarrassment, was in his tone. He advanced close to me while he spoke: –

"What voice was that which lately addressed you?"

He paused for an answer; but, observing my trepidation, he resumed, with undiminished solemnity, "Be not terrified. Whoever he was, he has done you an important service. I need not ask you if it were the voice of a companion. That sound was beyond the compass of human organs. The knowledge that enabled him to tell you who was in the closet was obtained by incomprehensible means.

"You knew that Carwin was there. Were you not apprised of his intents? The same power could impart the one as well as the other. Yet, knowing these, you persisted. Audacious girl! But perhaps you confided in his guardianship. Your confidence was just. With succor like this at hand you may safely defy me.

"He is my eternal foe; the baffler of my best-concerted schemes. Twice have you been saved by his accursed interposition. But for him I should long ere now have borne away the spoils of your honor."

He looked at me with greater steadfastness than before. I became every moment more anxious for my safety. It was with difficulty I stammered out an entreaty that he would instantly depart, or suffer me to do so. He paid no regard to my request, but proceeded in a more impassioned manner: –

"What is it you fear? Have I not told you you are safe? Has not one in whom you more reasonably place trust assured you of it? Even if I execute my purpose, what injury is done? Your prejudices will call it by that name, but it merits it not.

"I was impelled by a sentiment that does you honor; a sentiment that would sanctify my deed; but, whatever it be, you are safe. Be this chimera still worshiped; I will do nothing to pollute it." There he stopped.

The accents and gestures of this man left me drained of all courage. Surely, on no other occasion should I have been thus pusillanimous. My state I regarded as a hopeless one. I was wholly at the mercy of this being. Whichever way I turned my eyes, I saw no avenue by which I might escape. The resources of my personal strength, my ingenuity, and my eloquence, I estimated at nothing. The dignity of virtue and the force of truth I had been accustomed to celebrate, and had frequently vaunted of the conquests which I should make with their assistance.

I used to suppose that certain evils could never befall a being in possession of a sound mind; that true virtue supplies us with energy which vice can never resist; that it was always in our power to obstruct, by his own death, the designs of an enemy who aimed at less than our life. How was it that a sentiment like despair had now invaded me, and that I trusted to the protection of chance, or to the pity of my persecutor?

His words imparted some notion of the injury which he had meditated. He talked of obstacles that had risen in his way. He had relinquished his design. These sources supplied me with slender consolation. There was no security but in his absence. When I looked at myself, when I reflected on the hour and the place, I was overpowered by horror and dejection.

He was silent, museful, and inattentive to my situation, yet made no motion to depart. I was silent in my turn. What could I say? I was confident that reason in this contest would be impotent. I must owe my safety to his own suggestions. Whatever purpose brought him hither, he had changed it. Why then did he remain? His resolutions might fluctuate, and the pause of a few minutes restore to him his first resolutions.

Yet was not this the man whom we had treated with unwearied kindness? whose society was endeared to us by his intellectual elevation and accomplishments? who had a thousand times expatiated on the usefulness and beauty of virtue? Why should such a one be dreaded? If I could have forgotten the circumstances in which our interview had taken place, I might have treated his words as jests. Presently, he resumed: –

"Fear me not: the space that severs us is small, and all visible succor is distant. You believe yourself completely in my power; that you stand upon the brink of ruin. Such are your groundless fears. I cannot lift a finger to hurt you. Easier would it be to stop the moon in her course than to injure you. The power that protects you would crumble my sinews and reduce me to a heap of ashes in a moment, if I were to harbor a thought hostile to your safety.

"Thus are appearances at length solved. Little did I expect that they originated hence. What a portion is assigned to you! Scanned by the eyes of this intelligence, your path will be without pits to swallow or snares to entangle you. Environed by the arms of this protection, all artifices will be frustrated and all malice repelled."

Here succeeded a new pause. I was still observant of every gesture and look. The tranquil solemnity that had lately possessed his countenance gave way to a new expression. All now was trepidation and anxiety.

"I must be gone," said he, in a faltering accent. "Why do I linger here? I will not ask your forgiveness. I see that your terrors are invincible. Your pardon will be extorted by fear, and not dictated by compassion. I must fly from you forever. He that could plot against your honor must expect from you and your friends persecution and death. I must doom myself to endless exile."

Saying this, he hastily left the room. I listened while he descended the stairs, and, unbolting the outer door, went forth. I did not follow him with my eyes, as the moonlight would have enabled me to do. Relieved by his absence, and exhausted by the conflict of my fears, I threw myself on a chair, and resigned myself to those bewildering ideas which incidents like these could not fail to produce.

V

Order could not readily be introduced into my thoughts. The voice still rung in my ears. Every accent that was uttered by Carwin was fresh in my remembrance. His unwelcome approach, the recognition of his person, his hasty departure, produced a complex impression on my mind which no words can delineate. I strove to give a slower motion to my thoughts, and to regulate a confusion which became painful; but my efforts were nugatory. I covered my eyes with my hand, and sat, I know not how long, without power to arrange or utter my conceptions.

I had remained for hours, as I believed, in absolute solitude. No thought of personal danger had molested my tranquillity. I had made no preparation for defense. What was it that suggested the design of perusing my father's manuscript? If, instead of this, I had retired to bed and to sleep, to what fate might I not have been reserved. The ruffian, who must almost have suppressed his breathings to screen himself from discovery, would have noticed this signal, and I should have awakened only to perish with affright, and to abhor myself. Could I have remained unconscious of my danger? Could I have tranquilly slept in the midst of so deadly a snare?

And who was he that threatened to destroy me? By what means could he hide himself in this closet? Surely he is gifted with supernatural power. Such is the enemy of whose attempts I was forewarned. Daily I had seen him and conversed with him. Nothing could be discerned through the impenetrable veil of his duplicity. When busied in conjectures as to the author of the evil that was threatened, my mind did not light for a moment upon his image. Yet has he not avowed himself my enemy? Why should he be here if he had not meditated evil?

He confesses that this has been his second attempt. What was the scene of his former conspiracy? Was it not he whose whispers betrayed him? Am I deceived? or was there not a faint resemblance between the voice of this man and that which talked of grasping my throat and extinguishing my life in a moment? Then he had a colleague in his crime; now he is alone. Then death was the scope of his thoughts; now an injury unspeakably more dreadful. How thankful should I be to the power that has interposed to save me!

That power is invisible. It is subject to the cognizance of one of my senses. What are the means that will inform me of what nature it is? He has set himself to counter-work the machinations of this man, who had menaced destruction to all that is dear to me, and whose coming had surmounted every human impediment. There was none to rescue me from his grasp. My rashness even hastened the completion of his scheme, and precluded him from the benefits of deliberation. I had robbed him of the power to repent and forbear. Had I been apprised of the danger, I should have regarded my conduct as the means of rendering my escape from it impossible. Such, likewise, seem to have been the fears of my invisible protector. Else why that startling entreaty to refrain from opening the closet? By what inexplicable infatuation was I compelled to proceed?

"Surely," said I, "there is omnipotence in the cause that changed the views of a man like Carwin. The divinity that shielded me from his attempts will take suitable care of my future safety. Thus to yield to my fears is to deserve that they should be real."

Scarcely had I uttered these words, when my attention was startled by the sound of footsteps. They denoted some one stepping into the piazza in front of my house. My new-born confidence was extinguished in a moment. Carwin, I thought, had repented his departure, and was hastily returning. The possibility that his return was prompted by intentions consistent with my safety found no place in my mind. Images of violation and murder assailed me anew, and the terrors which succeeded almost incapacitated me from taking any measures for my defense. It was an impulse of which I was scarcely conscious that made me fasten the lock and draw the bolts of my chamber door. Having done this, I threw myself on a seat; for I trembled to a degree which disabled me from standing, and my soul was so perfectly absorbed in the act of listening, that almost the vital motions were stopped.

The door below creaked on its hinges. It was not again thrust to, but appeared to remain open. Footsteps entered, traversed the entry, and began to mount the stairs. How I detested the folly of not pursuing the man when he withdrew, and bolting after him the outer door! Might he not conceive this omission to be a proof that my angel had deserted me, and be thereby fortified in guilt?

Every step on the stairs which brought him nearer to my chamber added vigor to my desperation. The evil with which I was menaced was to be at any rate eluded. How little did I preconceive the conduct which, in an exigence like this, I should be prone to adopt! You will suppose that deliberation and despair would have suggested the same course of action, and that I should have unhesitatingly resorted to the best means of personal defense within my power. A penknife lay open upon my table. I remembered that it was there, and seized it. For what purpose you will scarcely inquire. It will be immediately supposed that I meant it for my last refuge, and that, if all other means should fail, I should plunge it into the heart of my ravisher.

I have lost all faith in the steadfastness of human resolves. It was thus that in periods of calm I had determined to act. No cowardice had been held by me in greater abhorrence than that which prompted an injured female to destroy, not her injurer ere the injury was perpetrated, but herself when it was without remedy. Yet now this penknife appeared to me of no other use than to baffle my assailant and prevent the crime by destroying myself. To deliberate at such a time was impossible; but, among the tumultuous suggestions of the moment, I do not recollect that it once occurred to me to use it as an instrument of direct defense.

The steps had now reached the second floor. Every footfall accelerated the completion without augmenting the certainty of evil. The consciousness that the door was fast, now that nothing but that was interposed between me and danger, was a source of some consolation. I cast my eye toward the window. This, likewise, was a new suggestion. If the door should give way, it was my sudden resolution to throw myself from the window. Its height from the ground, which was covered beneath by a brick pavement, would insure my destruction; but I thought not of that.

When opposite to my door the footsteps ceased. Was he listening whether my fears were allayed and my caution were asleep? Did he hope to take me by surprise? Yet, if so, why did he allow so many noisy signals to betray his approach? Presently the steps were again heard to approach the door. A hand was laid upon the lock, and the latch pulled back. Did he imagine it possible that I should fail to secure the door? A slight effort was made to push it open, as if, all bolts being withdrawn, a slight effort only was required.

I no sooner perceived this than I moved swiftly toward the window. Carwin's frame might be said to be all muscle. His strength and activity had appeared, in various instances, to be prodigious. A slight exertion of his force would demolish the door. Would not that exertion be made? Too surely it would; but, at the same moment that this obstacle should yield and he should enter the apartment, my determination was formed to leap from the window. My senses were still bound to this object. I gazed at the door in momentary expectation that the assault would be made. The pause continued. The person without was irresolute and motionless.

Suddenly it occurred to me that Carwin might conceive me to have fled. That I had not betaken myself to flight was, indeed, the least probable of all conclusions. In this persuasion he must have been confirmed on finding the lower door unfastened and the chamber door locked. Was it not wise to foster this persuasion? Should I maintain deep silence, this, in addition to other circumstances, might encourage the belief, and he would once more depart. Every new reflection added plausibility to this reasoning. It was presently more strongly enforced when I noticed footsteps withdrawing from the door. The blood once more flowed back to my heart, and a dawn of exultation began to rise; but my joy was short-lived. Instead of descending the stairs, he passed to the door of the opposite chamber, opened it, and, having entered, shut it after him with a violence that shook the house.

How was I to interpret this circumstance? For what end could he have entered this chamber? Did the violence with which he closed the door testify the depth of his vexation? This room was usually occupied by Pleyel. Was Carwin aware of his absence on this night? Could he be suspected of a design so sordid as pillage? If this were his view, there were no means in my power to frustrate it. It behooved me to seize the first opportunity to escape; but, if my escape were supposed by my enemy to have been already effected, no asylum was more secure than the present. How could my passage from the house be accomplished without noises that might incite him to pursue me?

Utterly at a loss to account for his going into Pleyel's chamber, I waited in instant expectation of hearing him come forth. All, however, was profoundly still. I listened in vain for a considerable period to catch the sound of the door when it should again be opened. There was no other avenue by which he could escape, but a door which led into the girl's chamber. Would any evil from this quarter befall the girl?

Hence arose a new train of apprehensions. They merely added to the turbulence and agony of my reflections. Whatever evil impended over her, I had no power to avert it. Seclusion and silence were the only means of saving myself from the perils of this fatal night. What solemn vows did I put up, that, if I should once more behold the light of day, I would never trust myself again within the threshold of this dwelling!

Minute lingered after minute, but no token was given that Carwin had returned to the passage. What, I again asked, could detain him in this room? Was it possible that he had returned, and glided unperceived away? I was speedily aware of the difficulty that attended an enterprise like this; and yet, as if by that means I were capable of gaining any information on that head, I cast anxious looks from the window.

The object that first attracted my attention was a human figure standing on the edge of the bank. Perhaps my penetration was assisted by my hopes. Be that as it will, the figure of Carwin was clearly distinguishable. From the obscurity of my station, it was impossible that I should be discerned by him; and yet he scarcely suffered me to catch a glimpse of him. He turned and went down the steep, which in this part was not difficult to be scaled.

My conjecture, then, had been right. Carwin has softly opened the door, descended the stairs, and issued forth. That I should not have overheard his steps was only less incredible than that my eyes had deceived me. But what was now to be done? The house was at length delivered from this detested inmate. By one avenue might he again reenter. Was it not wise to bar the lower door? Perhaps he had gone out by the kitchen door. For this end, he must have passed through Judith's chamber. These entrances being closed and bolted, as great security was gained as was compatible with my lonely condition.

The propriety of these measures was too manifest not to make me struggle successfully with my fears. Yet I opened my own door with the utmost caution, and descended as if I were afraid that Carwin had been still immured in Pleyel's chamber.

The outer door was ajar. I shut it with trembling eagerness, and drew every bolt that appended to it. I then passed with light and less cautious steps through the parlor, but was surprised to discover that the kitchen door was secure. I was compelled to acquiesce in the first conjecture that Carwin had escaped through the entry.

My heart was now somewhat eased of the load of apprehension. I returned once more to my chamber, the door of which I was careful to lock. It was no time to think of repose. The moonlight began already to fade before the light of the day. The approach of morning was betokened by the usual signals. I mused upon the events of this night, and determined to take up my abode henceforth at my brother's. Whether I should inform him of what had happened was a question which seemed to demand some consideration. My safety unquestionably required that I should abandon my present habitation.

As my thoughts began to flow with fewer impediments, the image of Pleyel, and the dubiousness of his condition, again recurred to me. I again ran over the possible causes of his absence on the preceding day. My mind was attuned to melancholy. I dwelt, with an obstinacy for which I could not account, on the idea of his death. I painted to myself his struggles with the billows, and his last appearance. I imagined myself a midnight wanderer on the shore, and to have stumbled on his corpse, which the tide had cast up. These dreary images affected me even to tears. I endeavored not to restrain them. They imparted a relief which I had not anticipated. The more copiously they flowed, the more did my general sensations appear to subside into calm, and a certain restlessness give way to repose.

Perhaps, relieved by this effusion, the slumber so much wanted might have stolen on my senses, had there been no new cause of alarm.

VI

I was aroused from this stupor by sounds that evidently arose in the next chamber. Was it possible that I had been mistaken in the figure which I had seen on the bank? or had Carwin, by some inscrutable means, penetrated once more into this chamber? The opposite door opened; footsteps came forth, and the person, advancing to mine, knocked.

So unexpected an incident robbed me of all presence of mind, and, starting up, I involuntarily exclaimed, "Who is there?" An answer was immediately given. The voice, to my inexpressible astonishment, was Pleyel's.

"It is I. Have you risen? If you have not, make haste; I want three minutes' conversation with you in the parlor. I will wait for you there." Saying this, he retired from the door.

Should I confide in the testimony of my ears? If that were true, it was Pleyel that had been hitherto immured in the opposite chamber; he whom my rueful fancy had depicted in so many ruinous and ghastly shapes; he whose footsteps had been listened to with such inquietude! What is man, that knowledge is so sparingly conferred upon him! that his heart should be wrung with distress, and his frame be exanimated with fear, though his safety be encompassed with impregnable walls! What are the bounds of human imbecility! He that warned me of the presence of my foe refused the intimation by which so many racking fears would have been precluded.

Yet who would have imagined the arrival of Pleyel at such an hour? His tone was desponding and anxious. Why this unseasonable summons? and why this hasty departure? Some tidings he, perhaps, bears of mysterious and unwelcome import.

My impatience would not allow me to consume much time in deliberation; I hastened down. Pleyel I found standing at a window, with eyes cast down as in meditation, and arms folded on his breast. Every line in his countenance was pregnant with sorrow. To this was added a certain wanness and air of fatigue. The last time I had seen him appearances had been the reverse of these. I was startled at the change. The first impulse was to question him as to the cause. This impulse was supplanted by some degree of confusion, flowing from a consciousness that love had too large, and, as it might prove, a perceptible, share in creating this impulse. I was silent.

Presently be raised his eyes and fixed them upon me. I read in them an anguish altogether ineffable. Never had I witnessed a like demeanor in Pleyel. Never, indeed, had I observed a human countenance in which grief was more legibly inscribed. He seemed struggling for utterance; but, his struggles being fruitless, he shook his head and turned away from me.

My impatience would not allow me to be longer silent. "What," said I, "for heaven's sake, my friend, – what is the matter?"

He started at the sound of my voice. His looks, for a moment, became convulsed with an emotion very different from grief. His accents were broken with rage: –

"The matter! O wretch! – thus exquisitely fashioned, – on whom nature seemed to have exhausted all her graces; with charms so awful and so pure! how art thou fallen! From what height fallen! A ruin so complete, – so unheard of!"

His words were again choked by emotion. Grief and pity were again mingled in his features. He resumed, in a tone half suffocated by sobs: –

"But why should I upbraid thee? Could I restore to thee what thou hast lost, efface this cursed stain, snatch thee from the jaws of this fiend, I would do it. Yet what will avail my efforts? I have not arms with which to contend with so consummate, so frightful a depravity.

"Evidence less than this would only have excited resentment and scorn. The wretch who should have breathed a suspicion injurious to thy honor would have been regarded without anger: not hatred or envy could have prompted him; it would merely be an argument of madness. That my eyes, that my ears, should bear witness to thy fall! By no other way could detestable conviction be imparted.

"Why do I summon thee to this conference? Why expose myself to thy derision? Here admonition and entreaty are vain. Thou knowest him already for a murderer and thief. I thought to have been the first to disclose to thee his infamy; to have warned thee of the pit to which thou art hastening; but thy eyes are open in vain. Oh, foul and insupportable disgrace!

"There is but one path. I know you will disappear together. In thy ruin, how will the felicity and honor of multitudes be involved! But it must come. This scene shall not be blotted by his presence. No doubt thou wilt shortly see thy detested paramour. This scene will be again polluted by a midnight assignation. Inform him of his dangers; tell him that his crimes are known; let him fly far and instantly from this spot, if he desires to avoid the fate which menaced him in Ireland.

"And wilt thou not stay behind? But shame upon my weakness! I know not what I would say. I have done what I purposed. To stay longer, to expostulate, to beseech, to enumerate the consequences of thy act, – what end can it serve but to blazon thy infamy and embitter our woes? And yet, oh, think – think ere it be too late – on the distresses which thy flight will entail upon us; on the base, groveling, and atrocious character of the wretch to whom thou hast sold thy honor. But what is this? Is not thy effrontery impenetrable and thy heart thoroughly cankered? Oh, most specious and most profligate of women!"

Saying this, he rushed out of the house. I saw him in a few moments hurrying along the path which led to my brother's. I had no power to prevent his going, or to recall or to follow him. The accents I had heard were calculated to confound and bewilder. I looked around me, to assure myself that the scene was real. I moved, that I might banish the doubt that I was awake. Such enormous imputations from the mouth of Pleyel! To be stigmatized with the names of wanton and profligate! To be charged with the sacrifice of honor! with midnight meetings with a wretch known to be a murderer and thief! with an intention to fly in his company!

What I had heard was surely the dictate of frenzy, or it was built upon some fatal, some incomprehensible mistake. After the horrors of the night, after undergoing perils so imminent from this man, to be summoned to an interview like this! – to find Pleyel fraught with a belief that, instead of having chosen death as a refuge from the violence of this man, I had hugged his baseness to my heart, had sacrificed for him my purity, my spotless name, my friendships, and my fortune! That even madness could engender accusations like these was not to be believed.

What evidence could possibly suggest conceptions so wild? After the unlooked-for interview with Carwin in my chamber, he retired. Could Pleyel have observed his exit? It was not long after that Pleyel himself entered. Did he build on this incident his odious conclusions? Could the long series of my actions and sentiments grant me no exemption from suspicions so foul? Was it not more rational to infer that Carwin's designs had been illicit? that my life had been endangered by the fury of one whom, by some means, he had discovered to be an assassin and robber? that my honor had been assailed, not by blandishments, but by violence?

He has judged me without hearing. He has drawn from dubious appearances conclusions the most improbable and unjust. He has loaded me with all outrageous epithets. He has ranked me with prostitutes and thieves. I cannot pardon thee, Pleyel, for this injustice. Thy understanding must be hurt. If it be not, – if thy conduct was sober and deliberate, – I can never forgive an outrage so unmanly and so gross.

These thoughts gradually gave place to others. Pleyel was possessed by some momentary frenzy; appearances had led him into palpable errors. Whence could his sagacity have contracted this blindness? Was it not love? Previously assured of my affection for Carwin, distracted with grief and jealousy, and impelled hither at that late hour by some unknown instigation, his imagination transformed shadows into monsters, and plunged him into these deplorable errors.

This idea was not unattended with consolation. My soul was divided between indignation at his injustice and delight on account of the source from which I conceived it to spring. For a long time they would allow admission to no other thoughts. Surprise is an emotion that enfeebles, not invigorates. All my meditations were accompanied with wonder. I rambled with vagueness, or clung to one image with an obstinacy which sufficiently testified the maddening influence of late transactions.

Gradually I proceeded to reflect upon the consequences of Pleyel's mistake, and on the measures I should take to guard myself against future injury from Carwin. Should I suffer this mistake to be detected by time? When his passion should subside, would he not perceive the flagrancy of his injustice and hasten to atone for it? Did it not become my character to testify resentment for language and treatment so opprobrious? Wrapped up in the consciousness of innocence, and confiding in the influence of time and reflection to confute so groundless a charge, it was my province to be passive and silent.

As to the violences meditated by Carwin, and the means of eluding them, the path to be taken by me was obvious. I resolved to tell the tale to my brother and regulate myself by his advice. For this end, when the morning was somewhat advanced, I took the way to his house. My sister was engaged in her customary occupations. As soon as I appeared, she remarked a change in my looks. I was not willing to alarm her by the information which I had to communicate. Her health was in that condition which rendered a disastrous tale particularly unsuitable. I forbore a direct answer to her inquiries, and inquired, in my turn, for Wieland.

"Why," said she, "I suspect something mysterious and unpleasant has happened this morning. Scarcely had we risen when Pleyel dropped among us. What could have prompted him to make us so early and so unseasonable a visit I cannot tell. To judge from the disorder of his dress, and his countenance, something of an extraordinary nature has occurred. He permitted me merely to know that he had slept none, nor even undressed, during the past night. He took your brother to walk with him. Some topic must have deeply engaged them, for Wieland did not return till the breakfast hour was passed, and returned alone. His disturbance was excessive; but he would not listen to my importunities, or tell me what had happened. I gathered, from hints which he let fall, that your situation was in some way the cause; yet he assured me that you were at your own house, alive, in good health, and in perfect safety. He scarcely ate a morsel, and immediately after breakfast went out again. He would not inform me whither he was going, but mentioned that he probably might not return before night."

I was equally astonished and alarmed by this information. Pleyel had told his tale to my brother, and had, by a plausible and exaggerated picture, instilled into him unfavorable thoughts of me. Yet would not the more correct judgment of Wieland perceive and expose the fallacy of his conclusions? Perhaps his uneasiness might arise from some insight into the character of Carwin, and from apprehensions for my safety. The appearances by which Pleyel had been misled might induce him likewise to believe that I entertained an indiscreet though not dishonorable affection for Carwin. Such were the conjectures rapidly formed. I was inexpressibly anxious to change them into certainty. For this end an interview with my brother was desirable. He was gone no one knew whither, and was not expected speedily to return. I had no clew by which to trace his footsteps.

My anxieties could not be concealed from my sister. They heightened her solicitude to be acquainted with the cause. There were many reasons persuading me to silence; at least, till I had seen my brother, it would be an act of inexcusable temerity to unfold what had lately passed. No other expedient for eluding her importunities occurred to me but that of returning to my own house. I recollected my determination to become a tenant of this roof. I mentioned it to her. She joyfully acceded to this proposal, and suffered me with less reluctance to depart when I told her that it was with a view to collect and send to my new dwelling what articles would be immediately useful to me.

Once more I returned to the house which had been the scene of so much turbulence and danger. I was at no great distance from it when I observed my brother coming out. On seeing me he stopped, and, after ascertaining, as it seemed, which way I was going, he returned into the house before me. I sincerely rejoiced at this event, and I hastened to set things, if possible, on their right footing.

His brow was by no means expressive of those vehement emotions with which Pleyel had been agitated. I drew a favorable omen from this circumstance. Without delay I began the conversation.

"I have been to look for you," said I, "but was told by Catharine that Pleyel had engaged you on some important and disagreeable affair. Before his interview with you he spent a few minutes with me. These minutes he employed in upbraiding me for crimes and intentions with which I am by no means chargeable. I believe him to have taken up his opinions on very insufficient grounds. His behavior was in the highest degree precipitate and unjust, and, until I receive some atonement, I shall treat him, in my turn, with that contempt which he justly merits; meanwhile, I am fearful that he has prejudiced my brother against me. That is an evil which I most anxiously deprecate, and which I shall indeed exert myself to remove. Has he made me the subject of this morning's conversation?"

My brother's countenance testified no surprise at my address. The benignity of his looks was nowise diminished.

"It is true," said he, "your conduct was the subject of our discourse. I am your friend as well as your brother. There is no human being whom I love with more tenderness and whose welfare is nearer my heart. Judge, then, with what emotions I listened to Pleyel's story. I expect and desire you to vindicate yourself from aspersions so foul, if vindication be possible."

The tone with which he uttered the last words affected me deeply. "If vindication be possible!" repeated I. "From what you know, do you deem a formal vindication necessary? Can you harbor for a moment the belief of my guilt?"

He shook his head with an air of acute anguish. "I have struggled," said he, "to dismiss that belief. You speak before a judge who will profit by any pretense to acquit you who is ready to question his own senses when they plead against you."

These words incited a new set of thoughts in my mind. I began to suspect that Pleyel had built his accusations on some foundation unknown to me. "I may be a stranger to the grounds of your belief. Pleyel loaded me with indecent and virulent invectives, but he withheld from me the facts that generated his suspicions. Events took place last night of which some of the circumstances were of an ambiguous nature. I conceived that these might possibly have fallen under his cognizance, and that, viewed through the mists of prejudice and passion, they supplied a pretense for his conduct, but believed that your more unbiased judgment would estimate them at their just value. Perhaps his tale has been different from what I suspect it to be. Listen, then, to my narrative. If there be anything in his story inconsistent with mine, his story is false."

I then proceeded to a circumstantial relation of the incidents of the last night. Wieland listened with deep attention. Having finished, "This," continued I, "is the truth. You see in what circumstances an interview took place between Carwin and me. He remained for hours in my closet, and for some minutes in my chamber. He departed without haste or interruption. If Pleyel marked him as he left the house, (and it is not impossible that he did,) inferences injurious to my character might suggest themselves to him. In admitting them, he gave proofs of less discernment and less candor than I once ascribed to him."

"His proofs," said Wieland, after a considerable pause, "are different. That he should be deceived is not possible. That he himself is not the deceiver could not be believed, if his testimony were not inconsistent with yours; but the doubts which I entertained are now removed. Your tale, some parts of it, is marvelous; the voice which exclaimed against your rashness in approaching the closet, your persisting, notwithstanding that prohibition, your belief that I was the ruffian, and your subsequent conduct, are believed by me, because I have known you from childhood, because a thousand instances have attested your veracity, and because nothing less than my own hearing and vision would convince me, in opposition to her own assertions, that my sister had fallen into wickedness like this."

I threw my arms around him and bathed his cheek with my tears. "That," said I, "is spoken like my brother. But what are the proofs?"

He replied, "Pleyel informed me that, in going to your house, his attention was attracted by two voices. The persons speaking sat beneath the bank, out of sight. These persons, judging by their voices, were Carwin and you. I will not repeat the dialogue. If my sister was the female, Pleyel was justified in concluding you to be indeed one of the most profligate of women. Hence his accusations of you, and his efforts to obtain my concurrence to a plan by which an eternal separation should be brought about between my sister and this man."

I made Wieland repeat this recital. Here indeed was a tale to fill me with terrible foreboding. I had vainly thought that my safety could be sufficiently secured by doors and bars, but this is a foe from whose grasp no power of divinity can save me! His artifices will ever lay my fame and happiness at his mercy. How shall I counterwork his plots or detect his coadjutor? He has taught some vile and abandoned female to mimic my voice. Pleyel's ears were the witnesses of my dishonor. This is the midnight assignation to which he alluded. Thus is the silence he maintained when attempting to open the door of my chamber, accounted for. He supposed me absent, and meant, perhaps, had my apartment been accessible, to leave in it some accusing memorial.

SECOND PART

I

[As this part opens, the unhappy Clara is describing her hurried return to the same ill-fated abode at Mettingen. Hence kind friends had borne her after the catastrophe of her brother Wieland's "transformation." This was the crowning horror of all: the morbid fanatic, prepared by gloomy anticipations of some terrible sacrifice to be demanded in the name of religion, had found himself goaded to blind fury, by a mysterious compelling voice, to yield up to God the lives of his beloved wife and family; and had done the awful deed!

Though chained in his madhouse, he persists in his delusion; insists that it still remains for him to sacrifice his sister Clara; and twice breaks away in wild efforts to find and destroy her.]

I took an irregular path which led me to my own house. All was vacant and forlorn. A small enclosure near which the path led was the burying ground belonging to the family. This I was obliged to pass. Once I had intended to enter it, and ponder on the emblems and inscriptions which my uncle had caused to be made on the tombs of Catharine and her children; but now my heart faltered as I approached, and I hastened forward that distance might conceal it from my view.

When I approached the recess, my heart again sunk. I averted my eyes, and left it behind me as quickly as possible. Silence reigned through my habitation, and a darkness which closed doors and shutters produced. Every object was connected with mine or my brother's history. I passed the entry, mounted the stair, and unlocked the door of my chamber. It was with difficulty that I curbed my fancy and smothered my fears. Slight movements and casual sounds were transformed into beckoning shadows and calling shapes.

I proceeded to the closet. I opened and looked round it with fearfulness. All things were in their accustomed order. I sought and found the manuscript where I was used to deposit it. This being secured, there was nothing to detain me; yet I stood and contemplated awhile the furniture and walls of my chamber. I remembered how long this apartment had been a sweet and tranquil asylum; I compared its former state with its present dreariness, and reflected that I now beheld it for the last time.

Here it was that the incomprehensible behavior of Carwin was witnessed; this the stage on which that enemy of man showed himself for a moment unmasked. Here the menaces of murder were wafted to my ear; and here these menaces were executed.

These thoughts had a tendency to take from me my self-command. My feeble limbs refused to support me, and I sunk upon a chair. Incoherent and half-articulate exclamations escaped my lips. The name of Carwin was uttered and eternal woes – woes like that which his malice had entailed upon us – were heaped upon him. I invoked all-seeing heaven to drag to light and punish this betrayer, and accused its providence for having thus long delayed the retribution that was due to so enormous a guilt.

I have said that the window shutters were closed. A feeble light, however, found entrance through the crevices. A small window illuminated the closet, and, the door being closed, a dim ray streamed through the keyhole. A kind of twilight was thus created, sufficient for the purposes of vision, but, at the same time, involving all minuter objects in obscurity.

This darkness suited the color of my thoughts. I sickened at the remembrance of the past. The prospect of the future excited my loathing. I muttered, in a low voice, "Why should I live longer? Why should I drag a miserable being? All for whom I ought to live have perished. Am I not myself hunted to death?"

At that moment my despair suddenly became vigorous. My nerves were no longer unstrung. My powers, that had long been deadened, were revived. My bosom swelled with a sudden energy, and the conviction darted through my mind, that to end my torments was, at once, practicable and wise.

I knew how to find way to the recesses of life. I could use a lancet with some skill, and could distinguish between vein and artery. By piercing deep into the latter, I should shun the evils which the future had in store for me, and take refuge from my woes in quiet death.

I started on my feet, for my feebleness was gone, and hasted to the closet. A lancet and other small instruments were preserved in a case which I had deposited here. Inattentive as I was to foreign considerations, my ears were still open to any sound of mysterious import that should occur. I thought I heard a step in the entry. My purpose was suspended, and I cast an eager glance at my chamber door, which was open. No one appeared, unless the shadow which I discerned upon the floor was the outline of a man. If it were, I was authorized to suspect that some one was posted close to the entrance, who possibly had overheard my exclamations.

My teeth chattered, and a wild confusion took the place of my momentary calm. Thus it was when a terrific visage had disclosed itself on a former night. Thus it was when the evil destiny of Wieland assumed the lineaments of something human. What horrid apparition was preparing to blast my sight?

Still I listened and gazed. Not long, for the shadow moved; a foot, unshapely and huge, was thrust forward; a form advanced from its concealment, and stalked into the room. It was Carwin!

While I had breath, I shrieked. While I had power over my muscles, I motioned with my hand that he should vanish. My exertions could not last long: I sunk into a fit.

Oh that this grateful oblivion had lasted forever! Too quickly I recovered my senses. The power of distinct vision was no sooner restored to me, than this hateful form again presented itself, and I once more relapsed.

A second time, untoward nature recalled me from the sleep of death. I found myself stretched upon the bed. When I had power to look up, I remembered only that I had cause to fear. My distempered fancy fashioned to itself no distinguishable image. I threw a languid glance round me: once more my eyes lighted upon Carwin.

He was seated on the floor, his back rested against the wall; his knees were drawn up, and his face was buried in his hands. That his station was at some distance, that his attitude was not menacing, that his ominous visage was concealed, may account for my now escaping a shock violent as those which were past. I withdrew my eyes, but was not again deserted by my senses.

On perceiving that I had recovered my sensibility, he lifted his head. This motion attracted my attention. His countenance was mild, but sorrow and astonishment sat upon his features. I averted my eyes and feebly exclaimed, "Oh, fly! – fly far and forever! – I cannot behold you and live!"

He did not rise upon his feet, but clasped his hands, and said, in a tone of deprecation, "I will fly. I am become a fiend, the sight of whom destroys. Yet tell me my offense! You have linked curses with my name; you ascribe to me a malice monstrous and infernal. I look around: all is loneliness and desert! This house and your brother's are solitary and dismantled! You die away at the sight of me! My fear whispers that some deed of horror has been perpetrated; that I am the undesigning cause."

What language was this? Had he not avowed himself a ravisher? Had not this chamber witnessed his atrocious purposes? I besought him with new vehemence to go.

He lifted his eyes: – "Great heaven! what have I done? I think I know the extent of my offenses. I have acted, but my actions have possibly effected more than I designed. This fear has brought me back from my retreat. I come to repair the evil of which my rashness was the cause, and to prevent more evil. I come to confess my errors."

"Wretch!" I cried, when my suffocating emotions would permit me to speak, "the ghosts of my sister and her children, – do they not rise to accuse thee? Who was it that blasted the intellect of Wieland? Who was it that urged him to fury and guided him to murder? Who, but thou and the devil, with whom thou art confederated?"

At these words a new spirit pervaded his countenance. His eyes once more appealed to heaven. "If I have memory – if I have being – I am innocent. I intended no ill; but my folly, indirectly and remotely, may have caused it. But what words are these? Your brother lunatic! His children dead!"

What should I infer from this deportment? Was the ignorance which these words implied real or pretended? Yet how could I imagine a mere human agency in these events? But, if the influence was preternatural or maniacal in my brother's case, they must be equally so in my own. Then I remembered that the voice exerted was to save me from Carwin's attempts. These ideas tended to abate my abhorrence of this man, and to detect the absurdity of my accusations.

"Alas!" said I, "I have no one to accuse. Leave me to my fate. Fly from a scene stained with cruelty, devoted to despair."

Carwin stood for a time musing and mournful. At length he said, "What has happened? I came to expiate my crimes: let me know them in their full extent. I have horrible forebodings! What has happened?"

I was silent; but, recollecting the intimation given by this man when he was detected in my closet, which implied some knowledge of that power which interfered in my favor, I eagerly inquired, "What was that voice which called upon me to hold when I attempted to open the closet? What face was that which I saw at the bottom of the stairs? Answer me truly."

"I came to confess the truth. Your allusions are horrible and strange. Perhaps I have but faint conceptions of the evils which my infatuation has produced; but what remains I will perform. It was MY VOICE that you heard! It was MY FACE that you saw!"

For a moment I doubted whether my remembrance of events were not confused. How could he be at once stationed at my shoulder and shut up in my closet? How could he stand near me and yet be invisible? But if Carwin's were the thrilling voice and the fiery image which I had heard and seen, then was he the prompter of my brother, and the author of these dismal outrages.

Once more I averted my eyes and struggled for speech: – "Begone! thou man of mischief! Remorseless and implacable miscreant, begone!"

"I will obey," said he, in a disconsolate voice; "yet, wretch as I am, am I unworthy to repair the evils that I have committed? I came as a repentant criminal. It is you whom I have injured, and at your bar am I willing to appear and confess and expiate my crimes. I have deceived you; I have sported with your terrors; I have plotted to destroy your reputation. I come now to remove your terrors; to set you beyond the reach of similar fears; to rebuild your fame as far as I am able.

"This is the amount of my guilt, and this the fruit of my remorse. Will you not hear me? Listen to my confession, and then denounce punishment. All I ask is a patient audience."

"What!" I replied; "was not thine the voice that commanded my brother to imbrue his hands in the blood of his children? – to strangle that angel of sweetness, his wife? Has he not vowed my death, and the death of Pleyel, at thy bidding? Hast thou not made him the butcher of his family? – changed him who was the glory of his species into worse than brute? – robbed him of reason and consigned the rest of his days to fetters and stripes?"

Carwin's eyes glared and his limbs were petrified at this intelligence. No words were requisite to prove him guiltless of these enormities: at the time, however, I was nearly insensible to these exculpatory tokens. He walked to the farther end of the room, and, having recovered some degree of composure, he spoke: –

"I am not this villain. I have slain no one; I have prompted none to slay; I have handled a tool of wonderful efficacy without malignant intentions, but without caution. Ample will be the punishment of my temerity, if my conduct has contributed to this evil." He paused.

I likewise was silent. I struggled to command myself so far as to listen to the tale which he should tell. Observing this, he continued: –

"You are not apprised of the existence of a power which I possess. I know not by what name to call it. [1] It enables me to mimic exactly the voice of another, and to modify the sound so that it shall appear to come from what quarter and be uttered at what distance I please.

"I know not that everyone possesses this power. Perhaps, though a casual position of my organs in my youth showed me that I possessed it, it is an art which may be taught to all. Would to God I had died unknowing of the secret! It has produced nothing but degradation and calamity."

[1] Biloquium, or ventrilocution. Sound is varied according to the variations of direction and distance. The art of the ventriloquist consists in modifying his voice according to all these variations, without changing his place. See the work of the Abbe de la Chappelle, in which are accurately recorded the performances of one of these artists, and some ingenious though unsatisfactory speculations are given on the means by which the effects are produced. This power is, perhaps, given by nature, but is doubtless improvable, if not acquirable, by art. It may, possibly, consist in an unusual flexibility or extension of the bottom of the tongue and the uvula. That speech is producible by these alone must be granted, since anatomists mention two instances of persons speaking without a tongue. In one case the organ was originally wanting, but its place was supplied by a small tubercle, and the uvula was perfect. In the other the tongue was destroyed by disease, but probably a small part of it remained.

This power is difficult to explain, but the fact is undeniable. Experience shows that the human voice can imitate the voice of all men and of all inferior animals. The sound of musical instruments, and even noises from the contact of inanimate substances, have been accurately imitated. The mimicry of animals is notorious; and Dr. Burney ("Musical Travels") mentions one who imitated a flute and violin, so as to deceive even his ears.

THIRD PART

I

[After Carwin's confession of his powers of ventriloquism all the mysteries are cleared up – save one. The owner of the voice heard in Clara's chamber, on the first night after the wanderer appeared at Mettingen; the threatener on the edge of the precipice; the spy in Clara's closet, and would-be intruder; the manipulator of the vile plot that destroyed her lover's confidence – all these hidden identities have materialized in the person of this one unhappy man. But while confessing the prying disposition which led to these sins, in efforts to protect himself from discovery, Carwin still denies that Wieland's mad acts were perpetrated at his instigation.]

"I have uttered the truth. This is the extent of my offenses. You tell me a horrid tale of Wieland being led to the destruction of his wife and children by some mysterious agent. You charge me with the guilt of this agency, but I repeat that the amount of my guilt has been truly stated. The perpetrator of Catharine's death was unknown to me till now; nay, it is still unknown to me."

At that moment, the closing of a door in the kitchen was distinctly heard by us. Carwin started and paused. "There is some one coming. I must not be found here by my enemies, and need not, since my purpose is answered."

I had drunk in, with the most vehement attention, every word that he had uttered. I had no breath to interrupt his tale by interrogations or comments. The power that he spoke of was hitherto unknown to me; its existence was incredible; it was susceptible of no direct proof.

He owns that his were the voice and face which I heard and saw. He attempts to give a human explanation of these phantasms but it is enough that he owns himself to be the agent: his tale is a lie, and his nature devilish. As he deceived me, he likewise deceived my brother, and now do I behold the author of all our calamities!

Such were my thoughts when his pause allowed me to think. I should have bade him begone if the silence had not been interrupted; but now I feared no more for myself; and the milkiness of my nature was curdled into hatred and rancor. Some one was near, and this enemy of God and man might possibly be brought to justice. I reflected not that the preternatural power which he had hitherto exerted would avail to rescue him from any toils in which his feet might be entangled. Meanwhile, looks, and not words, of menace and abhorrence, were all that I could bestow.

He did not depart. He seemed dubious whether by passing out of the house, or by remaining somewhat longer where he was, he should most endanger his safety. His confusion increased when steps of one barefoot were heard upon the stairs. He threw anxious glances sometimes at the closet, sometimes at the window, and sometimes at the chamber door; yet he was detained by some inexplicable fascination. He stood as if rooted to the spot.

As to me, my soul was bursting with detestation and revenge. I had no room for surmises and fears respecting him that approached. It was doubtless a human being, and would befriend me so far as to aid me in arresting this offender.

The stranger quickly entered the room. My eyes and the eyes of Carwin were at the same moment darted upon him. A second glance was not needed to inform us who he was. His locks were tangled, and fell confusedly over his forehead and ears. His shirt was of coarse stuff, and open at the neck and breast. His coat was once of bright and fine texture, but now torn and tarnished with dust. His feet, his legs, and his arms, were bare. His features were the seat of a wild and tranquil solemnity, but his eyes bespoke inquietude and curiosity.

He advanced with a firm step, and looking as in search of some one. He saw me and stopped. He bent his sight on the floor, and, clenching his hands, appeared suddenly absorbed in meditation. Such were the figure and deportment of Wieland! Such, in his fallen state, were the aspect and guise of my brother!

Carwin did not fail to recognize the visitant. Care for his own safety was apparently swallowed up in the amazement which this spectacle produced. His station was conspicuous, and he could not have escaped the roving glances of Wieland; yet the latter seemed totally unconscious of his presence.

Grief at this scene of ruin and blast was at first the only sentiment of which I was conscious. A fearful stillness ensued. At length Wieland, lifting his hands, which were locked in each other, to his breast, exclaimed, "Father! I thank thee. This is thy guidance. Hither thou hast led me, that I might perform thy will. Yet let me not err; let me hear again thy messenger!"

He stood for a minute as if listening; but, recovering from his attitude, he continued, "It is not needed. Dastardly wretch! thus eternally questioning the behests of thy Maker! weak in resolution, wayward in faith!"

He advanced to me, and, after another pause, resumed: – "Poor girl! a dismal fate has set its mark upon thee. Thy life is demanded as a sacrifice. Prepare thee to die. Make not my office difficult by fruitless opposition. Thy prayers might subdue stones; but none but he who enjoined my purpose can shake it."

These words were a sufficient explication of the scene. The nature of his frenzy, as described by my uncle, was remembered. I, who had sought death, was now thrilled with horror because it was near. Death in this form, death from the hand of a brother, was thought upon with indescribable repugnance.

In a state thus verging upon madness, my eye glanced upon Carwin. His astonishment appeared to have struck him motionless and dumb. My life was in danger, and my brother's hand was about to be imbrued in my blood. I firmly believed that Carwin's was the instigation. I could rescue myself from this abhorred fate; I could dissipate this tremendous illusion; I could save my brother from the perpetration of new horrors, by pointing out the devil who seduced him. To hesitate a moment was to perish. These thoughts gave strength to my limbs and energy to my accents; I started on my feet: –

"Oh, brother! spare me! spare thyself! There is thy betrayer. He counterfeited the voice and face of an angel, for the purpose of destroying thee and me. He has this moment confessed it. He is able to speak where he is not. He is leagued with hell, but will not avow it; yet he confesses that the agency was his."

My brother turned slowly his eyes, and fixed them upon Carwin. Every joint in the frame of the latter trembled. His complexion was paler than a ghost's. His eye dared not meet that of Wieland, but wandered with an air of distraction from one space to another.

"Man," said my brother, in a voice totally unlike that which he had used to me, "what art thou? The charge has been made. Answer it. The visage – the voice – at the bottom of these stairs – at the hour of eleven – to whom did they belong? To thee?"

Twice did Carwin attempt to speak, but his words died away upon his lips. My brother resumed, in a tone of greater vehemence: –

"Thou falterest. Faltering is ominous. Say yes or no; one word will suffice; but beware of falsehood. Was it a stratagem of hell to overthrow my family? Wast thou the agent?"

I now saw that the wrath which had been prepared for me was to be heaped upon another. The tale that I heard from him, and his present trepidations, were abundant testimonies of his guilt. But what if Wieland should be undeceived! What if he shall find his act to have proceeded not from a heavenly prompter, but from human treachery! Will not his rage mount into whirlwind? Will not he tear limb from limb this devoted wretch?

Instinctively I recoiled from this image; but it gave place to another. Carwin may be innocent, but the impetuosity of his judge may misconstrue his answers into a confession of guilt. Wieland knows not that mysterious voices and appearances were likewise witnessed by me. Carwin may be ignorant of those which misled my brother. Thus may his answers unwarily betray himself to ruin.

Such might be the consequences of my frantic precipitation,

and these it was necessary, if possible, to prevent. I attempted to speak; but Wieland, turning suddenly upon me, commanded silence, in a tone furious and terrible. My lips closed, and my tongue refused its office.

"What art thou?" he resumed, addressing himself to Carwin. "Answer me: whose form – whose voice, – was it thy contrivance? Answer me."

The answer was now given, but confusedly and scarcely articulated. "I meant nothing – I intended no ill – if I understand – if I do not mistake you – it is too true – I did appear – in the entry – did speak. The contrivance was mine, but – "

These words were no sooner uttered, than my brother ceased to wear the same aspect. His eyes were downcast; he was motionless; his respiration became hoarse, like that of a man in the agonies of death. Carwin seemed unable to say more. He might have easily escaped; but the thought which occupied him related to what was horrid and unintelligible in this scene, and not to his own danger.

Presently the faculties of Wieland, which, for a time, were chained up, were seized with restlessness and trembling. He broke silence. The stoutest heart would have been appalled by the tone in which he spoke. He addressed himself to Carwin: –

"Why art thou here? Who detains thee? Go and learn better. I will meet thee, but it must be at the bar of thy Maker. There shall I bear witness against thee."

Perceiving that Carwin did not obey, he continued, "Dost thou wish me to complete the catalogue by thy death? Thy life is a worthless thing. Tempt me no more. I am but a man, and thy presence may awaken a fury which may spurn my control. Begone!"

Carwin, irresolute, striving in vain for utterance, his complexion pallid as death, his knees beating one against another, slowly obeyed the mandate and withdrew.

II

A few words more and I lay aside the pen forever. Yet why should I not relinquish it now? All that I have said is preparatory to this scene, and my fingers, tremulous and cold as my heart, refuse any further exertion. This must not be. Let my last energies support me in the finishing of this task. Then will I lay down my head in the lap of death. Hushed will be all my murmurs in the sleep of the grave.

Every sentiment has perished in my bosom. Even friendship is extinct. Your love for me has prompted me to this task; but I would not have complied if it had not been a luxury thus to feast upon my woes. I have justly calculated upon my remnant of strength. When I lay down the pen the taper of life will expire; my existence will terminate with my tale.

Now that I was left alone with Wieland, the perils of my situation presented themselves to my mind. That this paroxysm should terminate in havoc and rage it was reasonable to predict. The first suggestion of my fears had been disproved by my experience. Carwin had acknowledged his offenses, and yet had escaped. The vengeance which I had harbored had not been admitted by Wieland; and yet the evils which I had endured, compared with those inflicted on my brother, were as nothing. I thirsted for his blood, and was tormented with an insatiable appetite for his destruction; but my brother was unmoved, and had dismissed him in safety. Surely thou wast more than man, while I am sunk below the beasts.

Did I place a right construction on the conduct of Wieland? Was the error that misled him so easily rectified? Were views so vivid and faith so strenuous thus liable to fading and to change? Was there not reason to doubt the accuracy of my perceptions? With images like these was my mind thronged, till the deportment of my brother called away my attention.

I saw his lips move and his eyes cast up to heaven. Then would he listen and look back, as if in expectation of some one's appearance. Thrice he repeated these gesticulations and this inaudible prayer. Each time the mist of confusion and doubt seemed to grow darker and to settle on his understanding. I guessed at the meaning of these tokens. The words of Carwin had shaken his belief, and he was employed in summoning the messenger who had formerly communed with him, to attest the value of those new doubts. In vain the summons was repeated, for his eye met nothing but vacancy, and not a sound saluted his ear.

He walked to the bed, gazed with eagerness at the pillow which had sustained the head of the breathless Catharine, and then returned to the place where I sat. I had no power to lift my eyes to his face: I was dubious of his purpose; this purpose might aim at my life.

Alas! nothing but subjection to danger and exposure to temptation can show us what we are. By this test was I now tried, and found to be cowardly and rash. Men can deliberately untie the thread of life, and of this I had deemed myself capable. It was now that I stood upon the brink of fate, that the knife of the sacrificer was aimed at my heart, I shuddered, and betook myself to any means of escape, however monstrous.

Can I bear to think – can I endure to relate the outrage which my heart meditated? Where were my means of safety? Resistance was vain. Not even the energy of despair could set me on a level with that strength which his terrific prompter had bestowed upon Wieland. Terror enables us to perform incredible feats; but terror was not then the state of my mind: where then were my hopes of rescue?

Methinks it is too much. I stand aside, as it were, from myself; I estimate my own deservings; a hatred, immortal and inexorable, is my due. I listen to my own pleas, and find them empty and false: yes, I acknowledge that my guilt surpasses that of mankind; I confess that the curses of a world and the frowns of a Deity are inadequate to my demerits. Is there a thing in the world worthy of infinite abhorrence? It is I.

What shall I say? I was menaced, as I thought, with death, and, to elude this evil, my hand was ready to inflict death upon the menacer. In visiting my house, I had made provision against the machinations of Carwin. In a fold of my dress an open penknife was concealed. This I now seized and drew forth. It lurked out of view; but I now see that my state of mind would have rendered the deed inevitable if my brother had lifted his hand. This instrument of my preservation would have been plunged into his heart.

O insupportable remembrance! hide thee from my view for a time; hide it from me that my heart was black enough to meditate the stabbing of a brother! a brother thus supreme in misery; thus towering in virtue!

He was probably unconscious of my design, but presently drew back. This interval was sufficient to restore me to myself. The madness, the iniquity, of that act which I had purposed rushed upon my apprehension. For a moment I was breathless with agony. At the next moment I recovered my strength, and threw the knife with violence on the floor.

The sound awoke my brother from his reverie. He gazed alternately at me and at the weapon. With a movement equally solemn he stooped and took it up. He placed the blade in different positions, scrutinizing it accurately, and maintaining, at the same time, a profound silence.

Again he looked at me; but all that vehemence and loftiness of spirit which had so lately characterized his features were flown. Fallen muscles, a forehead contracted into folds, eyes dim with unbidden drops, and a ruefulness of aspect which no words can describe, were now visible.

His looks touched into energy the same sympathies in me, and I poured forth a flood of tears. This passion was quickly checked by fear, which had now no longer my own but his safety for their object. I watched his deportment in silence. At length he spoke: –

"Sister," said he, in an accent mournful and mild, "I have acted poorly my part in this world. What thinkest thou? Shall I not do better in the next?"

I could make no answer. The mildness of his tone astonished and encouraged me. I continued to regard him with wistful and anxious looks.

"I think," resumed he, "I will try. My wife and my babes have gone before. Happy wretches! I have sent you to repose, and ought not to linger behind."

These words had a meaning sufficiently intelligible. I looked at the open knife in his hand and shuddered, but knew not how to prevent the deed which I dreaded. He quickly noticed my fears, and comprehended them. Stretching toward me his hand, with an air of increasing mildness, "Take it," said he; "fear not for thy own sake, nor for mine. The cup is gone by, and its transient inebriation is succeeded by the soberness of truth.

"Thou angel whom I was wont to worship! fearest thou, my sister, for thy life? Once it was the scope of my labors to destroy thee, but I was prompted to the deed by heaven; such, at least, was my belief. Thinkest thou that thy death was sought to gratify malevolence? No. I am pure from all stain. I believed that my God was my mover!

"Neither thee nor myself have I cause to injure. I have done my duty; and surely there is merit in having sacrificed to that all that is dear to the heart of man. If a devil has deceived me, he came in the habit of an angel. If I erred, it was not my judgment that deceived me, but my senses. In thy sight, Being of beings! I am still pure. Still will I look for my reward in thy justice!"

Did my ears truly report these sounds? If I did not err, my brother was restored to just perceptions. He knew himself to have been betrayed to the murder of his wife and children, to have been the victim of infernal artifice; yet he found consolation in the rectitude of his motives. He was not devoid of sorrow, for this was written on his countenance; but his soul was tranquil and sublime.

Perhaps this was merely a transition of his former madness into a new shape. Perhaps he had not yet awakened to the memory of the horrors which he had perpetrated. Infatuated wretch that I was! To set myself up as a model by which to judge of my heroic brother! My reason taught me that his conclusions were right; but, conscious of the impotence of reason over my own conduct, conscious of my cowardly rashness and my criminal despair, I doubted whether anyone could be steadfast and wise.

Such was my weakness, that even in the midst of these thoughts my mind glided into abhorrence of Carwin, and I uttered, in a low voice, "O Carwin! Carwin! what hast thou to answer for?"

My brother immediately noticed the involuntary exclamation. "Clara!" said he, "be thyself. Equity used to be a theme for thy eloquence. Reduce its lessons to practice, and be just to that unfortunate man. The instrument has done its work, and I am satisfied.

"I thank thee, my God, for this last illumination! My enemy is thine also. I deemed him to be a man, – the man with whom I have often communed; but now thy goodness has unveiled to me his true nature. As the performer of thy behests, he is my friend."

My heart began now to misgive me. His mournful aspect had gradually yielded place to a serene brow. A new soul appeared to actuate his frame, and his eyes to beam with preternatural luster. These symptoms did not abate, and he continued: –

"Clara, I must not leave thee in doubt. I know not what brought about thy interview with the being whom thou callest Carwin. For a time I was guilty of thy error, and deduced from his incoherent confessions that I had been made the victim of human malice. He left us at my bidding, and I put up a prayer that my doubts should be removed. Thy eyes were shut and thy ears sealed to the vision that answered my prayer.

"I was indeed deceived. The form thou hast seen was the incarnation of a demon. The visage and voice which urged me to the sacrifice of my family were his. Now he personates a human form; then he was environed with the luster of heaven.

"Clara," he continued, advancing closer to me, "thy death must come. This minister is evil, but he from whom his commission was received is God. Submit then with all thy wonted resignation to a decree that cannot be reversed or resisted. Mark the clock. Three minutes are allowed to thee, in which to call up thy fortitude and prepare thee for thy doom." There he stopped.

Even now, when this scene exists only in memory, when life and all its functions have sunk into torpor, my pulse throbs, and my hairs uprise; my brows are knit, as then, and I gaze around me in distraction. I was unconquerably averse to death; but death, imminent and full of agony as that which was threatened, was nothing. This was not the only or chief inspirer of my fears.

For him, not for myself, was my soul tormented. I might die, and no crime, surpassing the reach of mercy, would pursue me to the presence of my Judge; but my assassin would survive to contemplate his deed, and that assassin was Wieland!

Wings to bear me beyond his reach I had not. I could not vanish with a thought. The door was open, but my murderer was interposed between that and me. Of self-defense I was incapable. The frenzy that lately prompted me to blood was gone: my state was desperate; my rescue was impossible.

The weight of these accumulated thoughts could not be borne. My sight became confused; my limbs were seized with convulsion; I spoke, but my words were half formed: –

"Spare me, my brother! Look down, righteous Judge! snatch me from this fate! take away this fury from him, or turn it elsewhere! "

Such was the agony of my thoughts that I noticed not steps entering my apartment. Supplicating eyes were cast upward; but when my prayer was breathed I once more wildly gazed at the door. A form met my sight; I shuddered as if the God whom I invoked were present. It was Carwin that again intruded, and who stood before me, erect in attitude and steadfast in look!

The sight of him awakened new and rapid thoughts. His recent tale was remembered; his magical transitions and mysterious energy of voice. Whether he were infernal or miraculous or human, there was no power and no need to decide. Whether the contriver or not of this spell, he was able to unbind it, and to check the fury of my brother. He had ascribed to himself intentions not malignant. Here now was afforded a test of his truth. Let him interpose, as from above; revoke the savage decree which the madness of Wieland has assigned to heaven, and extinguish forever this passion for blood!

My mind detected at a glance this avenue to safety. The recommendations it possessed thronged as it were together, and made but one impression on my intellect. Remoter effects and collateral dangers I saw not. Perhaps the pause of an instant had sufficed to call them up. The improbability that the influence which governed Wieland was external or human; the tendency of this stratagem to sanction so fatal an error or substitute a more destructive rage in place of this; the insufficiency of Carwin's mere muscular forces to counteract the efforts and restrain the fury of Wieland, might, at a second glance, have been discovered; but no second glance was allowed. My first thought hurried me to action, and, fixing my eyes upon Carwin, I exclaimed, –

"O wretch! once more hast thou come? Let it be to abjure thy malice; to counterwork this hellish stratagem; to turn from me and from my brother this desolating rage!

"Testify thy innocence or thy remorse; exert the powers which pertain to thee, whatever they be, to turn aside this ruin. Thou art the author of these horrors! What have I done to deserve thus to die? How have I merited this unrelenting persecution? I adjure thee, by that God whose voice thou hast dared to counterfeit, to save my life!

"Wilt thou then go? – leave me! Succorless!"

Carwin listened to my entreaties unmoved, and turned from me. He seemed to hesitate a moment, – then glided through the door. Rage and despair stifled my utterance. The interval of respite was past; the pangs reserved for me by Wieland were not to be endured; my thoughts rushed again into anarchy. Having received the knife from his hand, I held it loosely and without regard; but now it seized again my attention, and I grasped it with force.

He seemed to notice not the entrance or exit of Carwin. My gesture and the murderous weapon appeared to have escaped his notice. His silence was unbroken; his eye, fixed upon the clock for a time, was now withdrawn; fury kindled in every feature; all that was human in his face gave way to an expression supernatural and tremendous. I felt my left arm within his grasp.

Even now I hesitated to strike. I shrunk from his assault, but in vain.

Here let me desist. Why should I rescue this event from oblivion? Why should I paint this detestable conflict? Why not terminate at once this series of horrors? – Hurry to the verge of the precipice, and cast myself forever beyond remembrance and beyond hope?

Still I live; with this load upon my breast; with this phantom to pursue my steps; with adders lodged in my bosom, and stinging me to madness; still I consent to live!

Yes! I will rise above the sphere of mortal passions; I will spurn at the cowardly remorse that bids me seek impunity in silence, or comfort in forgetfulness. My nerves shall be new-strung to the task. Have I not resolved? I will die. The gulf before me is inevitable and near. I will die, but then only when my tale is at an end.

III

My right hand, grasping the unseen knife, was still disengaged. It was lifted to strike. All my strength was exhausted but what was sufficient to the performance of this deed. Already was the energy awakened and the impulse given that should bear the fatal steel to his heart, when – Wieland shrunk back; his hand was withdrawn. Breathless with affright and desperation, I stood, freed from his grasp; unassailed; untouched.

Thus long had the power which controlled the scene forborne to interfere: but now his might was irresistible; and Wieland in a moment was disarmed of all his purposes. A voice, louder than human organs could produce, shriller than language can depict, burst from the ceiling and commanded him – TO HOLD!

Trouble and dismay succeeded to the steadfastness that had lately been displayed in the looks of Wieland. His eyes roved from one quarter to another, with an expression of doubt. He seemed to wait for a further intimation.

Carwin's agency was here easily recognized. I had besought him to interpose in my defense. He had flown. I had imagined him deaf to my prayer, and resolute to see me perish; yet he disappeared merely to devise and execute the means of my relief.

Why did he not forbear when this end was accomplished? Why did his misjudging zeal and accursed precipitation overpass that limit? Or meant he thus to crown the scene, and conduct his inscrutable plots to this consummation?

Such ideas were the fruit of subsequent contemplation. This moment was pregnant with fate. I had no power to reason. In the career of my tempestuous thoughts, rent into pieces as my mind was by accumulating horrors, Carwin was unseen and unsuspected. I partook of Wieland's credulity, shook with his amazement, and panted with his awe.

Silence took place for a moment: so much as allowed the attention to recover its post. Then new sounds were uttered from above: –

"Man of errors! cease to cherish thy delusion; not heaven or hell, but thy senses, have misled thee to commit these acts. Shake off thy frenzy, and ascend into rational and human. Be lunatic no longer."

My brother opened his lips to speak. His tone was terrific and faint. He muttered an appeal to heaven. It was difficult to comprehend the theme of his inquiries. They implied doubt as to the nature of the impulse that hitherto had guided him, and questioned whether he had acted in consequence of insane perceptions.

To these interrogatories the voice, which now seemed to

hover at his shoulder, loudly answered in the affirmative. Then uninterrupted silence ensued.

Fallen from his lofty and heroic station; now finally restored to the perception of truth; weighed to earth by the recollection of his own deeds; consoled no longer by a consciousness of rectitude for the loss of offspring and wife, – a loss for which he was indebted to his own misguided hand, – Wieland was transformed at once into the MAN OF SORROWS!

He reflected not that credit should be as reasonably denied to the last as to any former intimation; that one might as justly be ascribed to erring or diseased senses as the other. He saw not that this discovery in no degree affected the integrity of his conduct; that his motives had lost none of their claims to the homage of mankind; that the preference of supreme good, and the boundless energy of duty, were undiminished in his bosom.

It is not for me to pursue him through the ghastly changes of his countenance. Words he had none. Now he sat upon the floor, motionless in all his limbs, with his eyes glazed and fixed, a monument of woe.

Anon a spirit of tempestuous but undesigning activity seized him. He rose from his place and strode across the floor, tottering and at random. His eyes were without moisture, and gleamed with the fire that consumed his vitals. The muscles of his face were agitated by convulsions. His lips moved, but no sound escaped him.

That nature should long sustain this conflict was not to be believed. My state was little different from that of my brother. I entered, as it were, into his thoughts. My heart was visited and rent by his pangs. "Oh that thy frenzy had never been cured! that thy madness, with its blissful visions, would return! or, if that must not be, that thy scene would hasten to a close! – that death would cover thee with his oblivion!

"What can I wish for thee? Thou who hast vied with the great Preacher of thy faith in sanctity of motives, and in elevation above sensual and selfish! Thou whom thy fate has changed into parricide and savage! Can I wish for the continuance of thy being? No."

For a time his movements seemed destitute of purpose. If he walked; if he turned; if his fingers were entwined with each other; if his hands were pressed against opposite sides of his head with a force sufficient to crush it into pieces; it was to tear his mind from self-contemplation; to waste his thoughts on external objects.

Speedily this train was broken. A beam appeared to be darted into his mind which gave a purpose to his efforts. An avenue to escape presented itself; and now he eagerly gazed about him. When my thoughts became engaged by his demeanor, my fingers were stretched as by a mechanical force, and the knife, no longer heeded or of use, escaped from my grasp and fell unperceived on the floor. His eye now lighted upon it; he seized it with the quickness of thought.

I shrieked aloud, but it was too late. He plunged it to the hilt in his neck; and his life instantly escaped with the stream that gushed from the wound. He was stretched at my feet; and my hands were sprinkled with his blood as he fell.

Such was thy last deed, my brother! For a spectacle like this was it my fate to be reserved! Thy eyes were closed – thy face ghastly with death – thy arms, and the spot where thou lyedst, floated in thy life's blood! These images have not for a moment forsaken me. Till I am breathless and cold, they must continue to hover in my sight.

Carwin, as I said, had left the room; but he still lingered in the house. My voice summoned him to my aid; but I scarcely noticed his reentrance, and now faintly recollect his terrified looks, his broken exclamations, his vehement avowals of innocence, the effusions of his pity for me, and his offers of assistance.

I did not listen – I answered him not – I ceased to upbraid or accuse. His guilt was a point to which I was indifferent. Ruffian or devil, black as hell or bright as angels, thenceforth he was nothing to me. I was incapable of sparing a look or a thought from the ruin that was spread at my feet.

When he left me, I was scarcely conscious of any variation in the scene. He informed the inhabitants of the hut of what had passed, and they flew to the spot. Careless of his own safety, he hasted to the city to inform my friends of my condition.

My uncle speedily arrived at the house. The body of Wieland was removed from my presence, and they supposed that I would follow it; but no, my home is ascertained; here I have taken up my rest, and never will I go hence, till, like Wieland, I am borne to my grave.

Importunity was tried in vain. They threatened to remove me by violence, – nay, violence was used; but my soul prizes too dearly this little roof to endure to be bereaved of it. Force should not prevail when the hoary locks and supplicating tears of my uncle were ineffectual. My repugnance to move gave birth to ferociousness and frenzy when force was employed, and they were obliged to consent to my return.

They besought me – they remonstrated – they appealed to every duty that connected me with Him that made me and with my fellow-men – in vain. While I live I will not go hence. Have I not fulfilled my destiny?

Why will ye torment me with your reasonings and reproofs? Can ye restore to me the hope of my better days? Can ye give me back Catharine and her babes? Can ye recall to life him who died at my feet?

I will eat – I will drink – I will lie down and rise up – at your bidding; all I ask is the choice of my abode. What is there unreasonable in this demand? Shortly will I be at peace. This is the spot which I have chosen in which to breathe my last sigh. Deny me not, I beseech you, so slight a boon.

Talk not to me, O my reverend friend! of Carwin. He has told thee his tale, and thou exculpatest him from all direct concern in the fate of Wieland. This scene of havoc was produced by an illusion of the senses. Be it so; I care not from what source these disasters have flowed; it suffices that they have swallowed up our hopes and our existence.

What his agency began, his agency conducted to a close. He intended, by the final effort of his power, to rescue me and to banish his illusions from my brother. Such is his tale, concerning the truth of which I care not. Henceforth I foster but one wish: I ask only quick deliverance from life and all the ills that attend it.

Go, wretch! torment me not with thy presence and thy prayers. – Forgive thee? Will that avail thee when thy fateful hour shall arrive? Be thou acquitted at thy own tribunal, and thou needest not fear the verdict of others. If thy guilt be capable of blacker hues, if hitherto thy conscience be without stain, thy crime will be made more flagrant by thus violating my retreat. Take thyself away from my sight if thou wouldst not behold my death!

Thou art gone! murmuring and reluctant! And now my repose is coming – my work is done!

Fitzjames O'Brien

The Golden Ingot

I had just retired to rest, with my eyes almost blind with the study of a new work on physiology by M. Brown-Sequard, when the night bell was pulled violently.

It was winter, and I confess I grumbled as I rose and went downstairs to open the door. Twice that week I had been aroused long after midnight for the most trivial causes. Once, to attend upon the son and heir of a wealthy family, who had cut his thumb with a penknife, which, it seems, he insisted on taking to bed with him; and once, to restore a young gentleman to consciousness, who had been found by his horrified parent stretched insensible on the staircase. Diachylon in the one case and ammonia in the other were all that my patients required; and I had a faint suspicion that the present summons was perhaps occasioned by no case more necessitous than those I have quoted. I was too young in my profession, however, to neglect opportunities. It is only when a physician rises to a very large practice that he can afford to be inconsiderate. I was on the first step of the ladder, so I humbly opened my door.

A woman was standing ankle deep in the snow that lay upon the stoop. I caught but a dim glimpse of her form, for the night was cloudy; but I could hear her teeth rattling like castanets, and, as the sharp wind blew her clothes close to her form, I could discern from the sharpness of the outlines that she was very scantily supplied with raiment.

"Come in, come in, my good woman," I said hastily, for the wind seemed to catch eagerly at the opportunity of making itself at home in my hall, and was rapidly forcing an entrance through the half- open door. "Come in, you can tell me all you have to communicate inside."

She slipped in like a ghost, and I closed the door. While I was striking a light in my office, I could hear her teeth still clicking out in the dark hall, till it seemed as if some skeleton was chattering. As soon as I obtained a light I begged her to enter the room, and, without occupying myself particularly about her appearance, asked her abruptly what her business was.

"My father has met with a severe accident," she said, "and requires instant surgical aid. I entreat you to come to him immediately."

The freshness and the melody of her voice startled me. Such voices rarely, if ever, issue from any but beautiful forms. I looked at her attentively, but, owing to a nondescript species of shawl in which her head was wrapped, I could discern nothing beyond what seemed to be a pale, thin face and large eyes. Her dress was lamentable. An old silk, of a color now unrecognizable, clung to her figure in those limp folds which are so eloquent of misery. The creases where it had been folded were worn nearly through, and the edges of the skirt had decayed into a species of irregular fringe, which was clotted and discolored with mud. Her shoes – which were but half concealed by this scanty garment – were shapeless and soft with moisture. Her hands were hidden under the ends of the shawl which covered her head and hung down over a bust, the outlines of which, although angular, seemed to possess grace. Poverty, when partially shrouded, seldom fails to interest: witness the statue of the Veiled Beggar, by Monti.

"In what manner was your father hurt?" I asked, in a tone considerably softened from the one in which I put my first question.

"He blew himself up, sir, and is terribly wounded."

"Ah! He is in some factory, then?"

"No, sir, he is a chemist."

"A chemist? Why, he is a brother professional. Wait an instant, and I will slip on my coat and go with you. Do you live far from here?"

"In the Seventh Avenue, not more than two blocks from the end of this street."

"So much the better. We will be with him in a few minutes. Did you leave anyone in attendance on him?"

"No, sir. He will allow no one but myself to enter his laboratory. And, injured as he is, I could not induce him to quit it."

"Indeed! He is engaged in some great research, perhaps? I have known such cases."

We were passing under a lamp-post, and the woman suddenly turned and glared at me with a look of such wild terror that for an instant I involuntarily glanced round me under the impression that some terrible peril, unseen by me, was menacing us both.

"Don't – don't ask me any questions," she said breathlessly. "He will tell you all. But do, oh, do hasten! Good God! he may be dead by this time!"

I made no reply, but allowed her to grasp my hand, which she did with a bony, nervous clutch, and endeavored with some difficulty to keep pace with the long strides – I might well call them bounds, for they seemed the springs of a wild animal rather than the paces of a young girl – with which she covered the ground. Not a word more was uttered until we stopped before a shabby, old-fashioned tenement house in the Seventh Avenue, not far above Twenty-third Street. She pushed the door open with a convulsive pressure, and, still retaining hold of my hand, literally dragged me upstairs to what seemed to be a back offshoot from the main building, as high, perhaps, as the fourth story. In a moment more I found myself in a moderate-sized chamber, lit by a single lamp. In one corner, stretched motionless on a wretched pallet bed, I beheld what I supposed to be the figure of my patient.

"He is there," said the girl; "go to him. See if he is dead – I dare not look."

I made my way as well as I could through the numberless dilapidated chemical instruments with which the room was littered. A French chafing dish supported on an iron tripod had been overturned, and was lying across the floor, while the charcoal, still warm, was scattered around in various directions. Crucibles, alembics, and retorts were confusedly piled in various corners, and on a small table I saw distributed in separate bottles a number of mineral and metallic substances, which I recognized as antimony, mercury, plumbago, arsenic, borax, etc. It was veritably the apartment of a poor chemist. All the apparatus had the air of being second-hand. There was no luster of exquisitely annealed glass and highly polished metals, such as dazzles one in the laboratory of the prosperous analyst. The makeshifts of poverty were everywhere visible. The crucibles were broken, or gallipots were used instead of crucibles. The colored tests were not in the usual transparent vials, but were placed in ordinary black bottles. There is nothing more melancholy than to behold science or art in distress. A threadbare scholar, a tattered book, or a battered violin is a mute appeal to our sympathy.

I approached the wretched pallet bed on which the victim of chemistry was lying. He breathed heavily, and had his head turned toward the wall. I lifted his arm gently to arouse his attention. "How goes it, my poor friend?" I asked him. "Where are you hurt?"

In a moment, as if startled by the sound of my voice, he sprang up in his bed, and cowered against the wall like a wild animal driven to bay. "Who are you? I don't know you. Who brought you here? You are a stranger. How dare you come into my private rooms to spy upon me?"

And as he uttered this rapidly with a frightful nervous energy, I beheld a pale distorted face, draped with long gray hair, glaring at me with a mingled expression of fury and terror.

"I am no spy," I answered mildly. "I heard that you had met with an accident, and have come to cure you. I am Dr. Luxor, and here is my card."

The old man took the card, and scanned it eagerly. "You are a physician?" he inquired distrustfully.

"And surgeon also."

"You are bound by oath not to reveal the secrets of your patients."

"Undoubtedly."

"I am afraid that I am hurt," he continued faintly, half sinking back in the bed.

I seized the opportunity to make a brief examination of his body. I found that the arms, a part of the chest, and a part of the face were terribly scorched; but it seemed to me that there was nothing to be apprehended but pain.

"You will not reveal anything that you may learn here?" said the old man, feebly fixing his eyes on my face while I was applying a soothing ointment to the burns. "You will promise me."

I nodded assent.

"Then I will trust you. Cure me – I will pay you well."

I could scarce help smiling. If Lorenzo de' Medici, conscious of millions of ducats in his coffers, had been addressing some leech of the period, he could not have spoken with a loftier air than this inhabitant of the fourth story of a tenement house in the Seventh Avenue.

"You must keep quiet," I answered. "Let nothing irritate you. I will leave a composing draught with your daughter, which she will give you immediately. I will see you in the morning. You will be well in a week."

"Thank God!" came in a murmur from a dusk corner near the door. I turned, and beheld the dim outline of the girl, standing with clasped hands in the gloom of the dim chamber.

"My daughter!" screamed the old man, once more leaping up in the bed with renewed vitality. "You have seen her, then? When? Where? Oh, may a thousand cur – "

"Father! father! Anything – anything but that. Don't, don't curse me!" And the poor girl, rushing in, flung herself sobbing on her knees beside his pallet.

"Ah, brigand! You are there, are you? Sir," said he, turning to me, "I am the most unhappy man in the world. Talk of Sisyphus rolling the ever-recoiling stone – of Prometheus gnawed by the vulture since the birth of time. The fables yet live. There is my rock, forever crushing me back! there is my eternal vulture, feeding upon my heart! There! there! there!" And, with an awful gesture of malediction and hatred, he pointed with his wounded hand, swathed and shapeless with bandages, at the cowering, sobbing, wordless woman by his side.

I was too much horror-stricken to attempt even to soothe him. The anger of blood against blood has an electric power which paralyzes bystanders.

"Listen to me, sir," he continued, "while I skin this painted viper. I have your oath; you will not reveal. I am an alchemist, sir. Since I was twenty-two years old, I have pursued the wonderful and subtle secret. Yes, to unfold the mysterious Rose guarded with such terrible thorns; to decipher the wondrous Table of Emerald; to accomplish the mystic nuptials of the Red King and the White Queen; to marry them soul to soul and body to body, forever and ever, in the exact proportions of land and water – such has been my sublime aim, such has been the splendid feat that I have accomplished."

I recognized at a glance, in this incomprehensible farrago, the argot of the true alchemist. Ripley, Flamel, and others have supplied the world, in their works, with the melancholy spectacle of a scientific bedlam.

"Two years since," continued the poor man, growing more and more excited with every word that he uttered – "two years since, I succeeded in solving the great problem – in transmuting the baser metals into gold. None but myself, that girl, and God knows the privations I had suffered up to that time. Food, clothing, air, exercise, everything but shelter, was sacrificed toward the one great end. Success at last crowned my labors. That which Nicholas Flamel did in 1382, that which George Ripley did at Rhodes in 1460, that which Alexander Sethon and Michael Scudivogius did in the seventeenth century, I did in 1856. I made gold! I said to myself, 'I will astonish New York more than Flamel did Paris.' He was a poor copyist, and suddenly launched into magnificence. I had scarce a rag to my back: I would rival the Medicis.

I made gold every day. I toiled night and morning; for I must tell you that I never was able to make more than a certain quantity at a time, and that by a process almost entirely dissimilar to those hinted at in those books of alchemy I had hitherto consulted. But I had no doubt that facility would come with experience, and that ere long I should be able to eclipse in wealth the richest sovereigns of the earth.

"So I toiled on. Day after day I gave to this girl here what gold I succeeded in fabricating, telling her to store it away after supplying our necessities. I was astonished to perceive that we lived as poorly as ever. I reflected, however, that it was perhaps a commendable piece of prudence on the part of my daughter. Doubtless, I said, she argues that the less we spend the sooner we shall accumulate a capital wherewith to live at ease; so, thinking her course a wise one, I did not reproach her with her niggardliness, but toiled on, amid want, with closed lips.

"The gold which I fabricated was, as I said before, of an invariable size, namely, a little ingot worth perhaps thirty or forty-five dollars. In two years I calculated that I had made five hundred of these ingots, which, rated at an average of thirty dollars apiece, would amount to the gross sum of fifteen thousand dollars. After deducting our slight expenses for two years, we ought to have had nearly fourteen thousand dollars left. It was time, I thought, to indemnify myself for my years of suffering, and surround my child and myself with such moderate comforts as our means allowed. I went to my daughter and explained to her that I desired to make an encroachment upon our little hoard. To my utter amazement, she burst into tears, and told me that she had not got a dollar – that all of our wealth had been stolen from her. Almost overwhelmed by this new misfortune, I in vain endeavored to discover from her in what manner our savings had been plundered. She could afford me no explanation beyond what I might gather from an abundance of sobs and a copious flow of tears.

"It was a bitter blow, doctor, but nil desperandum was my motto, so I went to work at my crucible again, with redoubled energy, and made an ingot nearly every second day. I determined this time to put them in some secure place myself; but the very first day I set my apparatus in order for the projection, the girl Marion – that is my daughter's name – came weeping to me and implored me to allow her to take care of our treasure. I refused decisively, saying that, having found her already incapable of filling the trust, I could place no faith in her again. But she persisted, clung to my neck, threatened to abandon me; in short, used so many of the bad but irresistible arguments known to women that I had not the heart to refuse her. She has since that time continued to take the ingots.

"Yet you behold," continued the old alchemist, casting an inexpressibly mournful glance around the wretched apartment, "the way we live. Our food is insufficient and of bad quality; we never buy clothes; the rent of this hole is a mere nothing. What am I to think of the wretched girl who plunges me into this misery? Is she a miser, think you? – or a female gamester? – or – or – does she squander it riotously in places I know not of? O Doctor, Doctor! do not blame me if I heap imprecations on her head, for I have suffered bitterly!" The poor man here closed his eyes and sank back groaning on his bed.

This singular narrative excited in me the strangest emotions. I glanced at the girl Marion, who had been a patient listener to these horrible accusations of cupidity, and never did I behold a more angelic air of resignation than beamed over her countenance. It was impossible that anyone with those pure, limpid eyes; that calm, broad forehead; that childlike mouth, could be such a monster of avarice or deceit as the old man represented. The truth was plain enough: the alchemist was mad – what alchemist was there ever who was not? – and his insanity had taken this terrible shape. I felt an inexpressible pity move my heart for this poor girl, whose youth was burdened with such an awful sorrow.

"What is your name?" I asked the old man, taking his tremulous, fevered hand in mine.

"William Blakelock," he answered. "I come of an old Saxon stock, sir, that bred true men and women in former days. God!

how did it ever come to pass that such a one as that girl ever sprung from our line?" The glance of loathing and contempt that he cast at her made me shudder.

"May you not be mistaken in your daughter?" I said, very mildly. "Delusions with regard to alchemy are, or have been, very common – "

"What, sir?" cried the old man, bounding in his bed. "What? Do you doubt that gold can be made? Do you know, sir, that M. C. Theodore Tiffereau made gold at Paris in the year 1854 in the presence of M. Levol, the assayer of the Imperial Mint, and the result of the experiments was read before the Academy of Sciences on the sixteenth of October of the same year? But stay; you shall have better proof yet. I will pay you with one of my ingots, and you shall attend me until I am well. Get me an ingot!"

This last command was addressed to Marion, who was still kneeling close to her father's bedside. I observed her with some curiosity as this mandate was issued. She became very pale, clasped her hands convulsively, but neither moved nor made any reply.

"Get me an ingot, I say!" reiterated the alchemist passionately.

She fixed her large eyes imploringly upon him. Her lips quivered, and two huge tears rolled slowly down her white cheeks.

"Obey me, wretched girl," cried the old man in an agitated voice, "or I swear, by all that I reverence in heaven and earth, that I will lay my curse upon you forever!"

I felt for an instant that I ought perhaps to interfere, and spare the girl the anguish that she was so evidently suffering; but a powerful curiosity to see how this strange scene would terminate withheld me.

The last threat of her father, uttered as it was with a terrible vehemence, seemed to appall Marion. She rose with a sudden leap, as if a serpent had stung her, and, rushing into an inner apartment, returned with a small object which she placed in my hand, and then flung herself in a chair in a distant corner of the room, weeping bitterly.

"You see – you see," said the old man sarcastically, "how reluctantly she parts with it. Take it, sir; it is yours."

It was a small bar of metal. I examined it carefully, poised it in my hand – the color, weight, everything, announced that it really was gold.

"You doubt its genuineness, perhaps," continued the alchemist. "There are acids on yonder table – test it."

I confess that I DID doubt its genuineness; but after I had acted upon the old man's suggestion, all further suspicion was rendered impossible. It was gold of the highest purity. I was astounded. Was then, after all, this man's tale a truth? Was his daughter, that fair, angelic-looking creature, a demon of avarice, or a slave to worse passions? I felt bewildered. I had never met with anything so incomprehensible. I looked from father to daughter in the blankest amazement. I suppose that my countenance betrayed my astonishment, for the old man said: "I perceive that you are surprised. Well, that is natural. You had a right to think me mad until I proved myself sane."

"But, Mr. Blakelock," I said, "I really cannot take this gold. I have no right to it. I cannot in justice charge so large a fee."

"Take it – take it," he answered impatiently; "your fee will amount to that before I am well. Besides," he added mysteriously, "I wish to secure your friendship. I wish that you should protect me from her," and he pointed his poor, bandaged hand at Marion.

My eyes followed his gesture, and I caught the glance that replied – a glance of horror, distrust, despair. The beautiful face was distorted into positive ugliness.

"It's all true," I thought; "she is the demon that her father represents her."

I now rose to go. This domestic tragedy sickened me. This treachery of blood against blood was too horrible to witness. I wrote a prescription for the old man, left directions as to the renewal of the dressings upon his burns, and, bidding him good night, hastened toward the door.

While I was fumbling on the dark, crazy landing for the staircase, I felt a hand laid on my arm.

"Doctor," whispered a voice that I recognized as Marion Blakelock's, "Doctor, have you any compassion in your heart?"

"I hope so," I answered shortly, shaking off her hand; her touch filled me with loathing.

"Hush! don't talk so loud. If you have any pity in your nature, give me back, I entreat of you, that gold ingot which my father gave you this evening."

"Great heaven!" said I, "can it be possible that so fair a woman can be such a mercenary, shameless wretch?"

"Ah! you know not – I cannot tell you! Do not judge me harshly. I call God to witness that I am not what you deem me. Some day or other you will know. But," she added, interrupting herself, "the ingot – where is it? I must have it. My life depends on your giving it to me."

"Take it, impostor!" I cried, placing it in her hand, that closed on it with a horrible eagerness. "I never intended to keep it. Gold made under the same roof that covers such as you must be accursed."

So saying, heedless of the nervous effort she made to detain me, I stumbled down the stairs and walked hastily home.

The next morning, while I was in my office, smoking my matutinal cigar, and speculating over the singular character of my acquaintances of last night, the door opened, and Marion Blakelock entered. She had the same look of terror that I had observed the evening before, and she panted as if she had been running fast.

"Father has got out of bed," she gasped out, "and insists on going on with his alchemy. Will it kill him?"

"Not exactly," I answered coldly. "It were better that he kept quiet, so as to avoid the chance of inflammation. However, you need not be alarmed; his burns are not at all dangerous, although painful."

"Thank God! thank God!" she cried, in the most impassioned accents; and, before I was aware of what she was doing, she seized my hand and kissed it.

"There, that will do," I said, withdrawing my hand; "you are under no obligations to me. You had better go back to your father."

"I can't go," she answered. "You despise me – is it not so?"

I made no reply.

"You think me a monster – a criminal. When you went home last night, you were wonderstruck that so vile a creature as I should have so fair a face."

"You embarrass me, madam," I said, in a most chilling tone. "Pray relieve me from this unpleasant position."

"Wait. I cannot bear that you should think ill of me. You are good and kind, and I desire to possess your esteem. You little know how I love my father."

I could not restrain a bitter smile.

"You do not believe that? Well, I will convince you. I have had a hard struggle all last night with myself, but am now resolved. This life of deceit must continue no longer. Will you hear my vindication?"

I assented. The wonderful melody of her voice and the purity of her features were charming me once more. I half believed in her innocence already.

"My father has told you a portion of his history. But he did not tell you that his continued failures in his search after the secret of metallic transmutation nearly killed him. Two years ago he was on the verge of the grave, working every day at his mad pursuit, and every day growing weaker and more emaciated. I saw that if his mind was not relieved in some way he would die. The thought was madness to me, for I loved him – I love him still, as a daughter never loved a father before. During all these years of poverty I had supported the house with my needle; it was hard work, but I did it – I do it still!"

"What?" I cried, startled, "does not – "

"Patience. Hear me out. My father was dying of disappointment. I must save him. By incredible exertions, working night and day, I saved about thirty-five dollars in notes. These I exchanged for gold, and one day, when my father was not looking, I cast them into the crucible in which he was making one of his vain attempts at transmutation. God, I am sure, will pardon the deception. I never anticipated the misery it would lead to.

"I never beheld anything like the joy of my poor father, when, after emptying his crucible, he found a deposit of pure gold at the bottom. He wept, and danced, and sang, and built such castles in the air, that my brain was dizzy to hear him. He gave me the ingot to keep, and went to work at his alchemy with renewed vigor. The same thing occurred. He always found the same quantity of gold in his crucible. I alone knew the secret. He was happy, poor man, for nearly two years, in the belief that he was amassing a fortune. I all the while plied my needle for our daily bread. When he asked me for the savings, the first stroke fell upon me. Then it was that I recognized the folly of my conduct. I could give him no money. I never had any – while he believed that I had fourteen thousand dollars. My heart was nearly broken when I found that he had conceived the most injurious suspicions against me. Yet I could not blame him. I could give no account of the treasure I had permitted him to believe was in my possession. I must suffer the penalty of my fault, for to undeceive him would be, I felt, to kill him. I remained silent then, and suffered.

"You know the rest. You now know why it was that I was reluctant to give you that ingot – why it was that I degraded myself so far as to ask it back. It was the only means I had of continuing a deception on which I believed my father's life depended. But that delusion has been dispelled. I can live this life of hypocrisy no longer. I cannot exist and hear my father, whom I love so, wither me daily with his curses. I will undeceive him this very day. Will you come with me, for I fear the effect on his enfeebled frame?"

"Willingly," I answered, taking her by the hand; "and I think that no absolute danger need be apprehended. Now, Marion," I added, "let me ask forgiveness for having even for a moment wounded so noble a heart. You are truly as great a martyr as any of those whose sufferings the Church perpetuates in altar-pieces."

"I knew you would do me justice when you knew all," she sobbed, pressing my hand; "but come. I am on fire. Let us hasten to my father, and break this terror to him."

When we reached the old alchemist's room, we found him busily engaged over a crucible which was placed on a small furnace, and in which some indescribable mixture was boiling. He looked up as we entered.

"No fear of me, doctor," he said, with a ghastly smile, "no fear; I must not allow a little physical pain to interrupt my great work, you know. By the way, you are just in time. In a few moments the marriage of the Red King and White Queen will be accomplished, as George Ripley calls the great act, in his book entitled 'The Twelve Gates.' Yes, doctor, in less than ten minutes you will see me make pure, red, shining gold!" And the poor old man smiled triumphantly, and stirred his foolish mixture with a long rod, which he held with difficulty in his bandaged hands. It was a grievous sight for a man of any feeling to witness.

"Father," said Marion, in a low, broken voice, advancing a little toward the poor old dupe, "I want your forgiveness."

"Ah, hypocrite! for what? Are you going to give me back my gold?"

"No, father, but for the deception that I have been practicing on you for two years – "

"I knew it! I knew it!" shouted the old man, with a radiant

countenance. "She has concealed my fourteen thousand dollars all this time, and now comes to restore them. I will forgive her. Where are they, Marion?"

"Father – it must come out. You never made any gold. It was I who saved up thirty-five dollars, and I used to slip them into your crucible when your back was turned – and I did it only because I saw that you were dying of disappointment. It was wrong, I know – but, father, I meant well. You'll forgive me, won't you?" And the poor girl advanced a step toward the alchemist.

He grew deathly pale, and staggered as if about to fall. The next instant, though, he recovered himself, and burst into a horrible sardonic laugh. Then he said, in tones full of the bitterest irony: "A conspiracy, is it? Well done, doctor! You think to reconcile me with this wretched girl by trumping up this story that I have been for two years a dupe of her filial piety. It's clumsy, doctor, and is a total failure. Try again."

"But I assure you, Mr. Blakelock," I said as earnestly as I could, "I believe your daughter's statement to be perfectly true. You will find it to be so, as she has got the ingot in her possession which so often deceived you into the belief that you made gold, and you will certainly find that no transmutation has taken place in your crucible."

"Doctor," said the old man, in tones of the most settled conviction, "you are a fool. The girl has wheedled you. In less than a minute I will turn you out a piece of gold purer than any the earth produces. Will that convince you?"

"That will convince me," I answered. By a gesture I imposed silence on Marion, who was about to speak. I thought it better to allow the old man to be his own undeceiver – and we awaited the coming crisis.

The old man, still smiling with anticipated triumph, kept bending eagerly over his crucible, stirring the mixture with his rod, and muttering to himself all the time. "Now," I heard him say, "it changes. There – there's the scum. And now the green and bronze shades flit across it. Oh, the beautiful green! the precursor of the golden-red hue that tells of the end attained! Ah! now the golden-red is coming – slowly – slowly! It deepens, it shines, it is dazzling! Ah, I have it!" So saying, he caught up his crucible in a chemist's tongs, and bore it slowly toward the table on which stood a brass vessel.

"Now, incredulous doctor!" he cried, "come and be convinced," and immediately began carefully pouring the contents of the crucible into the brass vessel. When the crucible was quite empty he turned it up and called me again. "Come, doctor, come and be convinced. See for yourself."

"See first if there is any gold in your crucible," I answered, without moving.

He laughed, shook his head derisively, and looked into the crucible. In a moment he grew pale as death.

"Nothing!" he cried. "Oh, a jest, a jest! There must be gold somewhere. Marion!"

"The gold is here, father," said Marion, drawing the ingot from her pocket; "it is all we ever had."

"Ah!" shrieked the poor old man, as he let the empty crucible fall, and staggered toward the ingot which Marion held out to him. He made three steps, and then fell on his face. Marion rushed toward him, and tried to lift him, but could not. I put her aside gently, and placed my hand on his heart.

"Marion," said I, "it is perhaps better as it is. He is dead!"

My Wife's Tempter

I

A PREDESTINED MARRIAGE

Elsie and I were to be married in less than a week. It was rather a strange match, and I knew that some of our neighbors shook their heads over it and said that no good would come. The way it came to pass was thus.

I loved Elsie Burns for two years, during which time she refused me three times. I could no more help asking her to have me, when the chance offered, than I could help breathing or living. To love her seemed natural to me as existence. I felt no shame, only sorrow, when she rejected me; I felt no shame either when I renewed my suit. The neighbors called me mean-spirited to take up with any girl that had refused me as often as Elsie Burns had done; but what cared I about the neighbors? If it is black weather, and the sun is under a cloud every day for a month, is that any reason why the poor farmer should not hope for the blue sky and the plentiful burst of warm light when the dark month is over? I never entirely lost heart. Do not, however, mistake me. I did not mope, and moan, and grow pale, after the manner of poetical lovers. No such thing. I went bravely about my business, ate and drank as usual, laughed when the laugh went round, and slept soundly, and woke refreshed. Yet all this time I loved – desperately loved – Elsie Burns. I went wherever I hoped to meet her, but did not haunt her with my attentions. I behaved to her as any friendly young man would have behaved: I met her and parted from her cheerfully. She was a good girl, too, and behaved well. She had me in her power – how a woman in Elsie's situation could have mortified a man in mine! – but she never took the slightest advantage of it. She danced with me when I asked her, and had no foolish fears of allowing me to see her home of nights, after a ball was over, or of wandering with me through the pleasant New England fields when the wild flowers made the paths like roads in fairyland.

On the several disastrous occasions when I presented my suit I did it simply and manfully, telling her that I loved her very much, and would do everything to make her happy if she would be my wife. I made no fulsome protestations, and did not once allude to suicide. She, on the other hand, calmly and gravely thanked me for my good opinion, but with the same calm gravity rejected me. I used to tell her that I was grieved; that I would not press her; that I would wait and hope for some change in her feelings. She had an esteem for me, she would say, but could not marry me. I never asked her for any reasons. I hold it to be an insult to a woman of sense to demand her reasons on such an occasion. Enough for me that she did not then wish to be my wife; so that the old intercourse went on – she cordial and polite as ever, I never for one moment doubting that the day would come when my roof tree would shelter her, and we should smile together over our fireside at my long and indefatigable wooing.

I will confess that at times I felt a little jealous – jealous of a man named Hammond Brake, who lived in our village. He was a weird, saturnine fellow, who made no friends among the young men of the neighborhood, but who loved to go alone, with his books and his own thoughts for company. He was a studious and, I believe, a learned young man, and there was no avoiding the fact that he possessed considerable influence over Elsie. She liked to talk with him in corners, or in secluded nooks of the forest, when we all went out blackberry gathering or picnicking. She read books that he gave her, and whenever a discussion arose relative to any topic higher than those ordinary ones we usually canvassed, Elsie appealed to Brake for his opinion, as a disciple consulting a beloved master. I confess that for a time I feared this man as a rival. A little closer observation, however, convinced me that my suspicions were unfounded. The relations between Elsie and Hammond Brake were purely intellectual. She reverenced his talents and acquirements, but she did not love him. His influence over her, nevertheless, was none the less decided.

In time – as I thought all along – Elsie yielded. I was what was considered a most eligible match, being tolerably rich, and Elsie's parents were most anxious to have me for a son-in-law. I was good-looking and well educated enough, and the old people, I believe, pertinaciously dinned all my advantages into my little girl's ears. She battled against the marriage for a long time with a strange persistence – all the more strange because she never alleged the slightest personal dislike to me; but after a vigorous cannonading from her own garrison (in which, I am proud to say, I did not in any way join), she hoisted the white flag and surrendered.

I was very happy. I had no fear about being able to gain Elsie's heart. I think – indeed I know – that she had liked me all along, and that her refusals were dictated by other feelings than those of a personal nature. I only guessed as much then. It was some time before I knew all.

As the day approached for our wedding Elsie did not appear at all stricken with woe. The village gossips had not the smallest opportunity for establishing a romance, with a compulsory bride for the heroine. Yet to me it seemed as if there was something strange about her. A vague terror appeared to beset her. Even in her most loving moments, when resting in my arms, she would shrink away from me, and shudder as if some cold wind had suddenly struck upon her. That it was caused by no aversion to me was evident, for she would the moment after, as if to make amends, give me one of those voluntary kisses that are sweeter than all others.

Once only did she show any emotion. When the solemn question was put to her, the answer to which was to decide her destiny, I felt her hand – which was in mine – tremble. As she gasped out a convulsive "Yes," she gave one brief, imploring glance at the gallery on the right. I placed the ring upon her finger, and looked in the direction in which she gazed. Hammond Brake's dark countenance was visible looking over the railings, and his eyes were bent sternly on Elsie. I turned quickly round to my bride, but her brief emotion, of whatever nature, had vanished. She was looking at me anxiously, and smiling – somewhat sadly – through her maiden's tears.

The months went by quickly, and we were very happy. I

learned that Elsie really loved me, and of my love for her she had proof long ago. I will not say that there was no cloud upon our little horizon. There was one, but it was so small, and appeared so seldom, that I scarcely feared it. The old vague terror seemed still to attack my wife. If I did not know her to be pure as heaven's snow, I would have said it was a REMORSE. At times she scarcely appeared to hear what I said, so deep would be her reverie. Nor did those moods seem pleasant ones. When rapt in such, her sweet features would contract, as if in a hopeless effort to solve some mysterious problem. A sad pain, as it were, quivered in her white, drooped eyelids. One thing I particularly remarked: SHE SPENT HOURS AT A TIME GAZING AT THE WEST. There was a small room in our house whose windows, every evening, flamed with the red light of the setting sun. Here Elsie would sit and gaze westward, so motionless and entranced that it seemed as if her soul was going down with the day. Her conduct to me was curiously varied. She apparently loved me very much, yet there were times when she absolutely avoided me. I have seen her strolling through the fields, and left the house with the intention of joining her, but the moment she caught sight of me approaching she has fled into the neighboring copse, with so evident a wish to avoid me that it would have been absolutely cruel to follow.

Once or twice the old jealousy of Hammond Brake crossed my mind, but I was obliged to dismiss it as a frivolous suspicion. Nothing in my wife's conduct justified any such theory. Brake visited us once or twice a week – in fact, when I returned from my business in the village, I used to find him seated in the parlor with Elsie, reading some favorite author, or conversing on some novel literary topic; but there was no disposition to avoid my scrutiny. Brake seemed to come as a matter of right; and the perfect unconsciousness of furnishing any grounds for suspicion with which he acted was a sufficient answer to my mind for any wild doubts that my heart may have suggested.

Still I could not but remark that Brake's visits were in some manner connected with Elsie's melancholy. On the days when he had appeared and departed, the gloom seemed to hang more thickly than ever over her head. She sat, on such occasions, all the evening at the western window, silently gazing at the cleft in the hills through which the sun passed to his repose.

At last I made up my mind to speak to her. It seemed to me to be my duty, if she had a sorrow, to partake of it. I approached her on the matter with the most perfect confidence that I had nothing to learn beyond the existence of some girlish grief, which a confession and a few loving kisses would exorcise forever.

"Elsie," I said to her one night, as she sat, according to her custom, gazing westward, like those maidens of the old ballads of chivalry watching for the knights that never came – "Elsie, what is the matter with you, darling? I have noticed a strange melancholy in you for some time past. Tell me all about it."

She turned quickly round and gazed at me with eyes wide open and face filled with a sudden fear. "Why do you ask me that, Mark?" she answered. "I have nothing to tell."

From the strange, startled manner in which this reply was given, I felt convinced that she had something to tell, and instantly formed a determination to discover what it was. A pang shot through my heart as I thought that the woman whom I held dearer than anything on earth hesitated to trust me with a petty secret.

I believed I understood. I was tolerably rich. I knew it could not be any secret over milliners' bills or women's usual money troubles. God help me! I felt sad enough at the moment, though I kissed her back and ceased to question her. I felt sad, because my instinct told me that she deceived me; and it is very hard to be deceived, even in trifles, by those we love. I left her sitting at her favorite window, and walked out into the fields. I wanted to think.

I remained out until I saw lights in the parlor shining through the dusky evening; then I returned slowly. As I passed the windows – which were near the ground, our house being cottage-built – I looked in. Hammond Brake was sitting with my wife. She was sitting in a rocking chair opposite to him, holding a small volume open on her lap. Brake was talking to her very earnestly, and she was listening to him with an expression I had never before seen on her countenance. Awe, fear, and admiration were all blent together in those dilating eyes. She seemed absorbed, body and soul, in what this man said. I shuddered at the sight. A vague terror seized upon me; I hastened into the house. As I entered the room rather suddenly, my wife started and hastily concealed the little volume that lay on her lap in one of her wide pockets. As she did so, a loose leaf escaped from the volume and slowly fluttered to the floor unobserved by either her or her companion. But I had my eye upon it. I felt that it was a clew.

"What new novel or philosophical wonder have you both been poring over?" I asked quite gayly, stealthily watching at the same time the telltale embarrassment under which Elsie was laboring.

Brake, who was not in the least discomposed, replied. "That," said he, "is a secret which must be kept from you. It is an advance copy, and is not to be shown to anyone except your wife."

"Ha!" cried I, "I know what it is. It is your volume of poems that Ticknor is publishing. Well, I can wait until it is regularly for sale."

I knew that Brake had a volume in the hands of the publishing house I mentioned, with a vague promise of publication some time in the present century. Hammond smiled significantly, but did not reply. He evidently wished to cultivate this supposed impression of mine. Elsie looked relieved, and heaved a deep sigh. I felt more than ever convinced that a secret was beneath all this. So I drew my chair over the fallen leaf that lay unnoticed on the carpet, and talked and laughed with Hammond Brake gayly, as if nothing was on my mind, while all the time a great load of suspicion lay heavily at my heart.

At length Hammond Brake rose to go. I wished him good night, but did not offer to accompany him to the door. My wife supplied this omitted courtesy, as I had expected. The moment I was alone I picked up the book leaf from the floor. It was NOT the leaf of a volume of poems. Beyond that, however, I learned nothing. It contained a string of paragraphs printed in the biblical fashion, and the language was biblical in style. It seemed to be a portion of some religious book. Was it possible that my wife was being converted to the Romish faith? Yes, that was it. Brake was a Jesuit in disguise – I had heard of such things – and had stolen into the bosom of my family to plant there his destructive errors. There could be no longer any doubt of it. This was some portion of a Romish book – some infamous Popish publication. Fool that I was not to see it all before! But there was yet time. I would forbid him the house.

I had just formed this resolution when my wife entered. I put the strange leaf in my pocket and took my hat.

"Why, you are not going out, surely?" cried Elsie, surprised.

"I have a headache," I answered. "I will take a short walk."

Elsie looked at me with a peculiar air of distrust. Her woman's instinct told her that there was something wrong. Before she could question me, however, I had left the room and was walking rapidly on Hammond Brake's track.

He heard the footsteps, and I saw his figure, black against the sky, stop and peer back through the dusk to see who was following him.

"It is I, Brake," I called out. "Stop; I wish to speak with you."

He stopped, and in a minute or so we were walking side by side along the road. My fingers itched at that moment to be on his throat. I commenced the conversation.

"Brake," I said, "I'm a very plain sort of man, and I never say anything without good reason. What I came after you to tell you is, that I don't wish you to come to my house any more, or to speak with Elsie any farther than the ordinary salutations go. It's no joke. I'm quite in earnest."

Brake started, and, stopping short, faced me suddenly in the road. "What have I done?" he asked. "You surely are too sensible a man to be jealous, Dayton."

"Oh," I answered scornfully, "not jealous in the ordinary sense of the word, a bit. But I don't think your company good company for my wife, Brake. If you WILL have it out of me, I suspect you of being a Roman Catholic, and of trying to convert my wife."

A smile shot across his face, and I saw his sharp white teeth gleam for an instant in the dusk.

"Well, what if I am a Papist?" he said, with a strange tone of triumph in his voice. "The faith is not criminal. Besides, what proof have you that I was attempting to proselyte your wife?"

"This," said I, pulling the leaf from my pocket – "this leaf from one of those devilish Papist books you and she were reading this evening. I picked it up from the floor. Proof enough, I think!"

In an instant Brake had snatched the leaf from my hand and torn it into atoms.

"You shall be obeyed," he said. "I will not speak with Elsie as long as she is your wife. Good night. You think I'm a Papist, then, Dayton? You're a clever fellow!"

And with rather a sneering chuckle he marched on along the road and vanished into the darkness.

II

THE SECRET DISCOVERED

Brake came no more. I said nothing to Elsie about his prohibition, and his name was never mentioned. It seemed strange to me that she should not speak of his absence, and I was very much puzzled by her silence. Her moodiness seemed to have increased, and, what was most remarkable, in proportion as she grew more and more reserved, the intenser were the bursts of affection which she exhibited for me. She would strain me to her bosom and kiss me, as if she and I were about to be parted forever. Then for hours she would remain sitting at her window, silently gazing, with that terrible, wistful gaze of hers, at the west.

I will confess to having watched my wife at this time. I could not help it. That some mystery hung about her I felt convinced. I must fathom it or die. Her honor I never for a moment doubted; yet there seemed to weigh continually upon me the prophecy of some awful domestic calamity. This time the prophecy was not in vain.

About three weeks after I had forbidden Brake my house, I was strolling over my farm in the evening apparently inspecting my agriculture, but in reality speculating on that topic which latterly was ever present to me.

There was a little knoll covered with evergreen oaks at the end of the lawn. It was a picturesque spot, for on one side the bank went off into a sheer precipice of about eighty feet in depth, at the bottom of which a pretty pool lay, that in the summer time was fringed with white water-lilies. I had thought of building a summer-house in this spot, and now my steps mechanically directed themselves toward the place. As I approached I heard voices. I stopped and listened eagerly. A few seconds enabled me to ascertain that Hammond Brake and my wife were in the copse talking together. She still followed him, then; and he, scoundrel that he was, had broken his promise. A fury seemed to fill my veins as I made this discovery. I felt the impulse strong upon me to rush into the grove, and then and there strangle the villain who was poisoning my peace. But with a powerful effort I restrained myself. It was necessary that I should overhear what was said. I threw myself flat on the grass, and so glided silently into the copse until I was completely within earshot. This was what I heard.

My wife was sobbing. "So soon – so soon? I – Hammond, give me a little time!"

"I cannot, Elsie. My chief orders me to join him. You must prepare to accompany me."

"No, no!" murmured Elsie. "He loves me so! And I love him. Our child, too – how can I rob him of our unborn babe?"

"Another sheep for our flock," answered Brake solemnly. "Elsie, do you forget your oath? Are you one of us, or are you a common hypocrite, who will be of us until the hour of self-sacrifice, and then fly like a coward? Elsie, you must leave to-night."

"Ah! my husband, my husband!" sobbed the unhappy woman.

"You have no husband, woman," cried Brake harshly. "I promised Dayton not to speak to you as long as you were his wife, but the vow was annulled before it was made. Your husband in God yet awaits you. You will yet be blessed with the true spouse."

"I feel as if I were going to die," cried Elsie. "How can I ever forsake him – he who was so good to me?"

"Nonsense! no weakness. He is not worthy of you. Go home and prepare for your journey. You know where to meet me. I will have everything ready, and by daybreak there shall be no trace of us left. Beware of permitting your husband to suspect anything. He is not very shrewd at such things – he thought I was a Jesuit in disguise – but we had better be careful. Now go. You have been too long here already. Bless you, sister."

A few faint sobs, a rustling of leaves, and I knew that Brake was alone. I rose, and stepped silently into the open space in which he stood. His back was toward me. His arms were lifted high over his head with an exultant gesture, and I could see his profile, as it slightly turned toward me, illuminated with a smile of scornful triumph. I put my hand suddenly on his throat from behind, and flung him on the ground before he could utter a cry.

"Not a word," I said, unclasping a short-bladed knife which I carried; "answer my questions, or, by heaven, I will cut your throat from ear to ear!"

He looked up into my face with an unflinching eye, and set his lips as if resolved to suffer all.

"What are you? Who are you? What object have you in the seduction of my wife?"

He smiled, but was silent.

"Ah! you won't answer. We'll see."

I pressed the knife slowly against his throat. His face contracted spasmodically, but although a thin red thread of blood sprang out along the edge of the blade, Brake remained mute. An idea suddenly seized me. This sort of death had no terrors for him. I would try another. There was the precipice. I was twice as powerful as he was, so I seized him in my arms, and in a moment transported him to the margin of the steep, smooth cliff, the edge of which was garnished with the tough stems of the wild vine. He seemed to feel it was useless to struggle with me, so allowed me passively to roll him over the edge. When he was suspended in the air, I gave him a vine stem to cling to and let him go. He swung at a height of eighty feet, with face upturned and pale. He dared not look down. I seated myself on the edge of the cliff, and with my knife began to cut into the thick vine a foot or two above the place of his grasp. I was correct in my calculation. This terror was too much for him. As he saw the notch in the vine getting deeper and deeper, his determination gave way.

"I'll answer you," he gasped out, gazing at me with starting eyeballs; "what do you ask?"

"What are you?" was my question, as I ceased cutting at the stem.

"A Mormon," was the answer, uttered with a groan. "Take me up. My hands are slipping. Quick!"

"And you wanted my wife to follow you to that infernal Salt Lake City, I suppose?"

"For God's sake, release me! I'll quit the place, never to come back. Do help me up, Dayton – I'm falling!"

I felt mightily inclined to let the villain drop; but it did not suit my purpose to be hung for murder, so I swung him back again on the sward, where he fell panting and exhausted.

"Will you quit the place to-night?" I said. "You'd better. By heaven, if you don't, I'll tell all the men in the village, and we'll lynch you, as sure as your name is Brake."

"I'll go – I'll go," he groaned. "I swear never to trouble you again."

"You ought to be hanged, you villain. Be off!"

He slunk away through the trees like a beaten dog; and I went home in a state bordering on despair. I found Elsie crying. She was sitting by the window as of old. I knew now why she gazed so constantly at the west. It was her Mecca. Something in my face, I suppose, told her that I was laboring under great excitement. She rose startled as soon as I entered the room.

"Elsie," said I, "I am come to take you home."

"Home? Why, I AM at home, am I not? What do you mean?"

"No. This is no longer your home. You have deceived me. You are a Mormon. I know all. You have become a convert to that apostle of hell, Brigham Young, and you cannot live with me. I love you still, Elsie, dearly; but – you must go and live with your father."

Nathaniel Hawthorne

The Minister's Black Veil

A PARABLE [1]

[1] Another clergyman in New England, Mr. Joseph Moody, of York, Maine, made himself remarkable by the same eccentricity that is here related of the Reverend Mr. Hooper. In his case, however, the symbol had a different import. In early life he had accidentally killed a beloved friend, and from that day till the hour of his own death, he hid his face from men.

The sexton stood in the porch of Milford meeting-house, pulling busily at the bell-rope. The old people of the village came stooping along the street. Children, with bright faces, tripped merrily beside their parents, or mimicked a graver gait, in the conscious dignity of their Sunday clothes. Spruce bachelors looked sidelong at the pretty maidens, and fancied that the Sabbath sunshine made them prettier than on week days. When the throng had mostly streamed into the porch, the sexton began to toll the bell, keeping his eye on the Reverend Mr. Hooper's door. The first glimpse of the clergyman's figure was the signal for the bell to cease its summons.

"But what has good Parson Hooper got upon his face?" cried the sexton in astonishment.

All within hearing immediately turned about, and beheld the semblance of Mr. Hooper, pacing slowly his meditative way towards the meetinghouse. With one accord they started, expressing more wonder than if some strange minister were coming to dust the cushions of Mr. Hooper's pulpit.

"Are you sure it is our parson?" inquired Goodman Gray of the sexton.

"Of a certainty it is good Mr. Hooper," replied the sexton. "He was to have exchanged pulpits with Parson Shute, of Westbury; but Parson Shute sent to excuse himself yesterday, being to preach a funeral sermon."

The cause of so much amazement may appear sufficiently slight. Mr. Hooper, a gentlemanly person, of about thirty, though still a bachelor, was dressed with due clerical neatness, as if a careful wife had starched his band, and brushed the weekly dust from his Sunday's garb. There was but one thing remarkable in his appearance. Swathed about his forehead, and hanging down over his face, so low as to be shaken by his breath, Mr. Hooper had on a black veil. On a nearer view it seemed to consist of two folds of crape, which entirely concealed his features, except the mouth and chin, but probably did not intercept his sight, further than to give a darkened aspect to all living and inanimate things. With this gloomy shade before him, good Mr. Hooper walked onward, at a slow and quiet pace, stooping somewhat, and looking on the ground, as is customary with abstracted men, yet nodding kindly to those of his parishioners who still waited on the meeting-house steps. But so wonder-struck were they that his greeting hardly met with a return.

"I can't really feel as if good Mr. Hooper's face was behind that piece of crape," said the sexton.

"I don't like it," muttered an old woman, as she hobbled into the meeting-house. "He has changed himself into something awful, only by hiding his face."

"Our parson has gone mad!" cried Goodman Gray, following him across the threshold.

A rumor of some unaccountable phenomenon had preceded Mr. Hooper into the meeting-house, and set all the congregation astir. Few could refrain from twisting their heads towards the door; many stood upright, and turned directly about; while several little boys clambered upon the seats, and came down again with a terrible racket. There was a general bustle, a rustling of the women's gowns and shuffling of the men's feet, greatly at variance with that hushed repose which should attend the entrance of the minister. But Mr. Hooper appeared not to notice the perturbation of his people. He entered with an almost noiseless step, bent his head mildly to the pews on each side, and bowed as he passed his oldest parishioner, a white-haired great grandsire, who occupied an arm-chair in the centre of the aisle. It was strange to observe how slowly this venerable man became conscious of something singular in the appearance of his pastor. He seemed not fully to partake of the prevailing wonder, till Mr. Hooper had ascended the stairs, and showed himself in the pulpit, face to face with his congregation, except for the black veil. That mysterious emblem was never once withdrawn. It shook with his measured breath, as he gave out the psalm; it threw its obscurity between him and the holy page, as he read the Scriptures; and while he prayed, the veil lay heavily on his uplifted countenance. Did he seek to hide it from the dread Being whom he was addressing?

Such was the effect of this simple piece of crape, that more than one woman of delicate nerves was forced to leave the meeting-house. Yet perhaps the pale-faced congregation was almost as fearful a sight to the minister, as his black veil to them.

Mr. Hooper had the reputation of a good preacher, but not an energetic one: he strove to win his people heavenward by mild, persuasive influences, rather than to drive them thither by the thunders of the Word. The sermon which he now delivered was marked by the same characteristics of style and manner as the general series of his pulpit oratory. But there was something, either in the sentiment of the discourse itself, or in the imagination of the auditors, which made it greatly the most powerful effort that they had ever heard from their pastor's lips. It was tinged, rather more darkly than usual, with the gentle gloom of Mr. Hooper's temperament. The subject had reference to secret sin, and those sad mysteries which we hide from our nearest and dearest, and would fain conceal from our own consciousness, even forgetting that the Omniscient can detect them. A subtle power was breathed into his words. Each member of the congregation, the most innocent girl, and the man of hardened breast, felt as if the preacher had crept upon them, behind his awful veil, and discovered their hoarded iniquity of deed or thought. Many spread their clasped hands on their bosoms. There was nothing terrible in what Mr. Hooper said, at least, no violence; and yet, with every tremor of his melancholy voice, the hearers quaked. An unsought pathos came hand in hand with awe. So sensible were the audience of some unwonted attribute in their minister, that they longed for a breath of wind to blow aside the veil, almost believing that a stranger's visage would be discovered, though the form, gesture, and voice were those of Mr. Hooper.

At the close of the services, the people hurried out with indecorous confusion, eager to communicate their pent-up amazement, and conscious of lighter spirits the moment they lost sight of the black veil. Some gathered in little circles, huddled closely together, with their mouths all whispering in the centre; some went homeward alone, wrapt in silent meditation; some talked loudly, and profaned the Sabbath day with ostentatious laughter. A few shook their sagacious heads, intimating that they could penetrate the mystery; while one or two affirmed that there was no mystery at all, but only that Mr. Hooper's eyes were so weakened by the midnight lamp, as to require a shade. After a brief interval, forth came good Mr. Hooper also, in the rear of his flock. Turning his veiled face from one group to another, he paid due reverence to the hoary heads, saluted the middle aged with kind dignity as their friend and spiritual guide, greeted the young with mingled authority and love, and laid his hands on the little children's heads to bless them. Such was always his custom on the Sabbath day. Strange and bewildered looks repaid him for his courtesy. None, as on former occasions, aspired to the honor of walking by their pastor's side. Old Squire Saunders, doubtless by an accidental lapse of memory, neglected to invite Mr. Hooper to his table, where the good clergyman had been wont to bless the food, almost every Sunday since his settlement. He returned, therefore, to the parsonage, and, at the moment of closing the door, was observed to look back upon the people, all of whom had their eyes fixed upon the minister. A sad smile gleamed faintly from beneath the black veil, and flickered about his mouth, glimmering as he disappeared.

"How strange," said a lady, "that a simple black veil, such as any woman might wear on her bonnet, should become such a terrible thing on Mr. Hooper's face!"

"Something must surely be amiss with Mr. Hooper's intellects," observed her husband, the physician of the village. "But the strangest part of the affair is the effect of this vagary, even on a sober-minded man like myself. The black veil, though it covers only our pastor's face, throws its influence over his whole person, and makes him ghostlike from head to foot. Do you not feel it so?"

"Truly do I," replied the lady; "and I would not be alone with him for the world. I wonder he is not afraid to be alone with himself!"

"Men sometimes are so," said her husband.

The afternoon service was attended with similar circumstances. At its conclusion, the bell tolled for the funeral of a young lady. The relatives and friends were assembled in the house, and the more distant acquaintances stood about the door, speaking of the good qualities of the deceased, when their talk was interrupted by the appearance of Mr. Hooper, still covered with his black veil. It was now an appropriate emblem. The clergyman stepped into the room where the corpse was laid, and bent over the coffin, to take a last farewell of his deceased parishioner. As he stooped, the veil hung straight down from his forehead, so that, if her eyelids had not been closed forever, the dead maiden might have seen his face. Could Mr. Hooper be fearful of her glance, that he so hastily caught back the black veil? A person who watched the interview between the dead and living, scrupled not to affirm, that, at the instant when the clergyman's features were disclosed, the corpse had slightly shuddered, rustling the shroud and muslin cap, though the countenance retained the composure of death. A superstitious old woman was the only witness of this prodigy. From the coffin Mr. Hooper passed into the chamber of the mourners, and thence to the head of the staircase, to make the funeral prayer. It was a tender and heart-dissolving prayer, full of sorrow, yet so imbued with celestial hopes, that the music of a heavenly harp, swept by the fingers of the dead, seemed faintly to be heard among the saddest accents of the minister. The people trembled, though they but darkly understood him when he prayed that they, and himself, and all of mortal race, might be ready, as he trusted this young maiden had been, for the dreadful hour that should snatch the veil from their faces. The bearers went heavily forth, and the mourners followed, saddening all the street, with the dead before them, and Mr.

Hooper in his black veil behind.

"Why do you look back?" said one in the procession to his partner.

"I had a fancy," replied she, "that the minister and the maiden's spirit were walking hand in hand."

"And so had I, at the same moment," said the other.

That night, the handsomest couple in Milford village were to be joined in wedlock. Though reckoned a melancholy man, Mr. Hooper had a placid cheerfulness for such occasions, which often excited a sympathetic smile where livelier merriment would have been thrown away. There was no quality of his disposition which made him more beloved than this. The company at the wedding awaited his arrival with impatience, trusting that the strange awe, which had gathered over him throughout the day, would now be dispelled. But such was not the result. When Mr. Hooper came, the first thing that their eyes rested on was the same horrible black veil, which had added deeper gloom to the funeral, and could portend nothing but evil to the wedding. Such was its immediate effect on the guests that a cloud seemed to have rolled duskily from beneath the black crape, and dimmed the light of the candles. The bridal pair stood up before the minister. But the bride's cold fingers quivered in the tremulous hand of the bridegroom, and her deathlike paleness caused a whisper that the maiden who had been buried a few hours before was come from her grave to be married. If ever another wedding were so dismal, it was that famous one where they tolled the wedding knell. After performing the ceremony, Mr. Hooper raised a glass of wine to his lips, wishing happiness to the new-married couple in a strain of mild pleasantry that ought to have brightened the features of the guests, like a cheerful gleam from the hearth. At that instant, catching a glimpse of his figure in the looking-glass, the black veil involved his own spirit in the horror with which it overwhelmed all others. His frame shuddered, his lips grew white, he spilt the untasted wine upon the carpet, and rushed forth into the darkness. For the Earth, too, had on her Black Veil.

The next day, the whole village of Milford talked of little else than Parson Hooper's black veil. That, and the mystery concealed behind it, supplied a topic for discussion between acquaintances meeting in the street, and good women gossiping at their open windows. It was the first item of news that the tavern-keeper told to his guests. The children babbled of it on their way to school. One imitative little imp covered his face with an old black handkerchief, thereby so affrighting his playmates that the panic seized himself, and he well-nigh lost his wits by his own waggery.

It was remarkable that all of the busybodies and impertinent people in the parish, not one ventured to put the plain question to Mr. Hooper, wherefore he did this thing. Hitherto, whenever there appeared the slightest call for such interference, he had never lacked advisers, nor shown himself averse to be guided by their judgment. If he erred at all, it was by so painful a degree of self-distrust, that even the mildest censure would lead him to consider an indifferent action as a crime. Yet, though so well acquainted with this amiable weakness, no individual among his parishioners chose to make the black veil a subject of friendly remonstrance. There was a feeling of dread, neither plainly confessed nor carefully concealed, which caused each to shift the responsibility upon another, till at length it was found expedient to send a deputation of the church, in order to deal with Mr. Hooper about the mystery, before it should grow into a scandal. Never did an embassy so ill discharge its duties. The minister received them with friendly courtesy, but became silent, after they were seated, leaving to his visitors the whole burden of introducing their important business. The topic, it might be supposed, was obvious enough. There was the black veil swathed round Mr. Hooper's forehead, and concealing every feature above his placid mouth, on which, at times, they could perceive the glimmering of a melancholy smile. But that piece of crape, to their imagination, seemed to hang down before his heart, the symbol of a fearful secret between him and them. Were the veil but cast aside, they might speak freely of it, but not till then. Thus they sat a considerable time, speechless, confused, and shrinking uneasily from Mr. Hooper's eye, which they felt to be fixed upon them with an invisible glance. Finally, the deputies returned abashed to their constituents, pronouncing the matter too weighty to be handled, except by a council of the churches, if, indeed, it might not require a general synod.

But there was one person in the village unappalled by the awe with which the black veil had impressed all beside herself. When the deputies returned without an explanation, or even venturing to demand one, she, with the calm energy of her character, determined to chase away the strange cloud that appeared to be settling round Mr. Hooper, every moment more darkly than before. As his plighted wife, it should be her privilege to know what the black veil concealed. At the minister's first visit, therefore, she entered upon the subject with a direct simplicity, which made the task easier both for him and her. After he had seated himself, she fixed her eyes steadfastly upon the veil, but could discern nothing of the dreadful gloom that had so overawed the multitude: it was but a double fold of crape, hanging down from his forehead to his mouth, and slightly stirring with his breath.

"No," said she aloud, and smiling, "there is nothing terrible in this piece of crape, except that it hides a face which I am always glad to look upon. Come, good sir, let the sun shine from behind the cloud. First lay aside your black veil: then tell me why you put it on."

Mr. Hooper's smile glimmered faintly.

"There is an hour to come," said he, "when all of us shall cast aside our veils. Take it not amiss, beloved friend, if I wear this piece of crape till then."

"Your words are a mystery, too," returned the young lady. "Take away the veil from them, at least."

"Elizabeth, I will," said he, "so far as my vow may suffer me. Know, then, this veil is a type and a symbol, and I am bound to wear it ever, both in light and darkness, in solitude and before the gaze of multitudes, and as with strangers, so with my familiar friends. No mortal eye will see it withdrawn. This dismal shade must separate me from the world: even you, Elizabeth, can never come behind it!"

"What grievous affliction hath befallen you," she earnestly inquired, "that you should thus darken your eyes forever?"

"If it be a sign of mourning," replied Mr. Hooper, "I, perhaps, like most other mortals, have sorrows dark enough to be typified by a black veil."

"But what if the world will not believe that it is the type of an innocent sorrow?" urged Elizabeth. "Beloved and respected as you are, there may be whispers that you hide your face under the consciousness of secret sin. For the sake of your holy office, do away this scandal!"

The color rose into her cheeks as she intimated the nature of the rumors that were already abroad in the village. But Mr. Hooper's mildness did not forsake him. He even smiled again – that same sad smile, which always appeared like a faint glimmering of light, proceeding from the obscurity beneath the veil.

"If I hide my face for sorrow, there is cause enough," he merely replied; "and if I cover it for secret sin, what mortal might not do the same?"

And with this gentle, but unconquerable obstinacy did he resist all her entreaties. At length Elizabeth sat silent. For a few moments she appeared lost in thought, considering, probably, what new methods might be tried to withdraw her lover from so dark a fantasy, which, if it had no other meaning, was perhaps a symptom of mental disease. Though of a firmer character than his own, the tears rolled down her cheeks. But, in an instant, as it were, a new feeling took the place of sorrow: her eyes were fixed insensibly on the black veil, when, like a sudden twilight in the air, its terrors fell around her. She arose, and stood trembling before him.

"And do you feel it then, at last?" said he mournfully.

She made no reply, but covered her eyes with her hand, and turned to leave the room. He rushed forward and caught her arm.

"Have patience with me, Elizabeth!" cried he, passionately. "Do not desert me, though this veil must be between us here on earth. Be mine, and hereafter there shall be no veil over my face, no darkness between our souls! It is but a mortal veil – it is not for eternity! O! you know not how lonely I am, and how frightened, to be alone behind my black veil. Do not leave me in this miserable obscurity forever!"

"Lift the veil but once, and look me in the face," said she.

"Never! It cannot be!" replied Mr. Hooper.

"Then farewell!" said Elizabeth.

She withdrew her arm from his grasp, and slowly departed, pausing at the door, to give one long shuddering gaze, that seemed almost to penetrate the mystery of the black veil. But, even amid his grief, Mr. Hooper smiled to think that only a material emblem had separated him from happiness, though the horrors, which it shadowed forth, must be drawn darkly between the fondest of lovers.

From that time no attempts were made to remove Mr. Hooper's black veil, or, by a direct appeal, to discover the secret which it was supposed to hide. By persons who claimed a superiority to popular prejudice, it was reckoned merely an eccentric whim, such as often mingles with the sober actions of men otherwise rational, and tinges them all with its own semblance of insanity. But with the multitude, good Mr. Hooper was irreparably a bugbear. He could not walk the street with any peace of mind, so conscious was he that the gentle and timid would turn aside to avoid him, and that others would make it a point of hardihood to throw themselves in his way. The impertinence of the latter class compelled him to give up his customary walk at sunset to the burial ground; for when he leaned pensively over the gate, there would always be faces behind the gravestones, peeping at his black veil. A fable went the rounds that the stare of the dead people drove him thence. It grieved him, to the very depth of his kind heart, to observe how the children fled from his approach, breaking up their merriest sports, while his melancholy figure was yet afar off. Their instinctive dread caused him to feel more strongly than aught else, that a preternatural horror was interwoven with the threads of the black crape. In truth, his own antipathy to the veil was known to be so great, that he never willingly passed before a mirror, nor stooped to drink at a still fountain, lest, in its peaceful bosom, he should be affrighted by himself. This was what gave plausibility to the whispers, that Mr. Hooper's conscience tortured him for some great crime too horrible to be entirely concealed, or otherwise than so obscurely intimated. Thus, from beneath the black veil, there rolled a cloud into the sunshine, an ambiguity of sin or sorrow, which enveloped the poor minister, so that love or sympathy could never reach him. It was said that ghost and fiend consorted with him there. With self-shudderings and outward terrors, he walked continually in its shadow, groping darkly within his own soul, or gazing through a medium that saddened the whole world. Even the lawless wind, it was believed, respected his dreadful secret, and never blew aside the veil. But still good Mr. Hooper sadly smiled at the pale visages of the worldly throng as he passed by.

Among all its bad influences, the black veil had the one desirable effect, of making its wearer a very efficient clergyman. By the aid of his mysterious emblem – for there was no other apparent cause – he became a man of awful power over souls that were in agony for sin. His converts always regarded him with a dread peculiar to themselves, affirming, though but figuratively, that, before he brought them to celestial light, they had been with him behind the black veil. Its gloom, indeed, enabled him to sympathize with all dark affections. Dying sinners cried aloud for Mr. Hooper, and would not yield their breath till he appeared; though ever, as he stooped to whisper consolation, they shuddered at the veiled face so near their own. Such were the terrors of the black veil, even when Death had bared his visage! Strangers came long distances to attend service at his church, with the mere idle purpose of gazing at his figure, because it was forbidden them to behold his face. But many were made to quake ere they departed! Once, during Governor Belcher's administration, Mr. Hooper was appointed to preach the election sermon. Covered with his black veil, he stood before the chief magistrate, the council, and the representatives, and wrought so deep an impression, that the legislative measures of that year were characterized by all the gloom and piety of our earliest ancestral sway.

In this manner Mr. Hooper spent a long life, irreproachable in outward act, yet shrouded in dismal suspicions; kind and loving, though unloved, and dimly feared; a man apart from men, shunned in their health and joy, but ever summoned to their aid in mortal anguish. As years wore on, shedding their snows above his sable veil, he acquired a name throughout the New England churches, and they called him Father Hooper. Nearly all his parishioners, who were of mature age when he was settled, had been borne away by many a funeral: he had one congregation in the church, and a more crowded one in the churchyard; and having wrought so late into the evening, and done his work so well, it was now good Father Hooper's turn to rest.

Several persons were visible by the shaded candlelight, in the death chamber of the old clergyman. Natural connections he had none. But there was the decorously grave, though unmoved physician, seeking only to mitigate the last pangs of the patient whom he could not save. There were the deacons, and other eminently pious members of his church. There, also, was the Reverend Mr. Clark, of Westbury, a young and zealous divine, who had ridden in haste to pray by the bedside of the expiring minister. There was the nurse, no hired handmaiden of death, but one whose calm affection had endured thus long in secrecy, in solitude, amid the chill of age, and would not perish, even at the dying hour. Who, but Elizabeth! And there lay the hoary head of good Father Hooper upon the death pillow, with the black veil still swathed about his brow, and reaching down over his face, so that each more difficult gasp of his faint breath caused it to stir. All through life that piece of crape had hung between him and the world: it had separated him from cheerful brotherhood and woman's love, and kept him in that saddest of all prisons, his own heart; and still it lay upon his face, as if to deepen the gloom of his darksome chamber, and shade him from the sunshine of eternity.

For some time previous, his mind had been confused, wavering doubtfully between the past and the present, and hovering forward, as it were, at intervals, into the indistinctness of the world to come. There had been feverish turns, which tossed him from side to side, and wore away what little strength he had. But in his most convulsive struggles, and in the wildest vagaries of his intellect, when no other thought retained its sober influence, he still showed an awful solicitude lest the black veil should slip aside. Even if his bewildered soul could have forgotten, there was a faithful woman at this pillow, who, with averted eyes, would have covered that aged face, which she had last beheld in the comeliness of manhood. At length the death-stricken old man lay quietly in the torpor of mental and bodily exhaustion, with an imperceptible pulse, and breath that grew fainter and fainter, except when a long, deep, and irregular inspiration seemed to prelude the flight of his spirit.

The minister of Westbury approached the bedside.

"Venerable Father Hooper," said he, "the moment of your release is at hand. Are you ready for the lifting of the veil that shuts in time from eternity?"

Father Hooper at first replied merely by a feeble motion of his head; then, apprehensive, perhaps, that his meaning might be doubted, he exerted himself to speak.

"Yea," said he, in faint accents, "my soul hath a patient weariness until that veil be lifted."

"And is it fitting," resumed the Reverend Mr. Clark, "that a man so given to prayer, of such a blameless example, holy in deed and thought, so far as mortal judgment may pronounce; is it fitting that a father in the church should leave a shadow on his memory, that may seem to blacken a life so pure? I pray you, my venerable brother, let not this thing be! Suffer us to be gladdened by your triumphant aspect as you go to your reward. Before the veil of eternity be lifted, let me cast aside this black veil from your face!"

And thus speaking, the Reverend Mr. Clark bent forward to reveal the mystery of so many years. But, exerting a sudden energy, that made all the beholders stand aghast, Father Hooper snatched both his hands from beneath the bedclothes, and pressed them strongly on the black veil, resolute to struggle, if the minister of Westbury would contend with a dying man.

"Never!" cried the veiled clergyman. "On earth, never!"

"Dark old man!" exclaimed the affrighted minister, "with what horrible crime upon your soul are you now passing to the judgment?"

Father Hooper's breath heaved; it rattled in his throat; but, with a mighty effort, grasping forward with his hands, he caught hold of life, and held it back till he should speak. He even raised himself in bed; and there he sat, shivering with the arms of death around him, while the black veil hung down, awful, at that last moment, in the gathered terrors of a lifetime. And yet the faint, sad smile, so often there, now seemed to glimmer from its obscurity, and linger on Father Hooper's lips.

"Why do you tremble at me alone?" cried he, turning his veiled face round the circle of pale spectators. "Tremble also at each other! Have men avoided me, and women shown no pity, and children screamed and fled, only for my black veil? What, but the mystery which it obscurely typifies, has made this piece of crape so awful? When the friend shows his inmost heart to his friend; the lover to his best beloved; when man does not vainly shrink from the eye of his Creator, loathsomely treasuring up the secret of his sin; then deem me a monster, for the symbol beneath which I have lived, and die! I look around me, and, lo! on every visage a Black Veil!"

While his auditors shrank from one another, in mutual affright, Father Hooper fell back upon his pillow, a veiled corpse, with a faint smile lingering on the lips. Still veiled, they laid him in his coffin, and a veiled corpse they bore him to the grave. The grass of many years has sprung up and withered on that grave, the burial stone is moss-grown, and good Mr. Hooper's face is dust; but awful is still the thought that it mouldered beneath the Black Veil!

Anonymous

Horror: A True Tale

I was but nineteen years of age when the incident occurred which has thrown a shadow over my life; and, ah me! how many and many a weary year has dragged by since then! Young, happy, and beloved I was in those long-departed days. They said that I was beautiful. The mirror now reflects a haggard old woman, with ashen lips and face of deadly pallor. But do not fancy that you are listening to a mere puling lament. It is not the flight of years that has brought me to be this wreck of my former self: had it been so I could have borne the loss cheerfully, patiently, as the common lot of all; but it was no natural progress of decay which has robbed me of bloom, of youth, of the hopes and joys that belong to youth, snapped the link that bound my heart to another's, and doomed me to a lone old age. I try to be patient, but my cross has been heavy, and my heart is empty and weary, and I long for the death that comes so slowly to those who pray to die.

I will try and relate, exactly as it happened, the event which blighted my life. Though it occurred many years ago, there is no fear that I should have forgotten any of the minutest circumstances: they were stamped on my brain too clearly and burningly, like the brand of a red-hot iron. I see them written in the wrinkles of my brow, in the dead whiteness of my hair, which was a glossy brown once, and has known no gradual change from dark to gray, from gray to white, as with those happy ones who were the companions of my girlhood, and whose honored age is soothed by the love of children and grandchildren. But I must not envy them. I only meant to say that the difficulty of my task has no connection with want of memory – I remember but too well. But as I take my pen my hand trembles, my head swims, the old rushing faintness and Horror comes over me again, and the well-remembered fear is upon me. Yet I will go on.

This, briefly, is my story: I was a great heiress, I believe, though I cared little for the fact; but so it was. My father had great possessions, and no son to inherit after him. His three daughters, of whom I was the youngest, were to share the broad acres among them. I have said, and truly, that I cared little for the circumstance; and, indeed, I was so rich then in health and youth and love that I felt myself quite indifferent to all else. The possession of all the treasures of earth could never have made up for what I then had – and lost, as I am about to relate. Of course, we girls knew that we were heiresses, but I do not think Lucy and Minnie were any the prouder or the happier on that account. I know I was not. Reginald did not court me for my money. Of THAT I felt assured. He proved it, Heaven be praised! when he shrank from my side after the change. Yes, in all my lonely age, I can still be thankful that he did not keep his word, as some would have done – did not clasp at the altar a hand he had learned to loathe and shudder at, because it was full of gold – much gold! At least he spared me that. And I know that I was loved, and the knowledge has kept me from going mad through many a weary day and restless night, when my hot eyeballs had not a tear to shed, and even to weep was a luxury denied me.

Our house was an old Tudor mansion. My father was very particular in keeping the smallest peculiarities of his home unaltered. Thus the many peaks and gables, the numerous turrets, and the mullioned windows with their quaint lozenge panes set in lead, remained very nearly as they had been three centuries back. Over and above the quaint melancholy of our dwelling, with the deep woods of its park and the sullen waters of the mere, our neighborhood was thinly peopled and primitive, and the people round us were ignorant, and tenacious of ancient ideas and traditions. Thus it was a superstitious atmosphere that we children were reared in, and we heard, from our infancy, countless tales of horror, some mere fables doubtless, others legends of dark deeds of the olden time, exaggerated by credulity and the love of the marvelous. Our mother had died when we were young, and our other parent being, though a kind father, much absorbed in affairs of various kinds, as an active magistrate and landlord, there was no one to check the unwholesome stream of tradition with which our plastic minds were inundated in the company of nurses and servants. As years went on, however, the old ghostly tales partially lost their effects, and our undisciplined minds were turned more towards balls, dress, and partners, and other matters airy and trivial, more welcome to our riper age. It was at a county assembly that Reginald and I first met – met and loved. Yes, I am sure that he loved me with all his heart. It was not as deep a heart as some, I have thought in my grief and anger; but I never doubted its truth and honesty. Reginald's father and mine approved of our growing attachment; and as for myself, I know I was so happy then, that I look back upon those fleeting moments as on some delicious dream. I now come to the change. I have lingered on my childish reminiscences, my bright and happy youth, and now I must tell the rest – the blight and the sorrow.

It was Christmas, always a joyful and a hospitable time in the country, especially in such an old hall as our home, where quaint customs and frolics were much clung to, as part and parcel of the very dwelling itself. The hall was full of guests – so full, indeed, that there was great difficulty in providing sleeping accommodation for all. Several narrow and dark chambers in the turrets – mere pigeon-holes, as we irreverently called what had been thought good enough for the stately gentlemen of Elizabeth's reign – were now allotted to bachelor visitors, after having been empty for a century. All the spare rooms in the body and wings of the hall were occupied, of course; and the servants who had been brought down were lodged at the farm and at the keeper's, so great was the demand for space. At last the unexpected arrival of an elderly relative, who had been asked months before, but scarcely expected, caused great commotion. My aunts went about wringing their hands distractedly. Lady Speldhurst was a personage of some consequence; she was a distant cousin, and had been for years on cool terms with us all, on account of some fancied affront or slight when she had paid her LAST visit, about the time of my christening. She was seventy years old; she was infirm, rich, and testy; moreover, she was my godmother, though I had forgotten the fact; but it seems that though I had formed no expectations of a legacy in my favor, my aunts had done so for me. Aunt Margaret was especially eloquent on the subject. "There isn't a room left," she said; "was ever anything so unfortunate! We cannot put Lady Speldhurst into the turrets, and yet where IS she to sleep? And Rosa's godmother, too! Poor, dear child, how dreadful! After all these years of estrangement, and with a hundred thousand in the funds, and no comfortable, warm room at her own unlimited disposal – and Christmas, of all times in the year!" What WAS to be done? My aunts could not resign their own chambers to Lady Speldhurst, because they had already given them up to some of the married guests. My father was the most hospitable of men, but he was rheumatic, gouty, and methodical. His sisters-in-law dared not propose to shift his quarters; and, indeed, he would have far sooner dined on prison fare than have been translated to a strange bed. The matter ended in my giving up my room. I had a strange reluctance to making the offer, which surprised myself. Was it a boding of evil to come? I cannot say. We are strangely and wonderfully made. It MAY have been. At any rate, I do not think it was any selfish unwillingness to make an old and infirm lady comfortable by a trifling sacrifice. I was perfectly healthy and strong. The weather was not cold for the time of the year. It was a dark, moist Yule – not a snowy one, though snow brooded overhead in the darkling clouds. I DID make the offer, which became me, I said with a laugh, as the youngest. My sisters laughed too, and made a jest of my evident wish to propitiate my godmother. "She is a fairy godmother, Rosa," said Minnie; "and you know she was affronted at your christening, and went away muttering vengeance. Here she is coming back to see you; I hope she brings golden gifts with her."

I thought little of Lady Speldhurst and her possible golden gifts. I cared nothing for the wonderful fortune in the funds that my aunts whispered and nodded about so mysteriously. But since then I have wondered whether, had I then showed myself peevish or obstinate – had I refused to give up my room for the expected kinswoman – it would not have altered the whole of my life? But then Lucy or Minnie would have offered in my stead, and been sacrificed – what do I say? – better that the blow should have fallen as it did than on those dear ones.

The chamber to which I removed was a dim little triangular room in the western wing, and was only to be reached by traversing the picture-gallery, or by mounting a little flight of stone stairs which led directly upward from the low-browed arch of a door that opened into the garden. There was one more room on the same landing-place, and this was a mere receptacle for broken furniture, shattered toys, and all the lumber that WILL accumulate in a country-house. The room I was to inhabit for a few nights was a tapestry-hung apartment, with faded green curtains of some costly stuff, contrasting oddly with a new carpet and the bright, fresh hangings of the bed, which had been hurriedly erected. The furniture was half old, half new; and on the dressing-table stood a very quaint oval mirror, in a frame of black wood – unpolished ebony, I think. I can remember the very pattern of the carpet, the number of chairs, the situation of the bed, the figures on the tapestry. Nay, I can recollect not only the color of the dress I wore on that fated evening, but the arrangement of every scrap of lace and ribbon, of every flower, every jewel, with a memory but too perfect.

Scarcely had my maid finished spreading out my various articles of attire for the evening (when there was to be a great dinner-party) when the rumble of a carriage announced that Lady Speldhurst had arrived. The short winter's day drew to a close, and a large number of guests were gathered together in the ample drawing-room, around the blaze of the wood-fire, after dinner. My father, I recollect, was not with us at first. There were some squires of the old, hard-riding, hard-drinking stamp still lingering over their port in the dining-room, and the host, of course, could not leave them. But the ladies and all the younger gentlemen – both those who slept under our roof, and those who would have a dozen miles of fog and mire to encounter on their road home – were all together. Need I say that Reginald was there? He sat near me – my accepted lover, my plighted future husband. We were to be married in the spring. My sisters were not far off; they, too, had found eyes that sparkled and softened in meeting theirs, had found hearts that beat responsive to their own. And, in their cases, no rude frost nipped the blossom ere it became the fruit; there was no canker in their flowerets of young hope, no cloud in their sky. Innocent and loving, they were beloved by men worthy of their esteem.

The room – a large and lofty one, with an arched roof – had somewhat of a somber character, from being wainscoted and ceiled with polished black oak of a great age. There were mirrors, and there were pictures on the walls, and handsome furniture, and marble chimney-pieces, and a gay Tournay carpet; but these merely appeared as bright spots on the dark background of the Elizabethan woodwork. Many lights were burning, but the blackness of the walls and roof seemed absolutely to swallow up their rays, like the mouth of a cavern. A hundred candles could not have given that apartment the cheerful lightness of a modern drawing room. But the gloomy richness of the panels matched well with the ruddy gleam from the enormous wood-fire, in which, crackling and glowing, now lay the mighty Yule log. Quite a blood-red luster poured forth from the fire, and quivered on the walls and the groined roof. We had gathered round the vast antique hearth in a wide circle. The quivering light of the fire and candles fell upon us all, but not equally, for some were in shadow. I remember still how tall and manly and handsome Reginald looked that night, taller by the head than any there, and full of high spirits and gayety. I, too, was in the highest spirits; never had my bosom felt lighter, and I believe it was my mirth that gradually gained the rest, for I recollect what a blithe, joyous company we seemed. All save one. Lady Speldhurst, dressed in gray silk and wearing a quaint head- dress, sat in her armchair, facing the fire, very silent, with her hands and her sharp chin propped on a sort of ivory-handled crutch that she walked with (for she was lame), peering at me with half- shut eyes. She was a little, spare old woman, with very keen, delicate features of the French type. Her gray silk dress, her spotless lace, old-fashioned jewels, and prim neatness of array, were well suited to the intelligence of her face, with its thin lips, and eyes of a piercing black, undimmed by age. Those eyes made me uncomfortable, in spite of my gayety, as they followed my every movement with curious scrutiny. Still I was very merry and gay; my sisters even wondered at my ever-ready mirth, which was almost wild in its excess. I have heard since then of the Scottish belief that those doomed to some great calamity become fey, and are never so disposed for merriment and laughter as just before the blow falls.

If ever mortal was fey, then I was so on that evening. Still, though I strove to shake it off, the pertinacious observation of old Lady Speldhurst's eyes DID make an impression on me of a vaguely disagreeable nature. Others, too, noticed her scrutiny of me, but set it down as a mere eccentricity of a person always reputed whimsical, to say the least of it.

However, this disagreeable sensation lasted but a few moments. After a short pause my aunt took her part in the conversation, and we found ourselves listening to a weird legend, which the old lady told exceedingly well. One tale led to another. Everyone was called on in turn to contribute to the public entertainment, and story after story, always relating to demonology and witchcraft, succeeded. It was Christmas, the season for such tales; and the old room, with its dusky walls and pictures, and vaulted roof, drinking up the light so greedily, seemed just fitted to give effect to such legendary lore. The huge logs crackled and burned with glowing warmth; the blood-red glare of the Yule log flashed on the faces of the listeners and narrator, on the portraits, and the holly wreathed about their frames, and the upright old dame, in her antiquated dress and trinkets, like one of the originals of the pictures, stepped from the canvas to join our circle. It threw a shimmering luster of an ominously ruddy hue upon the oaken panels. No wonder that the ghost and goblin stories had a new zest. No wonder that the blood of the more timid grew chill and curdled, that their flesh crept, that their hearts beat irregularly, and the girls peeped fearfully over their shoulders, and huddled close together like frightened sheep, and half fancied they beheld some impish and malignant face gibbering at them from the darkling corners of the old room. By degrees my high spirits died out, and I felt the childish tremors, long latent, long forgotten, coming over me. I followed each story with painful interest; I did not ask myself if I believed the dismal tales. I listened, and fear grew upon me – the blind, irrational fear of our nursery days. I am sure most of the other ladies present, young or middle-aged, were affected by the circumstances under which these traditions were heard, no less than by the wild and fantastic character of them. But with them the impression would die out next morning, when the bright sun should shine on the frosted boughs, and the rime on the grass, and the scarlet berries and green spikelets of the holly; and with me – but, ah! what was to happen ere another day dawn? Before we had made an end of this talk my father and the other squires came in, and we ceased our ghost stories, ashamed to speak of such matters before these new-comers – hard-headed, unimaginative men, who had no sympathy with idle legends. There was now a stir and bustle.

Servants were handing round tea and coffee, and other refreshments. Then there was a little music and singing. I sang a duet with Reginald, who had a fine voice and good musical skill. I remember that my singing was much praised, and indeed I was surprised at the power and pathos of my own voice, doubtless due to my excited nerves and mind. Then I heard someone say to another that I was by far the cleverest of the Squire's daughters, as well as the prettiest. It did not make me vain. I had no rivalry with Lucy and Minnie. But Reginald whispered some soft, fond words in my ear a little before he mounted his horse to set off homeward, which DID make me happy and proud. And to think that the next time we met – but I forgave him long ago. Poor Reginald! And now shawls and cloaks were in request, and carriages rolled up to the porch, and the guests gradually departed. At last no one was left but those visitors staying in the house. Then my father, who had been called out to speak with the bailiff of the estate, came back with a look of annoyance on his face.

"A strange story I have just been told," said he; "here has been my bailiff to inform me of the loss of four of the choicest ewes out of that little flock of Southdowns I set such store by, and which arrived in the north but two months since. And the poor creatures have been destroyed in so strange a manner, for their carcasses are horribly mangled."

Most of us uttered some expression of pity or surprise, and some suggested that a vicious dog was probably the culprit.

"It would seem so," said my father; "it certainly seems the work of a dog; and yet all the men agree that no dog of such habits exists near us, where, indeed, dogs are scarce, excepting the shepherds' collies and the sporting dogs secured in yards. Yet the sheep are gnawed and bitten, for they show the marks of teeth. Something has done this, and has torn their bodies wolfishly; but apparently it has been only to suck the blood, for little or no flesh is gone."

"How strange!" cried several voices. Then some of the gentlemen remembered to have heard of cases when dogs addicted to sheep- killing had destroyed whole flocks, as if in sheer wantonness, scarcely deigning to taste a morsel of each slain wether.

My father shook his head. "I have heard of such cases, too," he said; "but in this instance I am tempted to think the malice of some unknown enemy has been at work. The teeth of a dog have been busy, no doubt, but the poor sheep have been mutilated in a fantastic manner, as strange as horrible; their hearts, in especial, have been torn out, and left at some paces off, half- gnawed. Also, the men persist that they found the print of a naked human foot in the soft mud of the ditch, and near it – this." And he held up what seemed a broken link of a rusted iron chain.

Many were the ejaculations of wonder and alarm, and many and shrewd the conjectures, but none seemed exactly to suit the bearings of the case. And when my father went on to say that two lambs of the same valuable breed had perished in the same singular manner three days previously, and that they also were found mangled and gore- stained, the amazement reached a higher pitch. Old Lady Speldhurst listened with calm, intelligent attention, but joined in none of our exclamations. At length she said to my father, "Try and recollect – have you no enemy among your neighbors?" My father started, and knit his brows. "Not one that I know of," he replied; and indeed he was a popular man and a kind landlord. "The more lucky you," said the old dame, with one of her grim smiles. It was now late, and we retired to rest before long. One by one the guests dropped off. I was the member of the family selected to escort old Lady Speldhurst to her room – the room I had vacated in her favor. I did not much like the office. I felt a remarkable repugnance to my godmother, but my worthy aunts insisted so much that I should ingratiate myself with one who had so much to leave that I could not but comply. The visitor hobbled up the broad oaken stairs actively enough, propped on my arm and her ivory crutch. The room never had looked more genial and pretty, with its brisk fire, modern furniture, and the gay French paper on the walls. "A nice room, my dear, and I ought to be much obliged to you for it, since my maid tells me it is yours," said her ladyship; "but I am pretty sure you repent your generosity to me, after all those ghost stories, and tremble to think of a strange bed and chamber, eh?" I made some commonplace reply. The old lady arched her eyebrows. "Where have they put you, child?" she asked; "in some cock-loft of the turrets, eh? or in a lumber-room - a regular ghost-trap? I can hear your heart beating with fear this moment. You are not fit to be alone." I tried to call up my pride, and laugh off the accusation against my courage, all the more, perhaps, because I felt its truth. "Do you want anything more that I can get you, Lady Speldhurst?" I asked, trying to feign a yawn of sleepiness. The old dame's keen eyes were upon me. "I rather like you, my dear," she said, "and I liked your mamma well enough before she treated me so shamefully about the christening dinner. Now, I know you are frightened and fearful, and if an owl should but flap your window tonight, it might drive you into fits. There is a nice little sofa-bed in this dressing closet - call your maid to arrange it for you, and you can sleep there snugly, under the old witch's protection, and then no goblin dare harm you, and nobody will be a bit the wiser, or quiz you for being afraid." How little I knew what hung in the balance of my refusal or acceptance of that trivial proffer! Had the veil of the future been lifted for one instant! but that veil is impenetrable to our gaze.

I left her door. As I crossed the landing a bright gleam came from another room, whose door was left ajar; it (the light) fell like a bar of golden sheen across my path. As I approached the door opened and my sister Lucy, who had been watching for me, came out. She was already in a white cashmere wrapper, over which her loosened hair hung darkly and heavily, like tangles of silk. "Rosa, love," she whispered, "Minnie and I can't bear the idea of your sleeping out there, all alone, in that solitary room - the very room too Nurse Sherrard used to talk about! So, as you know Minnie has given up her room, and come to sleep in mine, still we should so wish you to stop with us to-night at any rate, and I could make up a bed on the sofa for myself or you – and – " I stopped Lucy's mouth with a kiss. I declined her offer. I would not listen to it. In fact, my pride was up in arms, and I felt I would rather pass the night in the churchyard itself than accept a proposal dictated, I felt sure, by the notion that my nerves were shaken by the ghostly lore we had been raking up, that I was a weak, superstitious creature, unable to pass a night in a strange chamber. So I would not listen to Lucy, but kissed her, bade her good-night, and went on my way laughing, to show my light heart. Yet, as I looked back in the dark corridor, and saw the friendly door still ajar, the yellow bar of light still crossing from wall to wall, the sweet, kind face still peering after me from amidst its clustering curls, I felt a thrill of sympathy, a wish to return, a yearning after human love and companionship. False shame was strongest, and conquered. I waved a gay adieu. I turned the corner, and peeping over my shoulder, I saw the door close; the bar of yellow light was there no longer in the darkness of the passage. I thought at that instant that I heard a heavy sigh. I looked sharply round. No one was there. No door was open, yet I fancied, and fancied with a wonderful vividness, that I did hear an actual sigh breathed not far off, and plainly distinguishable from the groan of the sycamore branches as the wind tossed them to and fro in the outer blackness. If ever a mortal's good angel had cause to sigh for sorrow, not sin, mine had cause to mourn that night. But imagination plays us strange tricks and my nervous system was not over-composed or very fitted for judicial analysis. I had to go through the picture-gallery. I had never entered this apartment by candle-light before and I was struck by the gloomy array of the tall portraits, gazing moodily from the canvas on the lozenge-paned or painted windows, which rattled to the blast as it swept howling by. Many of the faces looked stern, and very different from their daylight expression. In others a furtive, flickering smile seemed to mock me as my candle illumined them; and in all, the eyes, as usual with artistic portraits, seemed to follow my motions with a scrutiny and an interest the more marked for the apathetic immovability of the other features. I felt ill at ease under this stony gaze, though conscious how absurd were my apprehensions; and I called up a smile and an air of mirth, more as if acting a part under the eyes of human beings than of their mere shadows on the wall. I even laughed as I confronted them. No echo had my short-lived laughter but from the hollow armor and arching roof, and I continued on my way in silence.

By a sudden and not uncommon revulsion of feeling I shook off my aimless terrors, blushed at my weakness, and sought my chamber only too glad that I had been the only witness of my late tremors. As I entered my chamber I thought I heard something stir in the neglected lumber-room, which was the only neighboring apartment. But I was determined to have no more panics, and resolutely shut my eyes to this slight and transient noise, which had nothing unnatural in it; for surely, between rats and wind, an old manor-house on a stormy night needs no sprites to disturb it. So I entered my room, and rang for my maid. As I did so I looked around me, and a most unaccountable repugnance to my temporary abode came over me, in spite of my efforts. It was no more to be shaken off than a chill is to be shaken off when we enter some damp cave. And, rely upon it, the feeling of dislike and apprehension with which we regard, at first sight, certain places and people, was not implanted in us without some wholesome purpose. I grant it is irrational – mere animal instinct – but is not instinct God's gift, and is it for us to despise it? It is by instinct that children know their friends from their enemies – that they distinguish with such unerring accuracy between those who like them and those who only flatter and hate them. Dogs do the same; they will fawn on one person, they slink snarling from another. Show me a man whom children and dogs shrink from, and I will show you a false, bad man – lies on his lips, and murder at his heart. No; let none despise the heaven-sent gift of innate antipathy, which makes the horse quail when the lion crouches in the thicket – which makes the cattle scent the shambles from afar, and low in terror and disgust as their nostrils snuff the blood-polluted air. I felt this antipathy strongly as I looked around me in my new sleeping-room, and yet I could find no reasonable pretext for my dislike. A very good room it was, after all, now that the green damask curtains were drawn, the fire burning bright and clear, candles burning on the mantel-piece, and the various familiar articles of toilet arranged as usual. The bed, too, looked peaceful and inviting – a pretty little white bed, not at all the gaunt funereal sort of couch which haunted apartments generally contain.

My maid entered, and assisted me to lay aside the dress and ornaments I had worn, and arranged my hair, as usual, prattling the while, in Abigail fashion. I seldom cared to converse with servants; but on that night a sort of dread of being left alone – a longing to keep some human being near me possessed me – and I encouraged the girl to gossip, so that her duties took her half an hour longer to get through than usual. At last, however, she had done all that could be done, and all my questions were answered, and my orders for the morrow reiterated and vowed obedience to, and the clock on the turret struck one. Then Mary, yawning a little, asked if I wanted anything more, and I was obliged to answer no, for very shame's sake; and she went. The shutting of the door, gently as it was closed, affected me unpleasantly. I took a dislike to the curtains, the tapestry, the dingy pictures – everything. I hated the room. I felt a temptation to put on a cloak, run, half-dressed, to my sisters' chamber, and say I had changed my mind and come for shelter. But they must be asleep, I thought, and I could not be so unkind as to wake them. I said my prayers with unusual earnestness and a heavy heart. I extinguished the candles, and was just about to lay my head on my pillow, when the idea seized me that I would fasten the door. The candles were extinguished, but the firelight was amply sufficient to guide me. I gained the door. There was a lock, but it was rusty or hampered; my utmost strength could not turn the key. The bolt was broken and worthless. Balked of my intention, I consoled myself by remembering that I had never had need of fastenings yet, and returned to my bed. I lay awake for a good while, watching the red glow of the burning coals in the grate. I was quiet now, and more composed. Even the light gossip of the maid, full of petty human cares and joys, had done me good – diverted my thoughts from brooding. I was on the point of dropping asleep, when I was twice disturbed. Once, by an owl, hooting in the ivy outside – no unaccustomed sound, but harsh and melancholy; once, by a long and mournful howling set up by the mastiff, chained in the yard beyond the wing I occupied. A long-drawn, lugubrious howling was this latter, and much such a note as the vulgar declare to herald a death in the family. This was a fancy I had never shared; but yet I could not help feeling that the dog's mournful moans were sad, and expressive of terror, not at all like his fierce, honest bark of anger, but rather as if something evil and unwonted were abroad. But soon I fell asleep.

How long I slept I never knew. I awoke at once with that abrupt start which we all know well, and which carries us in a second from utter unconsciousness to the full use of our faculties. The fire was still burning, but was very low, and half the room or more was in deep shadow. I knew, I felt, that some person or thing was in the room, although nothing unusual was to be seen by the feeble light. Yet it was a sense of danger that had aroused me from slumber. I experienced, while yet asleep, the chill and shock of sudden alarm, and I knew, even in the act of throwing off sleep like a mantle, WHY I awoke, and that some intruder was present. Yet, though I listened intently, no sound was audible, except the faint murmur of the fire – the dropping of a cinder from the bars – the loud, irregular beatings of my own heart. Notwithstanding this silence, by some intuition I knew that I had not been deceived by a dream, and felt certain that I was not alone. I waited. My heart beat on; quicker, more sudden grew its pulsations, as a bird in a cage might flutter in presence of the hawk. And then I heard a sound, faint, but quite distinct, the clank of iron, the rattling of a chain! I ventured to lift my head from the pillow. Dim and uncertain as the light was, I saw the curtains of my bed shake, and caught a glimpse of something beyond, a darker spot in the darkness. This confirmation of my fears did not surprise me so much as it shocked me. I strove to cry aloud, but could not utter a word. The chain rattled again, and this time the noise was louder and clearer. But though I strained my eyes, they could not penetrate the obscurity that shrouded the other end of the chamber whence came the sullen clanking. In a moment several distinct trains of thought, like many-colored strands of thread twining into one, became palpable to my mental vision. Was it a robber? Could it be a supernatural visitant? Or was I the victim of a cruel trick, such as I had heard of, and which some thoughtless persons love to practice on the timid, reckless of its dangerous results? And then a new idea, with some ray of comfort in it, suggested itself. There was a fine young dog of the Newfoundland breed, a favorite of my father's, which was usually chained by night in an outhouse. Neptune might have broken loose, found his way to my room, and, finding the door imperfectly closed, have pushed it open and entered. I breathed more freely as this harmless interpretation of the noise forced itself upon me. It was – it must be – the dog, and I was distressing myself uselessly. I resolved to call to him; I strove to utter his name – "Neptune, Neptune," but a secret apprehension restrained me, and I was mute.

Then the chain clanked nearer and nearer to the bed, and presently I saw a dusky, shapeless mass appear between the curtains on the opposite side to where I was lying. How I longed to hear the whine of the poor animal that I hoped might be the cause of my alarm. But no; I heard no sound save the rustle of the curtains and the clash of the iron chains. Just then the dying flame of the fire leaped up, and with one sweeping, hurried glance I saw that the door was shut, and, horror! it is not the dog! it is the semblance of a human form that now throws itself heavily on the bed, outside the clothes, and lies there, huge and swart, in the red gleam that treacherously died away after showing so much to affright, and sinks into dull darkness. There was now no light left, though the red cinders yet glowed with a ruddy gleam like the eyes of wild beasts. The chain rattled no more. I tried to speak, to scream wildly for help; my mouth was parched, my tongue refused to obey. I could not utter a cry, and, indeed, who could have heard me, alone as I was in that solitary chamber, with no living neighbor, and the picture-gallery between me and any aid that even the loudest, most piercing shriek could summon. And the storm that howled without would have drowned my voice, even if help had been at hand. To call aloud – to demand who was there – alas! how useless, how perilous! If the intruder were a robber, my outcries would but goad him to fury; but what robber would act thus? As for a trick, that seemed impossible. And yet, WHAT lay by my side, now wholly unseen? I strove to pray aloud as there rushed on my memory a flood of weird legends –

the dreaded yet fascinating lore of my childhood. I had heard and read of the spirits of the wicked men forced to revisit the scenes of their earthly crimes – of demons that lurked in certain accursed spots – of the ghoul and vampire of the east, stealing amidst the graves they rifled for their ghostly banquets; and then I shuddered as I gazed on the blank darkness where I knew it lay. It stirred – it moaned hoarsely; and again I heard the chain clank close beside me – so close that it must almost have touched me. I drew myself from it, shrinking away in loathing and terror of the evil thing – what, I knew not, but felt that something malignant was near.

And yet, in the extremity of my fear, I dared not speak; I was strangely cautious to be silent, even in moving farther off; for I had a wild hope that it – the phantom, the creature, whichever it was – had not discovered my presence in the room. And then I remembered all the events of the night – Lady Speldhurst's ill-omened vaticinations, her half-warnings, her singular look as we parted, my sister's persuasions, my terror in the gallery, the remark that "this was the room nurse Sherrard used to talk of." And then memory, stimulated by fear, recalled the long-forgotten past, the ill-repute of this disused chamber, the sins it had witnessed, the blood spilled, the poison administered by unnatural hate within its walls, and the tradition which called it haunted. The green room – I remembered now how fearfully the servants avoided it – how it was mentioned rarely, and in whispers, when we were children, and how we had regarded it as a mysterious region, unfit for mortal habitation. Was It – the dark form with the chain – a creature of this world, or a specter? And again – more dreadful still – could it be that the corpses of wicked men were forced to rise and haunt in the body the places where they had wrought their evil deeds? And was such as these my grisly neighbor? The chain faintly rattled. My hair bristled; my eyeballs seemed starting from their sockets; the damps of a great anguish were on my brow. My heart labored as if I were crushed beneath some vast weight. Sometimes it appeared to stop its frenzied beatings, sometimes its pulsations were fierce and hurried; my breath came short and with extreme difficulty, and I shivered as if with cold; yet I feared to stir. IT moved, it moaned, its fetters clanked dismally, the couch creaked and shook. This was no phantom, then – no air-drawn specter. But its very solidity, its palpable presence, were a thousand times more terrible. I felt that I was in the very grasp of what could not only affright but harm; of something whose contact sickened the soul with deathly fear. I made a desperate resolve: I glided from the bed, I seized a warm wrapper, threw it around me, and tried to grope, with extended hands, my way to the door. My heart beat high at the hope of escape. But I had scarcely taken one step before the moaning was renewed – it changed into a threatening growl that would have suited a wolf's throat, and a hand clutched at my sleeve. I stood motionless. The muttering growl sank to a moan again, the chain sounded no more, but still the hand held its gripe of my garment, and I feared to move. It knew of my presence, then. My brain reeled, the blood boiled in my ears, and my knees lost all strength, while my heart panted like that of a deer in the wolf's jaws. I sank back, and the benumbing influence of excessive terror reduced me to a state of stupor.

When my full consciousness returned I was sitting on the edge of the bed, shivering with cold, and barefooted. All was silent, but I felt that my sleeve was still clutched by my unearthly visitor. The silence lasted a long time. Then followed a chuckling laugh that froze my very marrow, and the gnashing of teeth as in demoniac frenzy; and then a wailing moan, and this was succeeded by silence. Hours may have passed – nay, though the tumult of my own heart prevented my hearing the clock strike, must have passed – but they seemed ages to me. And how were they passed? Hideous visions passed before the aching eyes that I dared not close, but which gazed ever into the dumb darkness where It lay – my dread companion through the watches of the night. I pictured It in every abhorrent form which an excited fancy could summon up: now as a skeleton; with hollow eyeholes and grinning, fleshless jaws; now as a vampire, with livid face and bloated form, and dripping mouth wet with blood. Would it never be light! And yet, when day should dawn I should be forced to see It face to face. I had heard that specter and fiend were compelled to fade as morning brightened, but this creature was too real, too foul a thing of earth, to vanish at cockcrow. No! I should see it – the Horror – face to face! And then the cold prevailed, and my teeth chattered, and shiverings ran through me, and yet there was the damp of agony on my bursting brow. Some instinct made me snatch at a shawl or cloak that lay on a chair within reach, and wrap it round me. The moan was renewed, and the chain just stirred. Then I sank into apathy, like an Indian at the stake, in the intervals of torture. Hours fled by, and I remained like a statue of ice, rigid and mute. I even slept, for I remember that I started to find the cold gray light of an early winter's day was on my face, and stealing around the room from between the heavy curtains of the window.

Shuddering, but urged by the impulse that rivets the gaze of the bird upon the snake, I turned to see the Horror of the night. Yes, it was no fevered dream, no hallucination of sickness, no airy phantom unable to face the dawn. In the sickly light I saw it lying on the bed, with its grim head on the pillow. A man? Or a corpse arisen from its unhallowed grave, and awaiting the demon that animated it? There it lay – a gaunt, gigantic form, wasted to a skeleton, half-clad, foul with dust and clotted gore, its huge limbs flung upon the couch as if at random, its shaggy hair streaming over the pillows like a lion's mane. His face was toward me. Oh, the wild hideousness of that face, even in sleep! In features it was human, even through its horrid mask of mud and half-dried bloody gouts, but the expression was brutish and savagely fierce; the white teeth were visible between the parted lips, in a malignant grin; the tangled hair and beard were mixed in leonine confusion, and there were scars disfiguring the brow. Round the creature's waist was a ring of iron, to which was attached a heavy but broken chain – the chain I had heard clanking. With a second glance I noted that part of the chain was wrapped in straw to prevent its galling the wearer. The creature – I cannot call it a man – had the marks of fetters on its wrists, the bony arm that protruded through one tattered sleeve was scarred and bruised; the feet were bare, and lacerated by pebbles and briers, and one of them was wounded, and wrapped in a morsel of rag. And the lean hands, one of which held my sleeve, were armed with talons like an eagle's. In an instant the horrid truth flashed upon me – I was in the grasp of a madman. Better the phantom that scares the sight than the wild beast that rends and tears the quivering flesh – the pitiless human brute that has no heart to be softened, no reason at whose bar to plead, no compassion, naught of man save the form and the cunning. I gasped in terror. Ah! the mystery of those ensanguined fingers, those gory, wolfish jaws! that face, all besmeared with blackening blood, is revealed!

The slain sheep, so mangled and rent – the fantastic butchery – the print of the naked foot – all, all were explained; and the chain, the broken link of which was found near the slaughtered animals – it came from his broken chain – the chain he had snapped, doubtless, in his escape from the asylum where his raging frenzy had been fettered and bound, in vain! in vain! Ah me! how had this grisly Samson broken manacles and prison bars – how had he eluded guardian and keeper and a hostile world, and come hither on his wild way, hunted like a beast of prey, and snatching his hideous banquet like a beast of prey, too! Yes, through the tatters of his mean and ragged garb I could see the marks of the seventies, cruel and foolish, with which men in that time tried to tame the might of madness. The scourge – its marks were there; and the scars of the hard iron fetters, and many a cicatrice and welt, that told a dismal tale of hard usage. But now he was loose, free to play the brute – the baited, tortured brute that they had made him – now without the cage, and ready to gloat over the victims his strength should overpower. Horror! horror! I was the prey – the victim – already in the tiger's clutch; and a deadly sickness came over me, and the iron entered into my soul, and I longed to scream, and was dumb! I died a thousand deaths as that morning wore on. I DARED NOT faint. But words cannot paint what I suffered as I waited – waited till the moment when he should open his eyes and be aware of my presence; for I was assured he knew it not. He had entered the chamber as a lair, when weary and gorged with his horrid orgy; and he had flung himself down to sleep without a suspicion that he was not alone. Even his grasping my sleeve was doubtless an act done betwixt sleeping and waking, like his unconscious moans and laughter, in some frightful dream.

Hours went on; then I trembled as I thought that soon the

house would be astir, that my maid would come to call me as usual, and awake that ghastly sleeper. And might he not have time to tear me, as he tore the sheep, before any aid could arrive? At last what I dreaded came to pass – a light footstep on the landing – there is a tap at the door. A pause succeeds, and then the tapping is renewed, and this time more loudly. Then the madman stretched his limbs, and uttered his moaning cry, and his eyes slowly opened – very slowly opened and met mine. The girl waited a while ere she knocked for the third time. I trembled lest she should open the door unbidden – see that grim thing, and bring about the worst.

I saw the wondering surprise in his haggard, bloodshot eyes; I saw him stare at me half vacantly, then with a crafty yet wondering look; and then I saw the devil of murder begin to peep forth from those hideous eyes, and the lips to part as in a sneer, and the wolfish teeth to bare themselves. But I was not what I had been. Fear gave me a new and a desperate composure – a courage foreign to my nature. I had heard of the best method of managing the insane; I could but try; I DID try. Calmly, wondering at my own feigned calm, I fronted the glare of those terrible eyes. Steady and undaunted was my gaze – motionless my attitude. I marveled at myself, but in that agony of sickening terror I was OUTWARDLY firm. They sink, they quail, abashed, those dreadful eyes, before the gaze of a helpless girl; and the shame that is never absent from insanity bears down the pride of strength, the bloody cravings of the wild beast. The lunatic moaned and drooped his shaggy head between his gaunt, squalid hands.

I lost not an instant. I rose, and with one spring reached the door, tore it open, and, with a shriek, rushed through, caught the wondering girl by the arm, and crying to her to run for her life, rushed like the wind along the gallery, down the corridor, down the stairs. Mary's screams filled the house as she fled beside me. I heard a long-drawn, raging cry, the roar of a wild animal mocked of its prey, and I knew what was behind me. I never turned my head – I flew rather than ran. I was in the hall already; there was a rush of many feet, an outcry of many voices, a sound of scuffling feet, and brutal yells, and oaths, and heavy blows, and I fell to the ground crying, "Save me!" and lay in a swoon. I awoke from a delirious trance. Kind faces were around my bed, loving looks were bent on me by all, by my dear father and dear sisters; but I scarcely saw them before I swooned again.

When I recovered from that long illness, through which I had been nursed so tenderly, the pitying looks I met made me tremble. I asked for a looking-glass. It was long denied me, but my importunity prevailed at last – a mirror was brought. My youth was gone at one fell swoop. The glass showed me a livid and haggard face, blanched and bloodless as of one who sees a specter; and in the ashen lips, and wrinkled brow, and dim eyes, I could trace nothing of my old self. The hair, too, jetty and rich before, was now as white as snow; and in one night the ravages of half a century had passed over my face. Nor have my nerves ever recovered their tone after that dire shock. Can you wonder that my life was blighted, that my lover shrank from me, so sad a wreck was I?

I am old now – old and alone. My sisters would have had me to live with them, but I chose not to sadden their genial homes with my phantom face and dead eyes. Reginald married another. He has been dead many years. I never ceased to pray for him, though he left me when I was bereft of all. The sad weird is nearly over now. I am old, and near the end, and wishful for it. I have not been bitter or hard, but I cannot bear to see many people, and am best alone. I try to do what good I can with the worthless wealth Lady Speldhurst left me, for, at my wish, my portion was shared between my sisters. What need had I of inheritance? – I, the shattered wreck made by that one night of horror!